Books by Patrick Tilley

FADE-OUT

MISSION

MISSION

A NOVEL

MISSION

Patrick Tilley

Little, Brown and Company — Boston — Toronto

FIRST EDITION

LIBRARY OF CONGRESS CATALOGING IN PUBLICATION DATA
Tilley, Patrick.
    Mission.
    I. Title.
PR6070.I38M5 1981   823'.914   81-8214
ISBN 0-316-84541-8   AACR2

RRD
Designed by Susan Windheim

To
Pen-yr-Allt

MISSION

"Angels are the powers hidden in
the faculties and organs of Man."

Ibn al-'Arabi the Murcian
Greatest Master of the Sufi
1165–1240 A.D.

ONE

THE night I called at Manhattan General to pick up this lady doctor I was dating, something quite extraordinary happened.

For Miriam and me, it was the first in a chain of events that were to change our lives — mine especially — in a way that neither of us could possibly have imagined. For what we stumbled across that night was not the beginning of the story. If I am to believe what I have learned so far, the beginning was before and beyond Time as we know it. Our life-streams — along with those of the handful of other people who became involved — have established a brief interface with a cosmic event whose magnitude dwarfs the imagination.

If this is starting to sound heavy, hold on. I'm not kidding. This is going to change all our lives before it's over. Or end them. It's that big — and that simple. Even so, I don't guarantee to explain everything. You'll have to figure some of this out for yourselves. That's the way it works. But it's one hell of a story. I've got notes, photographs, tape recordings. All the evidence is locked in a safety deposit box registered in my name at the Forty-seventh and Madison branch of the Chase Manhattan Bank. I've put down everything I saw and everything that was said just the way it happened. It can all be checked against this account I am writing now. It's all true. Every word of it.

So help me God.

Before we go any further, I'd better tell you who I am. My name is Leo Resnick. I'm thirty-five years old and, at the time this thing started, I was a partner in the Manhattan law firm of Gutzman, Schonfeld and Resnick. The firm specializes in corporate legal work but occasionally handles divorce suits for its more favored clients. I was supposed to be making good as a claims attorney. How true that is, is not for me to say, but they put my name on the door last Christmas so I guess I must have been doing something right. Let's just say that it brought in enough to eat out in restaurants where they don't put the prices on the menus, run a three-liter Porsche Carrera, pay the bills on a nice apartment up on Seventy-fifth Street and a weekend place overlooking the Hudson. Except that to see the river, you have to stand on the roof.

Actually, the house at Sleepy Hollow was left to me by my uncle. Still, it added to my net worth and gave me problems like replacing shingles, cutting grass, buying heating oil and alarm systems. And so on. But there were a few bonuses too. If you had time to look, you got to see the leaves change color, clouds moving across a Panavision piece of sky, hear the wind in the trees, and split kindling for the log fire in the living room.

The whole Back-to-Nature bit.

To be honest, I didn't get up there all that often. I don't know about you, but I always got a little twitchy sitting around just listening to the grass grow. I needed the buzz from the streets, the big-city hype to get my nerve ends tingling. Some of that tangy, rush-hour traffic air in my lungs. It sharpens a guy up. Makes him feel human.

In town, most of my time was spent working. Either at the office or my apartment. Boning up on case law, laying the groundwork for suits. Looking for angles. I'm not married. I'd been going steady with this lady doctor for a couple of years. I guess you could say we were close but neither of us had let it get too serious. In other words, I was open to offers. Miriam — that's the lady doctor — knew they came my way now and then. She was not too wild about it but we always managed to avoid any heavy scenes.

So much for romance.

I've got a sister, Bella, who's married to a dentist up in Boston. She used to play cello with the Philharmonic but now she's into kids and clambakes. My parents live in Florida. They were always writing to tell me I should visit them more often and that I should holiday in Disney World. I didn't like to tell them that I preferred Fritz the Cat to Mickey Mouse and that I hadn't been to synagogue since Bella's wedding. End of life story. There's more, of course, but we don't need to get into that here.

Let's get back to where I got involved in this thing. The Manhattan General. I had arranged to pick up Miriam between nine-fifteen and nine-thirty. The plan was to have dinner and catch a late movie by that German guy Fassbinder. I find him a little heavy but Miriam is completely hooked on the European movie scene. It had been raining hard and I'd had some trouble in getting a cab. As a result, I didn't arrive at the Manhattan General until nine-fifty-ish. She wasn't waiting at the desk. The duty nurse, who knew who I was, phoned around and located Miriam in the morgue. I tried to figure out what she was doing there, because normally she works in Emergency and I know she hates losing out. Miriam told the nurse that she'd be right up.

I ducked out to look for another cab but there was nothing in sight. As I walked back into the building, Miriam stepped out of the elevator. I always liked seeing her in her white coat with a stethoscope round her neck. I guess it was because it made me feel like a responsible citizen and because I knew that my parents would approve if they'd known about her. Which they didn't. Or that when she got that white coat and the rest of her things off, she was a really great piece of ass.

We gave each other a hello-type kiss, then she took my arm and walked me away from the desk. "We may be stuck here for a little while. Did you make a reservation?"

"No," I said. "I wasn't planning on going anywhere fancy. Have you got some kind of crisis — or are we just going to sneak off and get stiff on lab alcohol?"

"Neither," replied Miriam. "Listen, an ambulance on an NYPD call brought in a man about half an hour ago. It turned out that he was a DOA who should have gone to the city morgue but —" She shrugged. "— maybe they thought we could give him the kiss of life. Anyway — there was something about him that really threw me. I want you to take a look and tell me what you think." She hit the elevator button.

I grimaced. "You mean — in the morgue?"

"Yes." She smiled. "Hey, that's something I've never asked you. Have you seen dead bodies before?"

"I've seen a couple of car crashes," I said. "But they were mainly blood and feet sticking out from under blankets."

The elevator came. Miriam ushered me in. "Don't worry. He's still in one piece."

I eyed her warily. "You promise? No messy exit wounds?"

"No. Nothing like that." She took hold of my hand and led me out of the elevator when it reached the basement. "This way, Dr. Resnick. I'll get you a white coat."

Smart move. Putting me in a white coat meant that I couldn't pass out without looking foolish. I composed myself as we entered the morgue and walked over to where this body lay half-covered by a sheet on an autopsy table. What they call the slab.

Miriam introduced me to the doctor who was carrying out the postmortem examination on the body. A guy called Wallis. A gray-haired chain-smoker who looked as though he'd seen it all. There was also a young intern with Harpo Marx hair hovering in the background. His named was Lazzarotti. He gave me the story so far. Two cops in a squad car had spotted the body in an alleyway over on the East Side.

It had been stripped naked. There were no clues as to the possible identity of the victim. Nobody in the immediate vicinity had seen or heard anything. The usual story. The cops had radioed for an ambulance, the crew of which claimed to discern lingering signs of life in the body. As a result, they had burned red lights all the way across town to the Manhattan General and had taken off again before the reception staff in Emergency discovered that they had been landed with a corpse.

I took a deep breath and looked at the body. Like Miriam had said, he hadn't been blown away but he was still a mess. The man was about thirty to thirty-five years old, medium build, lean hard body. In general, his features were of the type the police label Hispanic. He had a swarthy complexion and his skin was deeply tanned. He had a beard and straggly, shoulder-length hair. Like a hippie who'd done time on a kibbutz. There was a gaping, two-inch-wide stab wound in his left side just under his rib cage but the most unsettling thing was the bruises and lacerations. The guy had had the shit beaten out of him, then taken one hell of a whipping. The skin on his back had been cut through to the bone and there were deep raw stripes on the backs of his thighs as well. It also looked as if his attackers had beaten him over the head with a nailed piece of wood.

Miriam pointed to his feet. "See that?"

I nodded. "Yeah, what are they — bullet wounds?"

"No," replied Wallis. "Somebody drove a metal spike through them. Through his wrists too." He picked up an arm and showed me.

I swallowed hard. "Jeezuss . . . what kind of people would do something like this?"

"Animals," said Wallis. "New York's full of them." He squinted at me through the smoke of his cigarette. "You think this is bad? You want to stay on my tail for a week."

"Well, whoever it was really gave it to him, didn't they?" said Lazzarotti. "I wonder what the hell he did to deserve it?"

Wallis shrugged as he took the butt from his mouth and

lit another cigarette with it. "Probably a pusher who stepped on one of the big boys' toes. Or maybe he was carrying a consignment and decided to cut himself in. If you cross up the Mafia, they don't fool around."

"That's right," said Lazzarotti. "Remember that guy those two hoods hung on a meat hook and worked over with a blowtorch and cattle prod?"

"There are no needle marks on his arms," said Miriam.

"So he's an acidhead," replied Wallis. "Or maybe he screws Boy Scouts. Who cares? All I want to do is fill in this report and get the hell out of here. My wife is waiting in a restaurant uptown for an anniversary dinner. Not that I give a damn but I'm an hour late and I've canceled twice already."

"Would you like me to finish up for you?" asked Miriam. "I've done some PM work with your friend Ericsson."

Wallis hesitated, then scribbled his name at the bottom of what I presume was the autopsy report and death certificate. "Make sure you get a set of prints to send downtown to check against felons and missing persons."

"You got it," said Miriam. "Do you have any ideas about the cause of death?"

Wallis pulled on his cigarette and sniffed. "From what I can see, I'd say respiratory failure. The beating helped, but from the rope marks under his arms it looks as if this guy has been strung up somewhere. A few hours of that is all it takes. My guess is that the stab wound was inflicted after death occurred, but you may have to open him up to check that out. It's up to you. Personally, I don't think any of us need bust our ass over this one but don't let me stop you being zealous."

"Isn't that what practicing medicine is all about?" said Lazzarotti.

"It is indeed," replied Wallis. He closed up his bag and headed for the door.

Miriam called out to him. "How many years?"

Wallis paused with his hand on the push plate. "Years what?"

"How many years have you been married?"

"Twenty-seven," replied Wallis. The doors closed behind him.

Miriam turned to me. "You see? Some people do make it."

"Don't rush me," I said.

Lazzarotti, the intern, came out with another nauseous nugget. "You know, I've been thinking. Maybe it was a bunch of religious maniacs that did this. Remember that news item about that guy in England who had himself nailed to a cross on Hampstead Heath? Right through the palms of his hands. The police arrived just before his friends got to work on his feet. Happened about fifteen years ago."

"You must have been a really creepy kid," I said. "What did you use to keep under the bed — a Jack the Ripper scrapbook?"

Lazzarotti looked hurt. "No. I just read about it. Thought it might be relevant. After all, you never know."

"That's right," said Miriam. She eyed me then turned back to Lazzarotti. "Paul, get me an ECG and an EEG unit down here as fast as you can."

"But —" he began.

"Just do it, okay?" said Miriam. "Call me if there's any problem."

Lazzarotti left. Now for those of you who, like me, avoid watching open-heart surgery on TV, I should perhaps explain that ECG stands for electrocardiogram, and EEG for electroencephalogram. The first monitors heartbeats; the second, brain activity.

Miriam saw my puzzled frown. "You don't understand."

"I can understand you wanting to get rid of Lazzarotti," I said. "But why send him for an ECG unit? A pizza with sausages and peppers would have been more useful."

"We'll get to the pizza later," she replied. "Right now I want to run a couple of tests."

"I still don't get it," I replied. "What can they prove that you don't know already?"

"That this man isn't dead."

As you can imagine, that was a real jaw-dropper. "You've got to be kidding," I said.

"No. Something happened just as Wallis went out the door." Miriam motioned to the guy's left hand, which hung over the edge of the slab. There was a quarter-size drop of blood on the tiled floor beneath. Another drop fell beside it. Then another. The stab wound had begun to bleed too.

I turned to Miriam. "You're the doctor, but I have to ask — how can a mistake like this happen? I mean, my God — just think. If Wallis hadn't been in a hurry to get away from here, this poor bastard could have been sliced open from his neck to his navel."

Miriam gave me one of those pitying looks doctors reserve for laymen. "Leo, I was one of the people who checked him over in Emergency. He was dead. Believe me. Don't ask me to explain things. All I can tell you is he's alive now." She plugged the hole in his side and bandaged his wrists and feet. When she'd finished, she looked at me with this odd kind of expression. "This is going to sound a little crazy, but since you haven't remarked upon it I have to ask — doesn't he remind you of somebody?"

The question made me smile. "Is that why you sent Lazzarotti to fetch that equipment?"

"This is serious, Leo," said Miriam. "Answer the question."

I cast my eyes dutifully over the bandaged body. "Well — I know who you mean, but it's only because of what's happened to him."

"Take a look at his teeth . . ." Miriam opened up the man's mouth and showed me. "No fillings, or signs of any other dental work. He's also never worn shoes."

I shrugged. "So he's a barefoot freak who doesn't eat candy. That's not so unusual. Especially if he came from somewhere like Somalia, or the middle of Saudi Arabia. And in any case, the party you have in mind had his big moment two thousand years ago."

"I know. But just suppose . . ." Miriam let it hang there.

I could see that she thought that what she had been about to say was as outrageous as I did.

"I'm way ahead of you. It's a great idea but —" I shook my head. "Forget it. Things like that just don't happen."

The phone rang in the morgue attendant's office. He leaned backward and stuck his head around the door without moving his butt off the chair. "Lazzarotti . . ."

Miriam went across to take the call.

I turned back toward the body on the slab and found him looking at me. A chill shock wave rippled up my spine and I was still quivering when I reached the attendant's office.

Miriam lowered the phone. "What's the matter?"

I gestured wordlessly toward the body. But when we looked around, the cover sheet was lying flat on the top of the slab. The body had gone. My back had been turned for ten, maybe fifteen seconds.

Miriam eyed me, took a deep breath and spoke into the phone. "Paul, uhh — hold those units. I'll see you back up in Emergency."

Miriam and I went back to the slab, lifted up the cover sheet and looked at each other. "This is crazy," I said. "His eyes were open. What happened?"

She shrugged. "You tell me."

"Well, at least the blood's still here." I went down on one knee and reached out a finger.

"Don't touch it," said Miriam. "I want to put that on a slide." She folded the cover sheet over the foot of the table. There were smears on the slab where the lacerations on his back had started to bleed. She shook her head. I knew how she felt.

"There has to be a rational explanation," I insisted. "Just don't ask me what it is. But even if one buys the idea of the whole event, it doesn't add up. I mean — if the body disappeared, why didn't the blood go with it?"

Miriam gave me a look that spelled bad news. "That wasn't the only thing he left behind." She took her hand out of her coat pocket and offered it to me, palm upwards. "I found these stuck in his scalp when I looked him over upstairs."

She was holding three dark, inch-long spikes. I thought at first that they were nails. Then I looked again and saw that they were thorns.

Terrific. On top of which, we had a signed death certificate and no body to go with it. I handed the problem right back to her. "What do we do now, Doctor?"

Miriam decided that the best thing to do was play it straight down the line. The morgue attendant, who was totally absorbed in the twin activities of reading a paperback and picking his nose, had noticed nothing — and looked unlikely to move from his chair until payday. She therefore reasoned, with a kind of Polish logic, that as no one was likely to come looking for the body we might as well pretend that it was still there. While I held my breath, Miriam calmly filled out a card for the front of the freezer drawer that would hold our invisible corpse, then we put a combination of our fingerprints on the sheet that had to go downtown. Since the NYPD was not going to come up with a match for the dabs, we figured that the freezer drawer would stay closed until the time came to ship the body to the city morgue. And when somebody opened it and found it empty, that would be their problem.

Miriam transferred the blood from the floor onto glass slides then cleaned up the slab. We went back upstairs into Emergency where she did a quick snow job on Lazzarotti then we hung up our white coats and slipped out of the hospital.

Needless to say, we gave the Fassbinder movie a miss. We went back to Miriam's apartment on Fifty-seventh and First, brewed up some strong coffee, bolstered ourselves with an even stronger drink and looked at each other a lot. Occasionally, one of us would pace up and down and start a sentence that foundered somewhere between the initial intake of breath and the first three words. We were like a couple of characters from a play by Harold Pinter. In the second act, we withdrew into silence. I think we both thought that if we did not talk about the problem it would go away. A well-known tactic which, as you've probably discovered, doesn't work. Deep down, of course, we were both trying to figure out some kind of explanation that our dazed minds could accept. After all, we were normal people, leading normal lives, with a firm belief in the normal scheme of things. We both knew that thin-air disappearances just did not happen. And yet — there it was.

In the third act, when the words came, it was in the form of small talk that touched upon our lives but carefully side-stepped what had happened at the hospital. It was as if the event was a concealed Claymore mine which, if triggered by one careless word, might explode and blow our lives to pieces. And so we kept our distance until finally we could no longer resist playing the verbal equivalent of chicken. Jumping in with both feet but protecting ourselves by jokes — the New Yorker's defense against calamity. At least, I did. And we might have managed to laugh off the event if we'd been dealing with the inexplicable disappearance of an unknown Hispanic too poor to buy himself a pair of shoes. But all the black humor and skepticism I was able to muster could not shake Miriam's deep inner conviction that she had bandaged the wrists and feet of you-know-Who. And that really had me worried. Because on top of being a very down-to-earth doctor, this was a girl who had no time for religion. She came from a good solid family background, so naturally, like any nice Jewish girl, she had had a grounding in the faith. But, like me, she had left all that behind a long time ago. And again, like me, she was a very together person. She needed a religious experience like a hole in the head. But if she was right about who had done that Houdini act in the hospital morgue, there was only one possible explanation.

Somehow, at the instant of the purported Resurrection, the body of the man known as Jesus had been transported forward through time and had materialized for at least seventy-five minutes in Manhattan on Easter Saturday of the eighty-first year of the twentieth century.

"Instead of where?" I asked, when we reached this conclusion.

"Wherever he went to when he disappeared from the morgue," said Miriam.

"What kind of an answer is that?" I huffed.

"The kind you get when you ask that kind of question," she replied.

Now I am sure that some of you who have been following this may already have spotted what seems to be the deliberate mistake and maybe have even checked to see what it says in the Book. And the question you're asking is — if he rose on the third day, what was he doing in Manhattan on Saturday night? The answer is that the time in Jerusalem is seven hours ahead of New York. It was already Sunday over there.

I mention this now, but it didn't occur to me on that first fateful night. As I've said, we were both trying to find a way to dismiss the whole thing because, even if one set aside the nut-and-bolt practicalities of the time-travel hypothesis, it raised other issues that strained the limits of credibility.

To begin with, it meant accepting that the event described in the New Testament Gospels and which formed the cornerstone of the Christian faith actually took place. Until quite recently, I'd never taken that part of the story seriously but, after the publication of the latest scientific investigations of the Turin Shroud, I was prepared to accept the possibility that something quite extraordinary might have occurred. And if, as rumored, the alleged image of Christ had been sealed into the linen by some process involving cosmic radiation then, clearly, we were in a whole new ball game.

For it meant accepting not only the reality of time-travel, but also the simultaneity of time. Which meant, as I understood it, that Einstein had got it wrong. For if our tentative explanation was anywhere near the truth, then our own births, lives and deaths had occurred in the same instant as that in which the body of Christ had been transported from the first century A.D. to our own. And as he lay in the alleyway over on the East Side and later on that slab in the morgue, four Roman guards were lying blinded outside a rock tomb in a Jewish cemetery near Jerusalem and, if the scientists were right about the shroud, maybe even dying from radiation burns. While we sat in Miriam's apartment, his life and ours and all the events in between coexisted simultaneously along with every other event from the beginning to the end of the world — and the universe itself.

As you can imagine, the implications of such a concept were too stunning to even begin to contemplate. What we needed was reassurance. The comforting thought that our world was still as it had always been. That everything was as we perceived it to be. And so we tried to convince ourselves that what we had witnessed had not really happened. After all, visions of Christ, complete with stigmata, and of the Virgin Mary had appeared on numerous occasions to more than one witness. In some cases over periods of several hours. Days even. But to avail ourselves of this escape route meant explaining away the fact that the cops in the squad car, the crew of the ambulance, the admission personnel on duty in Emergency at Manhattan General, Wallis, Lazzarotti, the morgue attendant and the two of us had all been exposed to different segments of a unique hallucinatory experience.

Maybe Saint Teresa or Saint Augustine might not have had any trouble taking something like this on board, but ecstatic visions were definitely not part of our scene in spite of the highs we'd had while sharing the odd joint.

To be honest, we would have given anything to have been able to shrug the whole thing off, but no matter how our minds twisted and turned, the circumstantial evidence of our time-traveler remained. And while it could be destroyed, it could not be denied. The thorns that Miriam had picked out of the victim's scalp and the blood she had transferred onto three glass slides and had passed on for microscopic examination. And the photographs. Yes. They were a surprise to me too. One of the cops had taken four color Polaroids of the body before it had been moved from the alleyway on the East Side. We didn't know about the pictures on that first night but later, when they came into my possession, I remember saying to Miriam — "Have you any idea what these could be worth?"

You will find them with the other documents in my safety deposit box at the Chase Manhattan.

Sunday morning, April 19. The sun rose on schedule. The world around us, and presumably the universe, appeared to be still in one piece. Monday, the same thing. We went back to work and tried to forget what had happened. What the hell, life had to go on — right? We went out to dinner a couple of times. We made love. We even went to see the Fassbinder movie. But it was no good. Neither of us could shake off the image of that whipped and beaten body on the slab and its sudden inexplicable disappearance. And although I said nothing to Miriam, I was haunted by those eyes that had opened and the look they had given me.

Through a colleague, Miriam had gotten in touch with an obliging lady botanist who was able to identify the thorns as coming from a prickly shrub called *Palerius*. It was one of several similar types to be found in Israel and the Middle East generally. As evidence, it wasn't particularly conclusive, but it didn't help our mental campaign to turn the Saturday night mystery into a nonevent.

I asked Miriam if she was going to try and have the thorns carbon dated.

"No need," she replied. "Alison found traces of sap on the base of the thorns. She reckons that the branch they were growing on had been cut from the bush within the last couple of weeks."

Which, when you think about it, seemed to make sense.

It was with the blood sample that things got a little sticky and the story we concocted eventually fell apart but it was the best we could come up with at the time. Miriam had asked a friend of hers called Jeff Fowler to analyze it. He was the head of some research team or other that was working on blood fats. When he called Miriam back he had sounded distinctly twitchy so she fixed for the three of us to meet at my place.

As he came in through the door, he said, "Where did you get this sample from?" We hadn't even shaken hands.

"Before I answer I want to know one thing," I said. Stalling for time. "Is it human and, uhh — what would you like to drink?"

"The answer to your first question is a qualified yes. And I'll have some of that Jack Daniel's. On the rocks."

Miriam went into the kitchen to get the ice.

I put my back between Fowler and the bottle and poured out three thick fingers of sippin' whiskey. "That really surprises me. I thought it might be chicken blood. Or maybe pig."

"No, it's human," said Fowler. "Only more so. That's why I want to know who you got this from."

Miriam returned from the kitchen. I took the ice and sent her in to bat. "What exactly do you mean, Jeff?"

"Just what I've said," replied Fowler. "The blood is human but it differs from any other sample I've seen in two important respects. First, it appears to have been subjected to a heavy dose of radiation —"

"Not unreasonable." I handed over the Jack Daniel's in the hope that it might sap his zeal for the truth. "My client had been receiving cobalt therapy for cancer of the stomach."

Miriam eyed me and did her best to look as if she knew all about it. "And the second thing?"

"The red cell structure is abnormal," said Fowler. He didn't seem to have noticed that the ice cubes didn't touch the bottom of his glass.

"In what way?" I asked.

"Do you know anything about blood?"

I shrugged. "I know it retails at ten dollars a pint."

Fowler gave up on me. "It's too complicated to explain in

detail. What I really need is a bigger sample to run more tests but if the abnormality I found was reproduced throughout the body, it would arrest the aging process."

"I wish I knew the secret," said Miriam.

"I'm not kidding," said Fowler. "This is dynamite. Whose blood is it?"

I put on my blandest expression. "It, uhh — belongs to a gentleman who paid several visits to a center for psychic healing in the Philippines. As Miriam has probably explained, I'm a lawyer. My client's family had reason to believe that the treatment was fraudulent and we were preparing a lawsuit against the people involved."

"Got it," nodded Fowler. "Some of those guys are pretty smooth operators."

"Exactly," I said. "It took months of planning and skulduggery to obtain a sample of the blood that allegedly came from the stomach of my client after one of the 'operations.' The last thing I expected was that it would be human."

"Group O," said Fowler.

I grimaced disappointedly at Miriam. "My client's blood type . . ."

"Where is he?" asked Fowler. "Can we run some more tests?"

"I wish it were possible," I said. "He died last Friday. I'm acting for the family."

It was Fowler's turn to look disappointed. "I see. Has he, uhh — been buried yet?"

"No, cremated," I replied. "But if the blood cells were transformed in the way you suggest it would seem to imply that some of these people actually *do* have paranormal powers. If the word got around it might weaken our case. Apart from which it could be embarrassing for you."

"How do you mean?" said Fowler.

"Well —" I shot a sideways glance at Miriam. "You want to come out in public for faith healing? Even if it worked? Isn't your research program funded by one of the big multinational drug companies?" I sat back and let the poison do its work.

Fowler's eyeballs bounced off the rims of his glasses as he figured out the implications. "You're right," he mused.

I shrugged. "No point in rocking the boat."

"No," said Fowler. "And anyway, why should I help line the pockets of those dinks. Screw 'em."

"Good thinking," I said. Then added helpfully, "Jeff — why don't we play it like this? You keep the samples. Junk them or work on them all you want, but let's agree to keep this whole thing under wraps. It's going to make life a lot simpler. Okay?"

Fowler looked at each of us then nodded. "Okay. But don't be surprised if you hear from me again. I'm going to stick with this until I come up with a satisfactory explanation."

I threw up my hands and quoted the Bard. "There are more things in heaven and earth, Jeff. Let me give you a refill." I gave my fellow conspirator a loaded look.

Miriam smiled sweetly. "Leo — why don't you call Carol and see if she can make up a four for dinner?"

Carol was my friendly neighborhood nymphomaniac. If she got on Fowler's case he would soon forget about abnormal blood samples. In fact, by the time she was through, he wouldn't even remember the difference between red and white corpuscles.

Luck was certainly on our side on that particular night. Or so I thought. Now, of course, I know better. But don't let's jump the gun. Not only was Carol free, she was bowled over by Fowler's blend of academic diffidence and Old World courtesy that he probably picked up from watching *Upstairs, Downstairs* on Channel 13. Frankly, I found Fowler to be something of an asshole but with the aid of some spurious goodwill we managed to pass an agreeable evening over some Szechuan specialities then sent them both off in a taxi to finish what they had started under the tablecloth.

Miriam and I went back to my place with similar intentions but I made the mistake of first seeking praise for the way I'd handled Fowler's questions about the blood.

"Yes, it was very good," she said flatly.

"Very good? It was a goddamn stroke of genius," I crowed. "All we have to do now is keep him sedated with heavy doses of stunned admiration."

"Yes," said Miriam. "Unfortunately, Fowler isn't our only problem."

I stopped nibbling her ear. "How do you mean?"

"Well," she began, "I meant to tell you earlier but then Jeff arrived and — et cetera. The thing is, I was having coffee this morning with some of the hospital administrators and just by chance somebody mentioned the ambulance."

I felt my lustful passions wilt. "What ambulance?" As if I didn't know.

"The ambulance that answered the NYPD call — and brought the body to Manhattan General. Instead of taking it to the city morgue."

My eyes were riveted on hers. "Go on . . ."

"It was stolen from Gouverneur Hospital," she said. "The two paramedics who drove away with the body did all the right things but nobody knows who they are. It certainly wasn't any of the regular crews. I asked Lazzarotti about them. All he can remember is that they were both tall slim guys. Like basketball players."

"How about the police?" I asked.

"You mean the squad car that escorted them to the hospital? They don't know any more than we do," she said, then added with a shrug: "Listen — an ambulance is an ambulance. When one answers a ten-fifty-four, who asks questions?"

I reached for a cigarette and stiffened my nerves with a quick drag. "Has it been found yet?"

"Yes, the same night," said Miriam. "They left it parked outside Manhattan General." She borrowed my cigarette for a couple of puffs then put it back between my lips. "I'm going to make some coffee."

I followed her mechanically into the kitchen. My mind was in overdrive. Figuring all the angles. "Do you realize what this means?"

She nodded as she put some beans into the grinder. "I think so. But go ahead and tell me anyway."

For once I had to force the words out. "It means that — that someone must have known he was — coming."

"Exactly," said Miriam. "The question is — who?"

Who indeed? I had been besieged with questions all week and now more were crowding into my overworked brain. How could they have known? What was their role in all this? Where had they come from? Were they people, like us — or had they come from beyond time and space as he had? Why, of all the hospitals in New York, had they chosen Manhattan General? And did whoever "they" were know about us? I can at least tell you one thing for sure. When something like this is dropped in your lap at one A.M. in the morning, all carnal thoughts fly out the window.

TWO ≡≡≡≡≡≡≡≡≡≡≡≡≡≡≡

THE following Saturday, I drove up to Sleepy Hollow. On top of the metaphysical turmoil created by the mystery man at the hospital, it had been a pretty heavy week at the office and on the back seat of the Porsche was a caseful of papers that I'd promised myself I'd read through by Monday morning. Miriam was working but hoped to make it upstate Sunday after lunching with her parents in Scarsdale. Normally, I'd have stayed in my apartment. I think the real reason I left town was because I wanted a moment of relative peace and quiet to reflect on what had happened. At least I like to think that was the reason. That I had a choice, and not because it had all been worked out for me.

Around five in the afternoon I was sitting at my worktable in the living room, reading through an inch-thick deposition on a patent infringement case I was preparing. I glanced idly out of the window toward the trees that mark the western edge of my modest spread. Between the house and the trees is this big open stretch of grass. Miriam likes to call it the lawn, but to me it's only lawn when it looks like Astroturf. This is grass. At least some of it is. My neighbor took great pleasure in telling me that most of the green bits were clover. Anyway . . . there I was, gazing through the window, thinking that (a) I would have to get the mower fixed, and (b) that it was time for another cup of coffee. I mention this because I am absolutely certain about what I did, or to be more precise, did not see.

As there were only thirty pages of the deposition left, I decided to finish it off first. I read through a couple more pages then looked out the window again. And there was this guy in a pale brown robe and white headdress walking across the grass toward the house. Now it had taken no more than a minute to read those two pages. There was no way he could have gotten to where he was unless he had stepped out of thin air. I sat there, glued to my chair, and watched him come closer. Then I saw the bandages and knew I was in trouble. It was our friend from Manhattan General . . .

Was I frightened? Yes, a little. I think what I really felt at that particular moment was a sense of wonder. Amazement. I just could not believe that this was really happening to me.

I used a slip of paper to mark my place in the deposition and went out onto the porch. I saw him pause to look at my car before he came on up the steps through the rock garden to the house. It was the same guy, all right, but he looked a lot better than he had at the hospital. The swollen bruises on his face had disappeared and his nose had been reset. He stopped a couple of yards away from me. His eyes were tawny brown; his gaze, which had haunted me, very direct. I stood there and eyed him back, trying to manifest a subtle air of assurance. Listen, it's not every day that you find the Son of God, or whatever you want to call him, standing on your doorstep. Because, believe me, that's who it was. Miriam had been right. It wasn't the victim of some gangland killing that the police had found in that alleyway. It was the body of the Risen Christ. And he'd come back. The Man was here. In front of me.

Impossible? Of course it was. That's what I tried to tell myself. It made no sense. Yet it had happened. Even so, my mind still refused to accept the evidence of my own eyes. And that was because an inescapable choice was being forced upon me. Something I hate. If I resisted up to the very last moment it was because of the fear that to accept his presence would totally change my life just when I had reached the point when I was happy with the way things were. I could live with the world's imperfections. Doing so enabled me to comfortably ignore my own.

He glanced back at the Porsche with an admiring nod. "Nice."

That really threw me. It was so totally unexpected.

"Your name is Leo Resnick, right?"

I gulped wordlessly and nodded.

"We met at the hospital," he said. "Do you know who I am?"

I finally managed to loosen my larynx. "Yes — I think so. What can I do for you?" What a question. But at the time, I had no idea where it was going to lead me.

The Man just stood there, weighing me up with those deep-set eyes. There was something unnerving about the way he would look at you. It reminded me of a falcon. The way they fix on you as they sit on their handler's gauntlet. After what seemed a long while he answered me. "I'm not sure yet."

I felt the bottom drop out of my stomach. It was the "yet" that did it. It meant that I was involved. That he not only knew my name but also had my number. And I remember cursing my luck and thinking — if only it hadn't been raining last Saturday I would have found a cab. I would have gotten to the hospital on time. Miriam and I would have left before the ambulance that brought him in had arrived. And maybe — who knows? — maybe I could have stayed out of all this. If you had been in my place you would probably have felt the same way.

But why me? Even now, it's a question I still ask myself. Why pick on me? But on the other hand, when you think about it, why not? After all, the first time around, The Man just hauled a bunch of fishermen off the end of the pier at Capernaum. I'm anybody — just like the next man. And as I said, we're all in this together, whether we like it or not.

The Man took in the view from the porch then turned

back to me. "This may sound a little strange but — where am I?"

That threw me too. I mean, you don't expect Jesus to be interested in Porsche Carreras but when he steps out of nowhere onto your lawn, it's not unreasonable to assume that he knows where he is.

"You're in a place called Sleepy Hollow in upstate New York," I said. "The east bank of the Hudson River is just over there."

"Ahh, thanks . . ." He glanced briefly toward the trees.

"New York is part of the continental United States," I added helpfully. "North America?"

He looked at me blankly. "How far is that from Jerusalem?"

I thought it over and, as I worked out the answer, I was also thinking — *Get a grip on yourself, Resnick. Don't crack up. This conversation is not actually taking place. You've just been overworking* — "Jerusalem?" I heard myself say. "I would guess that the place you're looking for is about five thousand miles and two thousand years away. Today is Saturday, April twenty-fifth, nineteen eighty-one."

He frowned.

"That's using the Gregorian calendar," I explained. "Year One was about seven years after your presumed date of birth. I don't know what year this is according to the Jewish calendar but I could find out if you're interested. Anyway, for what it's worth, welcome to the twentieth century."

The Man took the news with an impassive nod. "I think I'm in trouble."

That was where I made my second big mistake. What I should have said was — "That's tough, look, I'm busy" or "I only see people by appointment. Call my secretary." Or told him to take it down the street. I didn't. But even now, I still can't quite accept the idea that that option was not open to me. I was filled with a sense of foreboding but suddenly I wasn't frightened anymore. I felt this great longing to *know* well up inside me. To find out what had really happened way back when this thing had gotten started and what he was doing here. There had to be an angle, and there was only one thing to say — "You want to come in and talk about it?"

The first thing I did after I got him settled was to excuse myself and call Miriam from the phone in the kitchen. "He's back . . ."

"Who's back?" she said.

"Who do you think for Chrissakes? Uhh, I mean —" I lowered my voice and made a mental note to reprogram vocabulary. After all, The Man was in the next room. "The DOA we lost on Saturday night."

There was a stunned silence at the other end of the line. "Leo — are you putting me on?"

"I wish I was, Miriam," I said. "I really and truly wish I was." I meant it too, despite the curiosity that now consumed me. For either of us to have anything to do with this guy could only lead to trouble. In our circle of friends and business associates there were two surefire ways of committing social suicide: going broke and getting religion. And the last was the worst.

"But Leo," said Miriam. "This is absolutely fantastic."

"Yes," I said cautiously. "I guess it is."

"How did it happen?"

"Well, he didn't come by Checker Cab," I said. "How do I know? He just appeared. What can I tell you?"

"Okay, okay. What kind of shape is he in?"

"He's fine," I replied. "He looks great. He's sitting on the sofa in the living room."

"What doing?"

"Drinking. He was thirsty. I gave him a drink."

Her voice turned sharp. "What of? Water, coffee, Coke?"

Doctors . . . He was her patient already. "No," I replied. "A glass of red wine."

"Wine . . . ?"

"That's what he asked for," I said, irritated by her tone of voice. "Look — how soon can you get here?"

"Oh, wow . . . that's a problem. I just can't walk out of here. Look, umm —" She sounded confused. "I'll come as soon as I can."

"Okay. How soon is that?" I said, pleased to have regained the upper hand.

"Maybe not till tomorrow morning. It's tough to find someone to cover for you on a Saturday. I'll come out there as soon as I come off duty. My parents were expecting me over but —"

"Never mind about them," I said. "They'll still be there next week. Are you sure you can't make it any sooner? Tell the hospital your grandmother's been taken sick. Or that she's dying or something."

"Leo," she said, "this is not like cutting classes in junior high school. Saturday night's the busiest we have in Emergency. They come in by the busload. I don't have an excuse to pull out and if I told them the truth, they call up the men in the white coats."

"You don't have to tell me," I replied. "Why do you think I want you up here? I need someone to tell me I'm not having a nervous breakdown."

There was a slight pause at the other end of the line. "Do you wish you were?"

"I don't know," I said. "At the moment, I'm too confused to tell you *what* I feel. I need more time to think about it."

"Okay, listen," she said briskly. "I'll get there as soon as I can. Meanwhile don't let him out of your sight."

"Oh, gee, thanks, Doc," I said. "Just how am I supposed to do that? You saw what happened at the hospital. If he decides to take off again, there's no way I can stop him."

"I know that," she replied. "Just keep him talking. Ask him where he's been all week."

I thanked her for the suggestion and hung up. I went back into the living room half-expecting to find it empty. Half-hoping would be nearer the truth. But he was still there, standing by the window taking in the view, glass in hand. He turned toward me and eyed me silently.

"Hi, how are you doing?" I said. You know — just to get things going.

"Fine." He raised his empty glass. "Is it okay if I, er . . . ?"

"Sure. Help yourself."

"How about you?" he said.

"Yeah, great." I couldn't help smiling. "This may sound stupid but I can't get over the way you talk. Just like an American. The accent is not homegrown but you speak better than most of the *chalutzim* we get in town."

That made him smile too. "How did you expect me to speak? Like someone out of the Saint James's version of the Bible?"

"I don't know," I replied. "In Aramaic, I guess."

"If I did, you wouldn't understand a word I said." He filled both glasses to the rim and handed one over. "Talking to people is easy. It's getting through to them that's the problem. The introduction of language was a retrograde step. Designed by some friends of mine to keep people apart. To prevent them from understanding one another."

I made a mental note to ask him who his friends were. We sat down with the coffee table between us. He put his feet up on it. Miriam's bandages were still in place. Over them, he was wearing a pair of leather sandals with studded soles. They looked as if they had pounded down a few stony roads in their time.

He saw me looking at them. "Roman army sandals," he said. "The best there is. A centurion gave them to me after I cured his servant. The pair I had before this took me to Britain and back before they finally gave out."

"Amazing," I said. "I didn't know you went to Britain."

He nodded. "Oh, yes, I went all over. I was on the road for twelve years."

"It's not in the Book."

"No," he said. "It got edited out."

"In fact, if I remember correctly," I continued, "after the account of your birth there's nothing until that bit in Jeru-

salem when you are twelve, then we don't pick up on you
until you're around thirty."

"Thirty-four," he said.

I realized I was going to have to get hold of a copy of the
New Testament and bone up on the text so I could ask the
right kind of questions. We sipped wine in silence for a
while then eventually, with studied casualness, I put my feet
up on the table too. And I remember thinking that I would
have given anything for Rabbi Lucksteen, who bar-mitzvahed me, to walk in so I could introduce him. Then I saw
The Man looking at me and wondered if he could read
minds.

"That phone call was to Miriam," I explained. "She was
the doctor who bandaged your hands and feet and . . ."

He nodded. "Ahhh . . ."

"You look a lot better than when I last saw you," I said.
"How are the, er — how's the wound in your side?"

He smiled. "Oh, you mean where they stuck the spear?
Much better."

"You must let Miriam take a look at you. She'll be up here
tomorrow." I grinned. "In the meantime, I'm supposed to
keep you talking."

He looked at me over the top of his glass. "That's okay
with me, but I don't want to interrupt anything. I noticed
you have a heap of papers on the table over there."

"It's not important," I said. After all, I thought, I didn't
have to be in the office until Monday morning, and with any
luck he might be gone by then. "Just make yourself at home,"
I continued. "I've got a big garden. There's a bike in the
garage, a stack of books and color TV. You might find that
interesting if you want a quick update on what's going on."

And if he got bored, there was always the chance that he
might mend the rail around the porch, or put up a few
shelves.

"Thanks," he said. "The problem is, I'm not sure just how
long I've got."

I received the news with mixed feelings. "How do you mean?"

"I mean I'm not sure what's happening," he said. "As I understood it, I was supposed to be in Jerusalem." He rubbed his forehead. "What year did you say this was?"

"Nineteen hundred and eighty-one. If I remember correctly, certain religious historians put the date of the, er — of your death around the middle of March, A.D. twenty-nine."

He nodded. "The fifteenth year of the reign of Tiberius." He dropped his head onto the back of the sofa and closed his eyes. "What a mess." After a while, he raised his head and looked at me. "You must be wondering what I'm talking about."

I spread my palms. "Look — I'm just an ordinary guy. I can't even begin to understand what this is about, or what it has to do with me, and I realize that you may not have time to tell me but we have to start somewhere. Let's go back a week. What's the last thing you remember happening in Jerusalem?"

He sat up a little. "I was lying inside this rock tomb wrapped in a long strip of linen." He gestured with his hands. "One half was underneath me, the other half was folded down over my head."

Which was good news for fans of the Turin Shroud.

"I don't quite understand," I said. "How could you know about that? You were supposed to be dead."

He shook his head. "No. It was only Joshua's body that had ceased to function."

"*Joshua's* body?"

"Yes," he replied. "Joshua was the given name of my host-psyche. We both shared the same vehicle. The thing you call a body. To us, it's a mobile life-support system. It was really his. I just lived there. It wasn't an ideal arrangement, but there was no alternative."

Oh, boy, I thought. Wait till Miriam hears about this. "Maybe we could come back to that later," I said. "Okay, you were in the tomb. Then what?"

He shrugged. "The next thing I remember is opening my eyes and finding myself lying on the table in the hospital morgue and you standing over me."

"Wait a minute," I said. "What about the alleyway?"

He frowned. "Alleyway?"

"The crew of a police patrol car found you lying naked in an alleyway on the East Side of Manhattan. They called an ambulance — which brought you to Manhattan General where several people, including Miriam, examined you before your body was sent down to the morgue. Are you telling me you don't remember any of that?"

"No," he said. "Just waking up and seeing you."

"Oh, come on," I cajoled. "You can do better than that. Try and think back. The ambulance that picked you up was stolen from outside another hospital about fifteen minutes before the police found you. The two men who picked up your body must have known you were coming. Who were they? Why did they bring you to Manhattan General?"

He looked at me with the baffled frown of a man who did not know what I was talking about. "I'd like to help you, Leo, but — I can't. As I've tried to tell you, I'm not in control of this situation."

"Okay," I said. "But if you do find out who was involved, I'd like you to tell me. If I'm going to be part of this, I have a right to know what's going on."

"Absolutely," he replied.

I had a sneaking suspicion that he wasn't leveling with me but what could I do? Some words came into my mind — *What is hidden is hidden.* Hadn't he said that? Whether he had or not, he held all the cards. The whole situation was so bizarre, the only course open to me was to play it by ear while keeping an eye on the nearest exit. I resumed the interrogation. "Where did you go when you left the hospital?"

He smiled. "Back inside the rock tomb. This time, my two crewmen were waiting for me. My sudden disappearance had caused a certain amount of confusion. I explained where I'd been — or rather, where I'd found myself — then we made contact with the longship. We sent Joshua's body through first, then the three of us were beamed aboard."

I tried to keep a straight face. "You mean like in — ?"

He nodded. "Yes. Like in *Star Trek*."

I had to laugh. "How do you know about that?"

"From you. The images were in your mind."

"It must be hard to keep a secret when you're around," I said.

He shook his head. "Not really. I've just got good antennae. I can sense that you're bursting with questions you want to ask me and I'd like to answer them but —" He shrugged ruefully. "It's not that simple."

"You mean you can't describe the indescribable," I said. Thinking — *Here we go. The classic cop-out.*

He smiled. "No. It's not a cop-out, Leo. As long as you are locked into the physical world you will never be able to comprehend mine. You communicate with other human beings through the spoken word, and it's possible to reach them on another level through music. But can you go beyond that? Can you imagine beings who use a form of language which begins where music leaves off? The answer is 'No. You can't.' Your brain contains censor-blocks that prevent you from reaching this level of understanding. Man is capable of soaring flights of imagination but he can never fly high enough. That's why we have to come down to earth. But you must remember that the *Star Trek–Star Wars* terminology is no more than a verbal shorthand to help you understand what I'm talking about. Because the only way we can communicate is by using words and concepts you are familiar with."

"Like you did before."

He smiled. "Yes. But this time, I'll try and spare you the parables."

Reading this, you may think that I was handling the situation with an incredible amount of cool. Not so. My insides were quivering like Jell-O. But the truth was that, after the initial shock had worn off, The Man was a very easy person to be with. But don't misunderstand me. He was no push-over. And I was well aware that being around him could be bad for your health. The point I'm trying to make is this. You read about someone like him, or some other youthful over-achiever like Alexander the Great, and one gets a feeling of awe. But in the case of The Man, that feeling of awe is the result of two thousand years of relentless brainwashing by the people running the road show. Meeting him face-to-face was something else. Because, to all external appearances, he was just like any other ordinary human being. It was true he had the kind of eyes that could burn a hole right through you, but apart from that, he was no more remarkable than any of the hundreds of people you pass every day in the street on your way to work. If the sky over Sleepy Hollow had split open in a blaze of light and I had been deafened by heavenly organ music, or a Stan Kenton version of The Last Trump, I might have felt differently, but here he was, sitting on the sofa in my living room with his feet up on the coffee table. Splitting a bottle of wine with me.

Respect? Sure, that was something I felt even though he had gone out of his way to make me feel at ease. Caution? Yes, certainly. Especially now that I knew he could read my mind. And also because I had no way of knowing what might happen from one minute to the next. A sense of wonder? Yes, that too — for the first fifteen minutes or so. You have to remember that I'd spent most of the week being amazed at what had happened the previous Saturday at the hospital. These days, things change so rapidly; people learn to adjust. And let's face it. Awe is a difficult thing to sustain. Especially for a New Yorker.

"Let me try and get something straight," I ventured. "Does the fact that you went back to first-century Jerusalem when you disappeared from the hospital morgue mean that time is — ?"

"Simultaneous? Yes . . ."

Just like that.

The news was stunning. My mind couldn't react to all the implications. I just accepted the fact meekly. "So — does that mean that birth, life and death are simultaneous events?"

"That's right," he said. "In the same way that the beginning, middle and end of a book exists between the front and back covers — but you only live your life story one page at a time." He eyed me with a smile. "Does that bother you?"

"I'm trying not to think about it," I said. "Tell me about the starship."

"You mean the longship? The vessel that came to rescue me?"

"Yes."

"Okay," he said. "But first, you have to remember what I told you about word images. Because no matter how I phrase it, this story is going to end up sounding like a cross between a movie scenario written by George Lukas and Tolkien's *Silmarillion*."

"Don't worry," I said. "I'll try and read between the lines."

He paused and rubbed his forehead. "I'm trying to figure out how to give you this without confusing you. . . ." He sat up, put his glass on the table and his feet on the floor and used his hands to underscore what he was saying. "Three of us were sent here to make contact with a group of — let's call them 'colonists' — beings like us that came to Earth a long long time ago. There was no response to our signals on the way in, or after we'd gone into orbit, so I came down with one of my crewmen to find out what had happened. The landing module — and remember these are your words I'm using — developed a malfunction on touchdown. As a result, the two of us were marooned. The second crewman, who was piloting what you would call the command module, went to get help. And that took about thirty Earth-years to get here."

The words came out as casually as if he was telling me how the car he was driving had stalled on the exit ramp of the Brooklyn Bridge on the way in to the office in Manhattan.

I tried to accept it in the same way. Even so, my eyes were

like saucers. "I see. So what does that make you — some kind of spaceman?"

"Not really," he replied.

"What are you then?" I said gingerly. "An angel?"

He smiled. "Don't let it worry you. Let's just say that I'm from out there somewhere."

"You mean from another galaxy?" I insisted.

He shook his head, "No. From another universe."

I nipped the soft skin of my left hand with the thumb and forefinger of the right. Digging in the nails until it really hurt. To convince myself, once more, that I really was sitting there having this conversation. That it was not just a dream. At the back of my mind there lurked the idea that some jokester might have popped acid into my jar of instant coffee. But on the other hand, I had had a reasonably sane conversation on the telephone with Miriam, and there were none of the sensory or color distortions associated with a normal trip. I focused my attention back onto what The Man was saying.

". . . and so the crucial question was — what did we do until the rescue ship got here? The only way we could survive was by incubating inside a host body — like yours. Only there was no guarantee that we could escape from it unharmed." He shook his head, remembering. "The problems . . . I can't tell you." He unclenched his fists and tapped his chest. "You can't know what it's like to be trapped inside one of these things."

"How could I?" I said. "I've never known any other kind of existence. At least, not one I can remember. Was it bad?"

"Horrendous," he replied. "A thirty-year nightmare. And it *still* isn't over." He made a fist. "They promised me. Go through with the Crucifixion, the Resurrection, and that's it. Next stop home. Instead of which, I end up in the twentieth fucking century." He saw the look on my face. "I'm sorry. I guess I'm not supposed to talk like that. Your brain just went into spasm."

I swallowed hard. "Listen. As far as I'm concerned, you can

say whatever you like. I just think you ought to know that there are a few words in my memory bank that are not meant to be used in polite company. They don't upset me but there are a lot of people around who have very firm opinions about you. And they wouldn't be at all happy to hear you talk like that — even though the Book says that you came on a little strong now and then." I smiled at him. "Maybe some of the flavor got lost in translation."

"We lost a lot more than the flavor," he said. He relaxed a little. "But you're right. There were times when I got a little uptight. I didn't realize how hard it would be to get through to people. But that bit in the Temple was special. I was trying to get myself arrested. The vessel that had come to rescue me was in solar orbit between Earth and Mars. Just one of a whole fleet of ships strung out between here and the Time Gate. Everybody was waiting. I *had* to get them to kill me."

My brain tried vainly to grapple with these new disclosures. Every time he spoke, the cosmic canvas he was painting got bigger and bigger. I fastened onto his last words. "Why was it you had to die?"

"Because it was the only way I could escape from this thing." He tapped his chest again. "Joshua's body."

"But why did someone else have to kill you?" I asked. "Why didn't you just — jump off a cliff? Or cut your wrists?"

He shrugged. "Good question. All I can say is that was the way it had to be done. There were reasons. Let's leave it at that." He poured out some more wine.

I wanted to ask him what those reasons were but I decided to wait until he volunteered the information. After all, it was just a bare seven days since he'd been crucified, and although his body had been miraculously healed, the event was clearly very much on his mind. I tried a slightly different tack. "Tell me — if the main reason for the Crucifixion was to enable you to get out of your body — or rather, Joshua's body — why are you back in it now?"

"Ahhh, it's not the same," he said. "It's been — how shall we say — reconditioned? Unlike yours, it is no longer subject to the physical laws that govern Time and Space but, apart from that, under normal circumstances it's virtually impossible to spot the difference. That was the whole point of the Resurrection. It was to prove that I had power over death. That I was able to come back as a fully functional, three-dimensional human being. But nobody warned me that time-travel was part of it. That's why I'm not sure what I'm doing here. When I found myself on that slab in the morgue instead of on board the longship, I was somewhat dismayed —"

"Dismayed?" I interjected.

He smiled. "I'm thinking of my image. When I'd recovered from the surprise, my first thought was that there had been a technical hitch. Riding a beam is not the most foolproof method of transportation. But now that I'm back here again, I'm not so sure. The odds against hitting the same time-slot as a result of a malfunction are astronomical. I have a feeling that this may be another part of the mission they haven't told me about yet." He shrugged. "It wouldn't be the first surprise they've sprung on me."

"How do you mean?" I said.

"The breakdown of the landing module was rigged. I was dumped here. They broke the news to me about a year ago when the rescue fleet entered the galaxy." He gave me a wry smile. "Looking back, I suppose it was the only way to get me to go through with it."

I swallowed what was left in my glass. My face must have shown that my brain was going into overload.

"I guess it must be difficult for you to take all of this on board," he said.

"It is," I admitted. "We've barely started and already we've opened up several king-sized cans of beans. I just hope we're going to have enough time to go over some of these areas in more detail."

"Maybe we will, maybe we won't," he said. "At the moment, I have no way of telling. Cross-time communication is possible, but unless the longship knows exactly where I am, we can't make contact. In any case, it's just acting as a relay station. The control point for this phase of the mission is on the other side of the Time Gate." He paused. "I think I just lost you again."

"Totally," I replied. "But don't worry. Just keep going. I'll try and sort it out later. The exercise will be good for my brain. This 'Time Gate' — what exactly is it?"

"It's the movable interface between your world and mine," he said. "Between temporal and nontemporal space. The door through which we enter and leave the cosmos. Which opens only for the brief moment of our passing then vanishes with its closing. Invisibly sealing the fabric of the physical universe which will never again be opened at that point in space for the rest of time. It is thus that the Empire is protected from the forces that seek to destroy it."

As I listened to him, I was praying that he would hang around until Miriam got there. I wanted someone else listening in. Let's face it, this was pretty wild stuff. I knew that no one in his right mind was going to believe my unsupported testimony. On the other hand, after listening to us, they might throw us both in the nuthouse. I perceived a partial answer to my predicament. "Uhh — would it be okay with you if we got some of this down on tape?"

"Yes, sure, go ahead," he said.

I went to fetch the small IBM dictation machine that I carry around in my Samsonite, checked that it was working, and laid it on the table between us. Then I took a deep breath and started in again. I'd lost all count of time, and was hopelessly tangled in the various threads of the story. It was just too big to handle. In the end, I opted for the simplest question I could think of. "Listen," I said. "There's something Miriam wanted to know. What have you been doing all week?"

"Trying to convince my friends in Jerusalem that I'm a real live person," he replied, "— and not some kind of ghost."

"I can understand their problem," I said. "Let's face it, this is a pretty fantastic situation."

"It is for you perhaps, but I lived with these people," he

said. "Some of them were family. I *told* them I would be back. I explained what was going to happen — and yet most of them still can't believe it." He shook his head despairingly.

I chewed over my words carefully then finally screwed up the courage to say — "This must have been a really bad time for your mother."

He nodded, and drank some more wine.

"Did she know who you really were?"

"Yes, from the very beginning," he said. "But sometimes she, uhh —" There was a slight break in his voice. "— she found it hard to cope." He turned away and stared out of the window.

I didn't say anything. We just sat there and let the silence settle round us. The late afternoon sunlight angled in through the windows and highlighted his profile. He certainly wasn't any Robert Redford. A real writer would be able to give you a couple of pages of deathless prose describing him from head to foot but I'll keep it short and sweet. He looked like a cross between Martin Scorsese and a bearded Robert De Niro. The dark, heavy-browed look combined with De Niro's coiled-spring leanness.

I thought back over what he had told me so far and what had happened since that fateful Saturday at Manhattan General, and it occurred to me that he still had not positively identified himself — and indeed never did. He didn't need to. The instinctive knowledge of who he was had welled up from somewhere deep inside me, while at the same time another part of me was trying to stop me from accepting it. Trying to bury the feeling of certainty under layers of doubt. Looking for a way to avoid getting involved.

Intellectually, it was an intriguing idea to be sharing a bottle of wine with The Man while Pontius Pilate and the Sanhedrin had search parties out looking for him. It didn't require a rational explanation. Our minds had been conditioned by several decades of science fiction and fantasy literature and the concept of time-travel had been with us, on paper at least, since about 1840. But no one in his right mind would believe that it could actually happen. Especially the scientific community who, faced with the latest findings on the Turin Shroud, had withdrawn into a baffled silence. I found it hard to imagine The Man agreeing to submit to tests under laboratory conditions in the way Uri Geller had. But even if he did — how could he prove that he had journeyed from the first century to the twentieth and back again? Wouldn't we turn out to be just one more generation of vipers looking for an empirically provable sign?

The Man came out of his reverie. "Tell me, Leo. Is everybody like you nowadays?"

"How do you mean?" I said.

"Well — in the way you've just accepted me being here — and the things I've told you."

"I accept that you're here," I said. "And that you were also at the hospital. But it's still giving me a few problems. As for the rest, I'm not too sure just how typical I am. I like to think I'm open-minded and I suppose, because of that, I don't have any preconceived ideas about you. It's the same with those endless arguments over the existence, or nonexistence, of God. It's an interesting idea, but I have to tell you that religion is not something I have a lot of time for. That goes for a lot of other people too. But there are millions of others of various persuasions who take it very seriously indeed. And the irony is, you could be in big trouble with both groups if you went around telling people who you are."

"Tell me something new," he replied.

"No, really, it's a lot harder now," I said. "Since you died, there have been quite a few freaks who claimed they were the Messiah, uhh — not that I'm trying to suggest that —"

"Sure," he said, "I know that."

"You see," I continued, "Miriam and I *know* what happened. We don't need convincing. We saw it with our own eyes. But if you decided to make your presence known to a wider audience, we could encounter a serious credibility problem. Take the Jews for instance. If my people didn't believe you were you then, what's going to make them believe you are you now?"

He nodded thoughtfully. "I see what you mean. . . ."

"It's the same with the Christians," I said. "There are plenty of them around but they can't even agree among themselves as to who you were, what you did, what you said, or whether you meant it. I think I'd better tell you that while you've been away they've been rewriting the script. The Ten Commandments are out, and faggots are in. People still believe in you but they might not be too happy if they knew you'd come back. I have a feeling that most of them would prefer the myth to the real thing."

His eyes fastened on mine. "But in spite of what you've said, *you* believe me."

I wriggled uncomfortably under his gaze. "Look — uhh, I already told you. Religion's never been a big thing with me. Especially my own."

"Religion is not what it's about, Leo," he said. "That's something you people dreamed up. What I'm concerned with is awareness."

I grimaced. "You may have trouble in putting that across. I hate to tell you this but, in the last twenty years, 'awareness' has become one of the world's great clichés. It's been exploited by all the wrong kinds of people."

"I know," he said. "The other side has been busy."

"The — other side?" I ventured cautiously.

"Yes," he said. "Didn't you know there was a war going on?"

I hesitated, unwilling to respond to his question, but I couldn't think of a way out. "You mean — all those stories about a ceaseless conflict between the Forces of Light and the Forces of Darkness are true?"

"Yes," he said.

My brain began to backpedal. "Sounds interesting," I said flatly. "But I'm not clear on where *I* fit into any of this. I mean, this is big league stuff. What can I do?"

"That's something we still have to work out," he said.

My face must have been a picture.

"Leo," he said. "This is one fight where you can't stand on the sidelines. All of us are involved whether we like it or not. So you might as well get used to the idea."

Okay, I thought. *But don't expect me to volunteer for hazardous duty. I'm strictly a rear-echelon man.*

If he picked up my cowardly thoughts, he did not reveal it. The one thing I did not need was news of an imminent Armageddon. I decided to steer the conversation back to something more innocuous. "I imagine your people must be wondering where you are."

"Yes," he mused. "I wish there was some way I could make contact."

I must tell you, I found it odd that he couldn't. I mean, from the way he'd been built up by the Roman Church, you'd have expected him to have a direct line. But I didn't press the point. "Where were you when you made this last time-jump?"

"In a village a few miles from Jerusalem," he said. "A place called Bethany. I was talking to my brother James and some of the Twelve —"

"The disciples?" I asked.

"Yes," he nodded. "My mother was there too. I walked out of the house expecting to be beamed up to the longship and —" He snapped his fingers. "— there I was, outside this place."

I nodded sympathetically but tried to hold back on the concern. "The Book does mention your sudden disappearances in that period after the Resurrection but the writers are a little hazy about your movements. Which is understandable. They weren't there when it happened."

"Have you read the New Testament?" he asked.

"Not from cover to cover," I admitted. "But I know the general outline. And I can tell you one thing for sure. Nobody mentioned you had a sense of humor."

He smiled. "There were times when that was the only thing that kept me going."

"Well, the laughs aren't in the Book," I said. "But it's still sold a lot of copies. From what you've already told me it's clear they didn't get anything like the whole story. But let's face it, they're only human. Now that you're here, why don't we use what time you've got to set the record straight? Let's get as much down as we can, then you can decide what you want to do with it."

"Okay," he nodded. "Good idea . . ."

It had to be. I'd been watching the bottle of wine. I'd had two glasses. He'd had six. And it was still full . . .

THREE ═══════════════

I left The Man in charge of the magic bottle and went and made myself a cup of coffee. At the back of my mind was a hazy memory of him doing something like this before but I couldn't remember whether it was with a cask of wine, a pitcher of water or a jar of oil. I phoned Miriam from the kitchen and asked her to bring me a copy of the O&NT. She told me she'd managed to talk her way off the Saturday night detail and would drive up in a borrowed car. She thought she would probably reach Sleepy Hollow around eleven and asked me what I was doing about food.

I told her that I'd brought enough for the two of us and that I had the impression that our guest wasn't too concerned about his calorie intake. It was, of course, the wrong thing to say.

"He drinks, doesn't he?" she said severely. "What makes you think he doesn't eat?"

"Okay," I said. "If you want to play the Jewish mother, bring up a bag of bagels."

There was a withering silence at the other end of the line. "You still there?"

"I'll see you later," she said. And hung up on me.

I carried my coffee back into the living room and resumed my recorded conversation with The Man. "You mentioned coming from another universe. I know that's one of our word concepts but according to the dictionary, 'universe' means 'the totality of things which exist' — 'another universe' is a contradiction in terms. So what exactly are we talking about?''

"A universe that lies beyond the boundaries of external reality — which you use as a yardstick to prove the 'existence' of everything within it." He paused as he saw me frown. "Think of it this way — you're familiar with the one you can see —"

"You mean the one that falls within the spectrum of visible light?"

"Yes," he said. "The optical universe. And your radio-astronomers are busy mapping others composed of X-ray and other high-energy sources that give you, for instance, a very different picture of the sun. It's no longer just a yellow disc broken by the occasional solar flare. You accept this invisible aspect of the sun because scientific instruments have confirmed its existence. So it should be easy for you to accept the idea of a parallel universe, which 'exists' alongside your own but which you cannot see because it is on a different wavelength. Now — just as a host of short-, medium- and long-wave radio programs can pass through this room simultaneously, my world is superimposed upon the space-time continuum that you perceive as the physical universe. It interpenetrates yours completely, and it is able to do this because, like the radio programs, it does not take up any space. Even so, it is as 'real' as your own yet your mind does not admit of its existence. Why? Because your brain — which is like a radio set capable of receiving broadcasts from all over the world — has become permanently tuned to one channel. The local station you know as external reality. The finite world. And the received data is fed into your brain through the five physical senses. But many more worlds lie beyond this one and —" He looked at me with just the hint of a smile. "—something tells me that you are aware of this possibility."

"Well, I'm not a complete dummy," I replied. "I've read a

couple of books by Carlos Castaneda and dipped into a third. I believe we have a sixth sense and like to think that we actually *do* possess that legendary third eye. I can accept the idea of alternative realities just as I can accept the idea that we once knew more than we do now. My problem is that I find it impossible to envisage what form those alternate realities might take, or how I could exist within them or — and which is more to the point — what relevance they have to the one I'm part of."

The Man smiled again. "Take it from me, Leo. You don't belong exclusively to this world. Otherwise, I wouldn't be here."

I headed for shallower water. "Let's go back to when you first arrived here. Before you entered Joshua's body. Did you come in a starship, longship, or whatever — like the one that I presume is still hovering somewhere above first-century Jerusalem?"

"No, something smaller."

I waited expectantly but he did not elaborate. "Okay," I said. "I won't ask to see the blueprints but — who builds these things?"

"Nobody." He smiled as he saw my frown. "They're brought into being by The Power of The Presence. Think of them as thought-projections."

"You mean like the castles and landscapes that were conjured up by the power rings worn by the characters in Michael Moorcock's trilogy — *Dancers at the End of Time?*"

He shrugged. "Yes, something like that. I'm not trying to evade your questions. There are no words to describe the workings of our world or how it came to be. Just accept that it is so."

I nodded. "Okay, I understand. But it's still very frustrating. Never mind. Let's move on. You said that there were three of you on board."

"Yes. Two Envoys and myself."

"And I assume that you were mission commander."

"Yes. In Earth terms, the Envoys were subordinate to me

but they were both time-wise. I had never been through the Time Gate before."

"How did it feel?" I asked.

He chewed over his answer. "It was quite an experience. . . . It's only fair to tell you that a lot of our people become 'star-struck' on their first trip through the gate. And some of them never recover."

Who were they? I wondered. And what happened to them? Did they become wandering spirits — on the run from God's army? Or did they go over to the enemy? I pressed on with my original line of questioning. "Okay — so there are three of you inside this spacecraft, or whatever. What do you look like?"

I could see that this was another one of the hard ones. He rubbed his chin and gave me a long look. "What are you asking me to describe — my temporal or nontemporal aspect?"

"Both," I replied.

He shook his head. "I can't. It's like trying to describe a rose to a man who's been blind from birth. Words are useless to describe its color and form. The only way he can receive an impression of the rose is through his other senses. By touching its petals and inhaling its fragrance. You can only understand what we are like in the same way. Not by touch or smell, but by reaching a higher level of awareness. Or if you don't like that word, let's say by — enhancing your degree of perception."

"That's cheating," I said. "Are you trying to tell me that if I'd been there when you stepped out of the landing module I wouldn't have seen you? The shepherds who were watching their flocks saw something. Or so the story goes. Are you really sure you can't tell me what it was?"

He shook his head again. "You're the one who's trying to cheat, Leo. You want the answers but you're not prepared to make the effort to understand. Remember the story about the man who threw seed onto stony ground? The trick is to ask the right questions. When you do, you'll find that you already know the answers."

"You mean — 'Knock and the door shall be opened'?"

He smiled. "I couldn't have put it better myself."

"Oh, come on," I insisted. "Just give me a little hint. If I *did* have this higher level of awareness, what would the three of you have looked like? In your spacesuits, or whatever."

He sighed. "You're a hard man, Leo." He drank some wine and toyed with his glass for a moment. "The only way to describe us would be as — luminous beings. Our exact shape would depend on the condition of the observer. The received image is influenced by cultural and racial imprinting, as well as the degree of perception. In other words, you might see us as Persian angels — anatomical absurdities with seventy-two pairs of wings covered with eight thousand eyes — or something like the board of General Motors but with halos and white suits."

"Okay, I get the message," I said. "What kind of shape are you in on the other side of the Time Gate?"

The Man gave me a really odd look. As if I'd asked him something near the knuckle. "I am that I am," he replied.

Some answer.

I sat back and finished off my coffee. "These two Envoys that you mentioned as having already been through the Time Gate. Had they visited us before?"

"Several times," he said. "They're enshrined in Earth mythology under many names. The Persians knew them as Beshtar and Sorush. Your people know them as Michael and Gabriel. Mi——"

"Don't tell me," I interjected. "Michael stayed in the command module while you and Gabriel went for the landing. It's in the Book," I explained. "Gabriel's the one who broke the good news to your mother."

"I don't know whether she saw it like that at the time," he said. "I remember at one point, life became rather complicated."

I waved him down. "One thing at a time. Let's get back to the spacecraft."

"Leo," he said. "Let me give you some advice. Don't get hung up on the hardware. The longships, the star-sail boats, the transit shells that we're obliged to wear are not really what we're about. It's just a means of getting here. There was a time, in the First and Second Age, when we could move freely between our world and yours. We had no need to shelter behind the Time Gate. But in the Third Age, the Age of Darkness, all that changed. The physical universe is now a very dangerous place." He paused, searching for the words. "Perhaps it will give you some idea of what I mean if I tell you that space is not the airless void you imagine it to be. To us, the cosmos is like a vast ocean, the galaxies island-continents separated by the deeps — intergalactic space. The planes of rotation of each galaxy — interstellar space — are regarded as seas, encompassing the star-islands. Such as your sun with its necklace of nine planets. The space contained by each star-island and its circling archipelago is called 'the Shallows.' And so on. Michael and Gabriel know much more about this than I do. The point is, before the Age of Darkness, the Deeps, the Seas and the Shallows were crystal clear but now, to an unprotected Celestial, it's like swimming through Iranian crude. And the atmosphere on this planet, which, despite all the pollution, you find quite breathable, is absolutely unbearable to us. To be trapped in it without the protection of our transit shells or a host body is like drowning in a mixture of boiling tar and sulfuric acid. Except, of course, we do not breathe, and cannot die. But it would be like choking to death — forever."

I nodded to show that I'd got the picture. "Nasty. So is that what you call yourselves — Celestials?"

"No," he replied. "But that's the nearest we can get using your language."

"Okay," I said. "So — this place you come from — on the other side of the Time Gate."

"Think of that as the Celestial Empire," he said. "But don't be misled by the stereotyped images conjured up by

Star Wars. The Empire is boundless and timeless. It encompasses all of creation and all of eternity. It interpenetrates the smallest particle of the physical universe but is itself impregnable. It is here, in this room, within your grasp. Yet it is as far beyond the reach of your mind as Earth is from the most distant galaxy still to be discovered by your astronomers. Many of your most brilliant philosophers have dismissed it as an illusion but it is, in fact, the ultimate reality."

"It also sounds like the ultimate paradox," I said. "Let me check that I've got this straight. There are two universes —"

He shook his head. "No. The Celestial Empire contains *nine* universes. Seven of them lie beyond the Time Gate through which I came. Collectively, they are known as the World Above. The other two space-time universes are known as the World Below. The cosmos, the physical universe which you inhabit, and the Netherworld —"

I cut in to gain some breathing space. "The Netherworld . . . ?"

The Man nodded. "Yes. A mirror image of the cosmos, but fashioned from antimatter. We also refer to it as the First Universe. It can only be entered through what your Earth astronomers call the Black Holes."

The concept of a mirror universe composed of antimatter was not unfamiliar. The idea had been kicked around by physicists for several decades. It was only the name that was new. Even so, I could not accept the fact of its existence with the same ease with which The Man had dispensed the information. Those of us who gave any thought to the matter were still trying to grapple with the logistical problems involved in the creation of our own apparently limitless universe. Yet here I was, confronted with eight more of the goddamn things. It was too much to handle.

The Man eyed me and smiled. "You look worried."

"Not really," I replied. "I think what my system needs is another shot of caffeine." I went into the kitchen, turned on the percolator then spoke to him through the open doorway.

"Let me recap that last bit to help me picture it in my mind. The space occupied by this planet, the solar system, the stars and the galaxies beyond is only the second of nine separate universes . . . ?"

"That's right," he said. "But don't waste time trying to construct a four-dimensional model of it in your mind. This is something that the conceptual processes of the human brain are not equipped to handle."

"You mean because — the seven universes beyond the Time Gate are nondimensional and nontemporal," I replied. Trying to work out in my logic-bound mind how, if there were no dimensions, you could tell where one universe ended and the next began. The answer is, of course, we can't — but Celestials can. It was, as he had warned, a conceptual problem that could not be resolved by the conscious part of my brain, whose sole function was to deal with external reality. But this was something I did not fully understand until much later. At that moment, my brain hurt — and it showed.

He eyed me sympathetically. "If you need to give this thing form, just think of it as a symbolic, multilevel pyramid with the First Universe at the bottom and the Ninth at the top."

I nodded gratefully and returned to the percolator as the boiling water started to bubble through the ground coffee. "And which one do you come from?" I asked, as I returned to my seat facing him.

"The Ninth," he said, with disarming simplicity.

I'm sure there was a lot more he could have told me about the setup in the World Above but you'll just have to accept, as I had to, that knowledge of the Empire's internal organization is not necessary in order for you to be able to understand the rest of this story.

"Let me ask you something else," I said. "I'm coming around to the idea that it's impossible for me to visualize the World Above but how do you see ours? Is your perception of external reality very different from the images my brain receives when I open my eyes in the morning?"

He nodded soberly. "Very different. . . ."

"And you're going to tell me that it's too complicated to explain," I said.

He shrugged. "All I can say is that I have 'double-vision.' My temporal aspect is equipped with different levels of sense perception that allows my metapsyche — the Celestial 'me' — to receive a visual impression of the universe that would make no sense to you whatever. At the same time, by dropping into a lower gear, I am also able to see the world that you think you 'see.' " He paused, then added smilingly, "The only difference is that my perception of external reality may not be quite as rosy, or indeed as clouded, as yours."

"That's what make life bearable," I replied, feeling the need to score one for mankind in general. "Okay, let's get back to the mission. The three of you came looking for these — colonists. What kind of an operation were they running here?"

"They were seeding the prime. Implanting the genetic matrices from which all life throughout the cosmos springs."

"So does that mean you made us — like it says in the Book of Genesis?" I asked.

"Not exactly. Our people were involved in the development of an earlier model which, for the sake of this discussion, we can label 'Proto-Man.' " The next bit made him smile. "You're what the U.S. Army might describe as an unofficial field modification."

"Don't knock it," I said stoutly. "I'm all I've got. How many people did you have working here?"

"Twelve."

I looked at him in utter astonishment. "Twelve . . . ?"

"You must remember that we're not talking about human beings," he said. "These were Celestial powers. Aeons from the Seventh Universe."

"In other words, heavy cosmic dudes," I said.

He smiled. "It's a reasonably apt description. They might not be too happy with it but then, Aeons do tend to take themselves rather seriously. It's important to remember that the world was a very different place during the Second Age."

"When was that?" I said.

"Oh, a long, long time ago."

"How long?"

"Way back. Thousands of millions of years," he said, waving the question away. "The Aeons were already at work here before the dawn of geological time. More pointless information. Your mind cannot draw any meaning from such a vast span of time."

"It's still nice to know these things," I riposted. "I didn't realize we went back that far."

"You don't," he said. "But you can forget all that stuff Darwin is supposed to have proved. You did not evolve from walking apes. Your ancestors began life on another plane of existence. Another wavelength which, during the Age of Darkness, was absorbed into the wave band of external reality. They were like dream images that slowly acquired a solid, tangible shape from which, finally, they could not escape. In the Second Age, before this happened, the landscape was much more nebulous. There weren't the pressures there are now. This crushing force of gravity dragging everything down. If it were possible for you to see it through your twentieth-century eyes — or even through those of the people I've just left — you would think you were on another planet. Jupiter perhaps. In any case, it would be unrecognizable as the present Earth. And if you were to catch sight of Proto-Man as he was forged in the fire-clouds of the world's dawning, you would not recognize him either."

"In that case, I won't ask you for a description," I said. "Let's get back to the colonists. You said that you came here to make contact. How long had you been out of touch?"

"We lost contact with this galaxy during the Second War of Secession." He paused. "This is getting rather involved."

"Just give me the broad outline," I said. "If there's time, I'll bone up on the fine print later."

"Okay," he said. "But remember what I told you about George Lukas scenarios. I have to use your language but you must try to make your mind reach beyond the words."

"I'm trying," I said. "But don't expect miracles. I'm new at this game. Uhh, by the way—" I added hurriedly, "no offense intended."

"That's all right," he said. "Listen, Leo, before we go any further. You don't have to treat me like the president of Yale, or the dean of your law school. You're looking at one of the founder-members of the school of plain speaking. So just say whatever's on your mind. If I'd wanted the red-carpet treatment, I'd have asked for the address of the nearest college of Jesuits."

"You got it," I replied. "On with the prehistory lesson."

He took a deep breath. "Very simply, the Empire to which I belong was split by a rebellion which had its roots in the creation of the World Below. The forces supporting the Empire called themselves Loyalists, and the rebels were called the Secessionists. In Earth mythology, they are also known as the Black Legions, the Forces of Darkness, the Satanic Hosts — the list is endless."

"Don't tell me," I said. "They are the bad guys."

He shrugged. "That depends on your point of view. They've evolved a very persuasive argument that casts us as the villains of the piece and them as the protectors of the universe which — according to this novel thesis — we are out to destroy. A neat twist." He smiled. "Anyway, to cut a long story short, we won the First War of Secession. The rebels were banished to the Netherworld —"

"The universe of antimatter . . ."

"Yes," he said. "It was a prison. That was the sole purpose behind its creation. We couldn't go in there, and they couldn't get out — or so we thought. There was a period of relative calm during which we began the work of reconstruction, then the rebels broke out of the Netherworld through the Dark Gates and swept through the universe like a forest fire. The Second War of Secession has been raging for about two hundred million years."

"How's it going?" I said.

He grimaced. "We're not doing too well at the moment. But don't worry. It will all work out."

I wondered if he knew that, at that moment, I was not worried in the slightest degree who the eventual winner might be. I was busy telling myself there was no need to pick sides.

His voice broke into my thoughts. "One of our problems is that the power grid — the network of channels linking the Empire with the galaxy primes that serve as both sailing and signal lanes — was totally shattered in the first assault. We've been trying to reconnect the system ever since so that The Power of The Presence can once again flow through the cosmos. Until that day, it has to come in discrete packages — through people like me." He smiled. "All this may not seem important to you, but to the Celestials in the World Below, The Power of The Presence is the lifeblood of the universe. It's like the human body. Stop the circulation to any of the limbs and they begin to waste away."

"Is that what happened to the twelve Aeons you had working here?" I asked.

"In a way, yes," he said. "Except of course in our case, the condition can never be fatal. Just a lingering agony."

It had never occurred to me that immortality might have its drawbacks too. "Tell me about the Aeons who were stationed here."

"I will. But first, I'm going to have to throw a couple more names at you. Don't worry if you can't remember all this. It's a lot to take in first time around." He paused to give my brain time to catch up. "The word Aeon describes their degree of power in the World Above. All Celestials trapped in the World Below by the Second War of Secession are known generically as the Ain-folk. And the ancient name for Earth was Eardh-Ain. The last signal we received from Earth confirmed that the rebels had taken the galaxy and were poised for a final attack on the prime. This planet. The colony had turned down a last chance to surrender and was preparing to make a last stand. And that was it. End of message."

"And so, to continue the medical analogy, the colony begins to waste away until, a few zillion years later, you drop out of the clouds like the Flying Doctor," I said. Testing the limits of his good humor.

He shrugged. "That's one way of putting it."

"And when Michael and Gabriel had been here before, under different aliases, they were acting as paramedics. Checking the patient's pulse."

"Yes," he said. "But if I can use another, more aggressive analogy, they were like OSS agents sent in to organize the Resistance. Earth wasn't totally cut off from our influence. We managed to make the occasional power input; to slip a few of our people in under the wire. But it was mainly an undercover presence. We had human beings fronting for us. Noah — who was more than a floating zoo-keeper — Moses, Elijah, Zoroaster, Gautama Buddha. All making an input. Keeping up the pressure."

"Now that you've mentioned Moses," I said. "Were the Jews really the chosen people?"

"You were once," he replied. "You know the place called Atlantis?"

I nodded.

"Well, the myths about that particular long-lost continent have their genesis in the history of our Earth colony and its destruction by the rebels. Fortunately, a small nucleus of survivors managed to escape the final holocaust. The progenitors of what you now call the human race. And among them were the distant ancestors of the twelve tribes of Israel."

"So, in fact, what you're saying is that our forefathers — in whatever guise — came over on the Celestial *Mayflower*."

"In a sense, yes. But by the time I got here, the situation

had changed quite radically." He smiled. "To put it in modern terms — you no longer had an exclusive."

"Nevertheless," I insisted, "you still turned up at Bethlehem."

He shrugged. "I had to start somewhere."

"Oh, come on," I said. "We were expecting you."

He smiled and relented. "All right. It validated the prophecies and, in terms of world history, it was where the action happened to be. The point where Greek, Roman, Jewish, Egyptian and Persian culture overlapped. It was the right time and the right place for the message to create the maximum impact."

"So doesn't that make us the chosen people?" I might have renounced all forms of religious faith but I still cherished the notion that I and my Zionist brothers miight have an edge on the rest of humanity.

"What I meant was that you were no longer the chosen people in the strict Biblical sense. I hadn't come just to save the Jews," he said.

"But to redeem Mankind . . ." I concluded confidently.

"It depends on how you define Mankind," he replied. He clasped his hands together and leaned forward, elbows on his knees. "The truth is, Leo, when I first got here you people were the least of my concerns. Jews, Gentiles . . . in my book, you were all expendable. My mission was to rescue *our* people. The twelve Ain-folk who were inside you."

"Inside us?" I said. I don't know why, but the news came as quite a shock. "Are you trying to tell me that the human race has been occupied by your people?"

"Yes," he said. "That's where they've been hiding ever since Earth and the rest of this galaxy fell intò enemy hands. Remember what I said about Michael and Gabriel resembling agents of the OSS? The situation here is analagous to your own recent past. The Second World War. The universe is like occupied Europe. The Ain-folk are the underground resistance movement that we are helping to stay alive until the day of liberation. And it's the rebels — your new over-lords — who are the Nazis, stamping their *Sturm und Drang* philosophy on the cosmos." He sat back. "You don't look too happy."

I shrugged. "I may get used to it, but right now I'm not too sure I like the idea of being taken over."

He leaned forward again and looked at me intently. "Leo — you haven't been taken over. The Ain-folk *are* the human race. Your body is no more than a mobile life-support system. A vehicle in which they could shelter until the Empire was able to rescue them. Without them, you'd be just another race of termites. It is the Ain-folk who provide your guidance system; the controlling intelligence of their earthly hosts. Note the plural. From the very beginning, they used groups of hosts. A few hundred at first, then several hundred, then several thousand. Just as the movements of a shoal of fish appear to be directed by a group mind, so the host bodies possessed by each of the Ain-folk formed a cohesive unit. They provided him with a refuge from the attacks of the Secessionist forces — the 'evil spirits' of antiquity — and in return he used his powers and knowledge of the world to ensure their continuing survival."

I nodded to show that I had understood — even though I was still not too sure how I felt about my newly discovered role as a minuscule, misplaced cog from a dismembered Celestial machine that lay awaiting the arrival of that Big Mechanic in the Sky. "Am I right in thinking that this is where all those stories about guiding spirits, folk gods and the soul of a nation come from?"

"Yes," he said. "If you can bear with me, I'll explain how it happened. Conditions weren't too bad when the Ain-folk first went into hiding but, as the rebels strengthened their hold on the world, the Ain-folk were no longer able to exercise the same degree of control over their host bodies. As time passed — and we're talking here of millions of years — the situation got progressively worse. Galaxy after galaxy fell into the hands of the rebels. Finally, they wrested control of the World Below from the Empire and began to change the nature of the physical universe."

"Was this the change of wavelength you mentioned?" I asked.

"Yes. Man was forced to change too. And in adapting to the new environment, he became totally enmeshed in the physical world. Enslaved by the pain and pleasure of a purely material existence. And as 'Brax ground Man into the earth beneath his heel, the beleaguered Ain-folk began to give up all hope of rescue."

"And it was no good them trying to break out," I added. "Because there was no way they could have gotten home."

"Right. . . ." He paused and poured himself another glass of wine.

"Just one thing," I said. "Who is 'Brax?"

He sank half the glass before answering. "The self-styled Lord of Chaos."

"I understand you're related."

He nodded wearily.

"Every family has one," I said. "In ours, it's my cousin Samuel." I waited for a moment, but he refused to be drawn.

"Let's get back to the war."

"Okay," I said. "But how about a time check?"

"Hmmm . . ." He closed his eyes while he worked it out. "At this point, we're talking about events that took place ninety million years ago. In geological time it is the last quarter of the Cretaceous Period —"

I cut in. "You mean when dinosaurs were roaming around?"

"Yes — and when the Alps, the Rocky Mountains and the White Cliffs of Dover were in the process of being built. The next two segments of geological time brought more upheavals: separation of the continents through lateral shifts in the Earth's outer mantle; worldwide population movements due to climatic changes. Gradually, the cohesion of the original host groups was destroyed. They split up, intermingled, and gradually forgot their collective identity. Each Ain-folk fragment, hiding deep within its human host, no longer openly remembered it was part of a greater whole. Celestial reality became a distant dream buried deep within the subconscious." He paused and took a sip of wine. "And that brings us back to your question about folkgods. It was the hidden memory of this relationship that gave rise to the first primitive forms of religion and sacrifice. From the subconscious awareness of the Ain-folk that lived within them came the idea of a powerful god–father figure. They recognized this as a psychic force which their enemies also possessed. By killing their enemies in battle, or by sacrificing captives, they believed they released trapped psychic power that would make their own god stronger. And because that life power was believed to reside in the heart and the head, these came to be the favored sacrificial offerings. And since their gods also had to eat, animals and other foods were provided in ceremonies that became increasingly elaborate. And as proof of their allegiance and knowledge that they owed their existence to him, Earth-Men made the ultimate sacrifice — specially selected members of their own tribe."

"What happened to the Ain-folk fragment when its host died?" I asked.

"It was released into a shadow world of nightmarish oppression from which it could only escape by entering another newborn human being."

"But wait a minute," I said. "As I understand it, the spirits of dead people who speak through these mediums all say that they're happy and having a good time. There's a lady who claims that Beethoven and a clutch of classical composers are all hard at work writing music and that Bertrand Russell is busy revising his ideas about God."

The Man shook his head. "Don't you believe it. Like the *kami* that the Shintoists revere, there are a lot of disembodied spirit forces present in the World Below but they are not floating around disguised as historic figures from Earth's past."

I was struck by a sudden insight. "You mean because —

because of the simultaneity of time — Beethoven, Handel and all of these other guys are still alive. So these mediums who claim to be in contact with them must somehow be locking on to their creative subconscious. Is that it?"

He nodded. "You're on the right track."

"Okay," I said. "I'll pick it up later. Let's stay with the Ain-folk. They were in the process of forgetting who they were . . ."

"Yes." He downed some wine and took up the story again. "Slowly, the bond between each Ain-folk fragment and its host body deepened, became stronger through their shared experience. It marked the beginning of an individual sense of identity. The birth of Man's ego. The rebels did everything they could to encourage it in an insidious attempt to blot out all memory of the Empire. But despite their efforts, a dim awareness of belonging to a greater whole remained. A lingering memory of immortality; of another existence beyond the confines of Earth. This is why, throughout the ages, generation after generation of Men have turned their eyes to the skies — often without knowing why — and have yearned to be rescued. That's what lies behind Man's death wish. The desire to shuffle off these mortal coils. For despite all the efforts to destroy it, the flame of Truth endures. The inner knowledge of Man's true origins and destiny." He paused and looked me right in the eye. "The realization that you and I are one, Leo."

That was when I felt I needed a drink.

I got up and poured myself a stiff shot of bourbon and got some ice from the kitchen. I remember standing holding the open door of the refrigerator, watching the cubes swirl around in my glass. To give me time to collect my thoughts. He had been right to warn me about George Lukas and Tolkien. He could have thrown in Doris Lessing as well. The Man had just outlined the best scenario I'd heard since *Star Wars*. It had an engaging plausibility but there was no way I could prove whether any of it was true. I just had to accept whatever he chose to tell me. I was conscious of this tug-of-war going on inside me. An eager, almost childlike credulity fighting a seesaw battle with this hard-faced, dismissive cynicism. Why had his words had such a disturbing effect on me? And what was it? Regret for lost innocence? A nostalgic memory of a simpler time — for ideals long discarded? Whatever it was I did my damnedest to bury it under a mountain of indifference. Once again I asked myself the sixty-four-dollar question: Why me? Why was he here? Why was he telling *me* all this? Had I gone quietly crazy? Was I going to wake up in a flower-filled room to discover that everything I had seen and heard in the last eight days had been taking place inside my head? Or was I dead? Had I, like the central character in that story by Michael Frayn whose title I was unable to recall, been the victim of a traffic accident on the way to pick up Miriam at Manhattan General? Was this God's way of breaking the news to me? Or was it The Man who was crazy? Or maybe not even The Man at all but some metaphysical freak from another star system who, for opaquely alien reasons, had decided to take advantage of my guilt-laden Jewish consciousness by presenting himself as the Messiah?

I am telling you this to show you how my mind twisted and turned in an effort to get myself off the hook. It was all too much, and had come at totally the wrong time. Listen — a two-hundred-million-year war. The Black Legions. Atlantis. The news that *we* were the aliens. It's okay to speculate about such things in the privacy of one's own home but, even if it was true, there was nothing we could do about it. The Twentieth-Century Flier might be rocking dangerously on the rails but anyone who tried to stop the train would merely incur the wrath of his fellow passengers. He and I might indeed be one, but where did that get us? Life had to go on. Wasn't I due in court at eleven-thirty on Monday morning? Didn't I still have four depositions to read through? Was Resnick the Resolute going to ditch everything he believed in — fame, fortune and fornication — because some bearded golden-eyed wine-bibber had taken the wrong turning on the way back to his starship? Goddammit, it was only by accident he was here anyway. He said that himself.

I closed the door of the refrigerator, carried my drink back into the living room, and sat down with a resigned sigh. Because the better half of me knew the answers to most of those questions, and the blanks were filled in later. I wasn't crazy and neither was he. He was The Man and he spoke The Truth. This wasn't a drugged fantasy or deathbed vision, this was really happening. But part of me *had* been dead — and had been brought to life by his presence. I sat there under his gaze and hoped fervently that the road he might propose to lead me down would not be as stony as the route he'd chosen first time around.

When I'd proofed myself against adversity with the aid of the bourbon, I took up the thread of our conversation. "Just let me check to make sure that I've got this right. Are you saying that what I think of as *me*, is actually part of one of you?"

"Yes," he said. "It's your soul, spirit, psyche, or whatever you may wish to call it. The *animus*. The intangible essence that provides the life force. The power that enables you to express your humanity — as opposed to your biological functions. The part of you that continues to exist after clinical death turns your body into pot roast."

"So does that mean that part of us goes on?" I said. "That reincarnation is possible?"

"It's more than possible," he replied. "It's a necessity."

"To provide continuing protection for the Ain-folk that are trapped here. . . ."

He nodded. "Yes."

"So, in fact," I concluded, *"we* are the aliens. The extra-terrestrials."

"Yes. Except, as I've explained, the individual psyche is now composed of elements drawn from several of the Ain-folk. It's one of these things that is complicated to explain but it has something to do with planetary configuration at the time of birth — plus a host of other factors. That goes for Miriam, and everybody else too."

"Are any of the bad guys mixed up in there too?"

He shook his head. "No. They work in a different way. They get to your brain through your body. It's the easiest way to keep control. The way we manifest ourselves is through the intellect, imagination, instinct and the positive emotions. By that, I mean love, compassion; not desire and the urge to screw."

I mulled over this new disclosure. "What you've said could explain a lot of things. My star sign is Gemini. Now I have a plausible explanation for my latent schizophrenia. Would I be correct in thinking that these twelve Celestial sleepers are tied in with the signs of the Zodiac and the whole astrology bit?"

"They're tied in with everything, Leo. There isn't time to go into all of it now. Just believe me when I tell you that it all hangs together. If I seemed callous when I said that you were expendable, you must understand that I was talking about my feelings on the approach phase of this mission. From the Empire's standpoint — the overview, if you like — your bodies were, and are, just vehicles. Mobile homes. The only thing we are interested in is the drivers. It was only during my own journey through the world that I began to realize the depth and strength of the bond that had been forged between the Ain-folk and their host bodies — and the pressures that 'Brax had brought to bear on both of them. It was pretty discouraging to discover that most of them had accepted their fate. They'd had enough. They didn't want to be liberated. As far as they were concerned, someone else could fight the war. For them it was over." He smiled. "In the same way that you wish it was over. You resent my disturbing your comfortable routine."

"That's not fair," I protested. "I never said that."

"True," he said. "But do you deny it?"

I shrugged petulantly. "If you're reading my mind, you must also know I'm trying hard to come to terms with what you're telling me. At the moment, I'm not quite sure how it relates to the big wide world out there."

The Man smiled again. "Do you want to know something, Leo? Clever people, like you, are always the last to understand. The Truth is incredibly simple; but it's not easy to find The Way. You must first get rid of all the garbage that has collected inside your head. You have to create a clear path that leads to understanding. It takes time and a great deal of effort. The rebels are constantly laying down smoke screens. Creating diversions. Feeding you false information. They will do anything to stop The Truth getting out. It takes a brave man to stand up against them. They have immense power, and many ways to break you. They can sap your will, corrupt you, ridicule you and, if all else fails, they can destroy you."

It sounded as if I might do better to put my money on the other team. "Can't you do anything to stop them?" I asked.

"We've got the power," he replied. "It's right here in the air, the earth, the sea, rocks, trees and every other living thing. Our big problem is persuading people like you to use it."

FOUR

MIRIAM arrived about half an hour behind schedule in a borrowed Pontiac station wagon. She got out from behind the wheel looking nervous and excited. "Is he still here?"

"Yes, relax," I said. "I have a feeling he's planning to make a night of it." By this time I'd become adjusted to the idea of spending the weekend with Jesus. The trouble would come when he decided to apply for a Green Card. I put my arm around her shoulder. "Come on in and say hello."

"Hold on," she said. "I've got some stuff in the car." She opened up the tailgate. The rear of the Pontiac was packed to the roof with food.

"This must be the first time anybody's robbed a supermarket and taken the store instead of the money," I said.

Miriam gathered up two bulging bags. "Save the jokes. Just help me get it inside."

Actually, I'm exaggerating a little. There wasn't all *that* much. Just enough to feed a football team for a week.

She caught me rolling my eyes. "Listen, you told me you'd asked him to stay on here. Most of it can go in the freezer."

We ferried the food through the back door into the kitchen. The last item was a case of red wine. "Now that really *is* something we don't need," I said, as we dumped it on the counter. I told her about the magic bottle in the living room.

"Leo," she said primly, "that isn't very funny."

"Miriam," I replied, "it's true. I swear it. Honest to God." I reached for one of the bottles she'd brought. "What is it — French?"

"No. California."

I pulled out the bottle and checked the label. "If you're the soul of sensitivity should you really be serving him this brand?"

She began to put things away busily. "It was marked down. Listen — you can tell him about Chavez and the grape-pickers later."

We packed the refrigerator and the freezer and crammed the rest into the cupboards, then she freshened up her face with cold water from the sink tap and ran a comb nervously through her hair. I watched with amusement as she tucked her blouse neatly into her skirt and adjusted the sleeves of her jacket.

"Would you like me to go upstairs and put on a tie?" I asked.

"Don't be such a smart-ass," she hissed. "Go and see if he's still there."

I edged toward the door, glanced over my shoulder into the living room, then signaled his presence with a grave nod. She moistened her lips, swallowed hard, picked up her black bag, and allowed me to usher her into the living room.

The Man looked over his shoulder as we came in then rose to face us with a smile. "Hello, Miriam," he said.

I didn't bother to introduce him. They shook hands. Miriam didn't let go. She looked as if she'd fallen under a spell. And despite my confused, self-centered response to the situation, I knew how she felt. To come face-to-face with The Man with the full knowledge of who you were looking at was a unique and overwhelming experience — despite the lurking premonition that we might later pay dearly for the privilege.

When Miriam finally found her voice, the tone was blandly professional, but I knew from experience that she was hiding her emotions behind her matter-of-fact medical persona.

Deep down, she was a wide-eyed New Jersey kid whose own heart was pounding too loud for her to be able to hear anything through her stethoscope. "That's a good resetting job somebody did on your nose. No sutures or post-op bruising."

Listen — you have to start somewhere. If that makes you smile, put yourself in her place. After you'd got up off your knees what would *you* use for openers?

"I heal fast," he said.

"Good," said Miriam, swallowing hard. "Is it, uhh — okay if I check you out?"

"Yes, sure, whatever you want." Just like that.

Miriam threw me a nervous glance. I gave what I hoped was a discreet, reassuring nod. It didn't help to know that he was probably monitoring all this inner turmoil and quietly laughing up his wide, pale brown, woolen sleeve.

Miriam extended a hand and ushered The Man toward the stairs. I followed them up to the master bedroom and peeked around the door. "Is it okay if I watch?"

"Sure," he said. "Come in."

Miriam peeled the bandages off his wrists. There was no trace of the wounds we had seen on the previous Saturday. No scar tissue. Nothing. I've got to hand it to her. Her eyebrows went up a good inch, but apart from that she took it in her stride. "Oh-kay . . ." she said in a detached singsong voice. "Let's have a look at the feet."

I held my breath as the bandages came off. It was the same story. Nothing to show that an inch-square metal spike had been driven through both feet and then had torn the surrounding flesh as it had taken the weight of his exhausted body.

"Move your toes around," said Miriam.

As he wiggled his piggies, she flexed each foot in turn, gently probing the bone structure with her fingers. "Mmmm, that's amazing," she said. She glanced up at me. "The bones that were smashed are all completely sound and back in place."

"Yes, well — I guess they would be," I said lamely.

Miriam got up off her knees. "Uhh — would you mind taking off your robe? I'd like to have a look at your back."

He stood up, slipped his arms out of the wide sleeves, and pulled the robe over his head. Underneath, he was naked apart from a loincloth made out of a strip of white linen. The brown skin covering his lean torso was unbroken. The hideous bruising and lacerations had disappeared, along with the ugly stab wound just under the ribs on the left side.

"Incredible," said Miriam. She shook her head in disbelief and turned him gently around so that he was facing her. "You must tell me how it's done. It would certainly move things along at Manhattan General."

The Man smiled. "It's easy when you have The Power." He sat down on the edge of the bed and laid his hands on his knees, palms upward. "Look . . ."

If I had not seen it with my own eyes, I would never have believed it. His appearances and disappearances had been mind-boggling bits of magic but what followed was absolutely fantastic. A sharp dent appeared in the skin of both wrists. The dent got deeper, then suddenly the skin was punctured. There was only one way to describe it. Two invisible spikes were being driven through his wrists. The wounds began to bleed. I felt sick but I couldn't take my eyes away.

Miriam fell down on her knees and grabbed his wrists, covering the wounds with her hands. "Stop it — please!"

"It's okay," he said quietly. "It doesn't hurt. It's all in the mind. Take your hands away and you'll see what I mean."

Miriam slowly let go of his wrists. She had blood on the palms of her hands but the wounds had vanished. The skin was quite unmarked. I stood there with a mouth like a goldfish, my mind reeling. From my passing acquaintance with the Book I knew that if he had only done half the things he'd been credited with it was clear that, even on a bad day, he could outperform the combined talents of the AMA. But if, in his resurrected form, he could travel through time and pull strokes like this, he was unstoppable. There wasn't a man alive who could touch him. I'll never forget that small but telling demonstration of his power, or the look on Miriam's face as she knelt in front of him, brushing her fingers over the spot where the invisible spikes had punched through flesh and bone only seconds before.

He took her hands in his. "Is it okay if I get dressed?"

Miriam nodded and got to her feet. She popped the discarded bandages into her black bag and gave me an odd look. Almost as if everything that had happened had been my fault. I suppose that after years of medical school and six years on the job it must be tough when you run up against your first cast-iron miracle.

Miriam headed for the door. "I need a drink. See you downstairs."

The Man pulled his robe back on. "I didn't mean to upset her."

I shrugged and did my best to sound matter-of-fact. "All doctors are the same. They don't like being outsmarted by their patients. Let's face it, that was pretty spectacular." It was more than that, but I didn't go overboard. After all, there might be more to come. If so, I would need every superlative I could lay hands on. I showed him his room and the toilet just in case he might wish to use either; then we went downstairs.

Miriam was sitting by the fire with her hands cupped around a glass that held enough vodka to put a Cossack and his horse under the table. Drink usually makes her happy. This time, she looked a little subdued. But in view of what we'd just witnessed it was understandable. We turned down the lights and sat around the flames and talked — mainly about ourselves. The Man was curious to know where we were from, what we did and why, and how we had come to be together. Et cetera. With his ability to read minds he must have known what we were going to say. I can only think that he wanted to compare what came out of our mouths with what was going through our heads. So Miriam and I laid edited versions of our life stories on him. Maybe he reached into our memories and gathered up the bits we left out. If he did, he was kind enough not to ask any awkward questions.

Eventually, we moved on from True Confessions to America in general and the global situation. We told him that it was a mess and that, sooner or later, things would have to change radically. The trouble was no one was sure that things would change for the better. The major political systems of both East and West were now recognized to be morally and economically bankrupt. And it was no good looking to religion for salvation. Of the two major faiths, the Christian church had been spiritually bankrupt for centuries, and oil-rich Islam was suffering from fundamentalist schizophrenia; Judaism you couldn't give away.

"Ask almost anybody," said Miriam, "and they will tell you that the world is going mad. But nobody believes in anything strongly enough to actually start doing something about it. Resolve has been replaced with resignation."

I knew what she was talking about but I tended to take a more optimistic view. After all, people have been saying that the world was going down the tubes ever since God told Noah to build the Ark. Despite what Henry Ford said about history it did, at least, prove one thing. Man was the great survivor. When I pointed this out, it made The Man smile.

"With a little help from his friends," he said.

And that made her smile too. I gave her a whose-side-are-you-on? look, then we broke it up and went upstairs. It was about one-thirty. Miriam sat on the edge of the bed and listened attentively as I described his arrival, recapped our opening dialogue, and played back the recorded highlights. She listened with rapt attention for a good hour then switched off with a series of yawns like open manhole covers.

"Sorry," she said. "I had a tough day at the hospital."

"Don't apologize," I said. "I'd like to sleep on it too." I climbed into bed. "At least you know now I wasn't kidding about the wine."

"Okay, so you were right about that," she said. "It's just that sometimes your jokes are in rather bad taste."

That made me sit up. "Look," I said. "There's something we ought to get straightened out. This is a very laid-back guy we've got here. Okay, he's special. Some kind of spaceman, perhaps. I can even buy the idea that he may really *be* the Son of God. But he also spent a good bit of his time whooping it up with debt-collectors, hookers and guys who'd jumped *shul* —"

She put her hand over my mouth.

I pulled it away. "Will you let me finish? The point is, I've never talked to a god before. The only way I can handle this situation is to treat our friend down the hall like a normal human being. And I advise you to do the same — otherwise they are going to ship us to the banana factory."

"Okay." She kissed me tenderly. Somehow, only our lips touched.

I decided to push my luck. Let's face it: one way or another, it had been a pretty heavy evening. "I'm going to ask him about that water into wine bit. If he could do a number on a couple hundred thousand gallons from the Hudson River we could be in business. On the other hand," I said, "if he could turn it into oil . . ."

Miriam stood up. "I'll see you in the morning."

"Where are you going?" I said.

"You've got three bedrooms, haven't you?"

I couldn't believe it. "Come on," I said. "This is ridiculous." I grabbed her hand and kissed it submissively. "Okay. No more jokes. May I drop dead if I ever laugh again."

She gave me a hard-eyed look and relented. But when she finally came out of the bathroom she was wearing a nightgown. Something she'd never worn when we'd been in bed together. I sat up on the pillow with my arms folded as she got into bed and pulled the covers up to her chin.

"There . . . satisfied?"

"Not quite," I said. "I'm waiting for you to get undressed. I was sort of hoping that you might feel like parking your mobile home next to mine."

She treated me to a smile that was ten percent pity and ninety percent malice. "Put it on the slate, Resnick."

She wasn't kidding either.

When I woke on Sunday morning, Miriam was already up. I showered, shaved, put on a bathrobe, and took a peek in the guest bedroom. The bed hadn't been slept in. I almost broke my neck in my haste to get down the stairs. Miriam was in the kitchen, dressed in a plaid shirt, jeans and sneakers, with an apron on top. Her hair was pinned back under a headscarf, and she had the freshly scrubbed look of a sixteen-year-old.

"Where's The Man?" I said.

She gave me another absurdly chaste kiss. "Relax. He's out on the porch. Why don't you get dressed and take him for a walk before we have breakfast?"

I helped myself to some coffee from the pot on the stove and went out front. It was a nice warm spring day. Maybe it was my imagination but there may even have been a church bell tolling somewhere. The Man was sitting cross-legged on a mat with his back against the cedar shingles which I'd had put on the walls to save me the chore of painting the old clapboards. I remember wondering if the one-piece robe he had on was a replica or if someone had done a deal with the guy who'd won it at the foot of the cross.

"Hi," I said. "Is it okay if I join you?"

"Sure."

I sat down in my uncle's wooden chair which, like most of the other furniture, had come with the house. Miriam must have gotten it out of the garage for him, but I guess chairs were not something he was used to. I blew on my coffee. "You had me worried. When I saw the bed, I thought you'd left us."

He shook his head and smiled. "I read through the Bible that Miriam brought then came down and watched some TV."

"What — all night?"

"Yes," he said. "This body doesn't function in the way

yours does. It has no need for sleep." He looked down at this
flower he had in his lap and twiddled it around in his fingers.
I'm not sure what kind. Red. A geranium, I think. Do they
come out in April?

"How far did you get with the Book?" I asked.

"Ohh, I read all of it." He saw my look of surprise. "It's
not difficult. You see, whereas you can only absorb written
information line by line through your eyes, I am able to
absorb the totality of a book just by holding it in my hands."

I eyed him and got up. "This, I've got to see." I went into
the house and returned with the first book that had caught
my eye. A paperback copy of *Webster's New World Dictionary of the American Language*. I passed it over to him and
sat down. He glanced at the front and back cover then
gripped it firmly in both hands.

"Are you ready?" I said.

"Just a minute . . ." He closed his eyes, inhaled deeply
then let his breath out slowly, as if preparing to meditate. It
took about thirty seconds and he didn't frown once. He
opened his eyes. "Amazing language. Very 'Braxian. Okay,
shoot."

"Divine truth," I said. "What pages do those words appear
on?"

He held the book flat between the palms of his hands and
rested his chin against it. "Page 172 and 612." He offered me
the book. "Do you want the column and line number as
well?"

"No, that's good enough." I took the book and checked his
answers. He was absolutely right, of course. I leaned back
and laid the book on the rail of the verandah. "Fantastic," I
said. "I suppose you realize that if you could teach people
how to do that, you could make a fortune. But then — that's
not what you came for."

"No," he said. He picked up the red flower and gazed at it.

And something odd happened. It may have been just a
chain reaction of ideas but I had the feeling someone else's

finger was on the button. That The Man was beaming thought-waves into my brain. The point was, I found myself, almost involuntarily, reflecting on how, despite the fundamental role it had played in the development of modern society, money lay like a deadweight upon the world: distorting our true sense of values; suffocating our good intentions. If we had too little of it, we were utterly crushed by the burden of poverty. If we had too much of it, we went in fear of our lives. Living behind high wire fences and electronic alarms. Dogged by security guards. Driving with a gun in the glove compartment. Wealth could make the weak a power in the land; poverty could make slaves of the strong and deprive them of their manhood. Even so, good fortune was a fickle mistress. A mountain of cash had buried many a man and woman alive.

The fate of nations, too, hung on the mind-numbing manipulations of the money markets. Arabian Nights fortunes in recycled petrodollars, Deutschemarks, and cuckoo-clock currency were telexed across the globe to bankroll dictators or give the kiss of life to democracies with a bad case of the staggers. For a price, of course. Countries without salable resources or strategic bases to offer as collateral could find their credit lines cut short. While the breadlines got longer. It was sobering to think of the huge food and grain reserves of North America and the commodity mountains of Europe sitting there in silos and deep-freeze dungeons while, all over the world, people were going hungry. Yet the good that could alleviate the plight of the undernourished was not shipped, as a matter of course, from the fat nations to the thin. It stayed put, or was pulped, burned, or left to rot to keep up commodity prices and because it cost too much to move it. It was unfortunate that people had to die but at least the books balanced. The politicians, financiers and economists never seemed to consider the possibility that we might owe a collective debt to the whole human race.

But who was I to pass judgment? In the past year I had put

on a good inch around my waist and left enough food on restaurant plates to feed a family in Kampuchea or the Karamoja for weeks.

Looking back, I realize that it was the first session in a short course of mental hygiene; the object of which was to clear the highways and byways of the mind and, in the process, prick my social conscience. Making me more sharply aware of the Gadarene-swinishness of the Me Generation.

"What did you make of the New Testament?" I said.

He pursed his lips. "A very clever mixture of fact and fiction. Some of the distortions are very subtle, others are blatant bits of promotional material inserted to support the Apostolic Succession. And things like the story of Judas are a travesty of the truth. It wasn't like that at all."

"I can't wait to get the inside track on all this," I said. "But first, I want to read through it carefully so I'll know what I'm talking about. However, there is one question that occurs to me. Why didn't this 'Brax character — who you said was trying to stop The Truth from getting out — just destroy all the records? That way, no one would have known that you had ever been born in Bethlehem."

"What you have to understand," he said, "is that in the final analysis, 'Brax cannot destroy The Truth. He can only bury it under impenetrable layers of gobbledygook and bar the way to it by tempting people off the True Path into the morass of the material world where they sink under the weight of their desires and possessions. Don't make the mistake of equating 'Brax with brute force. He is devious and diabolically clever. He gets a tremendous kick out of knowing that each one of you holds the key to The Truth. The key that could free you from your 'Braxian cell but which you are too blind to see. And that, even if you *could* see it, the majority of you would not bother to try to unlock the door because he has convinced you that there is nothing beyond the prison walls — and that anyone who believes there is should be regarded with derision. That is why The Word still lives within the corrupted text of the New Testament.

It doesn't worry 'Brax because he knows that most people don't really believe in the being you call God, and those who do have been fed a pack of lies and half-truths. So what has he got to lose?" The Man broke off and gazed into the center of the red flower, as if to restore an inner harmony that had been disturbed by talking about 'Brax. He looked up at me with a smile. "Incidentally, I see what you mean about the laughs."

"There's also no mention of the starship — or longship, as you call it."

"No, I didn't tell them about it," he said. "What would have been the point? The Old Testament scribes had enough problems with Ezekiel's trip in the fiery chariot. They related my arrival to the Star of Bethlehem but I didn't go into what that really was. You can't explain space-time travel — especially our brand — in a language that can just barely cope with the wheel. These concepts have to be introduced at the right time. If at all."

"Does that mean you're against progress?" I asked.

He smiled. "Think of that city you live and work in. Has progress made that a better place? You've become prisoners of the technology you've created."

"Oh, wait a minute," I protested. "Don't knock it. What about the developments in science, medicine, transport and communications? Don't tell me they haven't made the world a better place to live in."

"Leo," he said. "Let me tell you something." He lifted up the flower again and inspected it, rotating the stalk between finger and thumb. "There was a time, before that war we spoke about, when Man knew more about the cosmos than your astronomers have discovered through their telescopes. When he was familiar with the innermost mysteries of matter which your physicists are still constructing theories to explain. When he understood the nature of this flower better than the most brilliant botanist. When The Power within protected him from those who wished him harm. When sickness had not yet entered the world and when it did, could be cured by the touch of a hand. When Man could transport himself to the four corners of the world. Or could touch the stones of power and see whatever he wished and send his inner voice soaring like a seabird across oceans and mountains to bring word of his coming or summon far ones to his hearth." He smiled at me. "You want to hear music? Here — take hold of my hand."

I reached out. His fingers tightened round mine. Incredible. It's a word I've used before. I'm afraid it crops up quite a few times in this story. But like he said, there *are* no words to describe these things. This music seemed to flow through me. I didn't so much hear it as sense it. It was what the ad-men call a "total experience." An exquisite, vibrant melody that I can't describe. It wasn't a symphony-type thing, or something put together on a Moog synthesizer. All I know is that I didn't want it to end. My heart felt as if it was going to burst with — well, there is only one way to describe it — pure joy.

And then he let go of my hand. And the music stopped. Just like that. And there were these tears rolling down my face. So I pretended I had something in my eye, like I do in the movies. You know — like when Dustin Hoffman dies on the bus at the end of *Midnight Cowboy,* or when Bambi's mother gets shot.

"Not bad," I said, stopping to blow my nose. "So much for progress." I kept my eyes on my handkerchief as I rolled it up into a ball. "Do your people think they're going to be able to get on top of this time-warp problem you have?" Coming after the previous passage, that may sound an odd question but I wanted to get back to a relatively simple subject before I broke down and cried for real.

"I'm not sure," he replied. "They sent a signal back up the line. We'll just have to wait and see what happens."

My heartbeat began to slow down to something like its normal rate. "Those guys up there who are manning the longships in the rescue fleet. Are they all Celestials — like you, Michael and Gabriel?"

"Yes," he said.

"Does that mean we're unique? Or are there other places where Celestials have occupied intelligent life-forms?"

He paused before replying. "There are — other Mannish worlds," he admitted.

"In this galaxy?" I asked.

He shook his head. "No. You're the only people we have in this one. Earth was the prime. The seedbed from which life was to be carried to the stars. But the program was interrupted by the Second War of Secession."

It was a chilling thought to realize that we were alone. All those billions of stars in the Milky Way spiraling around the incandescent core with their attendant planets and moons. Each with a "For Rent" sign in the window. "Tell me about the Mannish," I said. "Are they like us?"

The question seemed to amuse him. "There's a family resemblance." He turned his attention back to the red flower.

"Is that all?" I queried. "Where are they? What are they called? Do they have arms and legs, and everything else in the right places? What do they do for a living?"

He raised his eyes to mine. "You're not ready for the rest. The time when Man is to meet his brothers is still to come."

"You mean in another Age?" I said, determined to get an answer to something.

"Yes."

"Okay," I said. "How many Ages are there? If the past and the future exist now, you must at least be able to tell me that."

"There are seven Ages," he said evenly.

This is not exactly how it came out but I've written it down in the form of a list to make it easier to understand:

The Ages Past

1st Age — The Age of Light
2nd Age — The Age of Creation
3rd Age — The Age of Darkness

The Present Age

4th Age — The Age of Life

The Ages to come
5th Age — The Age of Love
6th Age — The Age of Wisdom
7th Age — The Age of Glory

Once again he declined to go into details, but I did manage to elicit one additional item of information. We are, apparently, nearing the end of the Fourth Age and I gathered that the Fifth Age is when the good times are supposed to roll. "Soon" was the word he used but what that means is anybody's guess. On the time scale the Empire is using that could be next Monday, or a million years from now.

I changed course yet again and tried to question him about the longships. "Come on," I said. "I saw *Star Wars* five times. Humor me."

He put the red flower to his nose and eyed me indulgently. "What can I tell you? That it is twice as big as Manhattan Island yet weighs less than a box of Kleenex? Or that it is commanded by a Proconsul of the Empire? You mustn't let your fascination with the hardware mislead you. As I told you before, that's not really what it's all about. The only thing you need to understand — fully, with the totality of your being — is who and what you are and your relationship to me. Once you acquire that knowledge, all your questions will be answered."

"Okay," I said. "I'll try and bear that in mind."

Miriam came out onto the porch. She gave a sharp sigh as she saw me sitting there in my robe. "I thought you were going round the garden."

I looked at The Man then up at her. "We decided to talk instead."

"Breakfast is ready. Are you going to eat like that or are you planning to get dressed?"

"Give me a couple of minutes and I'll make you proud of me." I gave her a sunny smile but she didn't see it. She was looking past me at The Man. And she didn't look sixteen anymore. I turned and saw why.

The mat was empty. But he'd left us the red flower. Miriam picked it up before I could get out of the chair. I suddenly felt cheated, but inside there was also this almost inconsolable sense of loss. I could see that Miriam felt it too. Perhaps even more than I did. What we both needed to do more than anything else at that moment was to put our arms around each other.

But we didn't.

I just bared my teeth and said, "You and your fucking breakfast. . . ." Which shows, I guess, just how much I still had to learn.

Needless to say, that slip of the tongue meant that the rest of the weekend was shot to hell. The silence that hung over the breakfast table would have earned us a free ticket to a Trappist monastery. It was Miriam who finally broke the ice, but it didn't help to raise the temperature.

"You look as if you've got a lot to get through here. I think I'd better drive over to Scarsdale. After all, they were expecting me."

Scarsdale was where her parents lived. "Sure. Good idea." It was the wrong thing to say but part of me enjoys being mean-spirited now and then. I shrugged. "Listen — if that's what you want to do."

Of course it was. She already had her coat on. Maybe I could have persuaded her to take it off, but it was too much hassle. Besides, it was true. I really did need to make up for the time I'd lost on the Saturday having my mind bent by footnotes from the Two-Hundred-Million-Year War. If that sounds flip, it is because I was doing my damnedest to play it down. What we had become involved in was absolutely incredible. What we had seen and heard was fantastic. Unforgettable. But the look I'd seen in Miriam's eyes when he'd produced the stigmata had scared the hell out of me. I might be long on questions and short on answers but I was sure of one thing. As two of the smallest cogs in the Celestial machine, we ran the risk of being ground to pieces. The only way to stay sane, whole and healthy was by keeping a firm grip on reality. And that's what I planned to do on behalf of both of us. Even if it meant playing the bad guy.

I opened the front door but didn't offer to carry her overnight bag. We walked down to where she had parked the Pontiac. We both chewed on our teeth until we got there. She tossed the bag into the back and got in.

I leaned against the inside of the door as she went to close it. The window was up and it was obvious that she wasn't going to roll it down. "Listen," I said. "I'm sorry I blew my top when The Man disappeared. I guess it's because I don't know why any of this is happening, or what it is we're getting into. Maybe we ought to take some time to work out where we go from here."

"Take all the time you want." She switched on the ignition.

"What do you want me to do with all the food?" I said.

She threw me a bleak glance. "Ship it to the Vietnamese Boat People."

If I could have stood the pain, I'd have left my arm in the door as she slammed it shut. Just to ruin her weekend. But as I'm a devout coward, I lifted it prudently out of the way. I stepped back and watched her do a tight-lipped three-point turn, then waved her out of my life. It wasn't the first time she hadn't waved back and I knew it would not be the last. And what made us so different? People had been arguing over The Man for centuries. I went back inside and immersed myself in the heady world of patent infringements.

Now I don't know how closely you've been following this but some of you may have detected a certain schizoid quality in my reactions to The Man and what he'd been laying on us. If you'd been there when it was happening, I think you might have been a little confused too. I no longer doubted the validity of the experience. I was just doing my level best — as I've already said — not to go overboard. I had suspended both belief and disbelief. I was trying to cling to the middle ground, somewhere between awe and derision, but the deep-seated cynicism with which I regarded most of the things of this world and certainly all of the next kept bringing me back to earth. I wanted to hear more; to discover all he knew. But I didn't want to be drafted into this Man's army and, despite the voice inside my head which kept egging me on, I was not about to volunteer.

And there was another problem. This game of chronological hide-and-seek we'd gotten mixed up in threatened to cut us off from the people around us. After all, The Man could come back again. For days instead of hours. How long could we conceal this historical time bomb that had been dropped in our laps just because some cosmic body snatcher didn't know his quarks from his mesons?

Suppose someone started backtracking from that empty drawer in the morgue toward us? Or if friend Fowler got visions of winning a Nobel Prize by going public with his analysis of that blood sample? And I could envisage the Monday morning small talk at the office. *Hi, Leo. Have a good weekend?* Mmm, I was up at Sleepy Hollow and a couple of friends dropped in. *Oh, yeah — anybody special?* No. Just Miriam and a guy called Jesus.

It was a terrifying thought but, as I sat there in front of those depositions, I couldn't think of one person Miriam and I could tell who wouldn't think we had flipped our lids.

I diluted my anxiety with a generous shot of bourbon, waded through the rest of my paperwork, then drove back into town to avoid the inevitable Monday morning foul-up. It was around eleven when I let myself into my apartment. I checked with the answering service but there was no message from Miriam. I toyed with the idea of ringing her in case she'd tried to reach me at Sleepy Hollow, then thought better of it. If and when she wanted to get in touch, she would know where to find me. I went to bed with the Good Book and checked over a few key passages before I turned the light out. At least I knew where he'd gone. The Man had a date with the rest of the boys in Bethany. To break some bread and show Thomas his stigmata. And according to the Book, Thomas, who'd been out of town all week, was even more impressed than we were.

FIVE

On the Monday morning, I spent an extra half hour in bed and thought about the exercises I should have been doing and about phoning Miriam. By the time the cab called for me — my regular eight A.M. pickup — I hadn't done either. But to even things up, I walked the last five blocks. I had a dime ready in my fingers but, as it happened, all the pay phones I passed were in use.

I rode up in the elevator with Joe Gutzman, the senior partner and founder of the law firm. Joe was a small, dapper, silver-haired man whose tan identified him as a dedicated sunlamp worshipper. His mind was as precise as the Cartier watch on his wrist and he cost as much by the hour. He always looked as if he was about to smile but rarely did. Joe had two great sorrows in his life. The first was his son David, who had swapped a law career for an Israeli Air Force Skyhawk jet and had gone down over the Sinai desert during the Yom Kippur War with a SAM-7 missile up his tailpipe. The second was his daughter Joanna who, at the age of twenty-eight, was still unmarried in spite of the fact that she could pass for Brooke Shields on a dark street. In her case, I was the joint cause of Joe's sorrow. He had tried everything he could think of to get us together short of throwing his daughter naked into my bath. Career-wise, the advantages were obvious. Joanna was also a nice intelligent girl. It just didn't jell. The chemistry wasn't right. But I valued Joe's fatherly interest in my career and his oblique, but affectionate, regard. In my arrogance, I liked to think that it was due to my innate talent. That I had earned my place in the sun without falling all over his daughter. But another part of me knows that sometimes, when he came into my office to talk, it was not me he saw but the shadow of his lost son.

Joe favored me with a quizzical glance. They're something he uses a lot in cross-examination and he likes to keep in practice. "Have a good weekend?"

This could have been my big moment. There were eleven people in the elevator, eyes averted, all minding their own business. I could have jolted them all with the news. Embarrassed the hell out of them. Emptied the elevator at the next floor. But I didn't. "Not bad," I said. "I've been gearing up on the Delaware case. We're in court today. Going for that injunction against Cleveland Glass."

"Oh, yes," nodded Joe. "Are we going to win that one?"

"Of course," I said smoothly. "I'm handling it exactly as you suggested." Rule One for rising young lawyers: If you don't marry the boss's daughter, learn how to kiss ass.

I took my share of mail from Nancy at the switchboard and dropped it on Linda's desk as I went through to my own office. Linda is my secretary. The cover was still on her typewriter. Linda is not a clock-watcher, which means she always starts late. But she stays late too. So things even out. On top of which she can spell. What more can you expect these days?

I didn't see him as I came in through the door. In fact I'm willing to swear that the office was empty but, as I put my Samsonite on my desk, turned and sat down, there he was. Sitting on the black leather chesterfield, wearing the same brown robe and white Arab-type headdress. The sudden shock jerked me out of my seat. I gripped the edge of the desk to steady myself and closed my eyes for a couple of seconds. When I opened them he was still there.

I crossed the room and shut the door that led in from Linda's office. "Did anyone see you come in?"

"No," he said. "I just got here. I'm sorry. I didn't mean to startle you."

"That's okay," I said. "Nice timing." My gut was still quivering. Let's face it: Sleepy Hollow was one thing, but visitations at the office were definitely unwelcome. I was quite prepared to enroll for a course of enlightenment but I had no wish to play Russian roulette with my career. "Is this another quick trip, or should I make plans?" I asked. Trying to sound friendly, briskly polite and distant all at the same time.

The Man shrugged. "I can't tell you yet. We were in contact with the Time Gate the Sunday before last —"

"The day of the Resurrection?"

"Yes," he nodded. "After I got back to Jerusalem and was transferred to the longship, I sent a message explaining what had happened and requesting rectification of the time fault or, failing that, a revised set of mission orders. But so far, nothing has come down the line." He shrugged. "Until we get the word, I guess we must all do the best we can."

It was at this point I remembered those famous words of Tonto's — *What do you mean "we," white man?* But what I said was, "Maybe you've been dumped again. You did mention that might be the answer."

"I know." He looked doubtful. "I can't believe this has been programmed. All our Earth missions up to now have been linear inputs."

"What are they?" I could have kicked myself for asking such a dumb question. The last thing I wanted to do was to get involved in another long conversation. I had a million things to do. Joe, or Dick Schonfeld, the other partner, or Corinne, his assistant, might walk in at any minute and then where would I be?

The Man must have known all this was buzzing around my brain yet it didn't stop him. But then, nothing ever did. "An input," he began, "is the periodic interaction between the

Empire and the World Below — in this case, Earth — either directly, or by proxy. And a linear input is one which accords with your own perception of time as a one-dimensional straight-line series of events."

"You mean like one of your people coming to live here for a given period of time — like your own life in Galilee and Judea for example?"

"Yes," he said. "Time, for you, has three components. The future, which you are able to visualize as a variable projection of the present — the fleeting, immeasurably brief second component — and time past. Which is a sense-memory made up of personal experience and received images from other sources. But even though past events can now be recorded and reviewed on film, only the elusive moment of time present exists as a concrete realization — which instantly slips through your grasp. But if your perception of time could be altered to embrace the concept and indeed the existence of simultaneity, then you would realize that all past events *are still taking place* within a series of overlapping time frames —"

"You mean in the way that the separate images on a strip of movie film still exist on the reel after they have passed through the projector?" I said.

"Not quite, but it's close enough. For you, the present would be one of the single frames that is projected fleetingly on the screen. What you have to imagine is a setup where the *whole film* is being projected simultaneously." He smiled. "That's the hard part. Plus the fact that — as I've demonstrated — it is possible, under certain conditions, to traverse time in different directions. What one might call 'lateral tracking.' "

"Must be an amazing experience," I said.

"It is," he replied. "Just don't ask me how it's done."

"Don't worry. I won't." Stuff like this is hard going at eight forty-five on a Monday morning. And anyway, if, as he had said, he didn't know why he had been mailed to Manhattan, he was unlikely to know how. But he had this annoying knack of opening up avenues that I could not help wanting to explore. And time-travel was a subject I found hard to resist. "Tell me something. I know that Time is regarded as being relative to the observer but how can it be multi-dimensional?"

He smiled. "Just accept that it can. Don't think of Time as a straight line running from past to future. Think of it as a continuous strip within which, at a given point across its width, the multiplicity of simultaneous events that make up the present exist side by side. Like the strands of yarn that interweave to make up a width of fabric. Just as your time-line is interwoven with Miriam's — and with others too. The width of the strip is infinite, but try to imagine it standing on edge. Not in a straight line, but folded into sections that zigzag from side to side throughout eternity with — let's say — a century between each fold."

"Okay, I've got that," I said. "What happens when you come to the end of the strip?"

"There is no end," he replied. "It zigzags around in a circle."

"Wait a minute," I said. "If the ends of the strip join up, it means that the far future is also our past. That doesn't make sense."

He treated me to another patient smile. "You're forgetting the rules of simultaneity. Don't think of Time as being made up of the past, present and future. Time *is*."

"For you maybe," I riposted. "How does time-travel fit into this model?"

"Very simply," he said. "If you visualize these century-long folds as lying close together, you can see that, under certain conditions, one could pass *through* the weave of the fabric — from one 'fold' to another. It would be possible to make a straight-line connection between any point in what you regard as a past century and one in the future. For you, whose life runs along the plane of the fabric, Time is still linear. But we Celestials are not bound to the temporal dimension — and therefore can travel through it."

"I think I get the idea," I said. "Tell me — would this explain the fleeting visions of you that people have had down the centuries? Could they have seen you as you passed through their time-strip, or track, or whatever — on your way between here and Jerusalem?"

He shrugged. "I suppose it's possible."

The significance of his noncommittal reply did not escape me. I pressed the point further. "Would it explain the visions of your mother?"

He seemed genuinely surprised. "You've seen her?"

"No," I said. "But I understand she's made a number of personal appearances. Several world tours, in fact."

I had the feeling I was on to something but before we could take it any further, Linda knocked on the door and walked in with the opened mail. She was surprised to see that I had someone in my office but she didn't make a big thing of it.

"Anything important?" I asked.

"Just the top three. I can handle the rest." She glanced back at The Man. "Is this anything I should have down in my book?"

"No," I said. "This gentleman's a friend of mine. He just flew into town and stopped by to say hello." I introduced her to The Man. "This is Linda Kovacs, my assistant."

"Hi," said Linda.

I didn't attempt to explain who he was. I just sat there and watched them exchange smiles.

Linda turned to me. "Do you want me to hold your calls?"

"For the moment," I said.

She paused halfway out the door. "Would you like me to bring you some coffee?"

I referred the question to The Man.

"Not for me," he said.

"In that case, I won't bother," I said.

Linda left us. I checked my watch and decided that the mysteries of Time and Space would have to wait. "Look — I don't want to seem rude, because I'd love nothing better than to sit here and talk some more, but I have to be in court at ten-thirty and I have quite a few things to get through before then. Are you really sure you have no idea how long you're going to be around?"

"No," he said. Just sitting there.

"Then I guess we'll just have to play it by ear." I let out a long-suffering sigh in the hope of making him feel bad. It was a problem. I couldn't just leave him sitting around the office, but what were the alternatives? Put him on the train for Sleepy Hollow? Supposing he lost his way? I thought of asking Linda to drive him up, but that would mean loaning her the Porsche. Which was out of the question. Besides, putting the two of them together in isolation could be dangerous. If I got onto a limo service, it would be the same thing. He might do a conversion job on the chauffeur. Too risky. But why? Why should I be worried about what he might say or do to anybody else? I'll tell you — although the answer does me little credit. I didn't mind him screwing up my private life with his unscheduled appearances, and I was quite happy for him to hand me the Secrets of the Universe — whatever they were worth. I just did not want to be associated with him in public. It was as simple as that. And the more people he got involved with increased the risk that this thing might come out into the open. And God knows what might happen then. He would attract every nut in Christendom. I had no desire to end up as a marked man, or part of a three-ring circus.

Miriam was the answer. But she would be tied up at the hospital and besides, we weren't speaking. On top of which, I didn't fancy her being alone with The Man until I'd had a chance to straighten her out. It was then it came to me. A hotel. Brilliant. I could book him into the Mayflower on Central Park West and tell him to stay in his room until I was through for the day. But what about luggage? Simple. The airline was still looking for it. It happens all the time. Wallet? Everything stolen. I was the lawyer handling his case. The rest was easy. But what if he suddenly hightailed it back to Jerusalem? That was a chance I'd have to take. Providing he didn't do it in a packed elevator, there shouldn't be any problem. Very few people notice what's going on around them these days. I would arrange for the hotel to charge the tab to me. The sooner they hauled him back over the time-tracks, the less it would cost.

So why, you ask, didn't I stash him away for free in my apartment? Listen. First, it was too small; second, the janitor was too nosy; and third, I had a Pearl Bailey–type cleaning lady who came in on Mondays and Fridays.

He probably knew it already but I explained the idea I'd had about checking him into a hotel. Where I would visit him after I'd gotten out of the courtroom. And how, if he got bored, all he had to do was cross the street and take a walk in Central Park — where he would have no problems provided he did not talk to anybody.

"I can take care of everything," I said. "There's just one little problem. We need a name. Something to give Linda and the desk clerk at the hotel. You know — that she can put down in the phone log if you decide to call." I hesitated. "This is a little delicate but — I feel that 'Jesus' is kind of, well — provocative. And I really don't think our switchboard operator could handle 'Mr. Christ.' "

"Sure. I understand," he said. "I never used that name anyway. It was the Greeks who hung that on me." He thought for a moment. "My earth parents called me Joshua. But I have been known by many other names."

"Such as?"

"Ya'el?" He pronounced it Yah-*ell,* accenting the last syllable.

At least it was different. I had been thinking of something along the lines of Joshua Josephson but frankly, it was a little too, well — ethnic. Too on the nose. Lamb? Too weak. And then I had it. Shepherd. Just right. Quiet, strong, dignified. I put it to him. Ya'el Shepherd. "Only we'll spell it Y-A-L-E S-H-E-P-P-A-R-D," I explained. "To make it easier for people to pronounce. It's not fancy, but the message is there for anyone who wants to look for it. Okay?"

"Yes," he nodded. "I'll buy that. After all, awareness is what this is all about. But tell me, Leo — why don't you want people to be aware of my true identity?"

It was the question I'd been dreading. I had been hoping he'd been inside my head and picked up the answer to that one. Maybe he had — and had decided that it wasn't good enough. I tried desperately to come up with some reasons that made me look less of a shmuck. "Let me put it this way," I began. "According to the Book, your next scheduled appearance is supposed to coincide with the end of the world. You know the bit: darkness over the face of the sun, the moon turning to blood, smoke, fire, the four horsemen. Is this it? Is that what's about to happen?"

"No," he said. "At least, nobody's mentioned it."

I breathed a quiet sigh of relief. "So that's one good reason for keeping a low profile. There's no point in scaring the shit out of everybody if it's going to be a false alarm. Besides which, it's going to blow your entrance later on. And it won't do the stock market any good either. That may not be something you particularly care about, but the economy's in enough trouble already. And there's another reason. You've said that you're not sure why you're here. If that is so, my advice is to remain incognito — as far as possible — until this problem is sorted out. Whether they're religious or not, the one notion people cling to is that, no matter how bad things get down here, God, at least, is supposed to know what he's doing. If it is a mistake, if somebody *did* throw the wrong switch, it might be better not to make any kind of input that will show up in the history books."

He smiled. "Don't worry, Leo. I won't embarrass you."

That got me on the raw. "Did I say anything about that? It just so happens that, for once, I'm more concerned with the effect this could have on other people." It wasn't all bullshit. There was a grain of truth in there somewhere. If he didn't handle it right, he really could cause a lot of trouble.

Would reactionary governments stand idly by while he espoused the cause of the poor and the oppressed? Would the multinational corporations put up the shutters if he denounced materialism? Would the pope, the chief rabbi, the grand metropolitan — which I hope is the head of the Greek Orthodox Church and not a hotel — the archbishop of Canterbury, the chief ayatollahs of Islam, the Hindu and Buddhist hierarchy — would *they* agree to act as his joint cheerleaders? Would kings, presidents and praesidiums defer to a supranational authority in the shape of a thirty-four-year-old Jewish woodworker?

Are you kidding? Hell would have to freeze over first.

The Muslims would cut off oil supplies and declare a jihad. The Christians would never reach a consensus. The Hindus would riot, and the Buddhists would set fire to themselves.

And the Jews? The Jews would never admit they had made a mistake. Or would they? Supposing the Christians turned him down? I pictured this bizarre scenario in which my people recognized him, belatedly, as the Messiah. The leader of Eretz-Israel. The final justification of their right to the Promised Land that stretched from Tel Aviv to the Euphrates. I could see it all. The sons and daughters of Zion massed outside the Mayflower Hotel waving placards which read "Come back, Jesus. All is forgiven." That really would set the Middle East on fire. And it could happen. Wasn't there a prophecy that the War To End All Wars would begin in the hills of Hebron? I dismissed that chilling thought and tuned back to The Man.

"You look worried," he said.

"Not really," I replied. "I've just been thinking you'll need a change of clothes. We can't sign you into the Mayflower dressed like an Egyptian camel driver." I opened my Samsonite, pulled out my checkbook, and made one out in Linda's name for three hundred dollars. "Now listen," I said. "And don't argue. My secretary will take you out and get you fixed up with something to wear, then book you into the hotel. I'll call you this afternoon around four when the court hearing is over. Then I'll come around and pick you up this evening. Sometime after six. Okay?"

He nodded. "Sure. . . ."

I buzzed Linda, and when she came in, I explained about Mr. Sheppard's lost luggage, wallet, et cetera, and what I wanted her to do. "The clothes don't have to be fancy," I said. "Just make sure he's got something to change into while the rest is with the hotel's valet service. And try to leave him with fifty dollars in his pocket." As I said it, I wondered what on earth he might spend it on.

Linda looked at the amount I'd made the check out for and raised an eyebrow.

I sighed. Women . . . "Is your checking account good for a hundred?"

"Just about."

"Okay. Use it if you have to. I'll square it with you later. Get Sally to take over your phone while you're gone."

"I'll get my coat," she said. She flashed a friendly smile at The Man on the way out.

I waited until the door closed. "Just do me one favor."

"What's that?" he said.

"Don't drag Linda into this. I know that may sound kind of impertinent but —"

He waved away my unfinished apology. "Supposing she asks me questions?"

"Tell her you're a writer," I said. "I know one or two. You flew in from Los Angeles. You write scripts. Tell her you're working on a big Biblical epic.

"I don't know anything about Los Angeles," he said.

"Don't worry," I replied. "We can fix that right now." I got up and selected a couple of paperbacks from my office bookshelf. He caught them as I dropped them into his lap. "The top one is a guidebook to the State of California; the bottom one is a street atlas of Greater Los Angeles and Orange County. You should be able to take both of those on board before Linda comes back from the ladies' room. The rest you can get from her. She spent a year out there working for a producer at Universal. All you have to do is rehash the information she's got inside her head."

He smiled. "You learn fast."

"I'm doing my best," I said. "Let's face it. The way things are, we can't afford to waste any time."

"True," he said. Sitting there as if he had forever. He held up the two books. "Shall I put these back on the shelf?"

I just couldn't believe it. "What, already?" I gaped. "Do you mean to say that you can take in *two* books at the same time?"

He shrugged. "A whole shelf-ful or a whole library if you like. It just takes a little more concentration, that's all." He got up and replaced the books.

I watched him, saucer-eyed. "But — you didn't even close your eyes!"

"Yes, I know," he said, tongue-in-cheek. "I didn't want to waste any time."

It was reassuring to know that he still liked to score one now and then. And it was true that, after Linda had brought in the mail, I had bounced back from the blue funk his presence had put me in, and had become a little pushy. In other words, I was acting normally.

Linda knocked and put her freshly combed head around the door. "Ready when you are."

"We'll be right out," I said. I got up and ushered him across the room. When we reached the door, I took hold of the handle and laid my other hand daringly on his shoulder. I have to tell you there was no tingle. No electric shock. Just a plain, ordinary shoulder. Well, not quite ordinary. But you know what I mean. "One last thing. If you decide to go into Central Park, there'll be quite a few people around. So please, don't do anything fancy. Stay on the main paths and keep clear of the bushes."

"Can I hire one of the rowboats?"

"Do whatever you want," I said. "Just don't go walking across the lake."

It is at this point I want to stop and say that I'm aware that some of you may have been upset by some of the things you've read. And that any Evangelical Christians who've got this far without throwing the book on the fire may be downright angry. Outraged even. But the plain fact is, whatever he, or I, or any of us said or did was bound to offend somebody.

Take for instance the small thing like what The Man should wear. What should I have told Linda to do? Fit him out with a Brooks Brothers three-piece in banker's gray — or a bleached pair of jeans, sneakers, and a T-shirt that read "JESUS SAVES"? That may make some of you laugh, but really it was no joke. The way I saw it, sacrilege just didn't come into it. From what he'd already told me, it was clear that The Man was above religion. Religion, and all the self-righteous attitudes that went with it, was something *we* had invented. And let's face it: where he had just come from, there were plenty of people who didn't give a damn who he was. Especially those goons who had been on the execution squad in the Fortress Antonia. This was not the soft-focus Catholic Repository image of the New Testament figure. This was the real thing. The being, or whatever he or it was, who had been the epicenter of a tenuous and imperfectly documented event that had sent shock waves around the world. Upon which, over the centuries, generation after generation of ecclesiastical rip-off artists had built a massive power structure, financed by extortion, murder and plunder from the East; riddled with corruption and intrigue, and centrally heated by burning heretics. A structure that, when impudent monarchs separated the functions of Church and State, and began killing people in the name of the King instead of in the name of Christ, had become increasingly hollow, meaningless and irrelevant. If The Man had come to cast it down, or open the windows and let in some fresh air, there would be a lot of prelates in urgent need of career counseling.

SIX ══════════════════════════════════

THE first day of the hearing didn't go quite as smoothly as I expected and I spent the lunch recess reviewing game plans with Delaware's staff lawyers. Which meant I didn't get to call the office or the hotel. When I returned just after four-thirty Linda was back behind her desk and looking busy.

She tailed me into my office.

"How'd it go?" I said.

"Fine. Your check covered everything. He's in Room Three-fifteen. It's a suite facing the Gulf and Western building. I couldn't get him anything overlooking the Park."

"That's okay," I said. "He's not going to be in town for long."

Linda gave me an odd look. "By the way — are you sure your friend writes for the movies?"

I braced myself for trouble. "Yes, why?"

"Well —" She hesitated. "He's, uhh — such a nice guy. I mean he really is, you know?"

"Of course he is," I said. "One of the best."

I've mentioned the fact that Linda had spent a year in L.A. It was a few years back. When her mother had gone out to the West Coast to nurse a sick relative. She had gotten the job at Universal through family connections and rubbed shoulders with some of the glossier folk in Tinseltown. Maybe even put a few dents in the odd casting couch. Who knows? Whatever it was, the West Coast magic failed to cast its spell. Which meant that I gained a good, but slightly soured, secretary on the rebound.

And then I saw her eyes brim over with tears. My heart sank. "What is it?"

"Nothing." She wiped her eyes and honked into a Kleenex.

"What did he say? What happened?"

"Nothing. We just went shopping." She shrugged. "Oh, by the way, there was thirty dollars' change. He didn't want a lot of stuff." She gave me a wobbly smile. "It's funny, you know. I've never met a guy like that before."

You can say that again.

"It was like —" She searched for the right phrase. "Like shopping with a child. It was almost as if he'd never been in a big department store."

I nodded. "I know what you mean. He's always struck me as a guy who prefers the simple life."

"Yes," she said. "Apparently, he's got this cabin up in the woods near Lake Tahoe. No telephone. No TV. In fact, I don't think he even owns a typewriter."

"He probably likes doing things the hard way." I sat down in my five-hundred-buck soft-hide swivel chair and lit a cigarette.

Linda folded the tissue over and wiped her nose again. "I know how he feels. We went around to two or three stores and, for the first time in my life, everything suddenly looked very tacky. You know? There was just too much of everything. And I found myself thinking — who needs all this junk?"

"I often ask myself the same question," I said. I did my best to bolster her belief in the consumer society with a few well-chosen words then asked her to rustle me up a cup of coffee. I glanced quickly through the paperwork that had found its way onto my desk during my absence and put in a call to The Man in Room 315. "Hi, how's it going?"

"Just great," he said. "I've got a really nice room but the clothes take a bit of getting used to."

"You hear the same thing in the lobby of the UN every time there's a big debate on the Third World," I said. I explained why I hadn't gotten through to him earlier. "I'll be around as soon as I finish up here. Give me about an hour."

"Okay," he said. "Take care."

It seemed an odd thing for him to say but I put the phone down and thought no more about it. I mulled briefly over his impact on Linda and fervently hoped that she had no inkling of who it was who had moved her to tears. He certainly had a way with women. And it was at this point that I tuned out and got on with the job in hand.

By the time I reached the elevators in the lobby, it was going on a quarter of six. Our offices are on the twenty-second floor. The building starts emptying at five with a big rush, which then slows to a steady trickle over the next hour, leaving a residue of midnight-oilers. Which usually includes me. The doors closed on two of the elevators as I got there, leaving the lobby empty. I hit the button on the middle one and the indicator lit up to show that it was on its way down.

As I stood there, about half a dozen people gathered behind me. There was the usual *ting* as the elevator arrived. The doors opened. I started to step forward — and saw to my horror that the car wasn't there. I glimpsed the void beneath me as I began to lose my balance, then a giant unseen hand slammed into my chest and hurled me backward. In the same instant, the empty elevator flashed past like a guillotine blade and plummeted down the shaft. I heard someone scream, then I crashed into the people behind me, knocking several of them to the floor.

"Jesus H. Christ," said a man. "Are you okay?"

I nodded as he helped me up. Fortunately nobody had been hurt as I'd cannoned into them, but a couple of ladies were pretty shaken up. As soon as I found my voice, I offered my apologies which were brushed aside. Everybody seemed to think they were lucky not to have been first in line.

I should have taken the next car but I was too chicken. I

went down the emergency stairs instead. I was still quivering when I reached the ground floor, and my bones felt as if they'd turned to jelly. I found the other escapees clustered around the building superintendent. Everybody was totally mystified. The elevator was now working normally and, as the superintendent explained for what he claimed to be the tenth time, there was no way that the elevator doors could have opened if the car wasn't there.

I knew a way. But there was no point in trying to tell him. I went out onto the street and flagged a cab.

When I got to the Mayflower, I called The Man's room from the house phone and asked him to come down and meet me. He stepped out of the elevator wearing olive-green cords, a plaid shirt that toned in nicely, and a black nylon windbreaker with blue and white shoulder-stripes. The Roman army-issue sandals had been replaced by a pair of jogging shoes. He looked more like a rising young cinéaste than the Good Shepherd. But why not? Once again, I had to remind myself that the blue-eyed firm-jawed Anglo-Saxon Sunday School Jesus was a PR image produced by Christian propagandists of the Roman persuasion. If anything, it was the figure portrayed in the Byzantine mosaics that most resembled The Man who now approached me. But even that was the wrong way to look at him. I realized I had to stop comparing him to any of the stereotypes that had been constructed from the available evidence and see him *as he was*. As a nonpracticing Jew, I had a head start, but it was amazing to discover the amount of subliminal conditioning I'd acquired by living in a predominately Christian world.

We shook hands. It was obvious that he already knew what had happened.

"I think you just saved my life," I said. "I don't know how but —"

He shrugged it off.

"Well, thanks, anyway. Who set me up?" I asked. "Was it 'Brax's mob?"

"Yes. They know I'm here." He sensed my alarm and patted me on the shoulder. "Don't worry. I'll figure something out."

"What about Miriam?"

"Miriam is going to be all right. Trust me." His eyes held mine. They were full of strength and sincerity, but none of it rubbed off on me.

"It's easy for you to say that," I bleated. "But what happens if he tries again? I mean, from what you've told me, this is the guy who never gives up."

"You're right," he said. Then shrugged. "That's one of the risks you have to take."

"Oh, tremendous," I said. "That's all I need." As if this guy hadn't caused me enough problems already. I wasn't an expert on the early Christian Church but I'd picked up enough to know that few, if any, of the Apostles had lived to collect their retirement pay.

He must have known what was going through my mind. "Come on," he said. "Snap out of it. I told you what the score was on Saturday."

"Yes, I know. But this is a whole different ball game."

He smiled. "Leo — no one ever said any of this was going to be easy."

"True," I replied. "But no one said that it was going to be lethal either." I mean, what the hell? If The Man had to land on somebody's doorstep, why couldn't he have picked Billy Graham's? The guy had done pretty well out of this stuff. Someone like him should be taking the flak, not me. Then another thought slithered out of the treacherous recesses of my mind. Suppose the whole thing was a put-up job? Engineered by The Man to persuade me to go along with some unrevealed plan?

I caught his eye and realized that he was reading me like a book. I suddenly felt embarrassed. He deserved better.

He gave me a look that was pure gold. "Stick with me," he said. "And I'll do my best to make sure you come out of this in one piece."

And he did. Though not quite in the way I expected.

I grabbed his arm and steered him toward the street. "Come on. I need a drink."

We went to the Gulf + Western building just a few yards down the sidewalk and took the elevator up to the forty-fourth floor. I rode up without the slightest qualm. The way I figured it, nothing was going to happen to me when The Man was standing right next to me. Even so, I made sure we stepped out of the elevator together when we reached the top. It was then that I think he used a little Celestial magic because when we walked into the bar we got a table right by the huge picture window — something that had *never* happened to me before. You get a fabulous view over the West Side to the Hudson River and the George Washington Bridge that links Manhattan with New Jersey.

I ordered bourbon on the rocks for both of us. As the waiter turned away, The Man asked him to add a large vodka and tonic.

"It's to save time," he explained. "I asked Miriam to join us. But she can only duck out for thirty minutes. Is that okay with you?"

"Sure," I said nonchalantly. I didn't even try to get into how he knew when I was going to pick him up, or where I planned to take him for a drink. Or the fact that, if Miriam was already on her way, he must have contacted her *before* I reached his hotel.

It was stunning proof of his powers of precognition but, even so, it was small beer compared to his guardian angel bit on the twenty-second floor.

Miriam arrived at the same time as the drinks but that, I am sure, *was* a coincidence. We both rose to greet her. As I took hold of her hand her fingers tightened briefly around mine and transmitted that special tingle which tells you you're still ahead in the only game in town.

"Hi . . ." She gave me a quick kiss on the cheek then went to shake The Man's hand. But he took hold of her shoulders and kissed her on the cheek too. She sat down about a second before her legs gave way. And any thoughts I had of getting lucky in bed collapsed with her.

The Man picked up his glass and sniffed it. "Grain alcohol?"

"Yes," I said. "Can your bio-system handle that? I don't want you burning a hole in the carpet."

He raised his glass to us with a smile. "To the years ahead."

"Does that mean I can tear up my life insurance?" The question earned me a kick on the ankle from Miriam.

"Just love one another," he replied. "And let tomorrow take care of itself."

I like to think that little shaft was aimed at Miriam. She was always making plans. But as we sat there, I couldn't help thinking of another saying of his. At least, I hope it is. Which was — *To find one's life, one has to lose it.* "Trust me," he had said. And I certainly intended to try, but when you examined his assurances, they fell a long way short of a cast-iron guarantee of safe-conduct through the minefield he'd dropped us into. In his resurrected form, The Man was probably fireproof, but Miriam and I were sitting ducks. But let's face it — what were we? Two insignificant ground-vehicles each housing a tiny spark from one of the luminous beings he was so intent on rescuing. We were no different from all the millions of other people on this planet who were playing unwitting host to the trapped Ain-folk. The Aeons whose divine nature now found expression through the human spirit. Perhaps it was for that reason, despite the never-ending catalogue of man-made horrors, it could not be extinguished. But we could. Hadn't he told me that we were expendable? At that very moment, 'Brax and his heavies might be gathering overhead like a dark storm cloud. Zeroing in on us from the four corners of the cosmos. Not that I thought for one moment he planned on doing something drastic like leveling New York. But he and his boys could still make life difficult. After all, this was the mob that the Empire had failed to keep the lid on. It was all very well for The Man to talk about a tomorrow, but if he didn't hold all the aces, we might not get to see the sunrise.

Don't panic, I told myself. Any minute now, the yo-yos in the longship who are trying to straighten out the Resurrection may yank him back to Jerusalem and that will be the last you'll see of him. But perversely, I didn't want that either. What I wanted was the privileged pleasure of his company without the attendant dangers. The crunch line is, of course, as many have found out before me — there is no way you can come to a comfortable accommodation with Christ.

And then I thought, what the hell? We live in New York. We don't push our luck. We try to steer clear of trouble. But what guarantee do any of us have that we're going to make it through the day? What does it take? A guy on a bike swallows his whistle instead of blowing it and wraps your spleen around his handlebars. A junkie in search of oblivion tries to cut your wallet out with a knife and takes your heart with it. A terminal cancer case skydives through a fiftieth-floor window to save hospital fees and uses you as a trampoline. A .357-magnum ricochet blows away your cheesecake and the face you were feeding it into as you sit at a fast-food counter that fate has positioned opposite a bank-heist shootout. It can happen. I can give you names and addresses of the next-of-kin. You want to live here, you play the percentages. It's the price you pay for putting the bite on the Big Apple.

As you can see, it doesn't take me long to bounce back. Miriam listened wide-eyed as I related my encounter with the missing elevator and the invisible fist. I kept it low-key to avoid alarming her and to reinforce the image I liked to project of myself as a man who, besides being smooth, sharp and sexually magnetic, was also endowed with a certain nonchalant machismo. Which mean omitting the fact that I had, momentarily, been scared shitless.

It was touching to see how she accepted the situation without seeking any assurances for her own future safety. What was slightly less touching was the fact that she did not seek any on my behalf either. But then, maybe she knew something that I didn't. Or maybe, women really are different from men in their reaction to danger — in that that their first thought is for their children. If so, her motherly instincts were directed not toward me but toward The Man.

"Will you be all right?" she asked him as I finished my story.

"Yes, don't worry," he said. " 'Brax can't harm me now. He can only make things more difficult."

"What do 'Brax's boys look like?" I asked. It was one of those questions that made him raise his palms and shrug his shoulders. Which I now knew meant that I was not going to get a clear answer.

"They come in all shapes and sizes," he said. "They like to work through people if they can, but they can manifest their power and presence in various ways. They can flatten a city in the guise of a hurricane or they put on their black magic outfit and scare the hell out of people with primal images drawn from the id —"

"You mean like the goat-headed rider on the black horse with eyes like red-hot coals, *incubi, succubi,* vampires, hobgoblins, and assorted monsters from the Pit."

He nodded. "Yes. On the other hand, they can look like the people next door. And often are. That's when it gets a little tricky. It makes them a lot harder to spot."

"Are they around all the time?" I asked.

"Some of them are," he said. "A prison has to have its jailers. 'Brax has several legions of elementals guarding Earth. There are garrisons scattered throughout the cosmos holding the Secessionist galaxies, marauding packs patrolling the Deeps, and scout ships everywhere. But their main force, under the great Black Princes, is held in reserve to counter any major intervention by the Empire."

"It sounds as if they've got you pretty well tied down," I said.

The Man swallowed some bourbon and allowed himself a quiet smile. "It's not as simple a task as it sounds. 'Brax's power is eternal in the sense that he cannot be destroyed, but his degree of power is finite. He can divide it into an infinitely variable hierarchy of lesser beings. Creatures of his will that he can dispatch to do his bidding. He can unmake the Black Princes and the Lords of Darkness that were banished with him from the Empire and refashion them at his whim. He can destroy life. He can corrupt it. But he cannot create it. Life is a gift of Empire. The only way 'Brax can increase his strength is by winning the allegiance of the Celestial powers trapped in the cosmos. And he will never do that because the Empire keeps sending messengers in under the wire to bring word to the Ain-folk that they have not been abandoned. Giving them hope, the will and the means to resist through The Power of The Presence. And 'Brax has an even bigger problem. Although Time is simultaneous the cosmic clock governing the World Below is still ticking. Everything in it is subject to the Law of Lapsed Time. Which, expressed very simply, means that you cannot be in two places at once."

"But —" I began.

He held up his hand. "I know what you're going to say. Under the rule of simultaneity, I am being born and crucified while we sit here talking. But *not* in the same *linear* time frames." He turned to Miriam. "Are you still with me?"

"I'm just about hanging on by my fingertips," she confessed. "But keep going. Leo can explain it to me later."

The Man looked at me. "Think back to that idea of linear time as a strip of film in which each frame represents a fleeting instant of Time Present that you think of as 'now.' When I moved through from the rock tomb to Manhattan General I dropped out of that section of the film — then reappeared in the post-Crucifixion sequence some two hours later. The same thing happened over the weekend, and with my trip here today. I'll be missing from an equal number of time frames in twenty-nine A.D. But I could drop out of the linear time dimension and reenter it *at the same moment* somewhere else. Say — San Francisco."

"Yet another paradox," I mused.

"Yes," said The Man. "But only because you lack the proper modes of perception. Like me, 'Brax is not bound by Time and Space but, when he is operating in the physical universe — the cosmos — he is subject to the Law of Lapsed Time like everyone else. Which means that his forces, which as I've said are finite, cannot be everywhere at once. And his war with the Empire is being waged not only along the linear time dimension but also *outside* it. Throughout *all eternity*."

Maybe now you will understand what I said right at the very beginning about being caught up in a big event.

I eyed Miriam expectantly.

"Go ahead," she said. "I can't tell the Milky Way from a Hershey bar."

I swallowed some bourbon to help me get my bearings and focused on The Man. "So what you're saying is — 'Brax has to keep switching his forces around; moving them through Space and Time to try and stop you making an input."

"Yes. And the bigger the input, the bigger the force needed to counter it. We enjoy a slight tactical advantage in being able to choose the time and place. But against that must be set the difficulties in getting through to the World Below without being detected and the problems of protecting the Time Gate."

I was beginning to get the picture. "So . . . the name of the game is trying to stay one jump ahead. In order to keep 'Brax off balance."

"Yes. It's a constant battle of wits. But every time we get the upper hand 'Brax finds some way to undermine our position." He thought about it, and shook his head glumly.

"Oh, come on now," I joshed. "Life isn't *that* bad."

"That's very true," he replied. "But who do you think deserves the credit for that — our side or 'Brax?"

"Thank you," said Miriam. As I sat there trying to think of a snappy answer. "I always enjoy seeing a smart New York lawyer at a loss for words. It restores my faith in God."

I managed to find my tongue. "I'm glad something does."

"You struck out, Resnick," she said. Her eyes flared, willing me into silence. She turned to The Man. "The Book says that after you'd been baptized, you met up with what they call the 'devil' — spelled with a small *d*. Was that 'Brax?"

The Man nodded. "He turned up eventually. His people had shadowed us from the moment of touchdown. And he was also waiting in the wings, so to speak, when Michael and Gabriel landed to set up what is known as the Resurrection. The transfer of Joshua's body and my metapsyche to the longship."

I glanced briefly over my shoulder to see if anyone behind was eavesdropping on our conversation. I needn't have worried. Nobody was paying the slightest attention. The quartet nearest The Man was discussing the plot of the latest Woody Allen movie. And let's face it, the way we were talking, we could have been discussing another. By Mel Brooks.

"So that means he must have known about your disappearance too," said Miriam.

"He certainly knew things hadn't gone as planned," replied The Man. "And that caused a certain amount of confusion on both sides. My people should have waited awhile. After all, the first time around, I was back in Jerusalem in under two hours."

"But they didn't," I interjected, with a feeling that I knew what was coming.

"No," he said. "They panicked and immediately launched a massive search operation. Every available vessel was dispatched through the time-tracks in both directions. Back into the distant past, and forward to the twentieth century and beyond."

"And 'Brax sent his main force after them," I said.

The Man nodded. "He must have. When I transferred from the tomb to the longship after coming back from Manhattan General, the massive forces 'Brax had gathered had disappeared from the post-Crucifixion time frames. When my resurrected form had been fully restored, Michael and Gabriel revealed that the search parties had already taken off and, for various reasons, could not be recalled without causing even more confusion. On top of which, our communication link with the Empire had been broken. There was nothing in our mission orders to cover this situation. Nevertheless, I still had to return to Jerusalem to finish instructing the Twelve. So we mounted a major effort to pinpoint the fault in the transfer process that had caused me to sidetrack by a couple thousand years." He threw up his hands. "The system checked out perfectly. *I* was the faulty component. The flaw in the system. Why, is a mystery. It may be due to the trauma of the Crucifixion. But, somehow, the temporal aspect of my metapsyche has become unstable." He smiled at us both. "In practical terms, and plain English, it means that this form I have assumed — this *body* I'm in — is no longer firmly anchored in linear time. As yours are. *That's* why I keep disappearing."

Miriam was the first to break the ensuing silence. "I don't know whether Leo has mentioned this but I'm a very down-to-earth person. I'm sure all this is terrifically relevant but the honest-to-God truth is I have about as much interest in cosmic events as Leo has in the workings of the lower intestine."

"She doesn't mean that," I interjected. "She's a very intelligent girl."

"Of course I am," said Miriam. "You don't have to tell *him* that. And you don't have to apologize for me either. The fact is, when you work in the boiler room of a cosmic *Titanic,* it's hard to get emotionally involved with what's happening up on the bridge."

"It's a nice image," I said. "But I think you picked the wrong ship. At least I hope you did. If we have to be aboard anything, I'd rather it was something like the USS *Nimitz* with its flight deck packed with warring angels."

The Man eyed me indulgently then took Miriam's hand. "I know how you feel. I spent thirty-four years in the boiler room myself. What is it you were going to ask me?"

"It may be something I missed," she said, "but — at this

point in time — whatever that means — are your people still looking for you?"

"Yes," he said. "In the end, we decided it was better to let the search continue just in case I got into a jam somewhere along the line and needed help. There was always the chance that one of our ships might pass through my time frame."

"And 'Brax and his baddies are on their heels," she concluded.

"Yes. And in some cases, ahead of them."

I began to put the pieces together inside my head. It was incredible. While the foursome behind us continued their review of W. Allen's unique brand of movie magic, and a fat-fingered man on my right reacted with monosyllabic compassion to a tale of woe from a red-headed dancer whose show had just bombed on Broadway, The Man had casually revealed that he was the subject of the biggest manhunt ever.

As the sky beyond the Hudson River began the slow mix through from evening into night, and the windows of the black paper cutout city began to glitter like boxed constellations of cut-rate stars, opposing fleets of metaphysical spaceships fashioned by powers in universes beyond our own were playing a cosmic game of tag through the woven strands of Time. Traveling through the unnumbered centuries toward the beginning and the end of the world in search of The Man who sat beside us cradling a glass of bourbon.

"Tell me," said Miriam, "does this mean that — all those flying saucers people claim to have seen are *real?* Are they —" Her hesitation was understandable. "Are they looking for you?"

"Yes," he said. And now there was no hint of a smile. "They're not really full of little green men, or shaped like trash can lids but — as in the case of angels — people see what they want to see."

"Now it begins to make sense," I said, warming to one of my favorite subjects. "That's why the sightings are so brief, and the descriptions so varied. Why there aren't any good pictures, no real attempt to communicate with us, or meet us face-to-face. We are of no interest. They're just passing through."

It all seemed to fit neatly into the pattern of saucer sightings I'd read about, and the theories that UFOs came from another dimension. Another plane of existence. Or from the depths of human consciousness. Didn't they often appear quite suddenly, hover briefly over an area, a vehicle, or plane, then accelerate to speeds of thousands of miles an hour, and vanish into thin air?

If 'Brax's ships had followed in the wake of the Star of Bethlehem boys, or maybe moved ahead of them, it would explain the steady increase in reported UFO sightings in the last half of this century while at the same time disposing of most of the aerial mysteries recorded by the scribes of Sumer, King Tut, and from there on up. The Man had now made three trips up the line, and two back down. And had doubtless appeared to people on the way. If either side had picked up his trail, it was obvious that they would eventually narrow their search down to the right century, then the right decade, then gradually zero in on the right year until they had his exact location spotted.

Right here in Manhattan, within arm's length of L. Resnick.

I finished the last of my bourbon. "I've understood everything so far," I began. "But something puzzles me. I can grasp the concept of temporal instability and your return to related time frames of first-century Jerusalem. Because, in a sense, that's where your temporal roots are. But if you are not in total control of your movements, why is it you keep coming back *here?*"

My question made Miriam snort in disgust. I don't know why. The answer concerned her just as much as it did me. As we both discovered later.

"Leo," he said, "at the moment, I can't tell you. But when I find out, you'll be the first to know."

For some reason that sounded more like a threat than a promise. And it led me to consider the ever-present threat of the Apocalypse which was the scriptural corollary of the Second Coming and the gloomy prediction I've mentioned before — that the final holocaust would begin in the hills of Hebron. As it certainly would if The Man ever went back there as an official guest of the Israeli government. And it struck me that maybe I was wrong. Maybe 'Brax might arrange to have Manhattan taken out after all. With détente a dead duck, the world in turmoil and the Pentagon rewriting its nuclear war strategy, it could happen. The bad news in Revelations could begin with a preemptive strike by 'Brax to take out The Man to whom I had unwittingly become host. He had assured me that his coming here was an accident. But suppose he wasn't leveling with me? Suppose this was it — with a capital *I T?* The good guys might win in the end, but what good would it do us to be on the side of the angels?

I took my eyes off the bottom of my glass and gave him a sideways glance. He broke off his conversation with Miriam and looked at me with disarming directness. He pointed at my glass and pulled one of my five-dollar bills out of his hip pocket.

"You look as if you could do with another drink. Let me get you one." He flagged the waiter as if he'd been doing it all his life. "Miriam . . . ?"

"Not for me," she said. "I'm going to have to get back to the hospital." She checked her watch. "Maybe I can catch up with you later."

"Sure," I said. "I'll call you and let you know what's happening."

She waved us back into our seats as she got to her feet. "Take good care of him," she said.

I nodded obediently. She gave me a smile that spelled forgiveness but her eyes told me I was still on probation. As she moved past The Man she briefly took hold of his raised hand. "You must come to the hospital some time."

"Yes," he said.

We watched her walk away across the room. She turned

and gave a quick wave as she reached the line of people waiting for seats. Then she was gone.

"Nice girl . . ." He drained his glass as the waiter arrived.

"Very," I said, quietly appalled at the prospect of what the New York press would make of the miracles he might perform in Emergency. I put my glass on the tray and looked up at the waiter. "Make mine a triple. . . ."

SEVEN

WE sipped our way leisurely through the second round and I
pointed out some of the more interesting items that formed
part of the cityscape below us. The bar faces west, with a
shorter window on the north side, so to see the Empire State,
the Chrysler Building, and the other high-risers of Lower
Manhattan you have to eat in the restaurant that occupies the
other half of the forty-fourth floor. Even so, The Man was
still knocked out by the sheer volume of the city, the densely
packed piles of masonry we'd managed to cram onto an island
that had been purchased for a row of beads. As well he might
be. First-century Imperial Rome might be a jaw-dropper to
your average Visigoth, but nothing short of the Celestial City
itself could have prepared him for the glittering spectacle of
nighttime New York.

When we'd finished, we left the Gulf + Western building,
cut through to Broadway and down to Times Square. As
usual, it was littered with folks in search of a good time. Shoals
of eager minnows with darting eyes; their faces rainbow-
tinted by the razzle-dazzle from the acres of neon graffiti that
hung in the night sky without visible means of support. The
fluorescent icons of the good life. And in their wake came the
night people with walled-up eyes. The hustlers, pimps and
pushers, moving coolly through the minnows like razor-
toothed pike. Waiting for a chance to score.

We plunged into the crowds that spilled off the sidewalk, pausing every now and then to look at the displays in the jam-packed entrances to the pleasure palaces, the fast-food joints and record stores, then we stood for a while on a street corner and watched the world go by.

It is, perhaps, a banal remark, but it really *is* fascinating to watch the behavior of individuals in a crowd. Some move purposefully; others aimlessly, letting the waves of people carry them back and forth along the sidewalk like uprooted seaweed caught in the ebb and flow of an incoming tide. Longing for a chance encounter to leaven the emptiness of their lives but not daring to reach out to one another. Just wandering; hands in pockets, or folded out of sight under their arms. Like multiple amputees; crippled by the fear of rejection. Their days and nights spent on the fringe of life, waiting for something to happen. Watching the takers. The minnows, jostling for a share of whatever was up for grabs. Sex, thrills, laughter; or drugs to deaden the need for all three.

Traffic flowed past. A rumbling glass and metal river of reflections. Pushers moved upstream against the press of the crowd; muttering the menu of the Paradise Cafe; coke, hash, speed, smack, poppers, acid . . .

I watched one of them until he disappeared in a sea of featureless faces drained of color by the canopies of light that reached out over the sidewalk. Like bleached grains of sand on a distant shore littered with unfulfilled dreams. I was conscious of a degree of detachment that I had never felt before. As if The Man was making me watch the world through *his* eyes but with the knowledge of my own past pursuits of pleasure. And it bothered me more than a little to think that he might know exactly how I had behaved on those occasions. Even though he had never offered a word of criticism, the thought of any form of censure suddenly made me feel rebellious. After all, I had never pretended to be perfect.

I conjured up what I hoped was an air of aggressive unre-
pentance. "Do you want to move on — or have you seen
enough?"

"No," he said. "Give me the full ten-dollar tour."

"Okay," I replied. "But don't hold me responsible."

I steered him across Broadway and down toward Forty-
second Street and made sure he kept close to me as we eased
our way through the logjam on the corner. The street itself
was teeming with people of every race and color. United by a
single creed: the exploitation and gratification of human
desire. Maybe I'm neurotic but, when I walk around that area
between Broadway and Eighth Avenue, I always experience
a certain frisson. Maybe it's because of the higher-than-aver-
age number of blacks and Puerto Ricans gathered in rap
squads along the curb — as if in readiness to repel boarders.
Maybe it's because, by some miracle, I've never yet been
mugged and, at the back of my mind, I knew that sooner or
later it had to happen. Preferably sooner, while one still has
the sense not to resist and the strength to get up. It isn't a
problem now, but the one thing I dreaded was the prospect
of shlepping my bones around for seventy crime-free years
only to fall prey to a twelve-year-old vandal and his kid
sister.

Perhaps my fear is a lurking remnant of my Jewishness. A
race-memory of pogroms past, or a touch of the guilts about a
society that enables me to live in style while others sleep six
to a room in cold-water walk-ups. Or whatever. All I know is
that some of the people who eye you on that street are really
evil-looking bastards.

And there's another kind, that look as if they've just
crawled out from underneath a rock; the kind it's hard to
imagine walking the streets in broad daylight. Graduates
from Dracula's Charm School. When I see them, I always ask
myself — what the fuck do they do? How do they earn a
living? I wouldn't even offer them a job in our mail room for
fear they'd give our clients gangrene through licking the flaps

on the envelopes. Maybe they do nothing; just exist on food stamps and welfare. Maybe some of them are even beyond that.

We stopped and looked into a bar drenched with blood-red light. Four topless go-go dancers stood on a ledge above the bottles of booze and worked the fat off their hips with the help of some funky rock. Their faces frozen behind masks of makeup; their unseeing eyes focused on infinity. Below them, the bartenders dispensed drinks with a staggering indifference.

"It's a local custom," I said, as we regained the street.

The Man nodded. "They had the same kind of thing in Rome. Only the music wasn't so loud."

"What were you doing there?" I asked.

He shrugged. "Just passing through. . . ."

We moved on and, before I could grab him, he stepped inside a bookstore retailing hard-core magazines and fun things for fetishists. I took a deep breath and plunged in after him. My one big worry was that he might go ape and start busting up the place, like when he overturned the tables of the moneylenders inside the Temple. But as it turned out, he was on his best behavior. He just eyed everything with a kind of bewildered amusement. I'd seen enough of the product not to be shocked but, even so, some of the stuff on display was pretty dreadful.

And somehow, very sad.

The defiant full-frontal had come of age about the same time as I had, but years of overexposure had dulled my initial delight at being afforded sharp-focus close-ups of the female pudenda. How many trees, I wondered, had been killed to provide the paper to print all this junk? How did little girls who had skipped to school, and posed prettily in pigtails and their first party dress — how did they end up fingering their private parts in front of a camera? What was the process of dissolution? The answer had to be more than just two hundred bucks an hour.

I glanced along the racks of magazines. Row upon row of

full-page pictures of what the trade called "split beavers." The Temples of Venus that had served as Muse to generations of ardent poets, inspiring them to produce lambent sonnets that had caused ladies to blush and virgins to swoon, along with more robust rhyming couplets such as those found in *Eskimo Nell*. It was a magnificent obsession; but there was little poetry to be found in the explicit anthologies for sale which, when isolated from the attendant anatomy, bore a depressing resemblance to the unstuffed gizzards of Thanksgiving turkeys.

I turned to The Man. "Not a pretty sight."

"It never was," he replied.

I took him by the arm. "Come on. Let's get some fresh air."

We went out into the street and wandered on. Wherever we looked, it was more of the same. Finally, we ended up in front of a Broadway movie house where they were screening *Deep Throat*. There was a small crowd gathering in front of the box office in readiness for the next performance.

The Man ran his eyes over the pictures in the lobby then turned to me. "Do we have time to take in a movie before Miriam comes off duty?"

"We do," I said. "But this isn't it. We can go to one of the places on Third Avenue." I took hold of his arm.

He didn't move. "What's wrong with this one?"

"Look," I said. "Enough is enough. You saw that stuff in the bookstore. This is the film of the book. You don't need to watch this kind of thing. You already know we're sick. It will only upset you."

"Leo," he said, "I've been around for a long time. For a lot longer than you can possibly imagine. People now aren't any different from what they were two thousand years ago. Only the scenery is new. Besides, what harm can it do me? Your head's still in one piece — and you've seen it three times."

I felt myself go red with embarrassment. "True. But that was years ago."

Some of you who haven't seen the movie are probably

familiar with its reputation. But for those people who are totally ignorant of its content, I should perhaps explain that with this particular work, skinflicks came of age. Its screening caused a minor sensation and a polarization of opinion among committed liberals in the same way that the Soviet invasion of Czechoslovakia following the "Prague Spring" of '68 caused a split between Euro-Communists and hard-line Stalinists. *Deep Throat* is not a movie that invites interpretation. It has all the subtlety of a visit to a slaughterhouse.

Despite my whispered protests, The Man joined the line and blew the last of my loan on two tickets. After that, there was nothing to do but follow him inside; which I did with some misgiving.

You may have guessed that, despite my triple exposure to the unique talent of Ms. Linda Lovelace, this was not my all-time favorite movie and certainly not one I would have chosen as an introduction to the art of the cinema. But there was no doubt that it told The Man where a goodly number of our heads were at. As I mentioned earlier on, Miriam was into Fassbinder, Varda, Wertmuller, and Kurosawa. The last time I'd seen this kind of picture was five or six years ago. The magic, you might say, had worn off.

We found a couple of seats on the aisle and, as we settled in, I wondered why he'd decided to put me on the spot like this. I've got a certain amount of chutzpah but I didn't have the brass neck to sit through this particular movie in the company of Jesus without feeling uncomfortable. And he knew that. It could only be because he wanted to teach me something.

The house lights dimmed and I found myself praying for another blackout to hit the East Coast. I waited but, by the end of the main title, I realized that God and his Son were ganging up on me.

It goes without saying that the whole sorry experience was colored by the presence of The Man but, looking back, I believe it only heightened my objectivity; the feeling of detachment that had invaded me while standing with him on the street corner. My perception of the city, the people, of life itself, had changed; sharpened; become less — worldly? Whatever it was, I knew that there was no going back. I had not yet found the Way but The Man had gently coaxed me to take an irrevocable step forward. And as we watched Ms. Linda take an incoming round while massaging her gums on the pillared flesh of a second faceless studio buck I could not help but reflect on the tawdriness of the spectacle and the spiritual poverty of the performers and producers. The explicitness of the farmyard action, the total lack of any ennobling emotion and the baseness of the motivation behind its conception suddenly seemed to epitomize the mind-shriveling nihilism that underpinned the permissive society.

I had come from a humane, wholesome family but, like my contemporaries, I had swung through the Sixties, stalked the singles bars in search of talent, watched the girls on the centerfolds of *Playboy* sprout nipples and pubic hair, had subscribed to the success of *Hustler*, and had treasured their famous breakthrough issue with the "Sniff me" cover.

I had plumbed the depths of eroticism in print and in practice and if, in the end, I had found it wanting, it was not for lack of trying. To be fair, my encounters had been limited to those available to an imaginative heterosexual but apart from that minor character defect I was a man of my time. A fully paid-up member of this crooked age. Like Conrad's hero, I had journeyed toward the heart of darkness only to recoil before it engulfed me. But the process of disengagement had, in all honesty, begun before The Man had arrived to bug me.

It was right that the web of hypocrisy surrounding our sexual relationships had been blown away but, as society had shed its inhibitions, it had become ensnared in a new web of deceit spun by the dream merchants. The new freedom they purported to represent was merely a new form of bondage. The expanding market created the need for new and ever more extreme forms of sexual imagery to stimulate the jaded appetites of its customers. But to satisfy the desires of some,

meant the exploitation of others. And they were not all con-
senting adults. Did the five-year-old kids cajoled into fellatio
ever recover? Did the South American slum whores killed in
snuff movies ever collect? The excesses of the permissive society were no more a celebration of life than a prison riot was
a celebration of the fellowship between the inmates and their
guards.

The vibrant world of instant, plasticized sex was a cruel
illusion and all attempts to turn it into reality merely increased the alienation between human beings. What we
needed was not sexual freedom but freedom from sexuality.
It was not a question of it being wrong, or bad, or sinful. It
was unnecessary. A blind alley that led us away from self-
realization; not toward it. But we had been conditioned to
think exactly the reverse. Virility and female desirability
were measured in terms of a person's sexual proclivity and
their on-the-job performance. And its importance extended
way beyond the basic biological requirements for the survival
of the species. The power of our animal magnetism and its
assiduous application assured us of a favored position in the
social pecking order.

I realized now what The Man had meant when he had said
that language had been designed to prevent us from understanding one another. For the misuse of language played a
major part in the all-consuming quest for self-gratification.
Speech had not been heaven-sent. It was a gift from 'Brax. It
made it possible for us to lie to one another, and fueled our
capacity for self-deception. We all knew what was going on
yet we remained party to the continuing conspiracy to deprive language of its true meaning. It had become a debased
currency and the supreme example of this relentless devalu-
ation was the word "love." A word which described everything that The Man stood for, and which had been taken
over by 'Brax.

Love, in its truest sense and purest expression, was a universal, self-denying emotion. Though it might, on occasion,
be the bedfellow of desire they were, in fact, discrete states

of being. Physical desire was an affirmation of self; its fulfillment meant the possession of another human being. From
experience, I knew that could produce some delectable moments but I also knew that, as a social activity, it manifested
itself in many guises: from a loving one-to-one relationship
all the way down to gang rape, child molestation, and the
Boston Strangler. And that because of it, a lot of people had,
quite literally, fucked up their lives.

"Making love" — when stripped of its 'Braxian camouflage,
described two aspects of sexual intercourse: procreation and
fornication. Both well known to the prophets of old. The im-
pulse to procreate is — as the exponents of socio-zoology tell
us — triggered by the implacable desire of our genes to reproduce themselves. Fornication, strictly defined, was sexual intercourse between the unmarried but, by extension, had come
to mean fucking — in any known permutation — for its own
sake instead of for the sake of the kids.

A way of making friends and influencing people.

Don't let's knock it but, at the same time, don't let us
delude ourselves by dignifying these twin buttock-heaving
modes of human behavior with the word "love." Love can
exist without sex, but sex often needs to cloak itself with
counterfeit love in order to make itself acceptable. Which
does not mean to say that you cannot love someone and also
desire them. Just don't kid yourself that they're the same
thing. There is, in fact, an acid test you can apply to your
relationship with the person you share your bed with. And
you don't need litmus paper. All you have to do is ask yourself the following question and answer it honestly: Would you
still want to be with them, sharing their joys and sorrows,
would you consider spending the rest of your life with them
if you were unable to have sexual intercourse? If the answer
is yes, then you may really be on the point of discovering
what love is all about.

When the movie ended, we shouldered our way out, back
onto the crowded strets. Word-images from The Man continued to flood into my mind. It was as if he was feeding me

enlightenment intravenously. I understood that love, raying outward from the soul, could pierce the hard, egocentric shell that held it captive. Its healing power could transform our lives, change the world and, in the final triumph of mind over matter, restore the balance between the opposing forces of the universe. The legendary Harmony of the Spheres without which everything, including the Celestial Empire, would go down the tube. Human consciousness was not a by-product of physical existence. It was not the result of biochemical processes but the thing that made those processes possible. It came from beyond Time and Space. From a higher realm of being of which The Man was part and to which he sought to bring us again by the power vested in him. And which was in all of us.

For each of us held the Key to the Kingdom. Where all things had been shaped by the Light of The Word. The indestructible, unifying force that flowed through the Cosmos and gave life to all within it. It could not be destroyed because it emanated from The One, The Presence, Y*W*H, Allah, the God-Head, the Creator, the Supreme Being, the Shekinah, the Unknowable, the Ultimate Principle; or Whatever. Which — according to The Man — was now locked into a life-and-death struggle with creatures spawned from its own being: the rebellious legions of 'Brax.

But while the power of Love could not be destroyed, it could be suppressed, perverted, misdirected. As when its energy was funneled through our sexual organs and our senses as desire for the things of this world; or transformed by the malevolent influence of 'Brax into hate.

It was not some grouchy moralism that had caused the ancient Hebrews to list our common failings among the seven deadly sins, but a more ancient wisdom. Lust, hate, pride, greed, envy were crippling deformations of the power of the spirit. They were the bars of the cage that imprisoned the soul. The chains that made the Celestial rider the slave of the earthbound host that carried him through the seductive dream caverns that 'Brax had woven about the world.

To keep us from The Light.

'Brax was playing for high stakes. He didn't want just what was on the table. He wanted the deeds to the casino and the rest of this galactic Las Vegas. And he was playing with loaded dice and a stacked deck.

One of 'Brax's major coups in this titanic struggle had been the forced creation of the ego from which had sprung the cult of the individual and an abhorrence of collectivism. The achievement of the individual was upheld as a triumph of the *human* will. The proof that Man was master of his own destiny and that rational science would unravel the mysteries of the universe. Belief in God was held to be the vestigial remains of a more primitive, irrational state of mind.

The emphasis on the individual belied the truth. Handel may have composed *Messiah*, but without a choir to bring it triumphantly to life it is nothing more than marks on pieces of paper. Even the most brilliant concert pianist was nothing without the generations of craftsmen whose collective skill had brought his instrument to its present peak of perfection. And there was a darker side to the supremacy of the individual human will. The Reverend Jim Jones could not have sown terror and death among his followers if they had not willingly subjugated themselves to his baleful personality. And if, instead of pandering to his lunatic ambitions, that fateful coterie of German generals and industrialists had told Hitler to take it down the street, the world might have been spared World War Two.

The egocentric behavior of the Me Generation; the obsession with doing one's own thing; the calculated selfishness that was required to claw our way to the top of the heap, discarding the people who were of no further use to us — all this was the reverse of The Man's teachings. We had turned our backs on the protocommunes that his disciples had created in the days immediately following the infusion of his power at the Feast of the Pentecost. *And they that believed were together and had all things in common; and sold their possessions and goods and parted them to all men as every man had need.* The only people who practiced that now were raggedy-assed Christian Anarchists. And who took any notice of *them?*

The trouble with niceness, self-sacrifice and goodness was that it was a real turnoff. And absolute goodness even more so. Like most people, I was capable of minor, unselfish acts but I was always careful not to let it get out of hand. After all, this is a tough world we live in. And in it, do-gooders usually end up by making everyone around them feel bad — or even inciting them to violence. I guess you could put it down to the perverseness of human nature.

Or 'Brax.

For behind any charitable feelings there lurks the insidious conviction that people usually get what they deserve; or should. Which helps us get over that attack of the guilts when we fail to write out a check for this week's good cause.

And what really gets us off the hook, gives us the excuse we need for not trying, is the discovery that even the good guys have feet of clay. It confirms our worst suspicions and makes us feel a helluva lot better to know that while Martin Luther King may have been to the top of the mountain and looked over the other side, he was also balling chicks in integrated motel rooms: That good old Ike, our open-faced soldier-President, had the hots for the peaches-and-cream English society girl–soldier who chauffeured him around wartime London. And when we fail to contribute to the fight against leprosy, we can do so in the comfortable knowledge that Nobel Doctor Albert Schweitzer was a tetchy, egocentric old fart who goose-stepped over his staff and patients. And if only we could get some dirt on Mother Teresa of Calcutta, our joy at eating out in expensive restaurants would be unconfined.

That was the problem with The Man. Apart from cussing a fig tree, he hadn't put a foot wrong. It was true he had put the hex on the Gadarene swine, but that was in a good cause. He'd also bad-mouthed the scribes and Pharisees, but everyone seems to agree that they were just a bunch of assholes.

Despite my ingrained skepticism, I had been struck by his essential goodness. As Miriam and Linda had been. There was a kind of basic integrity about the guy despite the fact that, up to now, he had reacted to everything with an intriguing passivity. But then if, as the Book said, he *was* the Son of God, he didn't have to *do* anything. His presence was enough; and from it, there radiated a quiet strength. Not an aura of physical force, but of incorruptibility. Which, in our day and age, was guaranteed to make people foam at the mouth.

I was jerked out of my ambulatory reverie by a sudden clamor across the street. A crowd of people stood back from a black guy spread-eagled in a doorway. Blood pumped out from under his body and snaked its way toward the curb. A cop, summoned by a distraught miniskirted hooker hurried along the outside of the line of parked cars with a drawn nightstick. The sound of approaching sirens cut a shrill swath through the noise of the traffic.

The Man took in the scene and started across the street.

I grabbed his arm and held him back. "Listen. Stay out of it. There's nothing you can do."

He tried to shake me off. "He's dying."

"Look," I said. "They'll have called an ambulance. Let that cop handle it. He'll know what to do."

He swung his arm up and twisted free. I swore under my breath and followed him across the street. We got separated by a couple of passing cars. By the time I reached the other curb, he was kneeling over the body. The crowd closed around him, leaving a narrow channel for the blood to drain into the gutter.

Dear God, I remember thinking, *don't let him start raising the dead.* The cop arrived. I stuck close behind him as he and the hooker made their way upstream.

The Man had rolled up the black guy's vest and put it under his head, and had ripped a couple of strips off his shirt to make a pad to staunch the flow of blood from the stab wound under the ribs. He got the cop to help him bind it into place, but I had an uneasy feeling that the Red Cross bandage bit was just to mask his magic.

"You a doctor?" asked the cop.

"No, a rabbi," said The Man. "But I do a little first aid on the side." He laid one hand on the victim's forehead and placed the other briefly over his punctured heart.

The black guy gave a little jerk, fluttered his eyelids, then rolled his eyes from side to side. Then he raised his head, looked down at his bandaged rib cage, and surveyed the ruins of his shirt. "Jeezuss, what d'you do that for, man? I paid sixty dollars for this fuckin' thing!"

The hooker, a caramel-colored fox with a Day-glo wig shaped like a giant nylon pan scourer, went down on her knees with a shrill cry of relief and cradled the ungrateful bastard's head. Two squad cars beat the ambulance into third place.

I hauled The Man up and made sure my fingers were riveted to his sleeve. "Come on. Let's get out of here."

We left the hooker to explain who had done what to whom and slipped through the three-deep ring of spectators as the paramedics hauled out their stretcher trolley. I glanced back and saw the black guy sit up unaided. I knew they wouldn't find a mark on him. And that could lead to a lot of awkward questions.

"What's the hurry?" said The Man as I hustled him across to the east side of Broadway.

"Just keep going," I said. "You and your goddamn miracles." All I wanted to do was grab a cab and put as much space as possible between us and the scene of the crime. But as always happens in situations like this, there was none available.

Someone called out behind us: "Hey — Rabbi!"

I held tight to The Man's arm and kept going. A greasy-looking, broad-shouldered guy in a leather bomber-jacket and tight jeans turned sharply and headed toward us from the other side of the street. His right hand was tucked inside his jacket. Which meant he either had fleas in his armpit, or a .38 Police Special.

The palm of somebody's hand slammed into my right shoulder. "Okay, you two — hold it right there."

It was the same voice as before. I looked back and saw it belonged to a young bearded guy in a flat tweed cap, with an Army surplus combat jacket over a red and black striped football shirt. He grabbed hold of The Man and spun him around, covering us both with his gun.

His friend in the leather jacket arrived. A real greaseball. He flashed his NYPD badge. "Drug squad. We're going to have to turn you over, friends."

Undercover narcs. It was insane. "Come on," I said. "What is this? Some kind of gag?"

Flat Cap waved his .38. "Don't get smart, shithead. Lay your hands on the roof of that car."

I looked at The Man. "Just do as they say."

We leaned against the roof of a white Volvo. Greaseball toed our feet apart and frisked us for concealed weapons. Starting with me.

"You're making a big mistake," I said. "I'm a lawyer. A member of the New York Bar Association. And this gentleman is one of my clients from out of town."

Greaseball made sure I was clean. "Okay, turn around." He snapped his fingers. "Identification."

I produced my wallet and showed him my driver's license and business card.

"Gutzman, Schonfeld and Resnick . . ." Greaseball ran his thumb over the raised ink on the card and passed it to Flat Cap. "They look expensive."

Flat Cap glanced at it then slipped it into a top pocket. "Check out the other guy."

I watched Greaseball frisk The Man and got my tongue into gear in readiness to explain away the absence of any means of identification. He turned The Man around and checked the inside pockets of the padded windbreaker.

"Bingo," said Greaseball. He exposed the left inside pocket of The Man's jacket and carefully pulled out a flat, transparent plastic bag full of white powder. He showed it to me, hefted it in his palm, then tossed it to Flat Cap. "I'd say that was a good six ounces."

Flat Cap nodded, then grinned at me. "I suppose you're going to tell me that your client's in the bakery business and that this is icing sugar."

A real comedian.

What the hell could I say? If the lab tests proved the contents to be six ounces of uncut coke or heroin, we were in big trouble. It had to be a setup. But how? Was it the black guy? Had he somehow palmed it off on The Man for friends to pick up later? And had the narcs seen the switch-play? Or had it been planted on him earlier? Perhaps in the store where he'd bought the jacket? Was this a ploy by 'Brax to put The Man on the spot? It was the only answer that made sense — in which case, Flat Cap and Greaseball might not be undercover cops at all but agents for a much more sinister organization. I was seized with alarm as my imagination began to run riot. If it was true, what could I do? I was helpless. How could I explain the situation to my friends in the DA's office — and to the judge and jury?

My legs wanted to run, but the fear of a paralyzing bullet in my back kept my feet glued to the sidewalk. In any case, now that they knew who I was, escape was impossible. And so it was, that from out of my cowardice, I was forced to find the courage to commit myself to the defense of The Man.

"My client's name is Yale Sheppard," I said. "He's an Israeli national who arrived today from Jerusalem. His passport, wallet and identification were stolen at John F. Kennedy. As his legal representative, I wish to know if you intend to arrest him — and on what charge."

Flat Cap showed the dope to The Man. "Do you deny ownership of this package and all knowledge that it was concealed on your person?"

The Man shrugged.

"Cuff him," said Flat Cap.

Greaseball pulled The Man's arms behind his back and clicked the bracelets shut over his wrists. I still couldn't believe it was really happening. Once again, we were surrounded by a ring of blank-faced sensation seekers. I was chilled by a curious sense of déjà vu; the thought that I might be witnessing a rerun of that scene in the Garden of Gethsemane.

Flat Cap pocketed the dope, read The Man his rights, then turned to me. "We're holding your client on suspicion until we get that package checked out. Start earning your fee, pal."

He holstered his .38, then both of them grabbed The Man by the arms and walked him into the street between the back of the Volvo and the car behind. As I followed them, a banged-up brown, '78 Dodge Charger cruised up and stopped alongside us. It all happened so quickly, I didn't get a proper look at whoever was behind the wheel. Greaseball got into the back with The Man. Flat Cap went in front.

I grabbed hold of his lowered window. "Hey, wait a minute. Let me ride downtown with you."

"Take a bus," said Flat Cap.

I held on to the window. "As this man's lawyer, I have the right to know the names of the arresting officers."

"Your client has not been arrested," said Flat Cap. "But I'm Ritger, he's Donati." He jerked a thumb over his shoulder.

"Where are you taking him?" I insisted.

"Seventh Precinct," said Flat Cap. "Now let go of this fucking car or I'll bust you for obstruction."

I shouted to The Man through the window: "Don't say anything until I get there!" The car pulled away, breaking my grip on the window. I watched with a sinking heart as it disappeared down the street. The small crowd that had gathered began to disperse, looking for some new event to satisfy their idle curiosity. It was nearly a quarter of ten. Normally, in moments of stress my brain works faster, becomes more incisive. That's what makes me a smart lawyer.

But not that night. I stood on the curb by the Volvo against which we'd been searched and fretted indecisively, torn between the desire to go immediately to the Seventh Precinct — which was on the eastern tip of Manhattan, south of Houston — and the need to discuss the situation with somebody. I might have found the moral courage I lacked but this was definitely not the time to make any rash moves. I walked back to Broadway and took a cab to Manhattan General.

Listen, even the best lawyers need to consult. Who else could I talk to?

EIGHT ===========

WHEN I reached the hospital I found Miriam up to her arm-pits in human suffering of one kind or another. It was one of those nights. She was always telling me what a kick she got out of being a doctor, but when she ducked out to see me after putting the last of fifteen stitches in somebody's scalp her face looked as crumpled as her white coat.

"Can we go somewhere and talk?"

As she led me through Emergency, I glimpsed some of the current crop of victims of life in the big city. Bleeding faces, broken limbs, burns, scalds; people who had been knifed or shot, in cold blood and in anger; zonked-out overdosed addicts with ulcerated arms; bewildered parents with taut, fraught faces, clutching kids who kicked and cried out of fear, or pain, and others who just lay there like rag-dolls, blank-eyed and unresisting.

We went into a small utility room. Miriam leaned back against the door and held it shut. She looked as if she was trying to keep the whole world out. "What is it? What's hap-pened?"

Women. How is it they always know? I told her about the miracle on Forty-second Street and the drug bust but left out our trip to the movies.

She bummed a cigarette off me. Her hands smelled of anti-septic. "What are you going to do?"

I shrugged. "I can't do anything until they charge him. Once they do that, we can get him out on bail."

"But he's innocent," she insisted.

"Look," I said. "You know that, and I know that, but it doesn't explain away a six-ounce bag of smack. Or whatever."

She eyed me reproachfully. "I just can't understand what possessed you to take him there in the first place."

I gritted my teeth. "He *asked* me to take him there."

"Leo," she said. "Come on. How would he know about Forty-second Street unless you told him?"

I prefaced my reply with one of those God-give-me-strength sighs. "I didn't need to tell him. He's been inside my head since Day One. And yours too. So lay off me — and drop the Goody Two-Shoes act before you contract a terminal case of moral rectitude."

Her eyes blazed. Hating me for having coaxed her into revealing some of her dark secrets and now throwing them back obliquely into her face. It's funny how we all strive to get the goods on one another yet try to maintain our own invulnerability. Take a tip from me: never give too much away. For, in the battle with the opposite sex, it is the whispered secrets of the bedroom confessional that provide the unkindest cuts of all.

A couple of seconds later, her better half resurfaced. "Supposing he disappears while he's out on bail? If he doesn't come back, it could cost you thousands."

"That's already occurred to me," I said. "There's a strong possibility that I may have to hock the Porsche and the place up at Sleepy Hollow just to raise the money."

"You could leave him in police custody."

I almost exploded. "Are you kidding?! You said yourself he was innocent. But that's not the point. I don't dare leave him there. If he disappears from a police cell —"

"So what if he does?" said Miriam. "That's their problem."

"It is — but suppose he reappears on my doorstep? The law does not look kindly upon people who knowingly harbor suspected felons."

"Oh, yeah . . . I hadn't thought of that," she said.

"Well think about it," I replied. "The last thing we need is an APB on Jesus of Nazareth and his mug shot circulated to every state in the nation."

Now, of course, she was full of wide-eyed sympathy. Not that it solved anything. "What's going to happen when he comes to trial?"

I waved the question aside. "That could take months. Listen. I don't want to even think about that. I've been beating my brains out trying to figure out a way of stopping this before it gets to the DA's office. If it was anyone else, I could at least have had a quiet word with Larry."

Larry Bekker, a buddy of mine from law school, was now deputy district attorney.

"Can't you have a word with him anyway?" said Miriam.

"What am I going to say to him?" I snorted. " 'Larry, I've got a little problem. I was on Forty-second Street with this client of mine called Jesus —'? Forget it." I gnawed at my thumbnail. "We're really over a barrel with this one. . . ."

"Where have they taken him?" asked Miriam.

"Seventh Precinct. . . ."

She raised an eyebrow. "I thought Forty-second Street came under Manhattan South."

"It does," I replied. "But the NYPD have dozens of different drug squads on the streets." I paused, then let go with the double whammy. "Always assuming that these guys are with the NYPD in the first place."

She frowned, then her eyes popped as she got it. "You mean — they may not be real people?"

"Oh, they're real enough," I said. "Well — let me put it this way: if they aren't, you and I aren't going to be able to tell the difference. What I mean is — they may be working for 'Brax."

Her eyelids dropped back into place as she got used to the idea. "But . . . what do you think he's trying to do?"

I exploded again. "How the hell do *I* know what his game plan is? He could play it two ways: he could maybe force The

Man to disappear and make sure that nobody knew he'd been here. In which case, you and I might find ourselves as popular as the people who made statements to the Dallas police after Kennedy's assassination. We could open the closet and find ourselves face-to-face with an unknown assailant who just happens to be an expert in karate —"

"Yukkk," said Miriam. "I don't think I like that."

I shrugged. "Listen. It could happen. The Man said that 'Brax will do anything to stop the truth getting out. And let's face it. There are lot of very powerful people around who'd be quite happy to help keep the lid on this. Think about it. I mean, we are involved, yet neither of us is exactly shouting the news from the rooftops."

"No," she said. "But only because we're trying to protect our own skins."

"Very true," I replied. "And there are others who are equally anxious to protect much bigger investments." I quickly outlined some of the problems I've mentioned earlier in this account: the worldwide social and political repercussions that could follow recognition of his presence; the panic that might ensue because of the predictions that linked his next public appearance with the Apocalypse; the inevitable head-on collision with the power centers of the Christian faith and competing religions. Had not the Vatican recently threatened to run leading theologians like Schillebeeckx and Kung out of town on a rail? How were they going to react to the news that the Star of Bethlehem was a spacecraft spun from the dreams of Empire, in synchronous orbit over the manger housing the newborn child of the Royal House of David, and his princely Celestial lodger?

(Don't look back, smart people. You did not skip a page. I put that bit together from what he'd already told me. We'll get to it in a greater detail later on.)

"Anyway," I concluded, "those are a few of the arguments for deep-sixing The Man's visit — and maybe us along with it. The incident with the elevator could have been a warning shot, to get us to back off. On the other hand, by having

The Man arrested, maybe 'Brax is trying to force him out in the open. To identify himself publicly as Jesus Christ. So that 'Brax can expose him as a fake."

"But wait a minute," said Miriam. "He *is* Jesus Christ."

"Sure," I said. "But who's going to want to believe that? Especially if he repeats some of the things he's already come out with. The ones who aren't foaming at the mouth will be rolling in the aisles."

She looked perplexed. "But — if you and I believe he's Jesus Christ, other people will too. After all, we are not even religious."

"Exactly," I said. "And neither is he, in the accepted sense. From what he's told me already, this guy is taking on all creeds and all comers. First of all, The Man has to prove who he is. And that could be more difficult than you think. The College of Cardinals in Rome is not going to just roll over with its legs in the air. The Mormon Tabernacle Choir is not going to rush to sing serenades under his window. And the Scientologists and the Moonies are not going to shut up shop and return all the money. If he goes public, everybody with a corner in the market is going to be jumping on his bones."

Miriam grimaced. "Ye-ess, I guess you're right."

"By the way," I added, "you've got it wrong. I don't *believe* he's Jesus. I accept it. There's a subtle difference."

She eyed me. "Of course. I forgot. You're a lawyer."

I knew what she meant. In terms of the endless word-game, we were the verbal cardsharps, skilled in the artful interpretation of motive, the subtle shades of innocence and guilt. Doctors didn't fool around with language in the same way. If they said you had cancer of the liver, it meant exactly that.

I checked my watch, then glanced over my shoulder and saw that the desk I'd been sitting on was equipped with a phone. "Can I use this to make an outside call?"

Miriam nodded. "Just dial nine."

I called Larry Bekker. I'd thought of one question I could ask him. He gave me a quick rundown drug enforcement scene and from it I was able to extract the relevant piece of information. Besides the local precinct officers who were detailed to make "street busts," there was a Narcotics Division team covering the Manhattan South Division. They were part of the Organized Crime Control Bureau, and were based in the Seventh Precinct. Which was where The Man had been taken. I thanked him, sent my love to his wife, learned that his daughter had had the braces removed from her teeth, accepted an invitation to bring Miriam to dinner but managed to fudge around the actual date.

"So — what now?" said Miriam.

I grimaced. "Better head downtown and see what the damage is. . . ."

She looked anxious. "Supposing —"

"You mean supposing 'Brax is behind this and not just the fuzz?" I shrugged. "We go on. What choice have we got? Our sweetmeats are already caught in the grinder."

"I wish I could do something," she said.

"Stand by," I replied. "You may hear me scream for help."

"Okay. Good luck." She squeezed my arm. "Call me."

"Sure. Take care." I kissed the tip of her nose.

She opened the door for me. "Why are you doing this, Resnick?"

I looked back at her. "What do you mean?"

"You know what I mean," she said. "What's your angle?"

I shrugged. "Good question. Maybe, for once in my life, I don't have one. Maybe it's because whatever I'm getting into just has to be better than the Delaware Corporation versus Cleveland Glass."

"I'm glad to hear it," she said. "There's hope for you yet."

I let it pass. It never does any harm to let them score now and then.

On the way downtown, I rehearsed legalistic responses to various imaginary scenarios then suddenly got a flash of inspiration. I got the cabbie to pull up at a pay phone, called Miriam, and explained my provisional game plan. At that moment in time I had no way of knowing if I would be able to engineer the opportunity to put it into effect but she agreed to stand by in case I managed to swing it.

The address Larry Bekker had given me turned out to be an old brownstone station house. You've seen buildings like it a thousand times in movies and on TV but it's a long time since the cops looked like Pat O'Brien. I paid off the cab and went in through the door. The desk sergeant was a florid, overweight barrel of Budweiser with leg-of-mutton arms bursting out of short blue shirt-sleeves and fat, stubby-fingered hands that looked as if they could tear your throat out. I explained my business. He told me that Detectives Ritger and Donati worked out of an office on the third floor.

I went up the stairs, braced for the worst. What happened was totally unexpected. As I reached the second floor, I met Ritger and Donati on their way down. Both of them were a good three inches taller than I was. Flat Cap, under any other circumstances, could have been quite a nice guy. Hard-nosed, but with a good intelligent face. I couldn't understand how he could work with such a slimer. Greaseball had donned a pair of orange shades. He swaggered down the stairs toward me with his elbows out, hands tucked in the front pockets of his bomber-jacket, and what looked like a coiled salami stuffed behind the zipper of his jeans. Someone must have told him he looked like Paul Michael Glaser. They should have pulled his badge for overacting. Just to look at him got my back up.

If I hadn't stepped in front of them, they'd have walked right past me. "We met on Forty-second Street," I said. "East of Broadway. You're holding a client of mine for illegal possession."

Flat Cap eyed me and ran his tongue around his teeth. "Ohh, yeah . . ." He glanced at Greaseball.

"His name's Sheppard," I said.

Greaseball jerked his head toward the floor above. "See Lieutenant Russell."

"What's happening? Has he been charged yet?"

"No," said Flat Cap. He went to move past me.

"Wait a minute," I said. "I'm going to need a copy of your arrest report. Have you made that out?"

The question seemed to amuse Greaseball. "Slow down, friend. Nobody's been arrested. Your client was pulled in on suspicion and strip-searched. That's all."

It still didn't dawn on me. "What d'you mean — 'That's all'?"

Flat Cap laid a hand on my arm. "It means that your client was clean. He was not in possession of any unlawful substance. Do I make myself clear?"

I looked at them both. "Wait a minute. Just what the hell's going on?"

The smile left Greaseball's face. "You're blocking the stairs, friend."

I stepped aside. Flat Cap was still holding my arm. He glanced around, then eyed me earnestly. "Let me ask you something. Do you want to ruin your client's trip to New York?"

"No," I said.

"Neither do we," said Flat Cap. "Do yourself a favor. Don't make waves. You've got enough problems."

I let it slip by me at the time, but I'm still wondering just what he meant by that remark. "Thanks for the advice," I said. I turned away from their mocking faces and went on up the stairs. I tried to figure out what could have happened and kept coming up with the same answer. They must have pocketed the bag of dope on the way down. If it really did contain six ounces of uncut coke, or heroin, the package had to be worth around fifty thousand dollars on the street. Not a bad night's work for Messrs. Ritger and Donati. It was a classic squeeze play. I couldn't accuse them of theft or raise the cry of police corruption without putting The Man on the spot. So much for Law and Order. But let's face it, it wouldn't be the first time that our boys in blue had cut themselves in on the street action.

A plainclothes cop directed me to Lieutenant Russell's office and told me in passing that he wasn't part of the drug squad. He knocked on Russell's door and checked to see if it was okay for me to go in. I heard a murmur of voices then the door opened and three guys in well-cut suits came out. They all gave me the once-over as they walked past. I don't know what it was, maybe it was their conservative taste in ties, but they left me with an odd impression. They looked more like bankers than cops. Or politicians. I never found out which. But maybe somebody else knows the answer to that part of the puzzle.

It turned out that Ritger had given Russell my business card and had warned him of my impending arrival. The lieutenant was not only pleased to see me, he wanted to ask me a few questions. The Man sat with his hands clasped in his lap, facing Russell's desk. Russell was a stocky, gray-haired guy in his mid-forties. Lined face; bushy eyebrows; washed-out blue eyes. The jacket of his three-piece plaid suit was hung over the back of his swivel chair. There was a dark-haired guy in a suit leaning against the wall to the right of Russell with folded arms. He had a thin slit of a mouth, with eyes to match, and his receding hairline had left him with a high domed forehead that made him look a bit like Ming the Merciless without the mustache.

Russell introduced him as Detective Frank Marcello, then pointed a finger at the fourth guy in the room. Rabbi Weinbaum. A small Levantine gnome; his face pale from countless hours of indoor study of the Scrolls. In his high black hat, yeshiva curl, and with his hollow-cheeked face half buried in a beard that covered his tie, he looked as if he'd come straight from an audition for a Broadway revival of *Fiddler on the Roof*.

Weinbaum eyed me over the top of his steel-rimmed glasses. *"Shalom."*

I nodded in reply and turned back to Russell. "Does this gentleman also work for the police department?"

"No," said Russell. "He's just helping us out."

"I don't quite understand," I said.

Russell exchanged a glance with Marcello. "When your

client was arrested, you forget to mention to the officers that he was only able to converse in Hebrew. All that we've had out of him so far are quotations from the Bible."

Rabbi Weinbaum nodded in solemn agreement.

"Got it." I looked at The Man. His eyes told me the whole story. I had to bite my cheeks in order to keep a straight face. "Is everything okay?" I said. Only it didn't come out that way. I heard myself asking him the question in Hebrew.

Now, if you're Jewish, you obviously pick up a few words here, the odd phrase there. But apart from the usual religious incantations, I had never put a colloquial sentence together in my life. Yet here I was, not only speaking it, but also aware of possessing an intimate knowledge of the language and the ability to speak it fluently. It was truly the Gift of Tongues. Pure magic.

"Yes," he replied. "These gentlemen have been very kind. Thank you for coming." His Hebrew persona was somehow more compelling than his twentieth-century image; his voice had more depth and resonance. But maybe I was responding to it on a more primal level. Something within me awakening to the voice of the God who had watched over our race since this struggle began.

I turned to Lieutenant Russell. "I understand that my client, who was held for questioning in connection with a suspected drug offense, is now not going to be charged. May I take it that he is now free to go?"

"Not exactly," said Russell. He shuffled the sheets of paper in front of him. From where I was sitting, I couldn't see what they were. Probably the rap sheet they had made out for The Man and a report from the two hoods who had pulled him in. He then looked up and fixed me with the stare that policemen usually reserve for wrongdoers. "There seems to be some confusion about Mr. Sheppard's actual identity."

Of course. It was such a stupid thing to do. I'd fed Ritger and Donati a variation of the same shit I'd laid on Linda. When they'd stopped us, my brain had stalled. It just hadn't occurred to me that they might check up on that part of the story. Now we were *both* in trouble.

Russell pulled out a piece of paper on which my lies had apparently been recorded. "There may have been some confusion in your mind at the time of the arrest," he began. Another wise guy. "But you are down here as saying that your client arrived today by air from Israel and had his identity papers stolen from JFK."

"That's correct," I said. "But —"

You don't need to be clairvoyant to guess what he enjoyed telling me. No one by the name of Yale Sheppard had arrived on any of the flights from Israel. Nor was there a Y. Sheppard listed as a passenger on any other flights arriving at JFK from overseas destinations. In fact, Immigration at JFK had no record of anyone with that combination of name and initial arriving in the last two weeks.

I didn't even bother to look surprised. I had exhausted my capacity for comic invention. I just sat there, trapped in my own web of lies, while Russell continued to review various, not unreasonable, hypotheses: such as the fact that my client was not on record as having arrived by air might explain why the theft of his wallet, passport and personal papers had not been reported to any of the airlines, or the airport police. Had he, perhaps, arrived by some other means of transport?

He had indeed, but I was not about to open that can of beans with Lieutenant Russell and the sphinx-like Marcello.

Weinbaum eased himself tentatively to his feet. "Excuse me. Is it all right if I go now? Mr. Resnick can translate any questions you want to put to his client."

"Sit down," said Russell. "We may want you to tell us what they are saying to each other."

Weinbaum subsided. But by now, I was badly rattled. I was in *shtuk* if I remained silent, and whatever I said would only put us deeper in the hole. Especially if it was the truth.

"Look," I said. "I really don't understand why we are pursuing this line of questioning. My client was arrested on suspicion of illegal possession. He was clean. I have been told there are no charges pending. If so, there is no case to answer. I am therefore asking you to release my client as of now, and I would like to point out that — unless you arraign him on some other pretext — neither of us are required to submit to further questioning. And one other thing. Not only were we manhandled and held at gunpoint without due cause, the two officers involved were also verbally abusive. I want to make it quite clear that if we are subjected to any further harassment, there is going to be a formal complaint on Larry Bekker's desk first thing tomorrow morning.''

One hundred percent pure bluster.

Russell was distinctly unimpressed. He waved me patiently back into my seat. "Come on. Let's cool it." He fingered the business card I had handed to Donati, and which was now stapled to the piece of paper on which my earlier misstatements had been recorded.

"Mr. Resnick," he said. "It says here that you're a lawyer. You must therefore be aware that, when acting in your professional capacity, you are an officer of the court, and that law enforcement officers tend to give credence to any statement you make in connection with an investigation by the police of a suspected felon or possible criminal activity." He treated me to a teddy bear smile. "In other words, we expect you to tell the truth. Or at the very least, an account of the relevant events which, while endeavoring to favor your client, has its basis on objective reality."

That was all I needed. A cop who read philosophy instead of watching ABC's *Wide World of Sports.*

"Okay," I said. "Where do we go from here?"

Russell shrugged. "You tell me. Immigration have asked us to hold your client overnight on suspicion of illegal entry into the United States. And if I don't start getting some joy from you, I'm going to hold you as an accessory. If you choose to consider that as harassment, I suggest you call Mr. Bekker." He nodded toward the phone.

I wondered if he knew that was the last thing I intended to

do. *Nyehhh*. What the hell, I thought. At least it will save me from another bad day in court. "I don't think there's anything I can say that will be of help," I said.

"Let me be the judge of that," replied Russell. "Let's try a few questions. It will save everybody's time in the morning."

What could I do? Tell him I wanted to call my lawyer? And then plead the Fifth Amendment?

"Where and when did you first meet Mr. Sheppard?"

I shot a quick glance at The Man and decided to stick as close as I could to the truth. "At Manhattan General Hospital. Nine days ago."

Russell received this with a nod. "So he didn't arrive from Israel today . . ."

"Look," I said. "All I can tell you is that he turned up in my office this morning. He told me that he'd been back to Jerusalem since our meeting at the hospital so I assumed that he'd come back the same way. By air. He indicated that he was in some kind of trouble and needed the help of a lawyer. I arranged to see him this evening to talk things over. We met for a drink, then walked down to Times Square and that's where he got lifted by two members of the drug squad that operates out of this building. End of story."

"Not quite," said Russell. "What were the circumstances of your first meeting with Mr. Sheppard at the hospital?"

I suddenly felt lucky. Russell had given me the chance to play my long shot. I took a deep breath and gave it my best Federal Grand Jury delivery. "I met him through a doctor I know who works in Emergency. Apparently, Mr. Sheppard had been brought in unconscious as the result of some kind of accident. This particular doctor knew that I was a claims lawyer and called me in with a view to acting for Mr. Sheppard whom, at this juncture, I was not able to speak with. I explained that I normally only handled corporate work but that I would endeavor to find him a suitable attorney."

"And did you?" asked Russell.

"No," I said. "I was busy. In fact, I didn't give it another thought until he turned up in my office this morning. As it happened, I was due in court on a big case. Dr. Maxwell had not called to advise me of his visit but I assumed that she had sent him along to me to follow up on my offer to find him an attorney. In the course of our conversation, it transpired that Mr. Sheppard had arrived at my office with no money, credit cards, or any means of identification. On top of which, he had this language problem. I didn't have time to go into it in detail. I had a really tight schedule. So I got my secretary to book him into the Mayflower Hotel and — as I've explained — made a date to see him later in the day. Which brings us back to here. All I know of Mr. Sheppard is derived from the information he has supplied to me."

Russell greeted my little speech with a series of sober nods. Marcello picked his nose, then studied his finger as he cleaned the nail with his thumb.

I looked at The Man and hoped to God that he would step in if I fell flat on my face. Then I smiled at Rabbi Weinbaum and apologized to him in my newfound language. "I'm sorry to take up so much of your time."

"It's a privilege," said Weinbaum. "Believe me."

I translated our brief exchange in Hebrew for Russell's benefit and couldn't help noticing that his earlier assurance was now besieged by doubt.

"Tell me, Mr. Resnick," he said, "are you in the habit of bankrolling strangers who walk in off the street and try to bum the services of an attorney?"

"Of course not," I replied. "It was only because I thought he had been sent along by this doctor — who happens to be a friend of mine — that I felt obliged to help. And also because he told me that he was a rabbi —"

"That's true," said Weinbaum. He looked at Russell and Marcello. "This man is a great scholar."

I smiled at Russell. "And as you are no doubt aware, we Jews have been known to help one another."

There was a moment's silence.

"Ring Manhattan General," I suggested. "Ask for Dr.

Miriam Maxwell. She may be able to give you some more information."

Russell eyed the three of us, glanced at Marcello, then lifted the phone and dialed the switchboard. "Get me a Dr. Maxwell at Manhattan General. And move it along, will you? I don't want to be here all night."

Maybe it was the way he slammed the phone back on the hook, but I got the impression that he would have preferred to call in the SS.

"Is Dr. Maxwell Jewish too?" he said.

I almost gave him the full ethnic shrug then decided not to overdo it. I raised my eyebrows instead. "You know how it is. The clever ones become doctors, rabbis, or musicians, and the others scrape a living as lawyers or comedians."

"You don't look as if you've had to scrape too hard," said Russell.

The phone rang just as I was about to get lippy. The switchboard operator had Miriam on the other end of the line. Russell explained who he was.

"Dr. Maxwell," he continued, "do you have any record of a patient by the name of Yale Sheppard? I understand that he was under your care some nine days ago."

I hid my hands under my arms and crossed my fingers as Miriam went into her number. I had no idea what story she had concocted. I just hoped it would be a good one. Russell was no dummy. But, on the other hand, it's amazing how people will go along with what doctors have to say. And that's what I was banking on.

Russell's eyes dwelled on each of us in turn as he "uh-huh-ed" several times into the phone, then said, "Yes, sure. We're holding him here right now." He listened some more then concluded by saying, "Third floor. I'll ring the desk and tell them to expect you. . . . Yeah. Thanks, Doc."

He rang off, then lifted the phone again and rang the desk. While he waited for them to answer, he looked at Marcello. "The guy's a yo-yo. . . ." The desk sergeant came through on the line. "Benny? . . . Russell. Listen. There'll be a Dr.

Maxwell — a dame, right? — from Manhattan General, arriving in the next fifteen to twenty minutes." He listened and shook his head. "No, Benny. We didn't kill anybody. We picked up one of their patients. Just send her on up. Okay?"

Russell put the phone down and looked at me. He almost smiled, then thought better of it. "You may have to forgo your fee on this one. Your client beat an intern over the head with a bedpan, stole some clothes, and broke out of the hospital sometime on Sunday night."

Beautiful. I contrived to look concerned. "I see . . ."

"What's more," said Russell, "his name is not Sheppard. That's something the doctor came up with to put on the bed chart. They don't know who the fuck he is. All they know is he shouldn't be loose on the streets."

I frowned, and gave Weinbaum and The Man a worried look. Real Actors Studio stuff. "Did they say what was wrong with him?"

"Psychotic cathexis," said Russell. "Whatever the hell that is." At least he was honest. He gathered up the few sheets of paper that constituted The Man's dossier and held them above his trash basket. "May I take it that you don't intend to sue us for violation of civil rights or any other kind of shit?"

"Forget it," I said. "I've wasted enough time."

Russell junked the paperwork. He pulled a couple of cigarettes out of a Lucky Strike pack, gave one to Marcello, then tossed the pack across the desk toward me. "Help yourself."

"Thanks." I offered it around. Weinbaum and The Man shook their heads. I took one as I passed it back, lit up, and took a deep drag in an effort to stop my heart pounding. "By the way," I said, "I'm sorry I unwittingly dragged Immigration into this. Will you call them and explain what happened?" I gave him an Honest Joe look of concern, then smiled. "I wouldn't want them to feel deprived."

"Don't worry," said Russell. "We'll take care of all that."

It was the right reply but I got the feeling that, sooner

or later, the bloodhounds would be back on our trail. I leaned toward Russell and indicated The Man with a sidelong glance. "I think maybe I should tell him what's happening. But I won't mention the doctor."

"Good idea," said Russell.

Once again I found myself speaking fluent Hebrew. Not that I needed to tell The Man what was going on. But we had to play it right down the line. I explained that the arrest had been a mistake; that Lieutenant Russell and Detective Marcello offered their apologies on behalf of the NYPD; and that a friend of mine was coming to pick us up in a car. I had the feeling that The Man had made a covert ally of Weinbaum but I kept it straight just to be on the safe side.

The Man absorbed the news with the frowning attention of someone trying hard to keep a grip on reality, then treated Russell to a jerky smile and asked if he could have a drink. If all else failed, it was clear that both of us had a future in summer stock.

Russell went to the door and bellowed an order for three Cokes and two coffees to someone called Tony. But this time, Miriam arrived before the refreshments. She had a raincoat over her white smock, and was carrying a black bag. I suppressed an insane desire to leap up and hug her. I just sat there and tried to sound like a man with a grievance. "Glad you could make it. . . ."

Miriam treated me to a consulting-room smile then put her bag on Russell's desk and flashed her hospital ID. "You Lieutenant Russell?"

"Yes," he said. "You by yourself?"

"Yes. Don't worry. He's not going to be a problem." She turned and treated The Man to a dazzling smile. "So — how are you, champ?"

"He doesn't understand English," I said. "You have to speak to him in Hebrew."

Her face soured. "Not necessarily," she replied. "It depends on who he thinks he is." She turned back to Russell. "How did he get here?"

Russell gave her a quick rundown on the arrest and my Good Samaritan act.

Miriam turned to me. "Didn't it occur to you to ring the hospital?"

"You weren't there," I said. "And Manhattan General only gives out information on patients to listed relatives or their own physician. Besides, when he turned up in my office, I naturally assumed he'd been discharged. If the guy's bananas, it's your job to keep him tied down."

Miriam waved me aside. "Yeah, okay, okay." She turned back to Russell and lowered her voice. "He looks harmless. I won't bother to give him a tranquilizing shot. We'll just walk him out of here."

"Sure, whatever," said Russell. "You got an ambulance outside?"

"No," said Miriam. "I didn't want to spook him. We'll take a cab."

"Are you sure you don't want a squad car?" said Russell.

Miriam shook her head. "A cab'll do fine."

I stubbed out my cigarette and addressed The Man in Hebrew. "Come on. It's time to go."

The Man and Rabbi Weinbaum rose together. Weinbaum took hold of The Man's left hand and patted it — as if to console him.

The Man gripped him by the shoulders and looked him straight in the eyes. "Walk in all His ways."

Only Weinbaum and I knew what he was saying.

"I will come and see you," said Weinbaum. "We must talk some more."

"What are they saying?" asked Russell.

"Goodbye," I said. Miriam and I moved toward the door with The Man between us.

"Uhh, just one thing, Doc," said Russell. "Who brought this guy into the hospital?"

I froze with my hand on the half-open door.

"That's something we haven't yet managed to find out," said Miriam. "I was called down to the morgue and found him lying naked on an autopsy slab with blood all over his back, wrists and feet."

Russell's nose wrinkled. "It's original. What's this, uhh . . . psychotic cathexis? Some kind of brain damage?"

"That's one way of putting it." Miriam eyed me briefly, then went on. "Cathexis is a term used by psychoanalysts. It's the accumulation of mental energy on some particular idea, line of thought or action. And it's described as psychotic when this kind of fixation is allied to a pathological mental state." She took a deep breath. "You see, Mr. Sheppard's problem is that he's convinced he's the Risen Christ."

Weinbaum groaned and muttered something under his breath in what I think was Yiddish.

"Oh, Jeezuss," said Marcello, breaking his silence.

Russell shook his head wearily and waved us toward the door. "That's enough," he said. "Just get him out of here."

The three of us walked out of the station house with Rabbi Weinbaum on our tail. He stood and watched us as we hailed a passing cab and ushered The Man into the back.

"Can we drop you somewhere?" I said.

Weinbaum shook his head. "To think such things could happen," he sighed. "To a man with such knowledge . . ."

I reverted to my native tongue. "Don't worry. He may get better." I shook his hand and climbed aboard. As we pulled away down the street I looked back out the window. Weinbaum was still standing on the curb, tugging at his beard; and no doubt reflecting on the futility of learning.

The cab was a new model without the iron curtain between the rear seat and the driver so we kept the conversation down to guided-tour small talk on the way uptown. New York after dark becomes another city as whole sections switch roles. Some not stirring until the trashman calls. Others blossoming like luminous night flowers, bursting into multicolored life. We crossed Twentieth Street, leaving the shuttered commercial section with its sculptured European facades and its deserted side streets full of ominous shadows, and headed north toward the sky-high blocks of mid-Manhattan where the random pattern of lighted windows glowed like jewels set in pillars of obsidian. By day or by night, the visual impact of New York was always stunning, but when darkness fell, there was more to it than just the razzle-dazzle. The night swallowed up the extraneous detail allowing the eye to focus on the pure form of the city's structures. Its essence. You became aware of the massive concentration of vitality, of worldly power; of the mother-lode that was there to be mined in those multistoried mountains of free enterprise. When you paused to consider what New York represented and what it had to offer, it wasn't hard to understand what drew men to 'Brax's dark banner.

At the Mayflower, The Man picked up his key from the desk and led us to the elevator with all the assurance of a blue-blazered lounge lizard. A silver-haired couple stepped in behind us so we rode up to the third floor in silence. By some curious coincidence their room was on the same floor. We politely let them leave the elevator first then found ourselves following them all the way down the corridor and down this dead end to the right. It was quite bizarre. With each step, the atmosphere became increasingly electric. I could feel the waves of apprehension coming off their backs. I wanted to say something to reassure them but I had the feeling that if I addressed even one word to them they would have heart attacks. If I'd been them, I'd have probably been scared too. The one place you don't want to be hit is in a lifeless hotel corridor; where there's no point in running because there's nowhere to hide; with all those closed doors that are going to stay closed no matter how hard you holler, until it's all over. This couple's ordeal ended at the door to Room 314. We left them, eyes averted, fumbling nervously for the key, and walked past to 315.

"That is very sad," said The Man, as he opened the door.

I shrugged. "It's the way things are." I ushered Miriam into the room then called out to the couple. "Good night." They didn't reply. They were still looking for their key. Or pretending to, while they waited for us to go inside. The Man was right. It was a sad state of affairs when you had to lock and chain yourself inside a hotel room and look through a peephole to make sure that the guy who announced himself as Room Service wasn't carrying the carving knife instead of the chicken sandwich.

Once inside the door, however, I pushed those thoughts aside. I grabbed Miriam and hugged her happily. "Doctor — you were absolutely fantastic."

As we parted, The Man grinned broadly and put his arms across our shoulders. And we each put an arm around him as if it was the most natural thing in the world to do. For one brief moment, we formed a victorious trio. We were like the Three Musketeers. All for one, and one for all. It felt great.

"Don't let's get too excited," said Miriam, as we became our separate selves again. "We're not out of the woods yet. If that guy Russell decides to check up at the hospital —"

I waved her worries aside. "He won't. He's like everybody else. One whiff of religious mania, and they tune out." I broke into a laugh. "And the incredible thing is that, in the end, what got us off the hook was the truth. Or, at least, ninety-five percent of it."

I took a look around The Man's hotel suite. After all, I was paying for it. It was a three-room unit. The living room had the usual sofa flanked by low tables and reading lamps, a couple of armchairs and the statutory color TV. The covers and the matching curtains were a nice flowered print in blue, white and green. The bathroom was small but had everything. The bedroom furnishings were standard and matched the colors in the living room. The bed itself was big enough for Bob, Carol, Ted and Alice. For a man who didn't sleep, or need it for anything else, it was a terrible waste of space.

When I came back to the lounge, Miriam had made herself at home on one of the armchairs. The Man had kicked off his shoes and was sitting cross-legged on the settee. I pulled the other armchair in closer, and told Miriam about my run-in with Ritger and Donati on the stairs and of my suspicions that they had pocketed the bag of dope to boost their take-home pay. By maybe as much as twenty-five grand apiece.

"But that's terrible," said Miriam.

"Absolutely," I said. "But, on the other hand, it saved me having to post bail. And gave you the chance to be a hero."

She gave me her outraged citizen look. "You mean to say you're not going to do anything about it?"

"Let New York's Finest take care of their own," I said. "We've got enough to worry about."

She frowned. "Such as?"

"Lots of things," I said. "Loose ends. Little things that don't add up. It may not turn out to be important, but it worries me because I can't put my finger on it."

"Come on," she said. "Surely you can give me a for-instance."

I leaned over and offered her a cigarette and got the use of her lighter in return. "I'll give you two," I said. "I've been going over what Larry Bekker told me. The Narcotics Division teams working out of the Seventh Precinct are only concerned with *organized* crime. Any arrests they make would normally be in pursuit of an ongoing undercover investigation. Random 'buy and busts' are handled by the Street Enforcement Unit based in the Twenty-third Precinct. Or guys on the drug detail at Manhattan South."

"You're getting too technical," said Miriam. "What is it you're trying to tell me?"

"The Man got arrested by the wrong people."

Miriam switched her eyes from me to The Man then back again. "Maybe they thought he was someone else. It could explain why they didn't press charges."

"Yes, maybe . . ." I looked at The Man expectantly. He gazed at me steadily, but didn't say anything. "It's the dope that really bugs me. When Ritger and Donati drove away, they knew I was a lawyer. Even so, that six-ounce bag went missing somewhere between Forty-second Street and the Seventh Precinct house. Let's assume Ritger and Donati stole it. Even if they didn't, they're involved. There's no doubt about that. But if The Man was just a face in the crowd, and they didn't know me from a hole in the wall, how did they know that, when I came down to bail out my client and found that he was miraculously 'clean,' I was not going to raise the roof with cries of 'police corruption'?"

She tried to puzzle it out. "Maybe they figured that you'd put your client's interests first."

"But Miriam," I said. "How did they *know* that? What made them so sure? As Russell reminded me, I'm an officer of the court. Those guys had ripped off a good fifty-grands' worth of uncut dope! A kid fresh out of law school could have done a deal with the DA's office over that. The Man could have turned State's evidence and walked. We might even have been federal agents. In which case, the shit would have really hit the fan. No matter how you slice it, the same question keeps coming up: how did they know I'd keep *shtum*? What made them think they could get away with it?"

Miriam eyed me. "I think the real problem is that smart lawyers think everyone else is as devious as they are. Maybe this Ritger and Donati are a lot dumber than you think. And has it occurred to you that the bag might not have been full of dope? Maybe, when they opened it, they found it really *was* icing sugar."

I frowned, then looked at The Man. "Was it?"

A smile crept into the corners of his mouth. "It was by the time we got downtown."

I laughed. And that made him laugh too. It was good to know that he could turn the tables on whoever had it in for us.

"It's not all that funny," said Miriam. "We still have to face the fact that 'Brax — or somebody — went to the trouble of planting that stuff. We know why. The question is how — or when?"

The Man shrugged. "It could have been in the store where we bought the windbreaker. Or in Times Square." He looked at me. "I was wearing it unzipped. It was pretty crowded down there."

"Yes," I said. "And you took it off in the movie theater, remember? You put it on the seat beside you."

He nodded. "That's right. And a guy came in halfway through and sat next to it."

"I want to ask you something," I said. "And if you can get inside our heads you must know the answer to this — were those cops real cops, or 'Brax's agents?" I kept my eyes fixed on his.

His eyes didn't waver. "They weren't demons in disguise, if that's what you mean. They were people, just like you. But it's not quite as simple as that. All of you, at one time or another, act as 'Brax's agents. He exercises a controlling influence over all your lives — yet most people remain blind to his presence. Because they are unaware of their inner self. Their *true* identity. They don't know they are held prisoner — and would laugh if you suggested the idea to them. Everybody has been brainwashed into believing that they are bound to the physical universe. That beyond the external world of sense perception there lies only the fathomless void of nonbeing. And his most recent achievement has been to persuade the majority of the world that he, 'Brax, does not exist. Thus enabling your materialist philosophers to prove, with the aid of 'Braxian logic, that the concept of a Supreme Creator is a groundless primal myth." He paused to let that sink in, then added, "By the way, I can't get into everybody's head. I told you up at Sleepy Hollow that it was easy to shut me out. If I've been inside yours, it's because your minds opened up to let me in."

His answer was instructive but it hadn't told me what I really wanted to know. "Are you trying to tell us that there isn't a way to head off trouble? That you didn't know you were going to get busted?"

"No. What I'm saying is that I can't stop it from happening."

"You stopped me from going down the elevator shaft," I said.

His golden eyes fastened on me. "Did I?"

I held my ground. "Didn't you?"

His look softened. "Don't be misled by what you've seen — or what you think you've seen. I may have the edge in the long run, but there are limits to my power in the temporal dimension." He smiled. "I may be batting on the side of the angels but — I have been known to miss a curve ball."

Tremendous.

"So in other words," I said, "all we can do is stand there and take it on the chin."

He waved his palms upward and outward. "It's what the Twelve had to do."

"Yes, but you gave them a big boost," I countered. "You put their brains into orbit at the Feast of Pentecost. When *they* got arrested and beaten, they didn't feel a thing. They even knew how to walk through locked doors."

He shook his head. "I can't give you a magic wand, Leo. "You've already got what it takes. It's up to you to learn how to use it."

He was right, of course, but that still left me with a backlog of unanswered questions. I couldn't get rid of the nagging suspicion that we were the victims of a well-intentioned snow job. I looked at my watch. It was after midnight. I got to my feet. "I hope you don't mind, but I'm going to have to leave it there. It's been quite a day."

"Yes, for me too." He uncrossed his legs and got up from the sofa.

I offered my hand to Miriam. She rose and took it obediently but her eyes told me she would have preferred to go on talking. The Man walked us to the door.

"I take it you know about Room Service," I said. "I mean if you want food, or anything, all you have to do is —"

He nodded. "Yes, I know."

I gripped his hand. "Listen — I'm going to be in court all

day again. And the same thing goes for the rest of the week. I'd like to duck out but it's a big case and, well — you know how it is."

"Sure," he said. "Don't worry. I may not be here anyway."

"Yeah, well, just in case you are . . ." I pulled out my wallet and handed over two fifty-dollar bills. I was turning into a real Daddy Warbucks. "I'll call you between four-thirty and five. If you've got any problems before then call Miriam — or Linda. But go easy with her. You had her in tears today."

"I'll bear that in mind." He bussed Miriam on the cheek. "Take care. . . ."

"You too," she said. This time, her knees didn't fold up under her. But then, she was a New Yorker too. Give us time to catch our breath and we can take anything and everything in our stride.

When we reached the street, it was such a nice night, we decided to walk up Central Park West to my apartment on Seventy-fifth Street. Hand in hand like fifteen-year-olds on their first date. But privy to the greatest secret in the world. I don't know what strange alchemy was at work but by the time we reached my front door, any lurking 'Braxian passion I harbored had quietly disappeared. Miriam made me an ice-box raider's sandwich and we took it to bed with two mugs of hot milk. She claimed to have eaten but she still managed to chisel me out of the third deck, which held most of the Polish salami.

Afterward, we snuggled down among the crumbs and embraced each other lovingly. Somehow, it seemed enough. As if, in some as yet unspecified way, we were now different. Special.

In the darkness, we gently untangled our limbs and turned on our sides to sleep. I felt Miriam's body hug the zigzag made by my own.

"Leo," she said.

"Yes?"

"You didn't tell me you went to the movies."

"Ohh — didn't I?" These blackout inquisitions are a big favorite with Miriam.

"No," she said. "What did you take him to see?"

"The Sound of Music."

"Ahhh . . . did he like it?"

I larded my voice with sleep. "Loved it. . . ."

NINE

BEFORE I left my apartment on Tuesday morning, I rang The Man at his hotel. I could hear muted TV jingle music in the background. "Sounds as if you've been up all night. Did you see anything good?" I asked. Fervently hoping he hadn't tuned into Channel J's Ugly George.

"Yes," he said. "One of the movies was *Five Graves to Cairo*. With Eric von Stroheim. It reminded me of a trip I made through North Africa."

"Don't you believe it," I replied. "It was all shot in California. Listen. Do me a favor. Muss up the bed a little so it looks as if it's been slept in. And do it every morning for as long as you're there."

"Okay," he said. "But it only makes extra work."

"It's included in the price of the room," I said firmly. "There's no rebate for not using the bed. Oh, by the way —" I added, "— there was something I forgot to ask you last night. Who were those three guys that came out of Russell's office as I arrived?"

"Nobody important," he replied.

It wasn't good enough but there wasn't time for a lengthy cross-examination. Miriam put her head around the bathroom door. "Give him my love." I passed it on.

"Have a nice day," he said.

There was no reason to think why I should but, as it turned out, I managed to pick up Monday's dropped passes and get our team back in the game. So much so that Mel Donaldson, the senior man on Delaware's backup team — who was a real worry-wart — actually told me he thought I'd done a good job. Not that I needed this rare accolade. When court recessed for the day, I knew that we were ahead on points because my clients were happy and relaxed enough to ask my advice about getting laid. I advised them to hit the bell captain of their hotel with a few bills. He was sure to have a line into the ladies who gave room service. Somebody asked me if they took credit cards.

I turned aside from their laughter, packed up my papers, and left them to it. The house rules for entertaining out-of-town clients allow us to point them in the right direction but spare us the task of procuring.

I got back to the office at four-thirty. Linda followed me into my room. I leafed through the telephone messages she'd put on my blotter then sat down and eased the knot in my tie. "No calls from Mr. Sheppard?"

"No," she replied. "But I stopped by the hotel during my lunch break."

I kept my head down and my voice casual. "Oh, yeah . . ."

"Yes," she said. "I picked his robe up from the cleaners."

Her words didn't filter through properly. "You did what?"

"I picked up his robe," she repeated. "He changed into the clothes we bought while we were at the store. Then after I'd checked him into the hotel, I took the robe to a dry cleaner's on my way back to the office. It's just around the block from here."

I nodded. "I see. Did he, er — say anything?"

She frowned. "Like what?"

"I don't know," I said. "I mean, what did you do? Leave the package at the desk — or take it up to his room?"

"I rang his room from the lobby and he told me to come on up." Linda raised her hands. "What's the matter? Did I do something wrong?"

I leafed through the papers in front of me. "What makes you say that?"

She shrugged. "I don't know. Suddenly it's a big production. You sent me shopping with him yesterday. I was just following through."

"Sure. Listen. Everything's fine." I pulled out my wallet. "Thanks for taking care of it. How much do I owe you?"

"Nothing. Forget it." She waved away my ten-dollar bill. "He, er — already paid me."

I had the feeling she was lying. "That still leaves the cab fare."

She shook her head. "I walked."

Now, if you include the crosstown blocks, there's a total of fifteen between the hotel and our office on Forty-ninth and Madison. So a two-way trip is quite a hike. And Linda, as I know from petty cash slips, is not a girl who likes walking. Most of the time she totters around on four-inch heels.

I smelt trouble. "Linda — ?"

"Is it okay if I sit down?" she said.

I motioned to her to pull up a seat and broke open a new pack of cigarettes.

"I was followed," she said.

I snapped my lighter shut and placed it carefully on my desk. "Tell me about it."

Linda took a deep breath. "It was after I picked up the robe —"

I flagged her down. "Whose name did you put on the ticket?"

"His —"

"Okay. Sorry — go on."

"Well, anyway," she continued, "this place I go to is run by a Cuban family. They're always bawling each other out in Spanish. So I go in and hand over the ticket to this young guy but when he checks the number, the robe is not hanging on the rack with the rest of the stuff that's ready for collection. Which is odd, because I'd brought it in the day before, and they clean things in a couple of hours — right?"

"Right . . ." I said.

"So he goes out back to check, and there's a lot of yakking goes on, and this woman sticks her head around the door and takes a good look at me, then finally the old man who owns the place comes out with the robe folded in tissue paper, and puts it in a bag for me."

I nodded. "Did he say anything?"

"Yes," said Linda. "He asked me if it was mine. So I said, 'No, it belongs to a friend.' So then he asked me if I knew where my friend had gotten it from. And I said I didn't know but that I thought it was probably from the Middle East because he'd just come back from there. It seemed like he was asking me a lot of questions but — well, I'm a pretty regular customer and he's always been a friendly guy. So I went along with it."

I kept my voice casual. "The address on the ticket. Was it for the office or — ?"

"The hotel," she replied. "Anyway — finally, when I get outside, the woman from the cleaner's is standing looking in the window of the next store. She was about fifty, gray hair, black headscarf and coat. You know the way they dress. And with a shopping bag. I was kind of surprised to see her because I thought she was still working out back, then I thought, 'What the hell? It's probably her lunch hour too.' So I started back toward Madison Avenue."

"And she followed you," I said.

Linda nodded. "Yes. I wasn't sure at first. I mean, when you walk along Madison at lunchtime, you can be in the same crowd of people for two or three blocks. So I kept going. I cut across the bottom of Central Park to the hotel, looked back when I reached the entrance — and there she was. About fifty yards behind me on the other side of the street."

"So what did you do?"

She shrugged. "I checked with the desk to see if he was in, rang his room, then went on up with the package. We talked for about ten or fifteen minutes. Mainly about the difference between New York, Los Angeles and the rest of America. He asked me a bit about my parents, and why we'd left Hungary. And that was it."

"What happened when you came out of the hotel?"

"She was still standing in exactly the same place across the street. Holding her shopping bag. Like an old black crow." She shuddered at the memory. "It was really creepy."

"I can imagine," I said. I dragged deeply on my cigarette, sat back and tried to work it out. There was nothing special about the robe — at least, as far as I knew. It was like one of those wide-sleeved djellabas you see Arabs wearing in holiday brochures for places like Morocco and Tunisia. Only this one didn't have a hood. Nothing fancy. Just woven from rough, pale brown wool. "Did you walk back here?"

"Part of the way," she said. "I mean, you can't really tell if anyone's tailing you if you're in a cab."

I nodded wisely. "Good thinking . . ."

"Yes," said Linda. "So I walked down to Fifty-seventh and Broadway. I looked back a couple of times but she hadn't moved from the park side of the street. Then I lost sight of her. I zigzagged over to Ninth then got a cab back to the office. For all I know she may still be there."

I picked up the phone and asked Nancy to get me Mr. Sheppard in Room 315 of the Mayflower Hotel. Then I lit another cigarette and eyed Linda. I mulled over the idea of letting her in on our big secret and decided against it. She only had to blab it round the office and I'd be finished. Joe Gutzman's benevolence allowed me a certain amount of license, but if he discovered that my newest client was Jesus Christ, he'd tell the sign-writer to get busy with a bottle of paint remover.

"Linda," I said, "why do you think this woman followed you?"

"I don't know," she replied. "I was hoping you might tell me."

Some chance.

The phone rang. It was Nancy. There was no answer from

Room 315. The hotel switchboard had checked with the desk. Mr. Sheppard had not left any messages.

"Okay, thanks, Nancy. I'll try again later." I rang off with a kind of blank feeling. Like when you're waiting for bad news. You know what I mean?

Linda stood up and put the chair back in place. I treated her to Resnick's winning smile. "If I solve the mystery, you'll be the first to know."

She walked to the door. "We could always go over to the store and ask the lady what the problem is."

"We could," I said. "But why make waves? You know how touchy these people are. There's no law against walking up Madison Avenue."

"I guess not." She left looking distinctly disappointed.

I tried to settle down and catch up with the paperwork, but the pressure wave generated by the implications of Linda's story made it difficult to concentrate. Yesterday the cops, today a Cuban dry-cleaning lady. But — despite what The Man had said, or rather what he had *not* said — were they real cops, or just reasonable fascsimiles? In the case of Mrs. el Cubano, the robe was obviously the catalyst, but was she a random element — or another external agency that had been geared up by 'Brax in a new effort to expose us? If so, the fact that she had stayed outside the hotel meant she had transferred her interest from Linda to the owner of the robe and that, in turn, meant that there was more to come.

Terrific.

I taped some letters and rang the hotel a couple of times but there was no reply from his room. At six o'clock I left a message with the desk and put him out of my mind. So much so that, when I wrapped it up around a quarter of eight, I stepped into an empty elevator and rode it down to the lobby in solitary splendor without giving it a second thought. It was only when I got outside that I realized what I'd done. I went a little rubbery at the knees then shrugged it off. What was the point of worrying? Like I said before, I'm a New

Yorker. And beyond that, what did I count for in the overall scheme of things? I was just a biodegradable bag of bones housing an unquantifiable chunk of one of the good guys. In the final analysis, when measured against the cosmic scale of the struggle in which The Man was involved, my life — or that of any individual — wasn't worth a dime.

Not that we, tied up in the day-to-day problems of living, saw it that way. To each of us, our own lives were our prime concern. To the young, the healthy, the thrusting individual, the most important thing was to go *on* living. It was the all-consuming passion. What the Eastern mystics had labeled *samskara* — "the thirst for existence." The desire to grab the goodies that the world had to offer.

I went into a bar I knew on Forty-seventh Street, ordered a bourbon on the rocks, and sat at the end of the counter near the window where I could survey both the interior and the street outside. And I tried to convince myself that what the people around me were talking about was important. That the man in the blue suit halfway down the bar was right to be concerned about the standing of the Mets. And that the three girls in the window swapping office gossip about a colleague who had man-trouble were not just wearing out their tongues. That their concerns, however trivial, had some intrinsic value. That their lives and mine, in their limited earthbound way, still had some meaning. That our rules of behavior were valid; our ambitions worthwhile.

I felt the need to make a conscious effort to maintain my grip on external reality, to combat the feeling of alienation that had been engendered by my contact with The Man and what he had told me. And which, if unchecked, threatened to destroy what I judged to be a promising career, a comfortable life and the pleasurable pursuits that were a part of it.

It was with this firm resolution that I returned to my reflection upon the human condition. I had decided to ring the hotel at nine o'clock so I had a good forty-five minutes in which to pierce some of the secrets of the universe. I asked the bartender to refill my glass to help things along. My eye wandered to the copy of the *New York Times* that was wedged between a couple of bottles, and which he kept for customers. One of the headlines was about yet another killing. All over the world, the slaughter went on. And so did the agonizing arguments about the retribution that our society should exact from the murderer. One of the cornerstones of our civilization was the belief in the sanctity of human life, yet, as we clawed our way to the top of our own particular heap, we had lost sight of the most important, most fundamental belief of all: the sanctity of the human spirit.

Most of us — and that included me — paid lip service to the idea of its presence within the human body but we regarded it as human, not divine. A facet of our individual personality which, in itself, was nothing more than the external expression of biochemical processes within the brain. A collage of genetic factors, and the complex interactions between inherited characteristics and environmental conditioning. But despite whatever we felt we might owe to our ma and pa, our grandparents, or to Uncle Walter, most of us still believed that the person we felt ourselves to be was an inseparable part of our bodies; and as unique as our fingerprints.

All well and good but, over the weekend, The Man had blown that comfortable idea apart, destroying many of the convenient excuses for our behavior in the process.

His somewhat revolutionary thesis that we were no more than carrier vehicles for a unit of consciousness that, in itself, was only a mere fragment of a greater being had a certain coherence. Many theologians had advanced the idea that we were part of a divine collective. And it also found expression in the language we used to describe personal relationships and the sometimes surprising immediacy with which they could occur. The sudden empathy you could feel toward a total stranger; that we qualified with terms like "kindred spirit" and "soulmate" and with phrases such as "on the same wavelength" and "putting out good vibes." Was the instinctive kinship we felt simply the bonding of like with like? The subconscious recognition of another vestigial trace of our larger-than-life Celestial self? And was the desire for reunification the driving force behind our emotional relationships?

It made sense but it was not an easy idea to live with. After all, most of us spend a good part of our lives trying to work out just who the hell we are and what we're doing here. Coming to terms with our God-given grab bag of assets and liabilities. Resolving the crisis of identity — usually with the crushingly expensive help of our analysts. Some people never make it no matter how much they spend. I felt I had — and had even walked away with some loose change. Which was why I was not overly pleased to learn that the impressively cool Leo M. Resnick that I knew and loved was only one of many pairs of legs in the umpteenth section of a Celestial millipede that, in the reunion celebration following the Day of Judgment, would samba through the Gates of Paradise to collect its back pay.

And yet. And yet . . .

What The Man's thesis didn't quite explain was the equally strong antipathy one could feel toward people. The way I'd been turned off by the sight of Greaseball Donati. But maybe that was caused by dissonant combinations of the twelve Ain-folk. Like when you make cocktails. The bottles all contain alcohol but they don't all blend agreeably together. And if you mix gin, vodka and brandy, it's a recipe for disaster.

On the other hand, it was possible that the trapped Ain-folk were not a close-harmony Sunday School set whose idea of letting their hair down was to play Frisbee with their halos. Despite The Man's talk about a Golden Age, it may not have been all sweetness and light. Even though the Ain-folk were cosmic luminaries of a high order, it was quite possible that, out of the twelve, there had been at least one who got everybody's vote as being a celestial pain in the ass. And if there was a big chunk of him inside Donati, it could have explained my instant dislike of him.

It was a typical 'Braxian thought, but one I enjoyed. The world mirrored the conflict and chaos he had sown throughout the Universe. Our combative nature drew its strength from our self-centeredness. The ego that had been forged by 'Brax in the fires of the world from our imprisoned souls. *This* was the meaning behind the allegorical language of the medieval alchemists. It was the ego that was the base metal which The Man, and the Initiates of the Mysteries in the Middle Ages, had sought to transmute into gold. The divine metal. The spirit, freed from its earthly impurities. Transcendent. Eternal.

The Tibetan Book of the Dead and various schools of philosophy concerned with the search for spiritual awareness all spoke of the death of the ego as the prerequisite step on the path to enlightenment. The elimination of the "I," the preoccupation with which was the undisputed basis of so much of our unhappiness. I was taken by the idea of the quest but had no strong desire to embark upon it. The acquisition of my ego had afforded me a great deal of not-so-innocent pleasure and, despite the advent of The Man, I intended to hang on to it for as long as possible.

It was a ploy that the old hands knew as "playing both ends against the middle." The Man would probably regard it as cheating but I knew 'Brax would understand. After all, he'd invented it.

I bought a third drink and told the bartender to keep the change. In return for which, he let me use the phone he kept under the bar. It saved me having to go all the way out to the back and meant that I could enjoy the sensation of calling The Man while keeping an eye on the trio who were still chatting in the window. One of them was a promising blonde with a sensational pair of breasts in free-fall under a "Save The Whales" T-shirt.

There was no reply from his room. The desk told me that my earlier message was still pigeonholed. I left another with my home number, then quietly finished my drink. As I twisted round off the bar stool, I saw two of the girls from the window seat walk out the door; leaving the blonde looking at me over the top of her cigarette. It was a tough decision but I like to think I did the right thing. Listen. Whales are an endangered species. I care about these things.

The nature trail took me to a little restaurant over on Third Avenue. I left the waiter pouring the wine and ducked out to phone Miriam. She was still on duty. I told her where I was, and she told me that she'd called my apartment and the hotel.

"Are you with The Man?" she asked.

"No, a client. Mel Donaldson. One of the Delaware law team. A real klutz." I injected a note of pain into my voice. "He wants me to take him to the Playboy Club."

"Good luck," she said.

I explained that The Man had apparently left the hotel sometime between two and four P.M. and that I had been unable to contact him.

"You don't sound very worried," said Miriam.

"I'm trying to convince myself it's a waste of time," I said. "Let's face it, if he's telling us the truth and the future already exists, what's going to happen will happen whether we like it or not." I paused, then added worriedly: "I just wish I knew what he's got lined up for us."

"Maybe he doesn't know yet," she said.

"Don't you believe it," I replied. "He knows. You can bet your bottom dollar on that." We exchanged brief verbal tokens of friendship then I went back to the table and raised my glass to the T-shirt. "Sorry about that. A client. Mel Donaldson. One of the Delaware law team."

"Oh," she said. "Is he from this big case you're on?"

"Yeah . . ." I injected a note of pain into my voice. "A real klutz." I dismissed my business problems with a casual wave then did the old finger-along-the-back-of-the-hand bit. The light touch. It's a great way of testing the water. The feedback from the Resnick Skinometer was Alpha-plus. Which to Monopoly fans is like "Pass GO and collect $200." Only better.

"After we've eaten," I said, "why don't we go on to the Playboy Club?"

Would you believe it if I told you that she had been waiting for someone to ask her that?

Just for the record, her name was Fran Nelson. She was born in Philadelphia, and she worked in the production department of a Madison Avenue ad agency. She was one of five children. Her father was an optician, and active in Republican ward politics. It was the first time I'd dated a Republican but, like they say, there's a first time for everything. The rest we don't need to go into here. If I mention the incident at all, it is to illustrate my inner turmoil. Which sounds good. Or my inherent duplicity. Which sounds a little more honest. Whether I enjoyed it or not is irrelevant. More than anything else, it was not so much the need to score but the need to demonstrate my independence. To prove that I still had control over my life no matter what the eventual cost. Let's face it: we all have the urge to press the self-destruct button at some time in our lives. There are some people whose fingers are never off it. And anyway, as it said in the Book, The Man liked a challenge. I was still prepared to help him but that didn't mean to say I had to buy the whole bill of goods. Right?

Right . . .

TEN

WEDNESDAY morning. I rang the hotel again before I left my apartment. Room 315 didn't answer. When I got to the office I tried again. The desk confirmed that my two earlier messages were still pigeonholed. I rang Miriam and found myself talking to Lewis Carroll's Dormouse.

"You sound as if you're still in bed," I said.

"I am," was the snug reply. When she works the late shift, Miriam's day starts at noon. "How did you make out last night?"

Her choice of words gave me an uneasy feeling. "Ohh, er — you mean with Donaldson? It wasn't too painful," I said. "They had a group from the West Coast playing some great jazz." I gave her a cleaned-up version of my evening, substituting M. Donaldson for F. Nelson throughout. Then I told her that I still hadn't gotten through to The Man.

"What do you think's happened?" Her voice was now wide-awake.

I had decided not to tell her about the woman in black who had followed Linda. There was no point in both of us worrying. Not at this stage, anyway. I tried to hide my own concern but my answer still sounded peevish. "How the hell do I know? It could be any one of a hundred things. Let's face it, we may not be the only people he's been speaking to.

My guess is he's probably taken the Time Express back to twenty-nine A.D. On the other hand, he may have been kidnapped by a snatch-squad from the Pentacostal Church of God."

There was short silence at the other end of the line. "You don't really think that, do you?"

"No, Miriam," I said patiently. "That was a joke. But if this gets too much for us, we could always give the Holy Rollers a call. They'd take The Man off our hands in ten seconds flat."

She greeted that with another silence. "Is that what you want?"

"No," I said. "That was another joke."

"Well, cut it out," she replied. "When you try to be flip, you can be a real pain."

"Okay, okay, I'm sorry." I should tell you — if you haven't guessed already — that Miriam is one of those people who only laugh when they think something is funny; as opposed to the other kind who laugh because they're anxious to please. It was this serious side to her nature which appealed to me and which, paradoxically, I had enjoyed debauching. Not that it was easy. It took me months to persuade her to give up her flute lessons so that she could spend more time in bed with me.

"So what are you going to do?" she asked.

Questions. Always questions.

"I'm not sure," I replied. "If he's gone, there's no point in paying for an empty room. Checkout time is eleven A.M. The sensible thing would be to have the hotel make out his bill before they hit me for another hundred dollars. On the other hand, I don't want to run the risk of him stepping back into Room Three-fifteen from first-century Jerusalem while someone else is in the bedroom, or taking a shower. He's liable to end up back in the slammer."

"I suppose it's possible," said Miriam. "But if the last two visits are anything to go by, he seems to be zeroing in on you."

"Yes, you could have a point there." I checked my watch. It was just after nine. "Miriam . . ."

"Is this going to involve getting up?" she said.

"Too much sleep is bad for you." I kept it short and sweet. "The desk clerk has a note to bill the office. We have a charge account with the hotel. All you have to do is explain that Mr. Sheppard has left town. But make sure you check the room — in case he left something."

"Before eleven . . ." She sounded put-upon.

I promised to take her somewhere nice for supper.

As I rang off, I held onto the phone and toyed briefly with the idea of calling my whaling companion. Then I thought better of it. Linda came through the door with the morning mail. She saw my look of surprise and explained that the reason she was early was because she'd been up all night discoing with some friends from out of town. They'd watched the dawn come up over Battery Park then she'd showered and breakfasted at the Health and Racquet Club and come straight to the office.

She tried to cover a yawn but her hand wasn't big enough. "Anything special you want me to do today?"

"Well, now that you're here, you could try keeping awake," I said. "Mr. Sheppard has left town, but there's a chance he might call and leave a message."

"Okay." She stopped halfway to the door. "Did you tell him about the woman who followed me?"

I shook my head. "I didn't get the opportunity."

"Has he gone back to California?"

"No, I don't think so," I said. "He was planning to take off for Jerusalem."

"Ahh . . ." She nodded. "Must be to do some more research for that big Bible story he's working on." It was clear from her wistful voice that she would have jumped at the chance to carry his luggage.

"Very probably," I said. "Could you close the door?"

The day in court went reasonably well. I picked up Miriam at nine-thirty from Manhattan General. She'd had the foresight to take a case with her to the hotel and had cleared out The Man's room. From the description she gave, it sounded as if he'd left behind all the clothes he'd acquired on his shopping spree with Linda. In a way, it was just as well. If he'd turned up in 29 A.D. Jerusalem in olive-green cords and jogging shoes, that really would have given the Roman historians something to write about.

I took Miriam to a *brasserie alsacienne* that had been cloned from a famous joint I'd been to in Paris and ordered champagne and two monstrous helpings of *Choucroute Imperiale*. She'd inherited the taste for sauerkraut from her grandfather who'd been lucky enough to escape from Germany before the future Allied Nations started turning Jews away. In fact, the old man's taste for sauerkraut was about all he managed to bring with him.

I raised my glass to her. "Enjoy . . ." I liked to please her. I got a kick out of making her happy. It also made me feel a whole lot better because, although we hadn't exchanged contracts, I felt I was cheating on her when I went with someone else. I suppose it was because she was the only person with whom I had come the nearest to being the real "me." And each time I concealed something, or told her less than the truth, I diminished our relationship.

It's strange but, in all the time we were together, she never once told me what it was that she found attractive about me. We were so different. While I had a wide range of interests, I was aware that, compared to her taste for European movies, art galleries and classical string quartets, my passion for mainstream jazz, the big band sound and the motivational simplicity of Clint Eastwood movies made me something of a cultural Philistine. On top of which she was part of a close and happy family while I was a voluntary exile from mine. Looking back, I can only think she regarded me as something of a challenge.

We upended the bottle of champagne and turned down all suggestion of dessert and coffee. It wasn't because I was trying to shave a few dollars off the bill. We just wanted to get to bed before the champagne sparkle wore off. However, I regret to say that, on this occasion, yours truly turned out to be a limp torpedo. Miriam was not too perturbed, but I found it very unsettling.

"It's that goddamn sauerkraut," I growled. But I knew, in my heart of hearts, that it was Ms. Nelson that had turned my belly into a lead cannonball. I lay there thinking of the fortune I had paid my fucking analyst to remove all traces of guilt and considered slapping a writ on him for culpable negligence.

"Never mind," said Miriam. "Let's talk."

"I was planning to," I replied. "But afterwards."

"Let me make some coffee and we'll take it from there." She got up and wrapped her nakedness in the robe I had bought her and pulled the covers back over mine.

I sat up on one elbow. "You really do have a nice body. You know that?"

She grimaced and pushed back her hair. "I know I should lose a good fourteen pounds."

"Oh, no, don't," I said. "That's why I'm going out with you. I've had it with skinny model girls."

She eyed me and went into the bathroom. When she came out, I saw she had fastened her hair back with a ribbon. It was a sign that she was through fooling around and that I was now talking to my friend the doctor. I padded over to the closet and donned the terry cloth robe she allowed me to leave in there. I kept a similar one for her at my place. It's the nearest we ever got to handing each other the keys to our apartments.

I joined her in the kitchen as she ladled some beans into the grinder and raised my voice as she switched it on. "It's hard to realize that it's only five days since he turned up at Sleepy Hollow. So much has happened."

"Yes . . ." She moved me gently aside so that she could open a cupboard door to get at the cups and saucers. My mother used to do exactly the same thing. She never said, "Pass me this," or "Bring me that." She'd let me lounge

around watching her with my hands in my pockets while she
did it all. Devotedly. But with an air of self-sacrifice that she
wore like a hair shirt.

Miriam produced two cups of black coffee and slid one
along the counter.

"Thanks," I said. "You know, it was only today I realized
that, despite all the talking, we hadn't gotten around to discussing what *you* think about all this."

She blew on her coffee, took a trial sip, then shrugged.

"Oh, come on," I said. "You were the one who got us into
it."

She stirred in another spoonful of sugar. "You really think
so?"

"Listen," I said. "You recognized him, didn't you? It was
you who got me down to the morgue. And when the penny
didn't drop, you spelled it out for me. You knew. You were a
hundred percent sure *before* he disappeared."

Miriam shook her head. "Not a hundred percent sure. I
can't explain how it happened. It wasn't a conscious mental
process of deduction. I just happened to get a look at him
when the paramedics brought him into Emergency. I was on
the point of leaving to get cleaned up for our date. That's
when I saw the thorns sticking into his scalp. And as I . . .
pulled the first one out, I had this kind of, uhh — I don't
quite know how to describe it. I felt I'd been punched in the
heart, but the blow was internal. There was no pain. Just a
violent muscular spasm. And at the same time, I had this sudden flash of recognition. But at first, I was too embarrassed
to mention it." She shrugged, and picked up her cup. "The
rest you know."

"Miriam," I said. "I know what happened, and what he
said, and what I told you. And I know that you put your job
on the line to get us off the hook with Lieutenant Russell.
But I still don't know why a nice Jewish girl like you would
want to get involved with someone who claims to be Jesus
Christ."

She lowered her cup. "I don't remember him ever claiming that."

"He's certainly never denied it," I said. "And don't get smart. *I'm* the lawyer around here. Are you saying he isn't?"

She rolled her bottom lip. "Maybe he is, maybe he isn't. I seem to remember your saying that religion was something we invented. You also said that his teaching cuts right across our separate faiths, and from what I've seen and heard myself, he's clearly more than the carpenter who became the fisher of men. He may be Jehovah's messenger. He may even be Vishnu, Buddha, Jesus and Muhammad rolled into one. I don't think it really matters which badge he's wearing. It does to you, because your approach to this event is on a much more intellectual level. What matters to me is that, when I'm with him, I'm aware of being in the presence of an extraordinary power. He radiates an aura of —"

"Yes, I know," I said. "Linda took a broadside."

"It's not a soft, saccharine-type goodness," continued Miriam. "It has an astringent quality. It's more of a —" She tried to claw the words out of the air. "A kind of — firm benevolence. It has a cutting edge. And there's this feeling of —"

I'd already driven this route. "Incorruptibility?"

She snapped her fingers. "Yes. That's part of it. But what I was going to say was 'renewal' — 'rebirth.' " She gestured helplessly. "I've never experienced anything like this before."

"That's understandable," I said. "It's a fairly unique situation."

Her mouth tightened. "But one which you find pretty funny."

"Not at all," I said stoutly. "The time I've spent with The Man has shaken me up too. I'm not kidding. He has really put my emotions through the wringer."

"I'm glad to hear it," she replied. "Because there are times when I get the impression that you look upon this as nothing more than a philosophical exercise."

Now it was my turn to get tight-lipped. "Thanks a bunch."

"You see, with me," she continued, "it's much more of a

gut reaction. I just feel a lot better when he's around. You know what I mean?"

"Of course," I laughed. "Do you think I haven't felt it too?"

"Ahh, but you're trying to fight it," she said.

"No. Not fight it. *Control* it."

She raised her eyes to the ceiling. "Lawyers . . ."

I put down my coffee. "Miriam, there's nothing wrong with the way I am, or the way I'm dealing with this thing. We've been dropped in the middle of a minefield. One false step and it's going to blow us away."

"Leo," she said. "Make up your mind. When you called me last night, you said the future already exists. If we're due to get blown away, that's it."

I waved her words away. *"Nyehhh . . .* that's what *he* says, but he hasn't proved it, and I don't think he can. The theory's been around for a long time but it doesn't make sense. 'Brax is not going to keep fighting if he already knows he's not going to win. We *have* to be able to make a choice. It's demonstrably obvious we are able to exercise free will. To choose either to do or not to do something. And the course of action we decide on shapes our future and that of others whose lives are affected as a direct consequence of that decision. The future is constantly being modified by the interaction of an infinite number of decisions that are being made every second of every hour of every day." I paused and fixed on her eyes. "It has to be — surely."

She shrugged. "I think that's one of those questions that only become important when you start thinking about it. I've managed to get this far quite happily without having to."

"Okay then," I said. "Whether — in the long run — we have a choice or not, I really feel we ought to try and stay together on this."

"So do I," she said. "The problem is, we don't look at the world in the same way."

"That's what makes it exciting, Doctor."

I could see she didn't agree. "Leo — you spend your day

poring over papers, dancing a courtly gavotte with writs, subpoenas and pleas of *nolo contendere*. Where the most violent thing that can happen to one of your fat-cat clients is that he gets slapped with an injunction —"

"Yeah, okay," I said tiredly. "I get the message."

"Good," she replied. "Then you know what I'm trying to say. You go to court against Ford or General Motors over a batch of faulty back axles. I get to fix the faces of drivers who've gone through the windshields. My day is spent patching people. Performing on-the-spot diagnosis of pain and sickness. Trying to hold down the statistics of fatal accidents, while your fee depends on the money you can claw back for the next-of-kin."

"Terrific. I hope you get a citation —"

She grabbed my hand before I could pull it away. "Leo, I'm not getting at you. I know you're a caring person. It's just that our jobs are very much part of our lives, and because of them, we have different interests, different priorities. I practice medicine because, as long as I can remember, my one consuming passion was to learn how to save people's lives. I like the immediacy and the variety of the problems we get in Emergency. But that doesn't make me a better person. I just happen to find it more rewarding than doing nose jobs or prescribing Valium to frustrated suburban housewives."

"Sure," I said. "Decisions like that are always easier when you don't need the money." It was a cheap crack which left me wishing I'd bitten my tongue off.

"That's true," she said, without rancor. "But I also know that I don't have the kind of stamina required to work in geriatrics, or terminal cancer wards."

It was breast-beating time. "Okay, so now you've made me feel terrible. But what has this got to do with you and The Man?"

"Everything," she said. "I'm not interested in all that stuff about starships, Time Gates, and 'Brax's Black Legions. It's irrelevant — like The Man says. I just want some of that healing power to flow into my hands. So I can put it to work.''

I groaned at the prospect of going steady with a miracle-worker. "Miriam, for God's sake — I hope you're not really serious about this. I mean, I'm not against a little surreptitious laying on of hands, but if you're planning to turn Manhattan into Lourdes U.S.A. . . . wow . . . that's big stuff! The City Fathers might be pleased but you could find yourself in big trouble with your colleagues at the AMA. I think you ought to hold off on that idea until we've had time to think it through.''

"All right,'' she said. "But if he offers it to me, I'm not going to say 'No.' ''

I became a mite irritated. "Yeah, okay. Let me know when it happens and I'll cue in the heavenly choir.''

"Leo,'' she said. "I'm not kidding.''

I nodded. "I know. That's what worries me. Do you have a cigarette?''

She opened a cupboard above the drainer and produced a carton of Camels from behind the All-Bran and the Special K. I caught the tossed pack and opened it while she put the carton back in its hiding place. "I thought you'd switched to low tar.''

"Only in public,'' she said. Our cigarettes met over a lighted match. "Okay, shoot . . .''

"You asked me what my angle was,'' I said. "What does your female intuition tell you about his?''

She poured us out some more coffee. "I'm not sure. But I'll tell you one thing. His coming here was no accident. Are you trying to tell me God makes mistakes?''

If you remember, it was a point I raised with The Man at Sleepy Hollow. "It's an interesting theological proposition. All I can say is — we're in trouble if he does.'' I took another pull and waved the smoke from my eyes. "However, at least we agree about one thing. I know nothing about the mechanics of time-travel but I'd say that for him to land here once is a miracle, twice is an unhappy coincidence, and three times means we should cancel our holiday arrangements. The question is — what do we do if he turns up again?"

She shrugged. "Why don't you worry about that when it happens?"

"I'm not *worried*," I said. "I just like to think ahead — get things worked out. Doctors practice preventive medicine, don't they?"

"They do," she replied. "However, the real question is not 'What do we do if,' but one I've raised before — do you *want* him to come back?"

I raised my cup to my lips and sniffed the aroma before drinking. Miriam makes good coffee from her own private blend. "Let me put it this way," I began.

"Cut out the bullshit," she said. "Yes or no?"

I took another sip. "It's not quite as simple as that. There are two sides to this."

"Jeezuss," she groaned. "No wonder lawsuits drag on forever."

"Keep quiet," I said. "You gave me the floor. Let's take the positive side. Yes — I would like to hear from him again. If only to satisfy my curiosity. I'd like to hear the rest of the story because nothing he's told us so far matches what's written in the Book. At least not in any obvious way. I know there's a theory that the four Gospels have both a literal and an occult meaning but it will take more than two quick readings to crack the code — even with the head start he's given me."

The clues were there right enough — if you read between the lines. The trick was to reconstruct the missing pieces of the jigsaw puzzle. If you approached the Gospels, Acts and Revelations as if they were the statements of witnesses to a crime, then you held in your hands the greatest detective story of all time. But only The Man knew all the answers to the tantalizing questions raised by the texts.

"Now, maybe you could call that an intellectual interest," I continued. "But that's not the way I see it. The solution to the Christ-Mystery — if that's what's being offered — could turn all our lives around and alter the world view of history. Now, okay — I admit I'm not too sure whether I really want that to happen, but the chance to get the inside story is irresistible."

She handed me an ashtray. "So what does that mean in simple language? Are you saying that The Man *is* the Messiah promised to us by the God of Israel?"

"No," I said. "I'm prepared to accept that he could be the historical figure known as Jesus, but beyond that I'd prefer to keep my options open."

Miriam threw up her hands. "That's all I need. A *Jewish* lawyer!"

"Listen," I said. "What do you want me to say? I know what he's done and what he's said — and the effect all that has had on me. But what real proof has he furnished as to his identity? He hasn't produced any evidence that would stand up in a court of law — or any investigative body you'd care to mention. Okay, he did that trick with his wrists — which are where some of the so-called experts say the nails would actually have been. But he also said, *'Don't be misled by what you've seen, or what you think you've seen'* —"

"I know," she interjected. "But he wasn't talking about the stigmata."

"Miriam," I said. "Do you have any idea how many cases there are on record of people bleeding from the hands and feet? Literally hundreds. Wounds in their side, lacerations on their backs, scalp wounds from invisible thorns. There are even certified statements by doctors who found the scar of a cross-bladed spear wound in the heart of a dead medieval saint! Medical opinion — when it can be persuaded to face up to the evidence — classifies the phenomena as a type of hysteria. Churchmen put it down to the power of God. They're impressed, but they're not going to go overboard if that's all he can come up with. As for your gut reaction — what one could call the 'Linda-effect,' I'd say that was highly circumstantial. Charisma, in itself, is not proof of divinity. If it was,

Charles Manson would be wearing a halo. I'm not arguing about The Man's superhuman powers. Both of us have seen enough to convince the most hardened skeptic. But would it stand up to rigorous scientific analysis? Do you remember how they tore into Uri Geller after the Stanford Lab experiments?"

"Yes," said Miriam. "But I'd say that The Man was in a different league, wouldn't you?"

"No question about it,' I said. "Don't get the wrong idea. I'm not knocking The Man. Everything I've done from the start has been on the basis of believing that he was something special. It's been to protect him — though why the hell I should think he needs us to do that, I can't imagine."

"Maybe he thinks we need him," said Miriam.

"We need something," I said. "Even so, I still find it difficult to relate to the idea that *we* are the aliens. The strangers in a strange land who lost their memory and went to pieces. But on the other hand, it squares with the basic principles of Judaism: Observance of the Torah; the idea of the divine presence in history; the emphasis on the solidarity of the community and moral virtues."

And also with Israel's God-given role — to become a kingdom of priests and a holy nation; *To be a light unto the nations, to open blind eyes, to bring out the prisoners from the prisons, and them that sit in darkness* . . . The long-forgotten words came back to me.

"You know, when you think about it," I said, "none of the major religions has a monopoly on the truth, but they all contain part of it. 'Brax has done a good job keeping everybody at arm's length."

"Or at each other's throats," observed Miriam. "If The Man comes back, I'd like the chance to ask some of the questions."

"Go ahead," I said. "But don't waste time with the biggies. God is unknowable, and we won't understand the Secret of the Universe until we graduate as sunbeams. But that still leaves you with quite a few questions."

She smiled at me. "What do you plan to do — write down the answers?"

I smiled back at her. "I would — if that was what he wanted. Taking dictation is easy. The hard part would be nailing him down long enough to get through from start to finish. You saw what happened on Sunday morning. His movements are totally unpredictable."

"Yes, it's a problem . . ." She tapped another cigarette out of the pack, switched off the plate under the coffeepot, and led the way back to the bedroom.

I pocketed the cigarettes and matches and followed, cup in hand. We got back into bed but kept our robes on. She put an ashtray between us. "Okay. Now tell me why you *don't* want him back."

"Awww, come on," I said. "We've been through most of this. Any reasons I have for wishing to avoid another encounter are inspired by my base animal instincts for self-preservation."

"That sounds like the male chauvinist piglet I've come to know and love," she said. She softened the blow with a kiss on the ear, then turned out the light and left me to finish my coffee in the dark.

I lay there and asked myself yet again why it was only our lives he'd chosen to turn upside down. In an effort to second-guess his next moves, I had combed the New Testament looking for clues but, after the Resurrection, there was not a lot to go on. The accounts in each of the four Gospels differed but it was possible to arrive at a limited consensus. The Man had disappeared when two women called Mary visited the tomb early on Sunday morning — Jerusalem time. Okay. We know where he was — in Manhattan. Two young men in white — probably Michael and Gabriel — appear to the women and tell them not to get too upset. Later, near the empty tomb, the same two women see The Man. At first, they don't recognize him. I have a hunch that what they saw was an image of The Man as he was at a younger age, conjured up from their own memories. Whatever the explanation, he told them not to touch him — ". . . *for I am not yet ascended to my Father*" (John 20:17). Which must have been right after he disappeared from the morgue. John mentions that it was still dark. Mark and Luke don't record this appearance. Luke has the two men in white, Mark only one. Matthew also only has one "angel" who rolls back the stone from the door to the tomb. But in chapter 28, verse 9, he has Jesus meeting the two Marys — one of whom was Mary Magdalene — and they fall to the ground and grab his feet. In Matthew this encounter takes place before dawn; in Mark, at sunrise; in Luke, early in the morning. So at least they're not too far apart in their timing.

Later that same day around sunset, Luke 24:13 recounts how The Man met up with two men heading along the road to Emmaus, a village west of Jerusalem on the road to the port of Joppa. These two were from the group of seventy-two subdisciples known as the Followers of The Way. As The Man walks with them, they talk about the Crucifixion and he points out how the whole thing relates to the Old Testament prophecies. But despite this extended conversation, the two men don't recognize him. They invite him into their house; he breaks bread with them and disappears. And in the same instant, they realized who they had been talking to — and knew that the promised Resurrection was a reality.

According to Luke, the two men — one of whom was named Cleopas — drop everything and high-tail it back to Jerusalem. Not so. The Man told me later they went to Bethany — which was also on the Joppa road. Ten of the disciples were hiding out there in a house belonging to friends. The Book mentions *eleven* disciples but Luke's arithmetic, as well as his timing, seems to be wrong at this point if you take John's gospel into account. Unless they were counting Mary Magdalene as ranking with the disciples (as indeed she did and of which more later), or because the number 11 was one of the code signals that are concealed in the Gospel texts. Anyway . . . Cleopas and his friend arrive but before they could catch their breath and break the good news, The Man appeared in their midst and almost caused a mass cardiac arrest. He calms them down, talks for a while, eats some *gefilte* fish and a little bread, shakes them all by the hand — and vanishes.

The week goes by. Nothing happens. Saturday; he turns up at Sleepy Hollow. Sunday morning we're on the porch then, POW! — back to Jerusalem. Because eight days after his first visit, he reappears in Bethany to show his stigmata to Thomas, the disciple who had missed him the first time around.

I thought about Miriam and The Man in the bedroom and wondered if Thomas had witnessed a similar demonstration. The Book didn't mention The Man's exit but I imagine that he must have walked through the wall or a locked door, because that was when he materialized in my office on Monday morning.

It was at this point that the trail ran out. The Gospel of Saint John records him as turning up at Lake Tiberias where the disciples were out fishing. The Man stands on the shore and guides them onto a huge shoal of fish. Later, while reading a commentary on the New Testament, I discovered that in the opinion of many Biblical scholars, this episode is out of context. I'm pretty certain that this was one of the many allegorical code messages, but I'll tell you what The Man said about that later on. One thing at a time. Even though it probably didn't happen, I like to imagine that he stood in the shallows, and had some kind of sonar built into his ankles. But John's gospel did end on an intriguing note. With something like — *And there are many things which Jesus did, which, if they were all recorded, the world could not contain all the books which would be written.*

I can now tell you what that means. The Man fed the disciples the same information he gave me — with one important difference. I got a brief outline, a word at a time; they got chapter and verse in one blinding megavolt transmission: the history of the Empire; the Wars of Secession; the creation of the Netherworld; the works. No wonder it blew their minds.

Let's face it. God's equivalent of Henry Kissinger's *White House Years* must run to quite a few pages.

There was, however, an additional clue to The Man's post-Resurrection movements. Chapter one of Acts related that The Man showed himself to his disciples — who had now been promoted to Apostles — over a period of forty days, at the end of which they were promised the gift of the Holy Spirit. The Ascension followed, and once more two men in white step out of nowhere and — in the text, at least — dismiss the Twelve in a rather peremptory manner.

Finally, at the Feast of the Pentecost, fifty days after the Crucifixion, the eleven Apostles and a new number twelve, recruited to take the place of the missing Judas, are in this building in Jerusalem. Suddenly the interior is swept by hurricane-force winds; the heads of the Twelve are surrounded by "cloven tongues of fire"; they fall down drunk and begin to babble in every language from Ashanti to Zoque.

And that, as they say, is where it all starts happening. Except that The Man drops out of the story. No one saw him after the Ascension although he was alleged to have made voice contact with Saul/Paul on the road to Damascus. Of which, again, more later.

As I lay there, listening to Miriam's sleep-filled breathing, I tried to figure out what might lie ahead. If what one might call the "yo-yo" effect continued, there was a strong possibility that The Man could pop up in Manhattan — and into our lives — anytime during the next five weeks.

And then what? After the Feast of Pentecost in first-century Jerusalem, he could head back to the Time Gate or he could come back here and set up shop on a more permanent basis. Depending on what he had in mind. He'd told me that — as far as he knew — this wasn't the end of the world, but you only had to look at the global scene to realize that all the ingredients were there.

So far, we had escaped any lasting embarrassment and public exposure. If we stayed lucky, I told myself, the five-week headache we could handle. Whatever happened, we would at least get a good story out of it. Little did I realize, as I sat there in the dark shortening my life with yet another cigarette, that The Man planned to give it such an unexpected twist.

ELEVEN

THURSDAY, the thirtieth of April, dawned with a bright, clear innocence. I grabbed a quick shower, shared a cup of coffee with Miriam — who went back to bed to drink hers — then rode over to my apartment to change before catching my regular cab downtown. I met Joe Gutzman in the lobby and told him how the case was going as we rode up in the elevator. Linda made it to the office with another saga of missed connections just as I was leaving the building. I found myself involved in an over-the-shoulder conversation in which both of us kept walking and ended up shouting at forty paces. Ridiculous.

In court, it was one of those *blecch* days. The case had reached the nit-picking stage with impenetrable statements by opposing sets of technical experts. I know this hasn't got anything to do with The Man but perhaps I should just explain that we were seeking to prove that Cleveland Glass was using an industrial glass-making process which was covered by patents filed by my clients — the Delaware Corporation. In other words they were ripping off the advanced technology for free instead of paying over large chunks of money for the privilege of using same. Really gripping stuff. But now you know how I fill the day. As I sat there listening to a description of molten-glass flow-control systems, I began mentally adding up the salary bill and overheads for the entire operation and could not help wondering if our talents might not be better employed elsewhere. I concluded that they could but that the world would have to be differently ordered. The only problem was that we had to wait until the Twentieth-Century Flier plunged into the ravine before we could build the New Jerusalem. Until that happened, there was only one thing to do: take the money and run.

I returned to the office after court recessed for the day and heaved a sigh of relief. Because — in case you hadn't thought of it — there was always the possibility that The Man could have turned up in the middle of the proceedings. Looking back, I realize that I was wrong to be worried. A public appearance would have made him everybody's problem; not just mine. The fact is, of course, I was worrying for all the wrong reasons. I was so scared that I might be exposed to scorn, ridicule and even physical danger, so concerned with the preservation of my professional standing and the benefits it conferred, that not once did I ever seriously consider the implications of why he had chosen to appear to me, and not on the steps of St. Patrick's Cathedral. Later, when his purpose was revealed to me, it all made sense but at this point, in the second week of this mind-blowing adventure, I was still totally blinded by self-interest.

Although he hadn't asked for anything, I had the feeling that he was waiting for a new "me" to emerge. I had begun waking up in the middle of the night, seized by the fear that he might suddenly fix me with those golden hawk-eyes and say, "Follow me." He'd tapped a lawyer called Philip to be one of the Twelve. I could only pray to God that The Man wasn't planning a new whirlwind ministry. Because if he was, I would have to take a raincheck. I didn't have what it takes — and I didn't want to have it either. I wanted to stay safely inside the fifty-percent-silk/fifty-percent-acrylic fiber cocoon I'd spun for myself. I had everything going for me. The Twelve might have been given the gift of the Spirit but, as I'd already had cause to reflect, it hadn't exactly enhanced their career prospects. Like them, I was now party to the secret that I was just a carrier bag for some jigsaw puzzle pieces of the imprisoned Ain-folk, but that fact did not make me any less eager to go on living. Correctly serviced, my body had another good thirty to thirty-five years on the road and I was determined to get the maximum mileage out of it. If I got hit by a truck, the ghost I gave up would only go into parking orbit, or maybe have its parts pigeonholed until it was called off the rank, or reassembled in the correct astrological configuration and slotted into a newly conceived fetus for another roller-coaster ride through the Earth-World Amusement Park. My death, I told myself, in his name — or in the name of any other cause — would have absolutely no effect on the outcome of the struggle between the Empire and 'Brax.

The Man had talked about the fragmented Ain-folk being consigned, upon the death of their human hosts, to a nightmarish plane of existence from which physical rebirth was the only escape. Perhaps this was the extradimensional world that Western devotees of the Hereafter had labeled Limbo. Maybe, in their desire to escape, some of the disembodied Ain-folk fragments tried to jump the line and ended up wrestling for control of the nascent embryo. It would explain those baffling cases of "multiple personality" where anything from two to a dozen or more distinct identities fought for elbow room within a single body. And if, in the confusion, some of the Old Testament–type demons managed to smuggle themselves aboard, the resulting conflict could manifest itself as violent insanity. Demonic possession could be a literal fact, not just a philosophical proposition or a psychological or neural disorder. And it would also make possible the birth of totally Satanic individuals. The historical Antichrists whose presence or impending arrival had exercised the minds of Christian scholars over the centuries.

The phone jerked me from my own private limbo. Linda had Jeff Fowler on the line. I told her to put him through.

"Hi, Jeff. How's it going?"

"Fine," he said.

"Good. How d'you make out with Carol?"

"Okay," he said. "You did me a real favor there. Are you going to be free later tonight? Say eight-thirty to nine?"

"I'll be at home," I replied. "What was it you wanted to see me about?"

"Blood," he said. And rang off. Just like that.

I put the phone down with a sense of foreboding, then picked it up again and asked Linda to try and get hold of Miriam or, failing that, to leave a message asking her to call me. I tried hard to concentrate on the pile of paperwork in front of me but the words wouldn't register in my brain.

Miriam rang back just before six. I told her about Fowler's cryptic phone call. "Have you any idea what it's about?"

"Nope," said Miriam. "I haven't seen him since we took him out to dinner with your ex-playmate Carol."

I tried to figure out what that little shaft signified, then gave up. "Are you going to be able to come over?"

"Uh-uh," she said. "I've got a date I can't break. I'm going out with a bunch of the guys to celebrate Ken Gallow's appointment as head of the teaching faculty. I told you about it — remember?"

"Ohh, yes, Ken Gallow," I said, with snide matter-of-factness. "*Your* ex-playmate."

She drove on over it. "You can handle Fowler. If he gets too close for comfort, pick him up on some technical point and pretend you don't understand. With luck, he'll launch into a lecture and lose track of what he was talking about. If not, tell him some more lies. You're very good at that."

I think it was a compliment, but it sounded like game, set and match.

When I reached my apartment at a quarter past eight, the first thing I did was to sink a good three fingers of bourbon. The idea was to totally bomb my neuromuscular system so that I could listen to whatever Jeff Fowler had to say without any outward demonstration of surprise, alarm or dismay.

Fowler hit the entry-phone button at eight-thirty on the

nose. I told him to come up and readied a Jack Daniel's. We settled in a couple of armchairs and I staved off the evil moment with some mild badinage about Carol Shiragawa who, I omitted to say (although it must now be obvious), is half-Japanese, stands as tall as Iowa corn (her father comes from Cedar Falls), and works as a reservation clerk for JAL. So — anyway, we finally got to it and I found myself regretting that The Man had not seen fit to help me out by arranging to have a wayward elevator cleave friend Fowler in two.

"Blood," I said.

"That's right." Fowler put his glass down with a delicately raised forefinger and pulled out a thin, Clint Eastwood cheroot. It looked ridiculous sticking out of his rather soft, doughy face but what the hell — we all dream, don't we? Fowler lit the cheroot with some ceremony then pointed it at me. "You are never going to believe this. I mean, it is *weird*. No, really."

"Sounds good," I said. "Why don't you run it by me?"

He retrieved his glass, took a thoughtful drag on the cheroot, and massaged his forehead. "Six-thirty, Tuesday evening, a Spanish priest turned up at the lab. Ordinarily, I wouldn't have known about it. It just so happened that he went down the wrong corridor and I met him on the way out of my section. Well — as we don't get many priests in our neck of the woods, I asked him what he wanted. He told me that he had a sample of liquid that he thought might be blood and wanted to have it analyzed. I explained that he'd come to the wrong place and that we were actually a specialist research unit. I mean, that thing I did for you and Miriam was a one-shot."

I nodded. "Sure . . ."

"So the priest says, 'This is special. It's from a statue.' "

"You're kidding," I said.

Fowler stabbed his cheroot in my direction. "My words exactly. So the next thing he does is produce a small corked phial and two color Polaroids of a statue about fifteen or so inches high."

"A statue of what?" I asked.

"Jesus Christ nailed to the cross," said Fowler. "You know, the usual thing. You see them all over Mexico. Made of plaster and painted with enamel. This particular one happens to come from Cuba. It's a family heirloom. Over a hundred years old."

A bell rang at the back of my mind but the memory circuits failed to connect. "And this statue is bleeding?"

Fowler sipped some JD and nodded. "From the head, side, hands and feet. Absolutely amazing. I've been around to see it myself. I've even had it off the wall. There are no pumps or tubes, or anything like that. The only possible way to fake it would be by a sealed unit inside. And the only way to check that would be to break it open, or to have it x-rayed. But the family won't let it out of the house."

"That figures," I said.

Fowler shook his head. "Forget it. These people aren't faking. This is authentic. And I understand from the priest that this kind of thing has happened before. Apparently there's a statue of Christ in a church in Pennsylvania that bled from the hands in nineteen seventy-five."

"Who owns this latest model?" The fact that Fowler was here meant I was involved, but I still couldn't see the connection.

"A fifty-three-year-old woman called Marguerita Perez. She and her husband operate a small dry-cleaning store in mid-Manhattan."

That was the connection. My stomach turned over. "When did this happen?"

"Monday," said Fowler. "According to Mrs. Perez, it all started when this girl brought in an ankle-length brown woolen robe."

"What has this robe got to do with the statue?" I asked. As if I didn't know.

"I'm coming to that," said Fowler. "I gather there was nothing really special about the robe. Just an Arab-type thing. But different from the normal run of garments that get handed over the counter in that it was made from home-spun wool and woven on a hand loom."

I shrugged. "So what? Ever since the *Whole Earth Catalog* hand looms have been big business."

"Sure," said Fowler. "But that's just a detail. The point is, when Mrs. Perez gets hold of this robe, puts it in the steam press and steps on the pedal, she finds herself standing on the hill at Golgotha, looking up at Jesus Christ nailed to the cross between the two thieves."

I forced out a laugh. "With or without the steam press?"

Fowler grinned. "Well, I did say that it was kinda weird."

I had to agree. Only there was now nothing to laugh at. It must have been Mrs. Perez who followed Linda to the May-flower Hotel. "Okay, then what?"

Fowler's grin broadened. "Production came to a halt. Mr. Perez finds his wife standing in front of the steam press, star-ing into space, tears streaming down her cheeks, invoking Father, Son, Holy Ghost and the Virgin Mary — and very clearly in some kind of religious trance."

"Yeah, well, she wouldn't be the first." I had decided to play it hard-nosed. Afraid that anything less might lead to the discovery of my guilty secret.

"Anyway," continued Fowler, "when he manages to snap her out of it, she tells him what she's seen, grabs hold of the robe, and starts babbling that it belongs to Jesus Christ."

Now why — I asked myself — did The Man have to pull a stroke like that? Or were he, the robe and everything else connected with him merely elements controlled by an even greater power? "What did Mr. Perez do?" I said. "Call a doctor?"

"No," said Fowler. "He called Father Rosado. He's their parish priest. When he got there, Mrs. Perez was saying her rosary in front of this statue. She has this little shrine set up on a big old chest, with candles and everything. And she'd got the robe folded up and placed on top of it, in front of this figure of Christ. So Father Rosado goes in to have a word with her and calm her down, and Mr. Perez is hovering in the background, hoping the priest can persuade his wife to let go of the robe so that he can have it ready in case the customer calls. Mrs. Perez grabs hold of Father Rosado and gives him an action replay of her vision of the Cross and, as she begins swearing to God that every word of it is true, the statue starts to bleed."

"Now that *is* weird," I said. And I meant it too. "The priest must have been pretty impressed."

Fowler nodded. "So was Mr. Perez. But I gather that the Vatican likes to play this kind of thing fairly close to the chest. Miracles and saints are something they like to check out to the last detail. And then they sit on it for a hundred years before going to press."

A policy I was not going to argue with.

"What happened to the robe?" I asked.

"Perez handed it over to the girl who brought it in. She collected it during the Tuesday lunch hour. The ticket was made out in the name of Sheppard at the Mayflower Hotel. Perez says the girl told him the robe belonged to a friend."

"Does Perez know who she is?" I asked. Doing my best to convey the impression that the question was of only marginal academic interest.

"He knows her by sight," replied Fowler. "She brings in stuff now and then. But he can't remember her name. Anyway — when she called in to pick up the robe Mr. Perez has to argue with his wife but finally he gets it away from her and —"

"And Mrs. Perez follows the girl," I said, trying to move things along.

"Yes." Fowler cocked his head on one side. "How did you know that?"

I smiled. "I always spoil movies for Miriam by telling her what's going to happen next. Okay, so the girl takes the robe to the Mayflower Hotel and delivers it to the person whose name is on the ticket."

"That's a reasonable assumption," said Fowler. "Mrs. Perez didn't go into the hotel. She waited across the street. When

the girl emerged about twenty minutes or so later, she didn't
have it with her."

"I see . . ." Mrs. Perez's version of the events squared with
Linda's estimate of the time she'd spent with The Man. Not
that, as far as I knew, she had any reason to tell me less than
the truth. "What did Mrs. Perez do then? Follow the girl?"

"No," said Fowler. "She just stood there. I know this
sounds crazy but — she was convinced that Jesus Christ was
going to appear." Fowler raised his eyebrows clear of the tortoiseshell rims of his glasses and looked at me with an owl-like
expression. As if trying to disassociate himself completely
from the statement he had just made.

I sensed I was getting deeper into trouble but I had this
insane desire to laugh. "And did he?"

"Yes," said Fowler. "Mrs. Perez claims he walked out of
the hotel, across the street and into Central Park."

"Do you believe her?" I asked.

"I'm convinced she believes it," said Fowler. "I *know* the
statue is bleeding because I've seen that myself and my obser-
vations have been confirmed by three other people. I can't
comment on her vision of Golgotha but, clearly, they are all
related events which, for the moment at least, cannot be
explained in a rational, scientific manner. And that rather
annoys me."

"Was she able to describe the person she saw?"

"Oh, yes," said Fowler. "Medium height, swarthy complexion, black beard, slim build, very piercing yellowy-brown
eyes. He was dressed in this pale brown robe that seems to
have triggered this whole thing off, white Arab-type headdress, bare feet, worn leather sandals."

I nodded. "What time was this?"

"About three o'clock in the afternoon."

I picked up Fowler's glass, poured in the remaining Jack
Daniel's, and handed it back to him. "What did she do — follow him into the park?"

"Yes." He took the glass. "Thanks. The only time I get to

drink this stuff is when somebody gives it to me as a Christmas present."

"Make it last," I said. "That's the end of the bottle." I refilled my own glass with bourbon and sat down. "Did she speak to him?"

"No," said Fowler. "But she claims he spoke to her." He smiled. "As you can imagine, she was in a, well — highly emotional state. I mean, it's not every day you run into Jesus."

Somehow, I managed to keep my face absolutely straight. "That's right."

Fowler tapped the ash off his dwindling cheroot. "Her story is that she followed him until he sat down on a bench by the edge of the lake. Mrs. Perez planted herself behind a tree about ten yards away." Fowler grinned. "You can imagine it, can't you? There he is, just watching the people go by. Nobody gives him a second glance, but they all look at her like she's crazy."

"They could be right," I observed.

"Yes, sure. Anyway," said Fowler, "she stands there for about fifteen minutes and finally summons up the courage to go and sit on the other end of the park bench."

"And?"

Fowler shrugged. "She says Christ spoke to her. In Spanish."

Of course. What else? "What did he say?" I asked.

Fowler swallowed hard. "He said — *Hello, Marguerita. How are you today?* But the poor bitch couldn't reply. She said her tongue was frozen to the roof of her mouth. So then he says — in Spanish again — *We don't have much time. Let me look at your hands.* She was so scared she didn't dare move but she says that her arms kind of unfolded by themselves. And he took hold of her hands. She has these arthritic knuckle joints. Or rather, she had. Anyway — he kneads the backs of her hands with his thumbs and she feels this surge of power go all the way up to her shoulder blades. Electricity was the way she described it. Then he put her hands one on top of the other, pats them and says, *Have a nice day* — and vanishes.''

I nodded soberly. "Just like that . . ."

"Yes," said Fowler. "Just like that."

"Amazing . . ." I sat back and braced myself for the inevitable crunch. It had to come, otherwise he would not have been telling me all this. But, as far as Fowler was concerned, there was, up to now, nothing in the story to link me with Mrs. Perez, or the girl and her mysterious friend Mr. Sheppard.

Fowler took a frugal sip of his JD. "I know how you feel. But I'll tell you what *is* amazing. By the time she got back to the store, the arthritis in her hands had totally disappeared. She showed them to me. There is no swelling. The joints are perfectly supple. Mind you, I didn't see them before the alleged treatment at the Central Park clinic, but her husband — who, I might add, is not too overjoyed at any of this — and Father Rosado both assured me that her hands had been quite badly deformed."

"Jeff," I said, "it may make the medical profession a little twitchy, but we both know cures like this happen every day of the week. At this time of the year, they're lining up at Lourdes by the busload to throw away their crutches. This is how the Vatican pays the rent."

"Sure," said Fowler. "Listen, don't get me wrong. I'm not saying I *believe* all this. I'm only telling you what *I* saw, and what these good people told me. Whether Mrs. Perez did or did not sit on a park bench with Jesus is not really something I want to get into —"

You should, Jeff, I thought. *You should . . .*

"— but the robe that triggered this whole thing off *exists*. And so does the girl who called for it and took it to the Mayflower Hotel —"

"Yeah, I'll accept that," I said. "There may be a causal connection between Mrs. Perez's vision of Christ and the robe she was pressing at the time, but what does that prove? I mean, really — how could it belong to Jesus? The person she claims she saw coming out the hotel and who spoke to her in Central Park could have been another hallucination. When women get religion, this is their big thing. Remember all those hysterical nuns in Ken Russell's film *The Devils?*"

Fowler nodded. "Yes, I accept that. But it still leaves us with the statue. And that *is* bleeding, and *I'm* not hallucinating."

"Yeah, that is weird," I replied. "But like you said, it's not the first time it's happened. Even so, it's a great story. I just can't figure out what it has to do with me."

"It's the blood," said Fowler. He left me hanging there while he lit another cheroot. "When I analyzed the blood from the statue, I realized that it was identical to the sample Miriam had given me."

That was a real stopper. I stared at him. He must have thought I didn't understand.

"The sample of your client's blood," explained Fowler. "The one who died after receiving fraudulent treatment in the Philippines."

"Yes, okay," I said hurriedly. "I know the one you mean."

He dispersed a cloud of smoke. "Don't you think that is amazing?"

I shrugged. "I think it's an amazing coincidence. But nothing more. I mean — how many blood groups are there?"

Fowler didn't let up on me. "You're missing the point. It wasn't just the same blood group. The same abnormality was present in both samples. I won't bore you with the technical details but the only way to describe it is — superhuman."

He was right. But I couldn't tell him that.

"And the chances of it happening twice in just over a week are, well —" He spread his hands. "— it's very odd. You know what I mean?"

"I can see that it bothers you," I said. "I just don't see how I can help you, Jeff. My client's dead. He's been cremated —"

"Who was he?" asked Fowler.

I grabbed at the first name I could think of. "Uhh — a man called Abraham Lucksteen. He died at his daughter's home in Los Angeles. What I mean to say is that *she* is my client. Since the death of her father, that is. Anything more at this stage would be a breach of confidentiality." Terrible. I really got my tongue in a twist.

Fowler took off his glasses and peered closely at the lenses. I was struck by the way that his owl-like eyes now resembled those of a mole. "Leo . . . uhh, I really don't know you too well, so I hope you'll excuse me asking you this but —" He put his glasses back on. "— are you being totally frank with me?"

"Jeff," I began, with all the sincerity a smart kid like me can muster, "I appreciate that this blood analysis thing is a special concern of yours but just ask yourself — what could I possibly have to hide? I mean, there is just no way my late client could have any connection with a bleeding statue above a dry cleaners on Forty-ninth Street. That kind of thing only happens in movies. Believe me." I lit another cigarette and sat back as if I didn't have a care in the world. "By the way — is the Perez family planning to give this story to the media?"

"No idea," said Fowler. "But I have."

The news sent a chill shock wave up my spine but I managed to stay in my seat. "You've — spoken to the press?"

"Not exactly," he said. "The girl who shares Carol's apartment is on the news staff of Channel Eight. Her name's Gale McDonald. D'you know her?"

"Never met the lady," I replied. "How long has she been sharing with Carol?"

"Since the rent went up. Gale's from out of town. She landed the job with Channel Eight about four weeks ago."

Terrific. That was all I needed. A TV newshound looking for the first big break. I tried to make my interest sound casual. "So, uhh — what's happening? Is she planning to follow up on this story?"

"She's already on it," said Fowler. "I spoke to her before I came over here. She was on her way to the hotel."

"Ahhh," I nodded. "Has that started to bleed too?"

"No," grinned Fowler. "She's trying to get a lead on this guy Sheppard. When she phoned, the desk told her he'd checked out of his room on Wednesday morning."

"Well, that proves one thing," I said. "He wasn't the guy who disappeared from the park bench. If he could vanish into thin air, why would he reappear to pick up his bill?"

Fowler aimed his cheroot at me. "You've got a point there."

I stood up. "Jeff, uhh, listen — I don't want to rush you but I'm due in court again tomorrow and I have a stack of stuff to plow through —"

"Sure." He checked his watch, then got up and drained his glass. "As a matter of fact, I've got to be somewhere too. I'll let you know if Gale manages to get any of this on the air."

"Do that," I said. "I'd hate to miss it." I steered him to the front door of my apartment. "It's amazing how much of this stuff goes on. Yet most of us never hear about it."

"Yes," he said. "Like the real truth about all those flying saucer sightings — the ones that can't be explained away."

"That's right." I shook his hand and gave his shoulder a friendly pat as he stepped out into the corridor.

Fowler smiled. "You may think I'm a little paranoid but — when I analyzed your client's blood sample, I did seriously consider that it could be, well — extraterrestrial."

I smiled back. "Really?"

Fowler nodded. "For about thirty seconds. But then, anyone who reads UFO Update in *Omni* knows that there is nothing out there."

"They'd better be right," I said. "Because if they land, I'm going to cancel my subscription." I stepped back inside my apartment and began to close the door.

Fowler took a step toward the elevator then stopped. "Leo — just tell me one thing. How did you know that the dry-cleaning store was on Forty-ninth Street?"

I forced a good-natured laugh out of my throat. "What is this — *Gangbusters?* Come on. Git outta here . . ."

The first thing I did after I'd closed the door was to pour myself another drink. The second thing I did was to call

Miriam. I found myself talking to her answering service. I left my name and number and a plaintive one-word message — "Help."

"Is that with or without an exclamation mark?" asked the amiable young lady who was manning the phone.

"Without," I replied. "I don't want to start a panic." It was ironic. If I had paid more attention to Carol as a person instead of just regarding her as a hot piece of Japanese take-out, I would have known whom she was rooming with before getting mixed up with friend Fowler. There was a lesson in there somewhere.

A spark of 'Braxian anger flared within me and I mentally barbecued Linda. If only she hadn't taken The Man's robe to the cleaners . . . But then I *had* asked her to look after him. I erased all thoughts of savage reprisals and tried to work out my next best move. I didn't know how bright or pushy this newslady might be but she didn't need to be Dick Tracy to find the connection between the miracle-working Mr. Sheppard and Leo N. Resnick. I'd left a trail that a blind Boy Scout could follow. One thing was certain. I had to get Ms. McDonald off the case. The problem was how to do it without spilling the entire can of beans.

I brewed myself a strong cup of coffee and sat down despairingly at my worktable where my loaded Samsonite lay with the lid open. I shut it to remove the stack of unread papers from my sight and buried my head in my hands. When I remembered my coffee, it was lukewarm. I didn't have a number or address for Fowler so I rang Carol on the off chance he might have gone there.

He had. "Hang on," said Carol. "I'll go and get him." She sounded rather breathless. But then she had let the phone ring fifteen times before answering it. "Oh, by the way," she said, lowering her voice, "I've been meaning to thank you for introducing me to this guy."

"My pleasure," I said. "Is he, er — okay?"

"Are you kidding?" She giggled. "A jackrabbit. Just unbelievable."

"Lucky you," I replied. "Let me speak to Jeff."

Fowler came on the line. He sounded out of breath too.

"You certainly don't waste any time," I said. "What were you doing — screwing on the doormat?"

He gave a prim cough. "No. I ran up the stairs."

I adopted a bantering tone. "Come off it, Jeff. It's common knowledge that all you medical people are sex maniacs. I'm going steady with a lady doctor, remember?"

"Yes, so I gather," he replied. "Even so, it's unwise to make sweeping generalizations based on a sample of one."

I let it go. The last thing I wanted to do was get his back up. "Jeff, uhh, I'll keep this short and sweet. I'm involved in a matter of some delicacy and I need your help."

His voice thickened. "Okay, tell me about it." God knows what Carol was doing to him. Probably eating him alive. I'm not kidding. Once you press her button, she's like a boa constrictor with St. Vitus's dance.

"Well, Jeff," I began. "The fact is that when you were at my place, I was not as forthcoming as I might have been."

"So-oh-ohh . . . what does that mean?" he replied.

Have you ever had the experience of talking to someone while he's getting his rocks off on the other end of the line? It can be very disconcerting. Especially when you can visualize the people and the apartment and know that the phone is in the hall.

"Jeff," I said, "what I'm trying to tell you is pretty important but something gives me the impression that I don't quite have your undivided attention."

He answered with what was either a gasp of pleasure or impatience. "Leo, for Chrissakes — say what you want to say or get off the fucking line, okay?"

"Okay, okay," I said hurriedly. "It's just that this Mr. Sheppard — you know — the one who owns the pale brown robe?"

"Ye-ess . . . ?" he grunted.

"Well, uhh —" I gritted my teeth. "He happens to be a client of mine."

The reply came in the form of a Stockhausen-type symphony of splintering bamboo and tinkling glass as the imported Red Chinese hall stand collapsed under the vectored thrust of their coupled bodies.

I plodded through my paperwork and called again an hour later. The phone was off the hook. I slammed the receiver down and turned my attention back to the sheaf of notes I was trying to transform into a coherent legal argument. But my mind kept wandering back to the problem The Man had left me with. From what Fowler had said, it seemed unlikely that Mrs. Perez would be able to produce any witnesses who could provide corroborating evidence of her miraculous encounter in the park. But if the story was aired by Channel Eight, some of the passersby might come forward. Even so, there was no direct evidential link between the person she claimed she saw and my client — Mr. Sheppard. If she chose to fixate on him, that was her problem, not mine. I started to feel a little better.

The real news story was the plaster cross hanging on Mrs. Perez's wall, with its bleeding figure of Christ. If this reporter could be persuaded to zero in on that, then we were off and running. But if the worst happened, if I was unable to steer McDonald away from The Man and the Mayflower Hotel, my involvement with him could be made to appear perfectly reasonable. All I needed was some plausible evidence to show that Mr. Sheppard was a duly registered member of our society with a job and a home to go to. And I also had to work out how best to square my evasions with Jeff Fowler. His relationship, via Carol, with Ms. McDonald made things very tricky. One whiff of a cover-up and the newslady's nostrils would start to quiver.

I worked on my notes with muddled slowness until midnight then went to bed plotting moves in the dark. Like a chess master playing several opponents simultaneously. Only in my case, the games were all being played out on the same board. I decided to make one last try to keep the lid on the whole affair and then, if that didn't work, I was prepared to let the whole thing blow and book myself into a clinic.

TWELVE

THE alarm woke me at seven. I yawned and stretched my way to the bathroom instead of doing my floor exercises, and postponed yet again my jogging session in the park. I did however resolve to arrange a game of squash to compensate for this double lapse in my fitness program, and finished my shower with the tap turned to cold. My mind and body now braced to meet the evils of the day, I made a cup of coffee and considered the plan of evasive action which had sprung almost fully formed into my waking brain. It is amazing how you can go to bed wrestling with an intractable problem and wake up with the answer.

Morning light pierced the weave of the drawn curtains. I opened them wide and let the sun flood in. The street below was lined with cars jammed nose to tail. A woman in curlers, slippers and an oyster-pink robe stood on the curb near the door to the apartment building across the street with a poodle on a lead. I watched her gaze loftily at the surrounding architecture while her mutt crapped under the rear fender of a blue Olds then signed off by peeing against one of the hubcaps. I suddenly became aware that the trees had blossomed pink and white. Some had already shed their tiny, confetti-like petals on the sidewalk. It's sobering to realize that there are times when you get so wrapped up in your life that you don't have a moment to notice such things. I've got time now. I can tell you that.

Miriam answered my cry for help at a quarter to eight. I recounted the highlights of Fowler's visit, the possible TV exposé, and my belated admission to a "professional" relationship with the missing Mr. Sheppard. "I should have settled the bill with hard cash," I said. "Never mind. Even if this Brenda Starr character discovers the tie-up between Linda, The Man and myself, there is no way she can build a convincing causal connection with what happened to Mrs. Perez and her plaster Jesus. And — remarkable though that is, I have a feeling that if word reaches Father Rosado's bishop, the ecclesiastical brass will move in to stage-manage the whole event. Which could include pretending that it never happened."

"Mmmm," said Miriam reflectively. "That sounds like what the White House people call 'the Best Case scenario.'"

"That's right," I said. "But you also have to keep your fingers crossed."

"They're crossed," she replied. "Now tell me the worst."

"Ahh," I said. "In the Worst Case scenario, the shit hits the celestial fan, Mrs. Perez is canonized, the dry-cleaning store on Forty-ninth Street becomes a shrine and is visited by the leaders of the Christian Church, the statue becomes a ninety-day media wonder and pictures of it are beamed by satellite into the homes of millions, and you and I are given white robes and condemned to a lifetime of lecture tours as Brother Leo and Sister Miriam."

"Do you have a plan?" said Miriam.

"A tentative one," I replied.

"Keep working on it," she said.

I changed the subject. "Are you going to be able to help me eat some of that food that's up at Sleepy Hollow this weekend?"

"I'll have to call you back on that," she said. "Two of our team are out sick and they're having to rearrange the work schedules."

"Aww, God, not again," I groaned. "You already do too much. You're never out of that goddamn hospital."

"It stops me feeling domesticated," she said.

I heard the smile that was wrapped around the words and decided it was as good a moment as any to sign off.

Before I left the office for the final session in court, I agonized briefly over whether I should have a word with Linda about a possible visit from Gale McDonald. I decided against it. She'd worked for me long enough to know the rules about questions from outsiders. If I told her to say nothing she might respond self-consciously to any questioning. If McDonald got the impression that she was covering up for me, it would only create further difficulties. And Linda would start asking questions too. The dangers — if any — lay in Linda's reaction to what Gale McDonald might choose to tell her about Mrs. Perez's miraculous encounter. Given her previous emotional response to The Man, there was no knowing what the news of bleeding statues and visions of Golgotha might do to her lapsed Catholic conscience.

What had happened so far only confirmed what I already knew: lies beget more lies; slowly and inexorably one becomes trapped in a spreading web of deceit. In my experience, if deception was necessary, the best thing was to say as little as possible; the next best thing was the creative use of the truth, something that lawyers excel at.

The last day in court was taken up by my closing speech and that of defending counsel. Despite the distractions and pressures of external events, I thought I managed to sum up our case with admirable cogency but the bench, in its wisdom, decided to withhold judgment until after the weekend because of the complex technical nature of much of the evidence. We were directed to reassemble at ten o'clock on the following Tuesday. I had a strong suspicion that the judge, who kept a forty-foot yacht up on Cape Cod, wanted to get away early to beat the traffic.

As the proceedings came to an end, the judge's clerk passed me a message to call the office. I took leave of my clients, accepted their optimistic assessment of the eventual judgment with a modest shrug, and left them to argue over whether they should go home for the weekend, invite their wives into town, or stick with the phone numbers their bell captain had come up with.

I called Linda from a pay phone in the corridor. She told me that a Ms. Gale McDonald from Channel Eight was awaiting my return.

"What does she want?" I asked. As if I didn't know.

"She didn't say," replied Linda. "Maybe you're about to become a celebrity."

"That's all I need," I said sourly. In my present paranoid state, remarks like that were too close for comfort. "Tell her I'll be back in about thirty minutes. Meanwhile send her out for a cup of coffee. I don't want her getting under people's feet. Especially Joe's."

On the way back to the office, I stopped off at a bookstore specializing in voluminous works on esoteric religions, arcane wisdom, and illustrated manuals on how to screw your way to instant enlightenment. It was one of those places which stocked something for all tastes. Everything in fact from the *Bhagavadgita* to *The Bermuda Triangle*. I bought a paperback reprint of Moses de Leon's *Zohar,* another on Gnosticism, and a secondhand volume on Jewish mystics.

The cab dropped me off level with the coffee shop which is adjacent to the entrance to our building. As I stepped out of the swing doors into the hallway, a voice behind me said, "Leo Resnick?"

I turned to find a girl in her mid-twenties standing behind me. The penny dropped. "Gale McDonald, Channel Eight . . ."

"Right." She gave me a brief, firm handshake.

I led the way to the elevators. "Did the police give you my picture?"

"No," she said. "Jeff Fowler told me roughly what you looked like. I was in the coffee shop when your cab pulled up. Something told me it was you." She shrugged.

We stepped into the elevator. "Do you always follow up your hunches?" I asked.

She smiled. "That's what makes a good reporter."

Terrific. Not only was I saddled with a young kid looking for the big break, I'd drawn one that was psychic.

I gave her the once-over as we lapsed into silence for the climb to the twenty-second floor. McD was a compact five-and-a-half-foot package with a Liza Minnelli crop of auburn hair and blue bug-eye shades. She wore a Highland-tweedy three-piece pantsuit with a matching Professor Higgins hat, a white silk shirt and square-toed boots with sensible heels. The only things missing were the pipe and a tie.

"Ahh, you've met," said Linda, as we walked into her office.

I nodded. "Were there any calls for me?"

Linda ran quickly through the telephone log. There had been eight calls from clients, only two of which she hadn't been able to deal with. "Oh," she added, "Jim Leander can't make that squash date tonight. He has to spend the weekend on the Coast with one of his authors. But Monday or Tuesday at six will be fine."

"Okay," I said. "Cancel the court."

"Shall I make a new reservation?" she asked.

"No, leave it," I said. "I may be tied up."

Like to a stake, for instance.

Linda nodded. "Incidentally, did Yale have any trouble at the airport?"

I frowned. "Yale — ?"

"Mr. Sheppard. I mean with everything being stolen," she explained. "His passport, and wallet and stuff."

I could have strangled her. "Oh — yeah . . . he, uhh, got back everything on Tuesday afternoon. The airport police found them when they were carrying out a random check on some baggage handler's lockers. Apart from the cash that is. And TWA found his baggage. He got it back just in time to catch his flight. Sorry, I forgot to mention it."

I ushered McDonald into my office, waved her over to the chesterfield and dealt with the two outstanding calls. As I

watched her out of the corner of my eye, McDonald produced a notebook and a portable tape recorder from her
leather shoulder bag, took off her hat, opened a pack of those
long thin cigarettes wrapped in dark brown paper and lit one
using a butane lighter with a dramatically long flame. I decided that she would not present any real problem. Her studied appearance gave me the impression that she was more
concerned with style than content.

I joined her on the chesterfield and declined the offer of a
brown paper cigarette. "What exactly is it you want to see me
about?"

"I'd like to ask you a few questions about a client of yours.
Mr. Sheppard." She kept her eyes on me. Maybe she thought
I'd jump a foot in the air at the mention of his name.

I gave nothing away. "Oh, yeah — is this anything to do
with Jeff Fowler's story about a statue and the lady from the
dry-cleaning store?"

McD nodded. "That's right. Mrs. Perez. I'm trying to establish what part Mr. Sheppard played in what is — on the
face of it — an extraordinary series of events."

I grimaced. "I suppose it makes a change from commuter
groups complaining about delays on the subway system and
the foul-ups down at City Hall. Always assuming that this
lady is telling the truth."

"Don't worry," said McD. "I've thought of that too."

"Good," I replied. "Before we go any further I want to
make three things quite clear. First — my client's involvement with Mrs. Perez is peripheral and quite coincidental.
Second, I am not at liberty to make any statement which
would breach client-confidentiality, and third" — I pointed to
the tape recorder — "I am not prepared to make an on-the-
record statement in reply to off-the-cuff questions. If you
want to tape an interview, I require advance notice of the
questions. In writing."

"I see . . ." She smiled. "I guess I should have thought of
that. I've never interviewed a lawyer before."

I turned on the Resnick charm. "Jeff mentioned you're an out-of-town girl. Where are you from, McDonald?"

"Miles City," she said.

I smiled apologetically. "I'm sorry. Should I know where that is?"

"It's in eastern Montana. North of the Yellowstone River and the Little Big Horn. Have you heard of that?"

"Ahh," I smiled. "A high plains drifter. Did you make it here in one jump?"

"No," she replied. "I put in some time on the *Reporter* in Billings, and with the *Herald* in Chicago."

"Ah, that's interesting," I said. Even though it wasn't. "The only thing I know about Montana is that the girls have straight backs and strong thighs."

"That's right." She flashed a line of sharp white teeth. "They also have a good nose for bullshit."

It turned out that in between learning shorthand and running copy for the Miles City *Star,* she had also been a Junior Rodeo champion. The nearest I'd gotten to a horse at the same age had been on a merry-go-round at Coney Island.

I looked at my watch while she was talking just to let her know that the session wasn't open-ended. "So tell me — how far have you got with this story? Have you seen the statue?"

"Yes," she said. "And I've also talked with Mrs. Perez, her husband, and the priest — Father Rosado."

"And — ?"

"I tracked down the doctor who had been treating her arthritis."

I nodded approvingly. "You've been busy. What do you plan to call your story — 'The Miracle of Central Park'?"

McDonald carefully tapped the ash off her long brown cigarette. "I'm not sure I've got one yet. But there is no doubt that Mrs. Perez is totally convinced that she met, and was cured by, Jesus Christ."

"Yes, well, she wouldn't be the first," I observed.

"No," said McD. "But she's the first I've talked to."

Montana was not, traditionally, considered to be part of the Bible Belt but I decided that until McDonald declared her faith, or the lack of it, it would be better to display a sincere spirit of inquiry. "Tell me honestly, do you think this Mrs. Perez is crazy — or do you believe these things can happen?"

McD took a long drag and thought it over. "Let me put it this way. I don't think it would do the world any harm if it happened more often."

"You may have a point there," I said. "So — bearing in mind my opening remarks — how can I help?"

McDonald pursed her lips. "To tell you the truth, Mr. Resnick, I'm not sure whether you can now. In fact, I wish Jeff hadn't put me onto the story. Like I said, I talked to the Perez family, but now they won't let me bring a camera crew to film the statue. Father Rosado has backed out of a studio interview, and the family doctor has also reneged on his promise to testify publicly about the apparently miraculous cure of her arthritic hands." She gestured helplessly. "The establishment is closing ranks."

I shrugged. "Come on McD, you know the score. It happens all the time. They feel threatened by this kind of thing. They like pat answers. Everything in neat little boxes." My plan, as you can see, was to show sympathy and understanding.

"Yeah . . ." She cocked her head to one side. "Tell me — have you seen the famous robe which is supposed to have triggered this whole thing off?"

"Yes. But it didn't." I dipped deep into my third-year psych seminar. "Don't let yourself get sucked in by Jung's theory of synchronicity."

She raised an eyebrow. "Which is . . . ?"

"The attempt to explain the apparently significant relationship between certain events which have no 'causal link.'"

McD nodded but I could see I had her temporarily baffled.

"Let me explain," I began. "Mrs. Perez was pressing the robe when she had the vision of Christ on the cross. So there was a correspondence between the physical act and her mental process. But that's all. There was no — what the scientists call 'causality.' The robe was just a robe. Something that my client picked up in an Arab bazaar while he was in the Middle East. It probably cost him less than twenty dollars." I smiled and let go the big one. "If it really belonged to Jesus Christ, I imagine it would be worth a lot more than that."

She nodded. "Ye-ess. Tell me — I couldn't help overhearing the conversation with your secretary. You mentioned TWA had lost his baggage. Had he just arrived from abroad?"

"No, California," I replied. Covering my tracks in case Linda had been shooting her mouth off. "He had his passport with him because he was going on to Israel."

"So he must have been wearing the robe when he arrived," she concluded.

I looked at her blankly. "So?"

"Well — don't you think that's rather strange?"

I smiled. "Come on, McD. I'm sure the news that there are a lot of strange people in California must have reached Montana by now. When he walked into my office, I didn't give it a second thought. A lot of people dress like that where he comes from."

She eyed me skeptically. "Okay. Let's take another point. I checked with the bell captain at the Mayflower. He says he remembers seeing an Arab in a white headdress and brown robe crossing the foyer at about the same time that Mrs. Perez claims she saw the man who healed her hands exit from the hotel and cross over into the park."

"Okay, where does that get us?" I asked, determined to make her do all the hard work.

"I checked with the desk," she said. "There were no Arabs staying at the hotel. The only person it could have been is your Mr. Sheppard."

The sly implication of complicity did not escape me. "It probably was," I admitted. "But I can't see what you're getting at. Mrs. Perez has a vision of the Crucifixion and a statue in her house starts to bleed. I believe it's happened before but I'd say that is news. Sheppard isn't. All that happened was that *my* secretary took *his* robe to the cleaners. That is the extent of his involvement. I can't really comment on Mrs. Perez but, from what Jeff told me, she seems to be a very devout Catholic and — dare I add — somewhat simpleminded? In my experience, the two things usually go together."

McD nodded. "Yes, I'll go along with that. But let's follow this through. Sheppard exits from the hotel. Mrs. Perez follows him into the park. He sits down and eventually she joins him. He speaks to her, cures her hands — and disappears."

"Hold on," I said. "That's what she *thinks* happened. You and I know that human beings do not just vanish into thin air."

"Not ordinarily, no," agreed McDonald. "But here's another curious coincidence. Although his bill was made out on Wednesday morning — and billed to you by the way — none of the staff on duty in the foyer remembers seeing him return to the hotel and his bed wasn't slept in on Tuesday night."

"That's right," I said. "He took a cab out to the airport to pick up his wallet and passport that the police had found, then flew out to Israel."

McD took off her blue shades and sucked one of the bows reflectively. "I see . . ."

"He called me from the airport," I said, slipping easily into the lie. "But that doesn't invalidate Mrs. Perez's encounter with Christ. Most people borrow physical prototypes for their fantasies. Take me, for instance. I've always imagined the Virgin Mary as looking like Deborah Kerr. When young, of course."

McD gazed at me with her deep-set eyes. "What kind of fantasy would someone like you have about the Virgin Mary?"

"I'd have to know you a lot better before I could answer that," I replied. "Next question."

McD lit another of her fashionable cigarettes and blew the smoke over her shoulder. "When Mr. Sheppard left for Israel on Tuesday afternoon, why did he leave some of his clothing in his room?"

"You've really been nosing around," I said, stalling for time. "What are you — gunning for the lead in a new series of *Police Woman?*"

She shrugged. "I like to cover all the angles."

I swallowed a smile as it came to me. "The answer's very simple. The airline had found his baggage. He didn't need the extra clothes I'd paid for. I had someone collect them and take them over to my place."

She accepted my reply with a nod. *I'm wasted*, I thought. *With this kind of talent, I should be working for the White House.*

"One last question —"

"I hope it is the last," I said, looking at my watch.

"What? Oh — yeah . . ." She recovered swiftly. "When Jeff Fowler told you about all this, why did you delay telling him that you already knew Mr. Sheppard and that it was your —"

I cut in again before it got too sticky. In the art of interrogation, the trick is to keep your opponent off balance. "I said nothing to Jeff because my professional relationship with Mr. Sheppard is none of his business. I'm involved in some very delicate negotiations on his behalf and I did not want to prejudice our position because of some uncontrolled media exposure. Mr. Sheppard is a very important property and the last thing we want is for him to wind up with a walk-on part in a Six O'clock News story."

I picked up her tape recorder and checked that it was off. "Here . . . put this away." McD stowed it away in her bag along with her unopened notebook. I lit another cigarette, eyed her through the smoke, and decided to play my ace in the hole. "Can you keep a secret?"

She shrugged. "It depends what kind . . ."

"Don't fool around, McD," I said. "What I have to say is strictly *entre nous.*"

"Okay — shoot."

I gnawed my lip to underline the gravity of the decision I was about to make. "You've heard of Uri Geller?"

"Not recently," she said. "But I know who you mean. Are you going to tell me that Sheppard is another spoon-bender?"

"No," I replied. "In any case, that was only one aspect of Geller's paranormal powers. Let me give you another name — Arrigo, the Brazilian psychic surgeon . . . ?"

McD shook her head. "I'm not really into all that stuff."

"Never mind," I said. "Arrigo cures people. So does Sheppard. But unlike Arrigo, he doesn't use a knife. Now for the moment, this is all under wraps. I am acting as Mr. Sheppard's legal adviser —"

"Who is he? Where does he come from?" asked McD.

"He's not an American citizen, and Sheppard is not his real name. I'm not at liberty to tell you any more than that. We're just putting the final touches to a million-dollar TV, publishing and lecture tour deal with some very big people out on the Coast. And one of the key clauses is no prepublicity." I paused for dramatic effect. "You see, McD, the fact is — my client *did* cure Mrs. Perez. He was crazy to do it, but there it is. Arthritis, rheumatism, slipped discs . . . anything to do with bones, joints, bad circulation —" I snapped my fingers. "He's an absolute wiz. Now perhaps you can understand why I didn't want to tell Jeff. I didn't want this thing to go off half-cocked. But when he told me he'd put you on the case . . ." I spread my palms.

McD gave me an understanding nod. "Yeah, got it."

I had the feeling she was on the hook. "I'd like to make you a deal, McD. If you give me your assurance that you will forget this conversation, and drop my client right out of whatever you want to make out of the Perez story, I will guarantee you a first crack at the big one when it breaks, plus an exclusive interview. What do you say?"

McDonald's face puckered thoughtfully. She stubbed out her cigarette. "Okay, it's a deal." She stood up and shouldered her bag. "Thanks for talking to me."

Although I was quietly pleased she had swallowed my glib

explanation, I hadn't expected her to give up so easily. The girl was a lot sharper than I'd bargained for. I could only hope that I had stopped her dead in her tracks. In fact, I was pretty sure I had. It was rather sad to see the light die in her no-nonsense slate-blue eyes. The crass commercialism of TV network deals and publishing tie-ins was something she could accept and understand only too well but it lacked the noble white-knight enchantment of the impenetrable mysteries of the spirit, the miraculous laying on of hands, and ecstatic visions. But then, it was a cruel world. It was no longer the bravest and the strongest that survived but the sharp-witted and the nimble-tongued. I got Linda to take down McDonald's office number and sent her on her way.

"Would you like a cup of coffee?" asked Linda.

"Strong and black," I said.

She brought it into my office a few minutes later. "I can't bear the suspense. Are you going to be on TV?"

"Not yet," I said. "She was more interested in Mr. Sheppard. The lady that followed you from the dry-cleaning store has been going around telling people he's Jesus Christ."

She took the news with a straight face. "I see . . . I guess it must be the beard."

"And the robe," I said. "She must have spotted the two of you when you went out shopping."

Linda thought it over. "Yes . . . So what did you say?"

"To McDonald? I told her that I'd known Mr. Sheppard for some time and was confident that this lady, whoever she was, was making a big mistake and probably needed her head examined."

"And did she believe you?" said Linda.

Looking back, that was a curious question, but at the time I took it in my stride. "If she didn't, I've been wasting my time, and she's about to waste more of hers. How long was she here before I called you?"

Linda raised her eyebrows. "Oh, uhh, about — ten, fifteen minutes."

"What did you talk about?" I sipped my coffee and watched

her mouth. She always loses control of it when she's telling less than the whole truth.

"Oh, gee . . ." Linda tried to remember. "She — asked me where I lived, how much the rent was on my apartment, how big it was — that kind of thing. She's sharing a place at the moment and wants to move out on her own. I gave her the name of a couple of good rental agencies and, er — asked her how she liked working in television." She shrugged. "And that was about it."

"Did you tell her you worked for Universal?"

Her mouth held firm. "Yes, I mentioned it in passing."

"Okay, thanks." I raised my cup. "I needed this."

Linda started for the door then turned to face me. "You needn't worry. I didn't say anything about Mr. Sheppard."

"Did she ask?"

"No," said Linda. "Do you think she might?"

I shrugged. "You know what reporters are like."

She nodded. "What should I say if she does?"

"Whatever you like," I said. "Just remember that Mr. Sheppard is now one of our clients."

The news surprised her. "Since when?"

"This afternoon," I replied. "He asked me to act as his attorney just before he left for Israel."

"Ahh, that's good." She smiled. "I'll open a file. Do you have an address for him?"

"No," I said. "I'll get him to give you one next time round." I slumped back in my chair with an audible sigh of relief as the door closed behind her. How long, I wondered, was I going to be able to keep this up? I could not remember lying with such agility since, at the age of fourteen, I began hanging out on street corners with *shiksas* instead of going to *schul*. I felt like one of those jugglers with thirteen plates spinning on top of long thin poles. It only needed one thing to go wrong to bring everything crashing down around me.

Now that The Man had backtracked to first-century Jerusalem life took on — outwardly at least — some semblance of normality. I managed to coax Miriam out of her white coat and into a little restaurant within beeping distance of the hospital. She listened to my account of McD's visit, told me I'd done a good job, turned down my offer of a country weekend, and was called away before the dessert. Undeterred, I drove up to Sleepy Hollow, made myself comfortable, and read the books I'd bought from cover to cover. It was an amazing experience. Page after page echoed The Man's story of the struggle between the Empire and 'Brax. Consider, for example, the ideas developed in the sixteenth century by Isaac ben Solomon Luria from the Zoharistic Kabbala.

Luria's theosophical vision centered on the idea that during the withdrawal of the Divine Light from the physical universe, a catastrophic event occurred during which luminous particles became trapped in shells of matter (*qelippot*) — a kabbalistic term that was also used to designate evil powers. The "withdrawal" could be interpreted as the Empire's retreat during the Second War of Secession and Luria's "luminous particles" could be an off-target description of the trapped Ain-folk, the twelve Celestial entities that had shaped the Earth colony during the Second Age.

Luria's mythical construct went on to posit the necessity of a rescue of the imprisoned particles and a return to their former state of being. This rescue, or "restoration" (*tiqqun*), was to be accomplished by the Jewish nation through strict observance of the traditions of the Torah, a rigorous asceticism, and an exemplary life founded on mystical prayer and contemplation. In this way, harmony, or "unification" (*yihud*) with the God of Israel, the transcendent power behind the universe, would be achieved.

Luria also reaffirmed belief in the successive reincarnation of the soul and its perfectibility, and he emphasized the need for an unceasing struggle against the powers of evil.

Once again, I was struck by this recurring theme of eternal conflict between the opposing forces of Light and Darkness that echoed the teachings of Zoroaster, the great reformer of religious thought in Persia. In the sixth century B.C. Zoroaster urged the abandonment of polytheism and revealed to his followers the identity of the supreme spiritual being — Ahura Mazdao — who was locked in conflict with Ahriman, the leader of the forces of evil. Zoraster proclaimed that Ahriman's influence upon the world manifested itself in the negative aspects of human existence and behavior.

The same idea was expressed in the beliefs of the Essenes: a closed Jewish community whose activities had come to light with the discovery of the Dead Sea Scrolls. The Essenes, who, according to the information released by Biblical scholars with access to their writings, lived a bleak, celibate existence, were believed to have flourished between the second century B.C. and the first century A.D. From the documents published to date, it appeared that they lived in daily expectation of the final cataclysmic battle in which the angelic Forces of Light would triumph and the chosen few would be saved — notably the Essenes themselves.

Apparently, they were wrong on both counts. Two thousand years later, the world was still waiting for the big event and — far from being saved — it was generally accepted that the Essenes were wiped out when the Romans steamrollered the Jews into the ground during the general uprising in 66–73 A.D. which brought about the destruction of the Temple in Jerusalem, the last-ditch epic at Masada, and the end of our hopes for unfettered nationhood.

But, as 'Brax knows, and as the opponents of civil rights learned in their turn, you cannot kill an idea whose time has come. Especially when it contains an eternal truth. The ideas of Zoroaster and the Essenes had resurfaced in the teachings of the Gnostics, the hugely influential Christian splinter group that had flourished in the first three centuries A.D. before its supporters were branded as heretics and its books burned by the agents of the early Roman Church in the best Nazi tradition.

It was the far-reaching impact of this event that led me to ponder the possibility that 'Brax might have been cunning enough to infiltrate the early Christian network as part of a long-term strategy to gain control and pervert The Man's original message. After all, the Russians had only just missed getting their man Philby into the top job with the British Secret Service. Why not a 'Braxian pope? No one could deny that, once Theodosius had declared Christianity to be the official religion of the Roman Empire, the bishops who had risen to positions of power via the Apostolic Succession had ignored The Man's injunction to "love thine enemies" and had proceeded to put the boot in with a vengeance.

But despite the tortures and the burnings and the massacres of sects like the Albigenses and the ever-mysterious Order of Knights Templar, they had not been able to suppress The Truth. The Word had been passed on from mouth to mouth. Clues had been inserted in written documents, paintings and carved inscriptions, camouflaged by intricate codes of mind-blowing complexity whose key was held by a select band of initiates whose sole task was to ensure that the ideas were handed on to the next generation.

The current Western standard-bearers of the Lurianic Kabbala were the Hasidim; Jewish communities like the Lubavitchers, over the bridge in the Williamsburg section of Brooklyn. The Hasidim, who drew their inspiration from the legendary doctrine of the itinerant, untutored eighteenth-century Polish rabbi Ba'al-Shem-Tov, believed that it was the duty of all Jews to aspire toward *devequt* — "being with God" — in every aspect of their daily lives. Ba'al-Shem-Tov held that true religion was not an ascetic withdrawal from the world but a knowledge of the immanence of God in all creation. The Hasidim placed great emphasis on the inner life of the believer and a close-knit, interdependent community life. Group leadership was provided by the *tzaddiqim,* the Just, or Righteous Ones, and the *wunder-rebbe,* the "miracle-working rabbi." There was also a belief which corresponded closely with what The Man had said; namely that the *tzaddiqim* contained a special "divine spark" and possessed superhuman faculties.

On top of which, let me add a brief historical footnote: Of all the Jewish groups persecuted by the Nazis, it was the

Hasidim that came the closest to being totally wiped out in the Holocaust. Whatever one might think of 'Brax, you had to give him credit for trying.

Hasidism was an attractive theory but, although their rigorous observance of Jewish ritual and the purity of their beliefs was above reproach, they were regarded with less than total enthusiasm by their more liberal Talmudic brethren. Even if groups like the Lubavitchers *were* on the right route to spiritual liberation as defined by The Man, their particular brand of self-denial was hardly likely to lead to the lightning conversion of the average fun-loving atheist.

I thought again of The Man's evasive reply to my question about the Jew's fundamental belief that they were the chosen people and wondered if their persecution throughout history had been the work of 'Brax. Instead of being destined to suffer because they had not recognized Jesus as the Messiah, it could have been because they still possessed — albeit unknowingly — an inner awareness of The Man's true identity and his relationship with the worlds beyond this one.

Was this the hidden truth that 'Brax wanted to suppress? The secret weapon that could bring his carefully constructed dream-world crashing round his head? Had the anti-Semitic measures of the later Roman emperors, the medieval monetary proscriptions against the Jews, the Inquisition, the Cossack-led pogroms in Poland and Russia which had culminated in the creation then the destruction of the ghettos of Eastern Europe, and the final horror of the death camps — had that been the work of Secessionist *einsatz-gruppen?*

And was the orchestrated hostility against the postwar State of Israel, whose prideful intransigence only served to increase the ever-present threat of its total destruction, yet another stage in 'Brax's Final Solution?

Why had the Jews — apart from a few periodic yawns of disinterest — clung doggedly throughout untold centuries to the idea of the One True God when greater and more powerful races — Babylonians, Assyrians, Egyptians, Indians, Greeks, Romans, Celts, Mayas, Aztecs, Norsemen and Teutons — had worshipped overpopulated pantheons of anthropo-morphic deities whose violent, sex-laden lives had provided the material for the world's first soap operas?

Since even our worst enemies would find it hard to deny that we were a creative people, our addiction to monotheism could hardly be ascribed to a lack of invention. It could only be explained by the fact that we Jews had been spiritually on the ball ever since our ancestors began the long march from Atlantis. If that is true, and I am right about 'Brax's part in all this, it goes a long way toward explaining why we have been forced to exchange our prayer shawls for flak jackets and may yet end making a last stand with our backs to the Wailing Wall.

My return to Manhattan on Monday brought an abrupt descent from the world of the spirit into that of the flesh. Some of which belonged to a guy called Ken Myers; a client who I had arranged to have lunch with at *Perigord*. Impressed with my handling of an industrial claim, Myers now wanted me to handle his divorce. I told him it was a pity he hadn't chosen to get divorced before I'd won him the million dollars because he now stood to lose a large slice of it in the settlement. Myers told me that he was so keen to get rid of his wife he'd be happy to give her the whole bundle. But then, he was on his third martini. I reminded him that since he was technically the guilty party, the problem was how to stop her asking for more.

Myers had become pixillated with, of all things, a leggy English showgirl whose father was a retired army major living in Berkshire and who went to Ascot for the races. Her mother had been one of the famed Bluebell girls — whoever they were. The name of this love-object was Edwina. Myers insisted on detailing her youthful anatomy and it was clear from his pain-wracked face that her Barbie Doll waist, boyish ass and athletic thighs were causing him a great deal of distress.

Edwina, in true stage-door tradition, was playing Myers like a marlin on a line. She had blown his mind with a private audition during a ski-lodge weekend at Vail, Colorado, but had refused a repeat performance without a ring and a written contract. His wife, on the other hand, had vowed to take him for everything he had. I learned that Edwina was twenty-three. Ken Myers was over fifty. He said she made him feel young again but his story put years on me. I mentally resolved that if it ever happened to me, I would have my dong cut off and stuffed upright in a sealed pickle jar to remind me of better days. But I couldn't tell him that. What I did was turn down the job with as much tact as I could muster and pick up the tab for lunch.

My conversation with Myers left me feeling vaguely depressed for the rest of the day but it ended with one small triumph. I twisted Miriam's arm and persuaded her to come with me to see my favorite double feature — *Dirty Harry* and *Magnum Force*. Clint may not provide much for the *Cahiers du Cinéma* crowd to agonize over, but for the real cognoscenti this is what it's all about.

"Come on now, be honest," I said, as we came out onto the street. "You've got to admit those were two really great movies."

She looked at me and shook her head. "It's at times like this that I wonder if I'm ever going to be able to do anything with you."

The news that she intended to remodel my character failed to dampen my enthusiasm; or my subsequent, silver-tongued ardor. At least there were no complaints about that. Monday then, finished on a high note. Which was just as well, because Tuesday was a day to remember.

THIRTEEN

I woke at half-past six with a pang of anxiety about the out-come of the case and decided to jog it out of my system. As you've gathered, I didn't have a fixed daily routine but I usually managed to make four days out of seven. It was part of my drive to give up smoking. The trouble was I needed a cigarette after the exercise to make me feel better. The squash, which I made an effort to play on the days I didn't jog, helped me work off my aggression. Football and baseball I got from TV. So much for sports.

As I was on the return leg, heading for the exit on Central Park West near Seventy-fifth Street, a beige Chevy cruised up from behind, matched my pace for a few yards, then pulled ahead and stopped. There are only two kinds of vehicles allowed in this section of the park: those belonging to the service department, and to the police. My stride faltered as I saw Detective Frank Marcello get out from behind the wheel and flag me down. As I trotted up to the car, he opened the door to the rear compartment. My friend Lieutenant Dan Russell was sitting in the back. He beckoned me to join him. Marcello regained his seat behind the wheel and sat with his back against the door where he could see me.

I eyed him then turned to Russell. "What's this all about?"

"I just wanted to have a little talk," said Russell. "You know what offices are like. Telephones, interruptions." He glanced casually out of the window. "I thought you might prefer someplace where we couldn't be overheard."

I wondered what he meant by that but decided not to pursue it. "Is this going to take long?" I asked. "Because I'm due in court this morning. And I have a cab picking me up at eight."

"Relax," replied Russell. "Catch your breath. You can be home from here in five minutes." He lit a cigarette and rolled down the window on his side. He had the air of a man about to play a cat-and-mouse game.

I decided to hurry things along. "What do you want to talk about?"

Russell inspected his cigarette as if he'd never seen one before. "I'm hoping it's *you* who will do the talking, Mr. Resnick. I'd like you to tell me why a lawyer of your standing has felt it necessary to be less than honest with me."

This was the moment I'd been dreading. "About what?"

Russell's voice changed gear. "Don't fuck around, Resnick. You and your lady doctor friend have already make a monkey out of me. I could book you both on a conspiracy charge. You could both end up out on the street. So think about that."

I did. And frankly, although I was worried for Miriam, I was more concerned with my own position. Although we had both abused our professional codes of conduct, what she had done was not that serious. But if I were called to account for my actions to the Bar Association, it could do real damage to my career. I took a deep breath and squared up to Russell. "What is it you want to know?"

Russell's expression became less aggressive but he still didn't relax. I guess he had me figured for a tricky customer. He flicked ash out of the window. "Let me tell you what I know already. That way you won't waste any of your valuable time telling unnecessary lies. One: Dr. Maxwell is assigned to Emergency. She does not handle any ward patients and she is not qualified for psychiatric work. Two: the hospital has no current records of any patient named Yale Sheppard. And three: while psychotic cathexis is an imaginative diagnosis, the Department of Clinical Psychology at Gouverneur Hospital tell me that it's not strictly kosher. You know what I mean?"

"Yes," I said. "But I can explain that."

"Good." Russell pulled a buff envelope from his inside pocket and dropped it into my lap. "Start right here."

I looked at him, then turned the envelope over in my hands.

"Go ahead, open it," said Russell. "I don't want you to miss your cab."

I untucked the flap of the envelope. Inside were four color Polaroids of a naked, rain-washed, bearded man. There were two full-length front and back shots of the bruised, lacerated body, a shot of the head and torso with the forearms laid across the chest, and a close-up of the battered face with its torn scalp and broken nose.

"Take a good look," said Russell. "And tell me who that guy reminds you of."

I leafed through the pictures a couple of times then put them back in the envelope and handed it to Russell. "It's some guy the police found in an alleyway over on the East Side about a couple of weeks ago. I saw the body at Manhattan General when I called to pick up Dr. Maxwell. She happened to be down in the morgue with a pathologist called Wallis."

Russell nodded. "Right. He signed the death certificate. But he tells me that Dr. Maxwell completed the examination. The records show that the body was put in Drawer Eleven. Would it surprise you to learn that Drawer Eleven is now empty?"

I shrugged. "Maybe somebody moved it."

"Yes," said Russell. "Maybe somebody did. The trouble is there's no record of it being shipped to the city morgue. Or anywhere else for that matter. And before you suggest a clerical error, let me tell you that Manhattan General is very careful about such things. Administration would not like it thought that unwanted bodies were being trucked away by dog-food manufacturers." Russell lifted the envelope and waggled it in front of my face. "So how does a man who is as dead as he is manage to (a) get himself a smart lawyer and (b) end up in my office ten days later?"

I gave a nervous laugh. "Wait a minute. Are you trying to tell me you think that corpse is my client?"

Russell looked at Marcello. "What d'you think, Frank?"

Marcello gave me a withering glance. "He's full of bull-shit."

"Okay, Resnick," said Russell. "You've got thirty seconds. Just what the hell is going on?"

What could I tell him? Any more lies would just drive me further into the corner. The only thing left was the truth. But that was even more unbelievable. How could I break the news to them that I was acting as the front man for a time-traveling Messiah? Reading this, you may think it would have been easy. It wasn't. Fear locked the truth in my throat. "Lieutenant," I said, "I'm not giving you any bullshit. But the fact is, I can't even begin to tell you what I'm involved in. It's so fantastic you just wouldn't —"

Russell's eyes suddenly popped wide open. He jolted back in his seat and paled visibly. "How the fuck — ?"

My stomach turned over too. The Man was sitting in the front seat next to Marcello dressed in the familiar brown robe and white headdress. Marcello was flattened against the door with his arms drawn back, his ass a good three inches off the upholstery and his head making a dent in the roof lining.

"Hi, Frank," said The Man. "Sorry — did I startle you?" He put his arm over the back seat, gripped my hand briefly, then smiled at Russell. "Hello, Dan, how's it going?"

"Jeezuss Christ," hissed Russell, shrinking back from the proffered hand.

"That's right," I said. "Now you know what I'm up against."

Marcello slowly subsided into his seat, his eyes fixed on

The Man. "Dan," he croaked, "is there a guy on the seat in front of you dressed like an Arab?"

Russell screwed up his eyes. Almost as if he hoped it might make The Man disappear. "Yeah. It's — it's the guy we saw at the precinct house. Sheppard . . ."

Marcello shook his head. "I still don't believe it."

Russell's eyes flickered between me and The Man. "Come on, Resnick — what is this? How'd he get in the car?"

"Why don't you ask him?" I replied. "He's the only one who knows the answer." I knew I was still in deep trouble but it made me feel better to see someone else going through the wringer. "Go ahead, shake hands with him. He won't bite."

Russell inched his hand out gingerly until it touched The Man's fingers. They shook hands but, when Russell tried to pull away, The Man didn't let go. "Oh, my God, he's real, Frank. Oh, shit — I must be going bananas."

The Man shook his head. "No, Dan. You're not seeing things. This is really happening."

"Well there's one way to find out," said Marcello. "If you're real, and we ain't crazy, we got ourselves a space-man—" He reached into his jacket and suddenly there was this gun in his hand.

"No," I bellowed.

The Man raised his hand and motioned me to be calm. "Put it away, Frank. If you try and shoot me, all you'll end up with is holes in the door. And how are you going to explain that?"

Marcello stared at The Man for a moment, then looked at his gun with a puzzled expression as if he couldn't work out how it had gotten into his hand. Then he slid it back into his shoulder holster.

"Give me your hand, Frank," said The Man. He was still holding on to Russell. He laid his golden hawk-eyes on each of them in turn. "I want both of you to keep quiet about this. Leo and I have work to do. Do you understand?"

Marcello nodded mutely. Russell's eyes glistened with tears. "Yes," he said, through trembling lips.

I was trembling too. *Dear God,* I thought, *don't ever put me on the spot like this again.*

"Okay, fellas, take it easy." The Man let go of their hands. "I'll call if I need you."

"Do that," said Russell. Both he and Marcello had completely relaxed. Not drugged, or hypnotized, or turned into a couple of robots. They just seemed to accept that it was quite in the natural order of things for The Man to suddenly appear on the front seat of their car.

The Man pointed to the envelope containing the Polaroids. "Why don't you let Leo keep those?"

Russell put the envelope into my hands without demur. "You'd better get a move on."

I looked at my watch. "You're right." I got out of my side of the car and nodded goodbye. "See you around . . ." I had no recollection of seeing The Man get out of the car, but when I straightened up, he was standing on the path beside me. I gripped his arm as we walked away from the car. "Thanks for helping me out. Those guys really had me backed into a corner." I grinned. "In fact, I was about to give up and tell them the truth."

"I know," he said. "That's why I thought it would be better coming from me."

"Are they going to be able to keep the news to themselves?"

The Man nodded. "Yes. The whole incident will seem like a dream that you know you've had but the details of which remain just out of reach."

I looked at my watch again. "Listen, I'm sorry, but I'm going to have to run."

"Go ahead," he said. "I'll see you there."

I looked at him uncertainly, then back at Russell's Chevy. It hadn't moved. I broke into a run. When I had gone about fifty yards, I glanced over my shoulder. The Chevy was still there, but The Man had disappeared.

When I let myself into my apartment, I found that he had

made himself at home in my favorite armchair. I opened the hall closet, pulled out the suitcase Miriam had used to collect his clothes from the Mayflower, and handed it to him on my way to the bathroom. "Do me a favor. Change into those."

"Do I have to?" he said.

"It would help," I replied. "A lady called Mrs. Perez — whom I believe you know — is probably out this very minute, pounding the sidewalks in the hope of catching sight of you. And there's a reporter from Channel Eight on your trail. A slim, twenty-five-year-old agnostic who cut her milk teeth on rawhide and goes by the name of Gale McDonald. She knows about the treatment you gave Mrs. Perez, and she's also very impressed with the statue. If we're not careful, this whole story could end up going nationwide. Do you get the picture?"

"I'm beginning to," he said.

"Good." I turned on the shower. "If you will now excuse me, I have five minutes in which to shower, shave, get dressed, and get downstairs before my cab arrives."

"You've got ten," he said. "Polish Henry is out sick. Jake's picking you up this morning, and he's running five minutes late."

He was right, of course. I pulled my damp hair into some semblance of a part, pocketed my wallet, keys and loose change, and grabbed my Samsonite. "Okay, stay here until I call you. There's some wine in the cupboard next to the refrigerator." I patted him on the shoulder as I hurried past. "Nice to have you back."

Now you are not going to believe this but — we lost the case. And not only did we lose it; the judge awarded costs to Cleveland Glass. For a minute or so I was completely speechless then, after going into a huddle with the Delaware team, I gave notice of our intention to appeal. As I gathered up my papers I found that, for the second time that day, I was shaking like a leaf. I had been totally convinced that we had everything sewn up. And so, up to that moment, had the legal boys from Delaware. Mel Donaldson, like the shmuck he was, immediately did a fast turnabout and told me he'd felt all along that I had been overly optimistic about our chances of winning but had deferred to my judgment even though — get this — he had been unhappy from the outset about my tactical handling of the case.

I didn't bleed too much. If we'd won, he'd have been the first to grab the credit. It wasn't the money they were worried about. Delaware was a rich corporation and the costs, though sizable, would only cause a hiccup in their annual accounts. No — the real problem lay in the fact that Delaware liked to think of its executives as winners, and the pressure to live up to that image was relentless. To have returned triumphant would have totally absolved them from any feelings of guilt they had acquired by screwing around on the company's time in the big city. Losing only served to compound it. Tough. I felt I'd been screwed too.

I called my apartment from outside the courtroom. The Man answered. "I suppose you know what's happened," I said with some bitterness. After all, he could have told me.

"Yes. Don't take it too badly."

His casual manner made me explode. "How the hell am I supposed to take it?! I know I told you to hold back on the miracles but — goddammit, you're supposed to be on my side!"

"I am," he replied. "But what has that got to do with it?"

"Everything," I said, simmering down a little. "Come on, you know what's been happening in the last two weeks. How the hell am I supposed to concentrate on anything with you on my back?"

He gave a quick laugh. "Is that the way you see it?"

Now I felt embarrassed at shooting my mouth off. "Look, you know what I mean. I'm like a guy with eleven holes in the dike and only ten fingers. At the very least you could have used a little influence to make sure I won the case. I mean, it's only fair."

"*Fair?* Leo, the case isn't important. What you do with your life is. I'll speak to you later." And with that he hung up on me. Great. That was all I needed. Jesus Christ telling me I was in the wrong job.

Midway through the afternoon, Linda told me that she had seen Donaldson and Hunnacker, his chief sidekick, coming out of Joe Gutzman's office. If they were avoiding me, it could only mean that they had come to lodge a complaint. I worked on, waiting for Joe's summons. It came half an hour later.

"Surprise decision," said Joe.

I agreed, and we reviewed the case in some detail and speculated on the reasons for the adverse ruling. "I'm sure we can get it reversed if we go for the appeal." And I explained to Joe that I had made the formal application right after the judgment but that, during the funereal lunch I'd had with the Delaware legal team, Donaldson had begun to cool off to the idea.

Joe shrugged. "Mel seems to think that you didn't give it your best shot."

"The man is an asshole," I replied. As you've probably gathered, I like to win too.

"I'm inclined to agree," said Joe. "However, he asked me if Dick, or maybe Wilkie, could handle the appeal."

Dick, was Dick Schonfeld, the second senior partner. Corinne Wilkie was his thirty-year-old assistant. She'd been breathing down my neck ever since she joined the firm a couple of years ago.

I reached for a cigarette then remembered that Joe didn't like people smoking in his office. "What did you tell him?"

"I told him that it was not our policy to switch horses in midstream," said Joe. "If they don't want to stick with you . . ." He completed the sentence with his shoulders.

Delaware's decision to go over my head was no surprise. Joe had handled their business since they'd started with two brick sheds and a subcontract from the Defense Department at the outbreak of the Korean war. When I began understudying Joe, I'd been one of four young attorneys vying for the main chance. My work with Delaware had helped me claw my way over the backs of the other three to Joe's right hand and, in the fullness of time, I had inherited them as clients. Joe had maintained his close personal links with the family that controlled the main board, and he held some of their blue chip stock. So I was keenly aware that his decision to back me was a remarkable and touching gesture of solidarity. And it made me feel lousy.

Joe leaned his elbows on the desk and slowly rubbed his hands together. "I'm sure it's possible to straighten this one out. Why don't you sit down and draft an analysis of the arguments in this case and how you think we can make them stick if it goes to appeal? If you can let me have that by the weekend, I can go through it, then we can put our heads together and —"

It gave me no pleasure to shaft my benefactor, but I had to say it. "Joe — I'm sorry — but I can't do it. I haven't changed my mind about Donaldson but maybe it *is* time they had a new attorney. Corinne would be fine for this. She's sharp, and she'd like nothing better than the chance to pick up a dropped ball."

Joe aimed one of his famous quizzical looks at me. "Leo — are you feeling okay? Or is there something you're not telling me?"

I chewed on his question and decided to come clean. "I think I need some time off, Joe."

"Leo," he said. "You're family. Trouble I should know about."

I shook my head with genuine regret. "I — I can't put it into words. And it's nothing you can help me with. I'm sorry."

Joe accepted my reply with a wry grimace. "Well, if you change your mind . . ."

Poor Joe. I knew what was going through his head. David, his son, had flown to Israel to enlist without even leaving a note. I was consoled by the thought that he probably knew that, at the ripe old age of thirty-five, no one was going to stick me in the seat of a Skyhawk.

"You'll be the first to know," I said, trying to sound as if I meant it.

Joe tried to look as if he believed me. "I ran into Ken Myers on Monday night. He told me you'd turned down his divorce case."

Myers was the man with show-girlitis. "I told him he was behaving like an asshole and advised him to stay married," I said. "On top of which, he got a free lunch. What's he complaining about?"

"Your attitude," said Joe. "Suddenly everybody who wants to do business with you is an asshole. So tell me — what does that make you?"

"Good question," I replied. "Maybe I'm beginning to crack up. That's why I'd like to tidy my desk in the next few days then take a couple of weeks off."

Joe's face reflected his genuine concern. "Take whatever time you need. But do me a favor. See a doctor."

I grinned. "I'm going out with one."

Joe threw his hands up in despair. "Leo — nobody was ever cured of anything by kissing a doctor's *tusch*. Go and see Sol Friedman."

"Okay, I will." Friedman was Joe's longtime friend and physician and one of the top guys in New York.

"And have him bill the office," said Joe. "It can come out of the overheads. And I want you to promise to call me at home if — well, you know . . ."

I nodded. "Yes. Thanks, Joe."

We both stood up. Joe came around from behind his desk, took my hand and held it all the way to the door. Almost as if he thought I might not make it unaided.

I opened the door with my free hand. "Listen — I appreciate your concern. And I want you to know that I'm not planning to try and solve whatever is wrong by running away."

Joe gave me a sad, knowing smile and patted me on the back as he saw me out.

I got back to my apartment around seven. The Man was sitting with his feet up in front of the TV set with a glass of wine in his hand and a bottle within easy reach. He was dressed in the clothes he'd bought with Linda.

He looked at me over the back of the sofa. "How did it go?"

"Not too badly," I said. "I feel marginally better than when I called you this morning."

He smiled. "Good . . ."

I dumped my case, peeled off my jacket and tie, and helped myself to a glass of wine. The Man switched off the TV set with the remote-control handset. I raised my glass to him as I sat down, and drank deep. "Where have you been — Jerusalem?"

He stretched, and sat up straight. "Yes."

"What's happening back there?"

"The Sanhedrin is still trying to cover up what's happened. The four soldiers who were guarding the tomb have been persuaded to change their story. Instead of the earlier wild talk about angels and blinding lights, they are now saying that they were overpowered by a group of my followers — who then made off with my body."

"There are a lot of people who still think that was probably what happened," I said. "Tell me — why did you just appear to the twelve Apostles — and to that other group, the, uhh —"

"The seventy-two Followers of The Way?"

"Yes," I said. "Why didn't you appear before Caiaphas, the High Priest, and the Council of the Sanhedrin? It would have made things a lot easier all round."

The Man shook his head. "It wouldn't have done any good. The Sanhedrin, as part of the ruling establishment, had reached an accommodation with the Romans. If they had embraced my message and incorporated it into the official doctrine, they'd have killed it stone dead. Nothing kills faith quicker than an educated mind. Scholarship prevents a man from acquiring true knowledge. Reason and logic are human faculties that were developed to make sense of the external world —"

"That is controlled by 'Brax," I interjected.

"Right," he nodded. "And 'Braxian logic cannot explain how I can be here, and also in first-century Jerusalem. It cannot cope with the questions raised by the concept of simultaneity. 'Braxian reason tells you that there are no such things as angels, miracles or timeless, dimensionless worlds beyond this one. 'Braxian rationality requires physical, scientific proof of existence as the basis for all belief. But Man's intellect, his intuition, his instinctive emotions enable him to make that leap that takes him beyond Time and Space. To experience God, or The Presence — or whatever name you choose to give *That Which Is*. To know the 'otherness' which is Man's true self and to which he belongs and will one day return. The untutored mind of a man that the scholars dismiss as ignorant can make that leap. So can the unspoiled mind of a child."

"Is that why you said, *'Suffer the little children to come unto me'?*" I asked.

"Yes." He smiled. "I can see you've been doing your homework. It's important to bear in mind that my mission was to free the Ain-folk. But that could only be achieved by first raising the level of awareness in each and every one of you. Your minds had to be unlocked before the Ain-folk could be roused from their drugged torpor. My words were to be the key. The message had to be spread by a revolutionary, subversive movement because it needed the fervor, the impetus and self-sacrifice that only a dedicated minority could provide. Whose evangelical zeal would carry the message beyond the borders of Israel and set the whole world on fire."

"And that was what you meant when you said that the Jews no longer had an exclusive," I said.

"That's right . . ." He leaned forward and refilled his glass. "Under the Sadducees, Palestine had become a theocracy. The priests were like the ayatollahs of Iran. The Temple controlled the money supply and the economy. It was like Fort Knox and the New York Stock Exchange rolled into one. And the people who ran it, through the Sanhedrin, ran the country. They were conservatives in every sense of the word. And they had allowed the flame of awareness that lay at the core of Judaism to be smothered with the dead weight of ritual and rigid observance of the Torah. True belief had become lost in the growing obsession with the minutiae of interpretation. The outward, measurable display of piety took preference over inner enlightenment. And among those Jews who were opposed to the collaboration between the rich ruling classes and the occupying power, the age-old struggle against 'Brax had become politicized. The long-awaited Messiah was no longer seen as the Heaven-sent instrument which would secure their spiritual liberation. The hopes of the revolutionaries were focused on the emergence of a priest-king who would combine the spiritual authority of Aaron and the generalship of David — who would lead the nation to victory against the oppressive *earthly* power of Rome."

I smiled at him. "I can understand why they were a little disappointed in you."

He smiled back. "They were doubly disappointed. I was anathema to the religious establishment and the business community because I challenged their authority and attacked their materialist philosophy, and I was regarded as worse than useless by the anti-establishment factions. Disparate groups like the Maccabees, the Sicarii, and the Zealots. And the Pharisees, who held the middle ground. The war they sought against the Romans was of no concern to me *or* the Empire. Ours was a struggle that was old before the world began. The only people on whom I made any real impact were the *'amme ha-'aretz* — the 'people of the land.' The unwashed peasants. The poor, impoverished sons of Canaan who had to work from dawn till dusk and were looked down upon because they neglected their ritual prayers and observances."

"And didn't pay their tithes to the Temple," I added.

He brushed my observation aside. "The Temple had more money than it knew what to do with."

I lit a cigarette and sat back. "So . . . what news of the Empire?"

The Man frowned. "How do you mean?"

"Well —" I hesitated to ask a question to which the answer might be bad news, but I was now committed. "— have you, uhh, had any confirmation that they know what's happening? Have they mailed you a new set of mission orders? Or are you finally going to come clean with me and tell me what's going on?"

He gazed at me silently over the top of his glass.

"I mean, it was great the way you bailed me out, this morning," I continued. "But please — don't tell me it was another accident. That really would be stretching coincidence too far."

"Yes, I guess it would . . ." He set his glass down. "It's really very simple —"

"Oh, really?" I said.

He smiled. "No, I mean that. Do you remember when we met at the beginning of last week after that elevator business and we talked about 'Brax — and I told you his forces were waiting in the wings when the rescue fleet arrived in the skies above first century Jerusalem?"

"I'm not likely to forget," I said.

"Well," he continued, "they weren't there to try and stop me going home. Nothing would have pleased them more. They were standing by in case we had some other move planned."

"Which, knowing you," I said darkly, "was more than possible."

He bit back a smile. "Do you remember our very first talk up at Sleepy Hollow — when I mentioned the power grid that once linked the Empire and the galaxy primes?"

"Yes," I said. "It was smashed by 'Brax after his breakout from the Netherworld and for the past hundred million years or so you've had Celestial linemen out trying to repair it."

He nodded. "That's right. It hasn't been easy. After 'Brax swept back into power his forces were dispatched to the farthest reaches of the cosmos. As the nature of the physical universe changed under their malevolent influence, we began to encounter what radio hams call 'signal impedance.' You may be able to visualize the problem better if you imagine The Power of The Presence being beamed out like a wireless signal and getting fouled up in an increasingly impenetrable cloud of static." He paused and sipped his wine thoughtfully. "Cloud is perhaps the wrong word. I don't want you to think of it as a towering mass of cu-nim hovering just beyond the Milky Way. It's a dark gray veil. A virulent miasma enveloping everything. Filling this room. Clouding your inner eye. Clogging your brain. And what we're trying to do is punch a hole through it to let the good news in."

"You're winning," I said. "I got the message."

"Good. So — to cut a long story short, the final phase of the Bethlehem mission included setting up a power transmission from the Empire to recharge Earth. In the way you boost the batteries of a car. But because of this problem of 'signal impedance' the rescue fleet was strung out in a line to act as relay stations for the beam, thus keeping it 'clean' and at maximum strength." He hesitated. "I was to be the final stage in the relay. The power was to be earthed through me."

Aha, I thought. *The Jewish Connection*. "Let me get this straight — was this operation to recharge the planet?"

"Yes."

I frowned. "What does the Earth need the power for?"

"To stay alive," he replied. "Not just to revive the Ainfolk. It's the life-force that permeates the natural world. Humans, animals, birds, fishes, insects, flowers, grass, rocks, trees, the earth, sea and sky all possess it in varying degrees. Earth is more than just a spinning ball of sea-girt rock, gift-wrapped in clouds. It's the mother of all life upon it. A conscious, living thing that holds within itself a memory of its past. It remembers everything that ever happened, records every emotion. And like you, it feels joy, sadness, pain, anger. It gets sick and purges itself. It was young, and will grow old."

"I never thought of the Earth as being alive," I said.

He smiled. "Have you never felt an inexplicable affinity with a rock you've picked up at random on a beach? Ever experienced a sense of place — the emotional charge stored in old houses, of battles lost and won recorded by the stones under your feet? Or discovered some spot where you feel an overwhelming rapport with the earth and sky? A sense of — unity?"

"Yes, I think I know what you're getting at," I said. "What Carlos Castaneda calls 'power places.' Is this what was meant by those words in the Book — *I will lift up mine eyes to the hills, O Lord, from whence cometh my help'?"*

He nodded. "There is a power-gradient that runs along the slopes of hills and mountains. And it was the earlier knowledge of these forces that degenerated into the idea of mountain-gods. There are other places too where the lines of force converge. When the whole system was working properly, these sites acted as cosmic terminals." He smiled. "What you might call Celestial gas stations."

"You mean like Glastonbury, in England?"

"That was one of them."

"Popular legend has you tied into the place." I said. "Joseph of Arimathea is believed to have taken the chalice you used at the Last Supper to Glastonbury where he and his party were taken under the protection of a Welsh king, Arviragus. Other mystical traditions link you with King Arthur, the search for the Holy Grail, Saint George and the Dragon. I'm told there's even a hymn which poses the question — *'And did those feet, in ancient times, walk upon England's mountains green?'"*

"They did," he replied. "But much as I admire your scholarship, we're getting off the point. As I said, the plan was to set up a power transmission but, in order to reduce interference to a minimum, we had to try and draw off 'Brax's forces from the point in time where it was going to happen."

"I'm beginning to get the picture," I said. "*You* were the decoy."

"That's right," he nodded. "As I was the only one who

could upset their plans, 'Brax had designated me as the prime target for surveillance. If I moved, they were bound to follow."

It finally dawned on me. "So it's not tag you're playing, but hide-and-seek. When you turned up at Sleepy Hollow with that stunned look on your face, you were lying to me. The lost time-traveler bit was just an act."

I could tell from his face that I'd said the wrong thing.

His eyes seemed to catch fire. "I've never lied to you, Leo. When I made those first two trips through the time-tracks, the Empire's plans for this part of the mission had not been revealed to me."

"So — the time-traveling was set up to look like an accident," I concluded.

The Man's face softened. "The crews of the rescue fleet still think it is. And because 'Brax is monitoring all communications between our ships and the Empire, their genuine confusion is helping to cover my tracks."

It was too much. "No wonder this war has been going on for two hundred million years . . ." I sat back and tried to slot this new piece of information into the cosmic jigsaw, then mentally tossed it aside. "Let me ask you something. You're into your second war, up to your armpits in trouble, wherever you look you've got problems — I just don't understand why you guys have to put up with it. If The Presence made 'Brax and all the other fallen angels, why doesn't he just un-make them?"

He digested my question. "It's not quite that simple. To do it, you'd have to undo everything."

I refilled my glass. "You mean — the Apocalypse?"

"You'd need to destroy more than the Earth," he said.

"The — universe?" I ventured.

"It wouldn't even end there," he replied.

It was a marvelously surreal situation. Out on the streets, people were worrying away at their lives as they made their way into town for a good time, or tried to get back to their brick or clapboard burrows, and here I was, sitting in a fourth-floor apartment on Seventy-fifth Street with The Man, casually discussing the disposal of the cosmos.

"How d'you mean — 'it wouldn't end there'?"

He spread his hands. "Because when this universe dies, the whole cycle starts all over again."

I raised my glass to him. "In that case, next time around, just count me out."

"I'll see what I can do," he said, returning my toast. "Let me quote you a few words from some unpublished material. Drawn from the elusive New Testament text that Biblical scholars have labeled 'Q.' "

From the German word *Quelle;* meaning "source."

His voice took on a new resonance and it was several seconds before I realized that he was speaking to me in Ancient Hebrew which, once again, I understood perfectly. But there was more to it than that. I knew, with absolute certainty, that this was the voice of Elijah, Moses and Abraham. The voice that had entered into them in the high places; whose vibrant echo had traveled down a three-thousand-year-long corridor of time and now filled my mind.

"Fear not, Wayfarer, but listen and be of good cheer for in Your Beginning, You were beyond Time and Space and neither shall hold you in thrall. For both came into being with the sundering of the Eye of The Presence, the Primal Fire which gave birth to the World Below. From that moment Recorded Time began and will continue until the far-flung realms of the Star-Kings and all that lies within and without returns to the point whence All Began, fusing into a single, incandescent mass of unimaginable density and brilliance. Yet None shall be crushed, and None shall be blinded for All shall be as Light and that Light shall shine forth from the Face of The Presence and all of Time Past shall be as a single heartbeat of Created Man. Then shall All begin again, and so it shall continue until The Work is as perfect as Its Maker. Only then shall the Bonds of Space and Time be broken. The World Below shall be as One with the World Above and All shall come to Glory."

The Man's words recalled the currently fashionable theory of the expanding universe that would, in time, collapse in upon itself, terminating its life in a gigantic thermonuclear holocaust. Were these the legendary hell fires to which unredeemed matter would be consigned while the Elect, freed from 'Brax's grip, rose clear of the ashes?

I tried to grasp the concept but it was too overwhelming. How many universes had been trashed before this one, which we had barely begun to comprehend? How many more would explode into life before the required degree of perfection had been achieved? All this was a far cry from the naïve, devotional simplicity with which The Man's life had been presented for popular consumption. The basic *"Blessed are the pure in heart"* bit still came through but, when one started to think about the supracosmic scale of the operation that The Man had outlined, the Christian claim that God, or Whoever, had sent his one and only Son to help pull us up by the bootstraps suddenly became inconceivable — and ludicrously impractical.

Were we the only breed in need of salvation? What about the mysterious Mannish that were out there somewhere? Among the numberless life-bearing planets circling the billions of stars in the billions of galaxies that lay beyond our own? If The Man came, as he claimed, from beyond Time and Space, from what had been termed the *Ungrund,* he could only be one of an infinite number of manifestations of the transcendent power of God. What we Jews termed the *Shekinah* and The Man referred to as The Presence. In saying this, I was not trying to destroy the widely held belief that he sat on the right hand of God. There just had to be more to it than that. He had already hinted at a hierarchical relationship in which Michael and Gabriel were of lower rank. And if one was to believe his story about the fleet that was now on station in the heavens above first-century Jerusalem, then he was clearly a top gun. Someone that the Empire had gone to a great deal of trouble to rescue — and whom 'Brax took very seriously indeed.

All well and good. But this new explanation still left me with several worrying loose ends. "Tell me," I said, "if the idea is to give 'Brax the slip, why take the risk of coming back here again? Especially since they knew you were here last week."

"It's not so much where I move to, but when," he replied. "They're bound to catch up with me eventually. The trick is to keep them guessing."

"But why keep homing in on me?" I insisted.

"Leo," he said, "has it occurred to you that you might have homed in on me? Don't you find it strange that when I landed in that alleyway on the East Side, none of the policemen who handled my body, or people at the hospital like Wallis, reacted to my presence. Yet you knew who I was."

"Not true," I replied. "It was Miriam who put the idea into my head."

He nodded. "And you rejected it. 'Braxian logic told you that it was impossible. But another part of your mind accepted the possibility of my existence and my presence in your world. And when I turned up at Sleepy Hollow, you recognized me."

My training as a lawyer got the better of me. "I admit I accepted that you were actually there — and that I wasn't going crazy."

He chuckled. "That's the bit I always find hard to understand. Why should believing in me be regarded as a sign of insanity?"

"Aww, jeez — what a question," I groaned. "Listen, you're just passing through. I have to live in that big wide world out there. From where I'm standing, God is, at best, an agreeable notion. And if he really *does* exist then he's got a lot of explaining to do. Like, for instance, why he left you out on a limb two thousand years ago."

He flagged me down. "There was a reason for all that. It was part of the mission."

"Okay, maybe it was," I said. "In which case I look forward to hearing about it. And perhaps you can also explain why it is that whenever people get themselves organized into a church with any kind of power structure, they always end up by giving religion a bad name. That goes for the guys selling awareness too. It's all a con game. The hustlers at the top cream off a fortune in cash and real estate, and the dummies at the bottom end up with empty pockets and a begging bowl."

"That's true," said The Man. "But you have to remember that 'Brax is doing his damnedest to turn people away from me. Let me give you the word on religion. There have been, and there will be, a lot of people who claim to have been given the power to preach The Word. Don't believe them. When you meet someone who is filled with The Power of The Presence, you'll know it without them having to say a word. James, John and Peter knew it when I came to them by the Sea of Galilee. You knew it up at Sleepy Hollow. The world is full of liars trying to sell you the soft option. Telling you that it's okay to go on hustling your way though life providing you go to church on Sunday. What you might call the 'Screw-you-Buster' brand of Christianity. The scenic route to God." He smiled and shook his head. "It's a dead end. There is only one True Path, and The Way is hard. Even so, you must beware of other false messiahs who will tell you that you have to renounce all material possessions in order to be saved. I can't argue with that. Too many people are crushed by the excess baggage they're carrying. By all means make an effort to shed the things of this world, but before you hand over your life savings, check the preacher's bank account. If he's richer, or lives in better style than the poorest member of his congregation, keep a tight hold on your wallet and run."

I nodded approvingly. "It's a pity you can't appear and say all this when one of these con artists is filling Yankee Stadium with their faithful subscribers."

The Man smiled again. "That's not my style. I never went in for preaching to big crowds."

I must say that surprised me. "What about the five thousand you fed with seven loaves and five fishes? Or was it four thousand, five loaves and only two fishes? I keep getting them mixed up."

"You're not the only one," he said. "The short answer is — it didn't happen. The original story concerned seven loaves, five fishes and four thousand people. But it was a code message for what you might call 'initiates.' The seven loaves and five fishes refer to the disciples. Five of whom were fishermen. You've probably already guessed that the twelve disciples were meant to symbolize the twelve trapped Ain-folk. The breaking up of the loaves and fishes into fragments to nourish the four thousand represented the fragmenting of the Ain-folk and their absorption into their multiple human hosts. As food enables the body to live, so their spirit-entities gave life to the soul."

"What about the fragments that were left over?" I asked, remembering the words in John's Gospel.

"Another code message," he said. "But this time, it referred to the rescue of the Ain-folk. The final liberation." He closed his eyes as he recalled the relevant passage: " '. . . *he said unto his disciples, Gather up the fragments that remain, that nothing be lost. Therefore they gathered them together, and filled twelve baskets . . .* ' " He opened his eyes. "And if I can paraphrase the next verse — '*This is the truth that I was sent to bring into the world.*' It's all there, Leo. You just have to look for it."

I nodded. "I'll have to read through it again. So — the twelve filled baskets represent the reassembled Ain-folk. But why all the double-talk? Why keep it a secret? Surely the whole idea was to get the message through to as many people as possible."

"Of course it was. But you must understand two things. First — we were working on a much longer time-scale than you appear to envisage. What the church calls my Ministry and Crucifixion took place not quite two thousand years ago. If you set that in the context of a war that has already lasted two hundred millions years . . ."

"Yeah . . ." I said. "I see what you mean."

"And second — what I had to say was not appropriate for mass audiences. In those days, there were no megaphones or public address systems. But even if I could have made myself heard, there is always someone on the edge of the crowd who gets it wrong. In any case, I couldn't talk to the *'amme ha-'aretz* as I'm talking to you. I had to keep it simple to prevent the message being garbled in transmission. So I adopted the storytelling forms that our people have used since they sat around the camp fires of Abraham. Many of those parables found their way into the Book. But there were many things I said more directly to the disciples in private."

"Did you pick them because they, uhh — had a higher level of awareness?" I asked.

He rolled his bottom lip. "I recruited them for several reasons. I suppose you could say they were receptive but — they all needed help."

"Was it difficult?"

He eyed me. Remembering. "It wasn't supposed to be. After all, I hadn't come to say anything that you didn't know already."

"You mean because you were not talking to us but to the Ain-folk *inside* us . . ."

"Yes," he said. "But 'Brax had made it impossible for me to reach them on what you might call the 'Celestial wavelength.'The bond between each Ain-folk fragment and its host body was now so tight, I could not make direct contact. I had to get into your heads first and open up the other channels into your mind. But I couldn't blast my way in on a shock wave of sound like some rock star screaming through two-thousand-watt speakers. It had to be done in a whisper." He fixed me with his eyes. "You see, Leo — the deepest truths cannot be communicated in the same way that you tell people the time, or what's for dinner. They have to be discovered. True knowledge comes from within. And by that I mean an awareness and understanding of the ultimate reality as opposed to external reality. That's why the word 'insight' is so aptly descriptive. Teaching is an unlocking process. But before the doors of perception can be opened, the mind has to be engaged. Tuned in. Switched on —"

"By drugs?" I said.

"No," said The Man. "Drugs only stimulate biological brain functions. The sensory distortions of a psychedelic trip do not lead to enlightenment. And any claims that it does are bogus. You can't mainline your way to the Ultimate Principle. The only sure path is through contemplation."

"Yes, well — I've given it a whirl," I said. "But there aren't many people who are able to sit around all day with their legs crossed."

"That's true," replied The Man. "But as a result, most people's minds shut down in early childhood and they sleep-walk through the rest of their lives —"

"Rather like the way I used to drive before I got the Porsche," I interjected. "I would arrive at Point B and suddenly realize that my last conscious memory was of leaving Point A. I'd driven the whole way in a kind of trance."

He nodded. "Most people's lives are like those car journeys of yours — boring and predictable. That's why you need to engage the mind. Preach from a soapbox on a street corner and people will walk right past you. But whisper a secret in someone's ear and tell them to guard it with their life . . ."

" 'Knowledge is power,' " I said, quoting the old adage.

"Francis Bacon," said The Man. "Very interesting man. I met him on the way here."

I let it pass.

"But," he continued, "if you offer to tell a man a secret that is also a mystery, then you've really got him interested. It's no good handing out the answers on a plate. The words just go in one ear and out the other. 'Brax knows this. First he created the spoken word to stop people communicating with each other, and now he has engineered the information explosion that has rocked the planet. He rules through the tyranny of the media. You now have TV, radio and newspaper coverage of the world but what has happened? Books and magazines pour off the presses like so many boxes of popcorn and are consumed just as mindlessly. People watch without seeing, they listen without hearing, they read without understanding. Knowledge has become just another product that is packaged and marketed like soap. And just as detergents are choking your rivers, so the garbage that is being pumped into your head through your eyes and ears is polluting your mind. Silting up the channels that lead into the crystal-clear stream of cosmic consciousness."

I had the feeling he was right but — short of a thermonuclear war — there was no way we could stop it now. Unless we turned to God for help. But in a way, that was just as dangerous because, if we didn't all speak with one voice, we could end by tearing each other apart like a pack of mad dogs.

"Let me ask you another question," I said. "I know that my 'Braxian logic may prevent me from ever understanding, but it's been worrying me. If, as you say, time is linear but also simultaneous — so that past, present and future all coexist — it follows that every event is predestined."

"Yes, it is," he said.

I took a deep breath. "So that means I didn't have any choice about whether I went downtown to get you out of jail. And in the same way, the disciples didn't have any choice whether they followed you or not. But if everything is already worked out — and has already happened —"

"Wrong," he interjected. "Nothing has happened. It is all still happening."

"Okay," I said. "It doesn't alter the fact that nothing can be changed. At some point farther along the linear time-track, in what Isaac Asimov christened the 'up-when,' 'Brax or the Empire is in the process of coming out on top. The victory celebrations are already taking place. Am I right?"

"Yes," he said. "You look confused."

I reached for my glass of wine. "It's your time-traveling that's bugging me. You're here now in the twentieth century and, from what you've said, you've obviously stopped off in-between here and first-century Jerusalem. So you must know how 'Brax fouls things up after you leave the Apostles to get on with the job. But if you *know* that — why don't you stop it before it happens and save yourself all these problems?"

"That's a good point," he said. "But you happen to have overlooked something. Way back at the beginning when we first started to talk about this, I compared the centuries of linear time to the pages contained between the covers of a book. With the beginning, middle and end existing simultaneously. And here we are on page nineteen eighty-one of one of the numberless chapters, sharing a glass of wine in your apartment while we wait for Miriam. Both of you, and all the other characters in the book, are living your lives line by line, page by page. But even though you know that your life is predestined it doesn't change anything —"

"You mean because I was predestined to acquire that knowledge?" I said. With a feeling that our conversation was turning full circle.

"Exactly," he replied. "And like all the other characters, you will either accept the idea or rebel against it, and go on making conscious decisions to change your life-situation or just drift with the tide. It's all down in the book. And that's why *I* can't alter the course of events. You see, this is where the Christians got it all wrong. I was not God, or The Presence — or whatever you want to call the author of this *roman fleuve*. I am from the Empire, yes. I come from beyond Time and Space. But I also happen to be another of the characters in the book. Who enters the story at the beginning of this chapter with his birth at a place called Bethlehem, drops out thirty-four pages later, travels forward in time, making the odd brief appearance on the way, then returns again in a major role near the end."

I held on tight to my glass as my brain tried to grapple with this new revelation. "Wait a minute, there's something wrong here. I accept that this life-between-the-covers-of-a-book idea is just an analogy but, if you logic it through, how can you — as one of the characters — know anything about the person who's written it?"

"Very easily," he said. "It's a well-known fact that all authors put something of themselves into the characters they create."

There really was no answer to that.

And I could not argue that it was impossible for the future to coexist with the present. There had been too many well-authenticated cases of specific predictions ranging from events a century or more in the up-when, by people like Nostradamus, and uncannily accurate short-range seers like Swedenborg. Later, I dipped into some other books and found that a noted Christian luminary, Saint Thomas Aquinas, had formulated a similar proposition: namely that "to God, all Time is eternally present." And Calvin had come to the same conclusion.

But in order for it to work — or rather, to satisfy my earthbound logic — 'Brax would also have to be one of the *dramatis personae* and not an unfettered external agency. It tied in with those much-quoted lines of Shakespeare's — "All the world's a stage / And all the men and women merely players."And I couldn't help wondering, as I reflected on our conversation, whether this was the fundamental truth which lay behind the opening lines of Saint John's Gospel — *"In the beginning was the Word, and the Word was with God, and the Word was God."* If this was so, and if one took into account The Man's disclosures about the birth and endless rebirth of the universe, it was clear that we and the whole of world history were a relatively minor incident in just one of an infinite number of drafts of an unpublished work.

I turned aside from this daunting prospect and cheered myself up with some more fruit of the vine. "So — does this mean that the issue is still in doubt?"

"In this chapter it is," said The Man. "That's why it's important that The Word is passed to this present age in a way people can understand."

"And is —" I hesitated. "— is that what you want me to do?"

He smiled that quiet infuriating smile. "Leo — I'm just here to explain the way things are. It has to be your decision."

I put my glass down and clawed air. "How can it be!?

You've just told me that my part has already been written! Whatever I decide to do has been already *decided!*"

"Yes, that's true," he said. "But now you're pursuing logic to the point of absurdity. You cannot have a system where every individual has total freedom of choice. Your decisions will always be influenced by factors beyond your control because each choice you make between alternative courses of action automatically limits the choices available to others. And the decisions made by others have a cumulative effect on the course of your own life. Economic, social or emotional pressures. The strengths and weaknesses of your own personality. Physical and mental factors influenced by heredity and environment. Always remember you cannot choose to be who you are. By the nature of your birth you have no control over your genetic makeup and are unable to alter the circumstances of your early childhood. All you can do is to work toward a realization and acceptance of the true nature of your being. When you achieve that, you will realize that free will is an illusion, cunningly woven by 'Brax to make you think that you are master of your own little universe."

It was unreal. A classic Catch-22 situation.

The Man sensed my mental disarray and raised his glass to me with a smile. "Just let it happen."

I didn't reply. What was the point? The Man knew exactly what I was thinking. However much we might kick against the idea of predestination, we had no choice but to go along with it. Because until we got to the bottom of our particular page, we couldn't tell how our lives were going to turn out. Our creator had cleverly arranged for each of us to experience the agony of choice, and the sweet or bitter consequences of our actions. And he had also given us the option to accept or reject the notion of his controlling presence.

FOURTEEN

MIRIAM turned up at my apartment just after nine. I took her coat and she gave me another of those chaste pecks on the mouth. I can only think she was trying to compensate for going overboard the night before.

"I brought a pizza." She thrust it at me and went in to greet The Man.

I put some plates and the pizza in the oven to warm, uncorked another bottle of Valpollicella and picked up a glass for Miriam then, as soon as I got a chance to butt in, I told her about my encounter with Russell and Marcello and showed her the color Polaroids the cops had taken of The Man.

She studied them in silence then handed them back. "I wonder how they knew you went jogging in the park?"

"I've been trying not to think about it," I said. "It means they must have been watching the apartment. They could have talked to the janitor. On the other hand, I may have had someone on my tail since we walked out of the Seventh Precinct. You too."

"Uhhh . . ." said Miriam. "I hadn't thought of that."

I shrugged. "They've obviously been asking questions. In fact the more you go into it, the worse it gets. The fact that Russell decided to check up on you means that he never swallowed our story. If so, why did he let us off the hook?"

Miriam shook her head. "You're being too devious again.

It's equally possible that Russell could have been telling someone about what happened. Let's face it — a nut who thinks he's the Risen Christ makes a good bar story. And during the discussion, someone could have queried my diagnosis. Psychotic cathexis may sound impressive to a layman but it wouldn't fool anyone in the profession."

"But how did he get hold of the pictures?" I insisted. "The Man was found in the Seventeenth Precinct."

"Leo," said Miriam, "if he checked up on me, it wouldn't be hard for him to work back from there. Come on, you know what these guys are like once they start picking away at something. Relax. It's all over. The Man fixed it this morning." She turned to him. "Right?"

"Yes," he nodded. "You can forget about Russell."

"Okay," I said. "But I still don't like the idea of being shadowed." I looked at them both. "I think it would be a good idea to cut down the public appearances — including that trip to Manhattan General."

Miriam's lips tightened. "Why don't we let The Man decide that? And why don't you go check the pizza?"

I trotted obediently into the kitchen. I have learned from experience that Miriam's mind cannot be changed by playing the macho male. Where that feminist monkey was concerned, this particular piglet had to tread very softly indeed.

When we'd finished our cartwheel sections of pizza, Miriam pushed her plate aside and said, "Okay . . . may I now ask some questions?" She sounded as if she meant business.

I took a tight hold on my glass and sat back. The Man eyed me with a smile and turned to Miriam. "What do you want to know?"

She lit a cigarette. "Let's backtrack to the point where you decided to regenerate inside a human fetus. Are we talking about what the Catholics call the 'Immaculate Conception'?"

"Yes," he said.

"So this was not the mental possession of a fetus of which Joseph was the biological father . . ."

"No," said The Man. "We altered the system a little."

"So, in fact, what we're talking about is parthenogenesis . . ."

"Yes."

Miriam saw my questioning look. "It's a reproductive process that does not require fertilization. Which, in the case we're discussing, would normally require penetration of the ovum by the male sperm. It usually only occurs in invertebrates and the lower plants."

"Thanks," I said.

The Man directed his explanation to both of us. "The manipulation of the genetic matrices and basic physiology were relatively simple. The one major problem — for me especially — was *karma*. The psychic accretion that every Ainfolk fragment acquires by cohabiting with its human host during each Earth-life. By the word 'fragment,' I mean the element which is regarded — by those who believe in these things — as the human soul, or spirit. Now to you perhaps, *karma* is a mystical abstraction. A notional mode of moral bookkeeping which adds up the negative balance on your life-account. And which has to be paid off during the cycle of reincarnation." He smiled. "Something else you may not believe in. We don't have that choice, however. To us, *karma* is an awesome reality. In physical terms, it is as if your bodies slowly became covered by a thickening sheath of coral until all movement became impossible. A crippling disability by any standards, but to us it is catastrophic. Because the acquisition of *karma* prevents us from reentering the higher levels of the Empire. You are permanently quarantined in the Third Universe and, if you become seriously contaminated, it's physically impossible to pass through the Time Gate."

"You mean 'spiritually impossible,' " I said.

He laughed. "Yes, sorry. It's this problem of language." He tapped his chest. "When I'm like this I tend to get a little confused now and then. In fact, at times, I find myself thinking the way you do."

"There's no need to apologize," I said. "After all, for thirty-four years, you were one of us."

Miriam gave me a thin-lipped look. "We were talking about regeneration . . ."

"That's right," said The Man. "As I think I mentioned earlier, Gabriel's reentry into the Third Universe did not pose any insuperable difficulties. He and Michael had done this kind of thing before. And they suggested that the problem of *my* reentry could wait until the rescue fleet arrived. As they pointed out, if it didn't, the question of reentry would become purely academic. The first priority was to get under cover. We had to find a couple of female hosts in good health and with a minimal degree of *karma* and then modify their reproductive systems to enable them to conceive unaided. Once that had been accomplished, we were able to fuse our metapsyches with the resulting embryo."

"Could you have done it without their cooperation?" asked Miriam.

"That's a difficult question," replied The Man. "Having them on our side made things a lot easier."

She nodded. "How did you go about finding these two women?"

"That wasn't as difficult as you might think," he said. "There isn't time to go into the history of the thing but — it was something that Gabriel had set in motion on an earlier mission."

"So you knew the process worked," said Miriam.

"It *had* — some nine hundred years earlier," he replied.

Something clicked inside my head. "Wait a minute — does that mean that Gabriel was Elijah?"

"Yes," he said.

Another piece of the puzzle dropped into place. Elijah, the greatest of the Hebrew prophets, who ranked equal first with Moses, had reaffirmed with unparalleled fervor that the only reality was the transcendent God of Israel. He'd also stressed the idea of salvation for a purified "remnant" of the Jewish people. At the end of his life, he had delegated his prophetic authority to Elisha and, according to the Book, had been taken up to heaven on a whirlwind. For whirlwind, read Five-Four-Three-Two-One-Zero, Ignition, Lift-off.

"I think I know what happened next," I said. "Gabriel volunteered to check it out."

The Man smiled. "How did you guess?"

"Well, it's not in the Book," I replied. "But when you said he'd once been Elijah, you gave me the answer. He was the child born six months before you were — and who grew up to be John the Baptist. His mother was called Elizabeth."

"Eliza," said The Man.

"Is he right?" asked Miriam, miffed at the way I kept horning in.

The Man nodded. "Yes. Gabriel approached her husband first. Zacharias. But he panicked at the contact so we had to put a temporary censor-block in his brain. It blanked out the memory of our presence but had the side effect of robbing him of his powers of speech. Eliza was forty-three years old but had had no children. Zacharias was a fifty-four-year-old priest. They were both strictly orthodox. A very devout couple."

"How did Eliza react?" asked Miriam. "Was she amazed, incredulous, frightened, or what?"

"She took it rather calmly," said The Man. "Rather in the way that you have adjusted to the idea of my being here. You have to remember that belief in miracles, visions and visitations from angelic messengers was part and parcel of Pharisaic Judaism. And although the Pharisees did not hold positions of power in the Sanhedrin or the Temple, their ideas still found a wide acceptance among the ordinary people of Palestine at the time we were there. Although, in the end, they were hostile toward me, the Pharisees' belief in the advent of a Messiah was quite intense. Michael and Gabriel, together with other Envoys, had gone to a great deal of trouble to keep the idea alive in each succeeding generation."

"So everything went smoothly," said Miriam.

The words brought a smile to his face. "I wouldn't say that.

It all came out right in the end but there were a few anxious moments. You see, the first, seven-week phase of the regeneration process is hypercritical. Because it's during that period that we are unable to control our host mothers or influence external events. After that first seven weeks, we are fully bonded to our human embryo hosts but we can detach our — let's call it our 'presence' — and can move around more or less at will. We can manifest ourselves as an externally observed form of our own choosing, or penetrate the human subconscious — such as in a dream."

"Got it," I said. "Is that how Gabriel was able to visit Mary while his host fetus was still being carried by Eliza?"

"Yes," said The Man.

"And he told her that she had been chosen to bear a child who — according to Luke — would be host to a spiritual being that he called the 'Son of God' and —"

Miriam cut me off. "And broke the news that her cousin Eliza was already pregnant with a similar child." She eyed me triumphantly.

"I'll go and make some coffee," I said. I kept the kitchen door and my ears wide open.

"Actually," said The Man, "Luke's story is pretty accurate at this point. Mary was in Nazareth when Gabriel broke the news to her. She had just turned sixteen and was engaged to Joseph — who was about thirty years old. It wasn't a love match. The marriage had been arranged between the two families. But in my 'divine ignorance,' I had overlooked the fact that local custom decreed that young ladies were not supposed to get pregnant before they were married. A month or so later, Mary told her mother. Who told her father, and —" The Man broke into a laugh as he recalled the scene. "It was so stupid. Gabriel and I should have known what would happen but, for some reason, it just didn't occur to us. Things are a lot different now, but back in those days, virgin brides were highly prized — and worth a great deal of money. And to make matters worse, before we could get to Joseph, he'd gone to Mary's parents to put himself in the clear and tell them exactly what he thought of their daughter. The trouble . . . I can't tell you." He waved the memory of it away. "But there is one particularly vivid moment I've always kept with me. And that's of stepping outside my mother and looking back at her. And seeing this small, frightened girl, just an inch or two over five feet, standing with her back to the wall inside the main room of her parent's house in Nazareth. With these big brown eyes brimming with tears. Facing her, around the other three sides of the room were her parents, aunts, uncles, the local rabbi, the yenta, numbed by the prospect of losing her commission, Joseph — looking hurt and angry — *his* parents, people from *his* family. And my mother just had to stand there and take it. Because if she had tried to tell them the truth, they would have stoned her for committing blasphemy."

I came to the door of the kitchen to put in my ten cents' worth. "Why couldn't you tell her family? Why did it have to be a secret?"

The Man looked across at me. "Why haven't you told Joe Gutzman, your mother and your sister about my visits?"

"That's different," I said, retiring to get the cups out and load them onto a tray.

"Anyway," continued The Man, "we managed to resolve the situation by tapping into Joseph's subconscious while he was asleep. Gabriel told him to take Mary as his wife and explained why. He did what we wanted. In those days, people took dreams much more seriously. But he always believed that it had been his decision."

I returned to the doorway. "You mean like mine to go downtown and spring you . . ."

Miriam looked over the back of her chair. "What happened to the coffee?"

"It's coming," I said.

The Man picked up the thread of the story. "As soon as they were married, I got Mary to visit Eliza in Bethlehem. They stayed together for about three months. They were both fully aware of their role in our mission but were quite happy to keep the news to themselves. And it also meant that I was living close to Gabriel who was able to give me the support and encouragement I badly needed." He grimaced at the memory. "Gabriel was an old hand at the game, but first time around, bonding one's self to a physical body can be a pretty hellish experience."

"Where was Michael all this time?" asked Miriam.

"Orbiting Earth in the vessel that had brought us into the galaxy," said The Man. "If I can use your space terminology again — and remember the word-concepts are *yours,* not mine — the situation was very like one of your Apollo moon missions. Michael in the command module, Gabriel and I down on the surface. Except we were marooned, and there had been no contact with Mission control since lift-off."

I brought in the coffee and laid the tray deferentially in front of Miriam. As we drank it, The Man explained that, during the fusion of their metapsyches with the host embryo, they had allowed the usual Ain-folk fragment to climb aboard to act as a chauffeur for their new vehicle. As a result, their host bodies were equipped with dual personalities: an earthbound soul that was only too happy to sink back into the relative comfort and security provided by a new human host, and a Celestial alter ego.

When Eliza gave birth to Gabriel's infant host, the child was called Johanan — meaning "Gift of God." The censor-block was removed from Zacharias's mind and he recovered his powers of speech. Gabriel now reentered his surrogate father's subconscious, and enlisted his cooperation in the mission. Mary, The Man's teenage mother-to-be, returned to Nazareth to wait out the remaining months of her pregnancy. Three weeks before her child was due, Mary and Joseph set out together for Bethlehem.

It was at this point that Michael placed the circling starship (my word for it, not his) into synchronous orbit directly overhead so as to maintain the closest possible link with his commander and colleague below. Communication by means of what The Man called the "mind-bridge" — presumably some form of Celestial telepathy — had become increasingly erratic due to the heavy static they were getting from 'Brax. Michael was powerless to help the grounded Celestials, but he had to remain in orbit until he received confirmation of the birth of The Man's human host.

To trained watchers of the skies, a new "star" had indeed been born. Among the Persian magi — the priest-astrologers in the lands east of the Jordan — there were several who had observed the orbiting starship and had correctly deduced that it signified the arrival of a new messenger from beyond the heavens. Among them were two who, for the sake of convenience, we can label Gaspar and Melchior in accordance with the sixth-century tradition. Gaspar resided in the northern city of Haran, the legendary birthplace of Abraham. Melchior was from Babylon. As students of the teachings of Zoroaster, and the ancient beliefs of the Jews that had left their mark upon the Persian religious psyche during the Captivity, both men knew that the appearance of this "star" heralded the imminent birth of a great Celestial power. They were convinced that this power would enter the world in the person of the long-awaited Messiah who, in accordance with the centuries-old prophecies, would be born in Bethlehem-Ephrata. The village that had been enshrined in Jewish history as the birthplace of King David. Balthazzar, the third of the magi who figure in this account, came from Alexandria, in Egypt. He too was a gifted astrologer and initiate of the body of esoteric knowledge known as the Ancient Wisdom.

Three months had passed between the Celestials' arrival in Earth-orbit and the moment when Johanan-Gabriel's mother had conceived. So it was eighteen months between the first recorded observation of the "starship" by the three magi and the birth of The Man in Bethlehem. More than enough time for Balthazzar to draw his own conclusions about the metaphysical origin of the event and its probable significance, and to concert a plan of action with his colleagues.

The three magi arranged to meet in Jerusalem where the

aging king, Herod the Great, had a palace of buttermilk marble. Herod was sixty-seven, stricken with arteriosclerosis, and surrounded with relatives who had inherited the family gift for intrigue and treachery. Herod, a favored vassal-king who had been accorded a large degree of autonomy by Rome, was, above all, a survivor. But the constant conspiracies of his ungrateful relatives and would-be revolutionaries had turned him into a malevolent despot who, in his determination to remain in power, had not hesitated to murder his second wife, her brother and mother, and several of his own sons.

It was at this point that The Man proceeded to demolish the rest of Saint Matthew's story. Apparently, the section dealing with the Nativity had been constructed to perform three separate functions. First: to carry another vital code message. Second: to establish the legitimacy of the claim — made by the early Judeo-Christians — that The Man was the direct descendant of David, Moses and Abraham. Third: as a crude piece of anti-Herodian propaganda.

One of the root causes of Herod's problems was the fact that he was not really a Jew. He was the son of a rich, influential Arab whose family had been forcibly converted to Judaism. This nagging challenge to his legitimacy continued to dog the three sons who assumed power after his death and led to the bad reviews the family got in the Gospels.

I knew it was Miriam's turn to ask questions but I could not help muscling in. "So — there was no meeting between Herod and the three magi."

"No," said The Man. "The literal interpretation of the promise of a child-king of the Jews from the house of David was just wishful thinking. The important part in that section is the phrase *'we have seen his star in the east.'* That's the code message. It was the Persian god, Ahura Mazdao, who was the 'star in the east.' Behind that line lay the truth that, with my birth, the power of Ahura Mazdao had entered the world to carry on the fight against 'Brax."

"That gets rid of one headache," I said. "I've been trying to work out how they could have seen Michael's ship in the east. He would have to be orbiting from west to east to match the speed of rotation in order to go into a geo-stationary orbit. Which means that the 'Star of Bethlehem' would have risen in the *west*. And then would have hung there as Gaspar and Melchior headed for Jerusalem."

The Man smiled. "Let that be a warning to you. Don't take everything too literally. You have got to dig below the superficial meaning of the words."

"What about this story that Joseph had to register at his place of birth?" I asked. "Were the Romans really holding a census?"

He gave a noncommittal shrug. "The reason why we went to Bethlehem was to be with Eliza, Zacharias and Johanan-Gabriel."

"Who was now what — six months old?" said Miriam.

"That's right," replied The Man.

I cut in on her next question. "Both Matthew and Luke stress the importance of Joseph's family tree. Matthew follows it as far back as Abraham. Luke tracks it all the way back to Adam, then God. But if Joseph wasn't your biological father, you could not have been a blood-relation of Abraham — which makes it a rather pointless genealogical exercise."

The Man nodded. "If it's taken literally. But if you visualize it as referring to some kind of spiritual seed being passed down through Adam to Abraham's line, generation after generation, then those passages begin to make some kind of sense."

I turned to Miriam. "I don't know how you're coping, but if we keep going at this rate, I'm going to have to put in for a brain transplant. He's been coming out with stuff like this since I got back from the office at seven."

"I know how you feel," she said.

"Yes, but do you really think anyone else is going to believe it?" I insisted. "That's what bugs me. The thought that he is telling us all these amazing things and it's all being recorded faithfully but, at the end of the day when we start playing back these tapes, people are going to say we made it all up."

Miriam exchanged a look with The Man. "Don't worry. I'm sure he'll think of some way to help us put the message across."

As I write this, I can't help asking myself: Did she know then? Is it possible that he had told her what was going to happen? Or am I, with hindsight, reading more into her words than was ever intended?

"Okay," I said. "Let's get to where you were born in the manger. You know — *'because there was no room in the inn.'*"

"Sorry," he smiled. "You'll have to delete the straw, the animals and the shepherds watching their flocks by night. That was all written in later to give the story popular appeal. To underscore the idea of rejection by a cruel, uncaring world and give you all a guilty conscience."

"So," said Miriam. "No manger."

He shook his head. "I was born in the same room of the same house as Gabriel. There were some animals in the barn underneath but . . ."

"When exactly was your birthday?" asked Miriam.

"Twenty-second of September in the thirty-seventh year in the reign of Augustus. Under your present dating system it works out at seven B.C."

"That makes you a Libra," said Miriam.

"A good sign," I said. A weighing in the balance. Justice. I checked through some books later. His birthday was well into the middle of Tishri, the seventh month in the Jewish calendar. Libra was also the seventh sign of the Zodiac. $7 + 9 + 22 = 38$, which by reduction $(3 + 8)$ became 11. I know critics of this unproven science say you can manipulate almost any combination to give the desired result but, to students of numerology, it was an interesting set of what were called 'cosmic numbers.'' Tishri was, by tradition, the month of plowing. The opening up of the soil to prepare it for the seed. And I was reminded that the Crucifixion had taken place in Nisan, the first month of the harvest, and that the gift of power to the Apostles had taken place in the month of Sivan — the period devoted to the tending of the vines.

I looked beseechingly at Miriam. "There's one more question I've got to ask." I turned to The Man. "Something that's been worrying me ever since we got onto this subject."

"What's that?" he said.

I hesitated, trying to frame the question as coherently as possible. "Well — if, as you suggest, 'Brax had created the conditions that left you marooned on this planet, had fouled up your communication link with Michael and had jammed all signals to the Empire — why didn't he try and wipe you out during that first period of regeneration when you were most vulnerable?"

"Yes," said Miriam. "I'd like to know the answer to that too."

He lifted his palms. "It's simple."

I really don't know why he kept saying that.

"The first thing to understand is that 'Brax could not actually 'wipe me out' in the sense that term implies. He didn't need to. He had already achieved his objective."

Miriam got in ahead of me. "You mean by forcing your regeneration within a human host?"

"Yes," said The Man. "You remember my telling you why I was reluctant to take that step. Because it meant that I would be subject to the law of *karma*. As long as I remained tied to a human host, I would be at the mercy of 'Brax — just like anybody else. Of course, I had more power to fight him with, but that only meant he would concentrate more of his energies against me. If I lost that fight and acquired a fatal degree of *karma*, I would be trapped in the World Below forever."

"Well — not quite forever," I said, remembering his words about the final triumph of Empire.

"That's true." He smiled. "But I would have become, like you, a prisoner of Time and Space. A tyranny you cannot fully understand until you return to the World Above. As you say, there is an end — but I would have had an awful long wait."

"Am I right in thinking that the Massacre of the Innocents never happened?" asked Miriam.

"Yes," he said. "But the ingredients of the story were there. If Herod *had* known about the arrival of the three magi and their claims that I was the newborn Savior of Israel, there certainly would have been a massacre. Herod certainly had no intention of allowing his line of succession be usurped by a dubious descendant of the Royal House of David. Herod was no fool. He knew that fulfillment of the prophecies was a cherished tradition among his Jewish subjects. The basis of their philosophy was the unshakable belief that their past had been shaped by the personal intervention of God, and that their future was in his hands. Herod, on the other hand, tended to believe that both he and his subjects would be better served by applying his own management skills to the task of shaping the nation's destiny."

"So the news never reached him," concluded Miriam. "But the three wise men *did* get to Bethlehem —"

"Yes," he said.

"With gold, frankincense and myrrh?" I added. Anxious to air my newly acquired Biblical expertise. "Or are you going to tell us they came empty-handed?"

He laughed again. "No. They came bearing gifts. But the value of them was mainly symbolic."

"Okay," replied Miriam. "Let's take them one at a time. Gold — that's easy to understand. I checked out the other two with my botanist friend who identified those thorns from your scalp. She told me they were both aromatic gum-resins that were burned like joss sticks. One from a tree, the other from a shrub. Why two lots of gum?"

He treated her to a patient smile. "They had different qualities. Frankincense was solely for burning. Myrrh was normally used in perfumes, and in medicines for its anti-septic qualities. It was also mixed with the wine given to criminals before their execution. To deaden the pain. To my parents, they were three welcome, practical gifts. But their symbolic significance formed another code message. To those who, like the magi, were versed in the Chaldean Mysteries, gold was the symbol of spiritual wisdom and the power of thought. Frankincense was the symbol for love and compassion. Myrrh symbolized incorruptibility — force of will. They represented the attributes of Ahura Mazdao, the leader of the Forces of Light whose transcendent power they believed had now been transferred to me."

"Was Ahura Mazdao someone else from the Empire — born into the world like you?" asked Miriam.

I answered for him. "No. He was a notional super-god that Zoroaster, the great Persian mystic, placed at the head of a pantheon of lesser deities, angels and demons. As I understand it, it was Zoroaster himself — who is sometimes known as Zarathrustra — who was the agent for the Empire in the sixth century B.C."

The Man confirmed my statement with a nod.

Miriam refreshed her memory with the aid of the Bible I had brought back from Sleepy Hollow. "Does this mean that there was also no trip to Egypt?"

"I'm afraid it does,' said The Man. "That was the last code message hidden in Matthew's account of my birth. What you might call 'the Egyptian connection.' The story of a three-year sojourn in the Lands of the Nile was inserted to underline the link between Thoth and myself."

Thoth, whose Greek name was Hermes Trismegistos, was one of the predynastic Egyptian gods, a spiritual entity who figured in their Creation legends and was the alleged inventor of numbers, arithmetic, geometry and astronomy. He was also credited with setting up an intriguing item known as the Siriadic Columns, on which were inscribed the history of all things past. When I dug out this information it seemed to tie in, albeit tenuously, with The Man's revelations about Mother Earth's encyclopedic memory banks.

I gathered our cups onto the tray and flashed a smile at

Miriam. "I'll go and make some more coffee. Keep talking."
A totally unnecessary instruction.

When I returned, it was time to put on a fresh tape. Joseph
had taken his young bride back to Nazareth where their infant star-child was playing happily among the wood shavings
of his father's workshop. At least, Joshua was. The Man's
metapsyche was commuting regularly to Bethlehem to compare notes with Gabriel.

Michael, who had been sitting out the double-barreled
delivery of his Celestial shipmates aboard the Star of Bethlehem, now began the return trip to the Time Gate. Which,
according to my calculations, meant that the "star" whose origins has confounded so many astronomers was a permanent
feature of the Mediterranean night sky until late December–
beginning of January. When I asked The Man why Michael
had stayed on station for so long instead of heading home to
get help, he explained that the three magi did not begin their
journey until the "star" had stopped its movement across the
heavens — thus confirming his arrival *and* his location.

According to the books, Herod the Great died on March
13, 4 B.C. I don't know about you but it always amazes me the
way historians confidently cite dates of this period. When you
discover the tinkering that went on with the Julian and Gregorian calendars right up to the eighteenth century it's a
wonder that any of us know which day it is. When this story
gets out I'm sure there will be more than one scholar who
will tell you that The Man got his dates wrong.

With Herod's death, the seemingly eternal problems of
Palestine returned to plague the Romans. The surviving
members of his family squabbled among themselves, each
trying to carve out the largest possible chunk of Herod's
palace-strewn real estate, his fortune in money and jewels, his
fifty-percent stake in the lucrative mining operations in Cyprus and his business interests in Rome. And his Jewish
subjects wanted out from under.

The Romans split Herod's kingdom between his three
surviving sons but they were as unpopular as their old man

despite everything he had done, and they continued to do, to court favor with their subjects — like rebuilding the Temple on Mount Zion in Jerusalem. A ninety-year labor of love that was still incomplete when the Romans leveled it in 70 A.D. along with the rest of the city.

It is depressing to discover that the current animosity between Arab and Jew was poisoning the body politic even then. And even more so when you considered how well the Jews fared under Islam — compared to their fate at the hands of Christians everywhere since Theodosius gave the Church of Rome its license to kill.

The province of Judea, with its prized city of Jerusalem, the political, religious and financial center of the nation, became the scene of sporadic uprisings, then, finally, open armed rebellion. Alarmed by reports that Palestine was coming apart at the seams, Varus — the Roman Governor of Syria — marched south with two full legions. About twenty thousand professional soldiers from the most powerful and best organized army the ancient world had ever known and which has only been matched for its machinelike efficiency and calculated ferocity by the *Waffen SS*.

The Man's face tightened as he recalled his memories of Varus's short, sharp, bloody campaign. Mary and Joseph had taken him to Bethlehem to visit Eliza and her son Johanan-Gabriel when news came that Varus's legions were heading south, one along the coast; the other through Galilee. Their objective was Jerusalem — where Eliza's husband Zacharias now held a modest post in the Temple hierarchy. Eliza went to fetch him. Mary and Joseph took Joshua-Ya'el and Johanan-Gabriel into the open country southwest of Bethlehem, setting up camp near the present-day Gaza strip.

"We waited there for weeks," recounted The Man, "hoping that Eliza and Zacharias would be among the stream of refugees coming from the direction of Jerusalem. Finally word came that the Romans had regained control of the province. So we started back toward Bethlehem. People we met on the road told us that the Romans were looting the towns and villages so we stayed in open country. Mary went into Bethlehem after dark and made contact with her relatives. They told her that Eliza had not returned from Jerusalem . . ."

The Man paused, reflecting on what, for a young child, must have been a harrowing experience. "We headed north. It was terrible. The Romans had crucified over two thousand people. The crosses were set up all the way around the walls of Jerusalem. Some of the bodies had hung there for weeks."

"Must have been a bad scene," I said, displaying my mastery of useless observation.

The Man looked across at me, his face suddenly haggard. "It was. The memory of it haunted me for the rest of my Earth-life. In fact, it still does."

And us too, I thought. The scene he had described was one that had been repeated time and time again. Different methods, different locations, new executioners. Variations on a theme by 'Brax. Masada, Auschwitz, Warsaw, Babi Yar. And Jerusalem.

Always Jerusalem . . .

He smiled wryly at Miriam. "Perhaps now you can understand why I almost did not have the courage to go through with it when it came to my turn."

Miriam leaned across from where she was sitting and touched his arm. "We don't have to talk about this if you don't want to."

The Man took her hand. "I *want* to tell you about it. It's important for you to know what happened."

"Was — was Zacharias one of the people who were crucified?" asked Miriam.

"No," said The Man. "He'd been killed earlier in the street violence — along with hundreds of others that the Romans didn't even bother to count. Gabriel and I were able to guide Joseph and Mary to where Eliza was hiding in a cellar. The atmosphere was still tense and there were troops on patrol everywhere. So we went on up to Nazareth in Galilee, where we had heard that things had stayed relatively quiet."

"I'm sorry," said Miriam. "But I have to ask this. Why did you let it happen? And if you couldn't stop it, why does God — I know that may not be the name of whoever you work for, but you know who I mean — why does he allow such things? It's easy to say that 'Brax is to blame for what we do to each other but — why must there be all this suffering in the first place?"

His reply reflected the gentle concern with which she had put the question. "Has it occurred to you that God might suffer too?"

Miriam shrugged. "We'll have to take your word for that."

Which, I thought, was a pretty good reply. After all, how could we know? And anyway, what kind of suffering could be experienced by a disembodied, transcendent being who, as far as I could gather, was safely separated from the nastiness of the World Below by the impregnable ramparts of the Empire? Were we talking about the spiritual equivalent of a finger and toenail-pulling session laid on by the Gestapo? Or the less traumatic self-inflicted agonies of doubt that besiege every artist who attempts to create a masterwork?

I know that both of us were too timid to press him on this point but the fact was that his answer begged the question.

I could only see one solution to the problem Miriam had raised. And that was to posit a situation in which God was neither omnipotent, nor unique. He might be the head of the Celestial Empire in the same way that Louis B. Mayer had been head of MGM. God could be imagined as the all-powerful producer who had come up with a great story idea which he'd given to 'Brax — a Celestial Eric von Stroheim — to direct. 'Brax had then departed with his film crew into the depths of the cosmos where he had promptly torn up the script, taken the telephone off the hook, and begun shooting his own version of the movie. What had begun as *The Sound of Music* now resembled *The Texas Chainsaw Massacre*.

The battle now in progress could be viewed as the struggle for creative control of the project: The Man, Gabriel, Michael *et al.*, as executives dispatched to the location by the

Head Office in an effort to talk — or beat — some sense into 'Brax. The problem was compounded by the fact that 'Brax could not be fired because he had a cast-iron contract with Celestial Studios, and the Head Office could not suspend production because everything they owned had been sunk into the locations, cast and costumes. And God — up there in the penthouse — kept telling his weary staff that there was nothing wrong with the original story. It was still a great idea. And that maybe, if they could just stop 'Brax from going completely overboard, when shooting was completed, they would be able to splice their own version together from the out-takes.

I liked this idea better than the Celestial blockbuster of which God was the sole author and in whose pages we were reduced to puppet status. As someone with a great idea that had gone wrong, God appeared — to me at least — a lot more lovable. It also shifted most of the blame onto 'Brax.

The trouble with the book analogy was that, if you thought it through, it meant that we were as insubstantial as the characters that populated the world of literature. It brought us right back to the *"I think, therefore I am/I am, therefore I think"* controversy. If the Hindus were correct in their ancient belief that the external world — which they called *Maya* — was an illusion, then you could posit a situation in which we, this wretched planet and the whole cosmic drama were nothing more than products of God's imagination.

Now I am aware that that statement may seem diffuse but, as a theory, it was no more untenable than the widely held alternative world view which consisted of looking up at the wonder of the star-lit heavens and accepting that it all existed without rhyme or reason. Or that, conversely, if it *had* any meaning then we wouldn't understand it — so why waste time trying? And it was infinitely preferable to the third, most popular, alternative, which consisted of keeping your nose stuck firmly in the trough and never thinking at all.

It was the knowledge that I had experienced these alternate states of mind in my feeble efforts to make sense of my own life that enabled me to appreciate, in some small measure, the difficulties The Man had faced then and the much greater problems he would encounter if he were to attempt the same task today.

We — the sum total of human/divine consciousness — might have started out as twelve pristine Celestial overminds, each with its own tidy flock of human hosts, but the situation now was completely out of control. It was true that Isaiah had utered the prophetic line *"For though thy people Israel be as the sand of the sea, yet a remnant of them shall return"* — but there were now over four *billion* people on this planet with more due every day.

That meant the Ain-folk element in each of us was now only a fraction of what it had been in less populous times. Was this all part of the plan, or was the injunction to *"Go forth and multiply"* a crafty bit of editing by 'Brax? The fact that our present share of the trapped Celestial presence was only a fraction of what it must once have been could account for the disappearance of those legendary powers our ancestors were said to possess: second sight, telepathic and healing ability, the understanding and mastery of the power stored in the stones, trees, earth and sky, an intuitive rapport with the world of nature and the ability to penetrate other planes of existence.

Nowadays, the vast majority of us had lost touch with the "otherworld." It was only the odd individual, or isolated groups, like the last true Mayans now living on the border between Mexico and Guatemala, who exhibited those strange powers that defied rational explanation. For the most part, they were derided or ignored by the rest of us who preferred to adopt the more comfortable unquestioning approach to life. To concentrate on the practical day-to-day problems of living. I had done the same thing myself quite happily for many years. I might pause now and then and ask myself, like Alfie, what it was all about. But asking questions does not necessarily entail a commitment to change. And even from where I'm sitting now, I know that speculating on just what the hell God is up to does not pay the rent. If you and I just sat around like the lilies of the field waiting until somebody clothed us we'd end up with double pneumonia.

I understand things a lot better now, but I still remember how I felt as we sat listening to The Man that evening in good old New York. It was easy for him to talk about the need to rouse the Celestial remnant that had taken refuge inside us. We, the poor earthbound vehicles, with our bald tires, rusty chassis and worn-out motors, had to face up to the brutal truth. Which was — to paraphrase President Nixon — in the battle for men's hearts and minds, 'Brax had us by the spark plugs. And had no intention of letting go.

So far, the only solution The Man had come up with was to cut them off — albeit metaphorically. I was aware that some of the early Christians had gone in for self-castration but, to be frank, it was not a solution you could sell to the hedonists of the twentieth century. Or to Jews with a penchant for metaphysical speculation. I had already made God a gift of my foreskin and, at that point in time, I had no intention of making any further donations.

FIFTEEN ═══════════════════

WEDNESDAY, the sixth of May, I arrived at the office at my usual time and spent the day tidying up more loose ends in preparation for my proposed two-week break. I had left The Man at my apartment with a plea to lie low. I did not tell Linda that he was back in town and, unless he walked in through the plate-glass door without opening it, I didn't intend to.

In the evening, Miriam came over and we sat through another family-album session with The Man. I won't go into the day-to-day details here. It's all down on the tapes I had been running since our first talk-fest up at Sleepy Hollow. But the broad outline was this: after Varus's legions had crushed the rebel uprising in Judea — in which Zacharias had died — Joseph, Mary and The Man-child Joshua returned to Nazareth in Galilee, taking the widowed Eliza and Johanan-Gabriel with them.

Just in case you've forgotten, Galilee was now ruled by Herod Antipas, the second of the old man's surviving sons, whose nickname was "The Fox."

Eliza and her son stayed with Joseph and Mary for the rest of that year then moved to a place called Aenon, near the village of Salim where there was a religious community run by the Essenes — the breakaway sect I mentioned earlier in this account. The enclosed, ascetic life-style of the Essenes had kept their collective *karma* to a minimum. It's something that's hard for us to appreciate, but the spiritual power generated by the community formed an umbrella of energy under which Gabriel was able to shelter from the will-sapping vibrations that 'Brax was beaming in from all sides. By taking cover in this way, Gabriel could keep his own *karma* down to a level which would allow him to pass back through the Time Gate.

The Man, however, elected to soldier on. He needed to acquire, at first hand, the experience of living in the world in order to appreciate the plight of the trapped Ain-folk.

A few weeks after The Man's fourth birthday, Mary gave birth to James, the first of her six other children. Four boys and two daughters. Benjamin, the last, was born when Joshua-Ya'el was eleven. His twelfth birthday was in 6 A.D., a year in which several things happened. Archelaus, the weak-kneed elder son of Herod the Great who had been appointed ethnarch of Judea, Samaria and Idumea, was deposed by the Romans and handed a one-way ticket to Vienne, in the Rhone Valley. His three-piece princedom was turned into a second-class Imperial Province ruled by a Roman procurator. Palestine, I gather, was not regarded as a popular posting among the soldiers and administrators of the empire. Its history of internecine discord plus the ever-present threat of sectarian violence and covert assassination by Jewish militants made it as attractive as the U.S. Marine's fire base at Ke Sanh.

Publius Coponius was the man who drew the short straw. He set up his headquarters at the port of Caesarea Sebaste (now just a heap of ruins near the fishing village of Sedot Yam midway between Haifa and Tel Aviv). Hold it — I've just realized that parenthetical remark needs some qualification. By "now," I mean "Now in 1981." Okay, back to the story.

The first thing Coponius did was to hold a census — something that struck dread into the heart of every Jew. A census of people, goods and property was the cornerstone of the Roman tax system. In their overseas territories, taxes were collected by an enterprising individual (or syndicate) known as a tax farmer, Roman money sharks who bid against each other for the license to milk a particular province. The leg work was done by the hated *publicani* — free-lance IRS men. Matthew-Levi was one of them until he got a better offer. The tax farmer and the procurator of a province worked hand in glove; the more they collected, the bigger the share that went to line their own pockets. The system was open to gross abuse but Rome didn't interfere as long as it got its share of the loot without having to send the troops in.

Since Augustus was still emperor when Coponius took office, my guess is that *this* is the census that the author of Luke mentions in his birth narrative and that somehow, with the passage of time, he got his dates mixed up. It's only one of several irreconcilable items in the four Gospels and is not crucial to the story. The important thing is that the stage was now set for the entry of Pontius Pilate who took over from Coponius in 26 A.D., ensuring himself a place in world history and creating jobs for a string of Hollywood actors.

The same year found The Man-child in Jerusalem and, as he told it, being punished for the first time by Joseph for misbehaving in the Temple. Son of God or no Son of God, you don't get lippy with the High Priest when you're only twelve years old.

This particular incident also occasioned the first meeting between The Man and Nicodemus, one of the younger members of the Sanhedrin — the supreme governing body that regulated Jewish affairs. Impressed by The Man-child's grasp of the Scriptures and his general level of intelligence, Nicodemus did his best to persuade Joseph and Mary to let their son be educated as a religious scholar. Joseph said, "No," turning down what was, on the face of it, a golden career opportunity. Which was either proof that he had a mind of his own, or that the Empire — through The Man — was continuing to move in its own mysterious way.

At first I thought it was strange that Mission Control would have turned down the chance to put The Man into a position where he could have remolded Jewish religious thought. Maybe even have been tapped for the post of High Priest. But then I remembered what he'd said about starting a grass-roots movement that had to break out of the strait-jacket of first-century Judaism and carry the flame of awareness to the world of the Gentiles. I can see now that because his theosophy drew together the disparate threads of all previous religious thought and welded them together into the shining strand of Truth from which each had sprung, it could not be contained within Judaism. It had to begin anew, drawing unto itself those who sought The Way. Leaving the corrupted, man-made structures to crumble like empty cornhusks.

When Joshua-Ya'el turned fourteen, he announced his intention of joining his cousin Johanan-Gabriel in the Essene commune on the banks of the River Jordan. This time, Joseph did not stand in his way. In any case, he now had four other young apprentices in the family and, since that first trip to Jerusalem, The Man had spent most of his time studying the Torah and arguing points of interpretation with the local rabbi. Who, it appears, was heartily relieved to see the back of his precocious pupil.

Upon his arrival at Aenon, The Man was immediately recognized as a "spiritual master" by the Essenes and was welcomed into the inner circle of Initiates where Johanan-Gabriel, despite his youth, had already established a commanding presence. Eliza, now fifty-eight, remained in the nearby community of adherents.

If you are not a student of arcane wisdom, ancient history, geography and the Kabbala, you may find parts of this next segment hard to handle but it's important to make the effort to understand because it has a direct bearing on our own situation. Some of you, I am sure, will know exactly what I'm talking about and may even be ahead of me.

It is almost impossible for us to comprehend through our physical senses the problems that The Man and Gabriel faced in trying to protect their metapsyches — their Celestial spirit forms — against the corrosive radiations beamed at them by 'Brax. Even now, the whole setup of the Empire and its billion-year struggle with the elemental forces of the Netherworld still remains, for me, a nebulous concept. But as I've already recorded, it is the ultimate reality. The war is taking place over us, through us and around us. 'Brax is as real as The Presence and we are all prey to his power.

For The Man and Gabriel, it took the shape of a malevolent spiral vortex in which they found themselves trapped, and which was trying to suck them down ever deeper into the physical world. While they, on the other hand, were trying to avoid this karmic accretion which coarsened their spirit beings. They were like seabirds struggling to free themselves from a glutinous oil slick.

We have all felt our will to succed in a given task or situation ebb away. Our self-discipline crumbles; we opt for an easier course — or do nothing at all. And maybe you've even had the impression that some external agency was sapping your mental and physical energies. It's no accident that it always seems to happen when the change you want to bring about is for the better. It's 'Brax who makes it easier to accept life rather than question it; to take rather than give; to deceive ourselves and others, rather than face up to the truth; to keep our hands in our pockets rather than offer help to a stranger; to envy rather than admire; to hate rather than love.

Man has been the target of 'Brax's negative influence since Earth fell into the hands of the Secessionists. We have been subjected to a relentless bombardment that has pounded the Celestial stowaway inside each of us into insensibility. It is this baleful barrage that we have to resist, with the help of The Power of The Presence. The force of will that the three magi acknowledged as an attribute of the newborn Man-child is not the drive that some of us possess to acquire material riches or political power. It is the will to renounce the desires and the false values of the 'Braxian world and, in doing so, to help change it. To win freedom for ourselves and victory for the Empire.

"Garbage," says that 'Braxian voice in our ear. And there is a natural tendency for most of us to agree with that assessment. Locked in our mobile homes, with our fogged-up windscreens, we can hardly see around the next bend. How can we even begin to imagine what it's like at the end of the road? We bump along, trying to get through the day, the week, the month; lurching from one year to the next, trying to make ends meet; make out; make some sense of our lives. Impose some kind of order on our own little corner of a disordered world. When you think of the labyrinthine reasonings of the theologists you can't help being struck by their total irrelevance to day-to-day living. I mean, really, when you come right down to it, who the fuck cares how many angels can stand on the head of a pin?

It's a hell of a lot easier to accept a less demanding analysis of our relationship to the rest of the cosmos. Namely: what's out there is out there and what's here is here. And that includes us. As to the greater mysteries of Creation and the concept of an omnipotent guiding intelligence, the answer was equally simple: if this is the best God can do, he should make way for a younger man; if he's trying to teach us a lesson, it's been a big waste of everybody's time; and if this is his idea of a joke then he can go screw himself.

It's not difficult for the 'Braxian mind to make out a case demonstrating the basic futility of The Man's message. The meek might be blessed but it was hard to see how they could ever inherit an earth threatened by radioactive weapons whose lethal aftereffects could last for thousands of years. Two-thirds of us risked going out with a bang and the remainder with a leukemic whimper.

Despite the bleatings of present-day democrats, every century, every year and every day furnished us with additional proof that it was only violence that paid off. It was bloody civil strife that had broken the rule of despotic monarchs, freed the slaves in the South and the serfs in Russia. It was the calculated savagery of freedom fighters that had driven the whites to surrender their resource-rich colonies in Africa. Mindless atrocities had given terrorists political clout, and murder had enriched gangsters everywhere. The Power of The Presence was, on the available evidence, no match for the power that came out of the barrel of a gun.

Man's violent nature, it could be argued, only mirrored the underlying ferocity of the natural world; the devastation that could be unleashed by the elements; the evolutionary predator-and-prey system of the reptilian and mammalian species; the relentless kill-and-be-killed cycle of the insects. We could wring our hands and hope that things would get better. Meanwhile, this way to the gas chamber.

A yawning chasm of willful incomprehension lay between the 'Braxian world and that of the Empire but it *was* possible to bridge it if you began to think of yourself not as just another intricately structured biochemical machine but as someone trapped *inside* that machine. The Celestial driver who had collapsed unconscious over the wheel and whom the Empire, through The Man, was doing its utmost to revive.

The deep coma into which our inner being had sunk had crept upon us by degrees after the World Below was plunged into the Age of Darkness. A Cloud of Unknowing descended upon our soul-minds, cutting us off from the Light of The Presence.

As the bond between the Ain-folk and their Earth hosts strengthened, there was an intermediate stage when control of the host groups was exercised through a human "demi-god" endowed with magical powers. This was the origin of the shaman. Later, when the parts became greater than the whole, the terrestrial leader of the race, or tribe, claimed as of right the qualities of the folk-god and became the mouth-piece and instrument of the divine will — now at one stage removed. The conditions had been created for dynastic suc-cession by divine right and for the emergence of theocratic forms of government through the person of the high priest and a self-serving hierarchy of acolytes. The conscious knowledge of their original pure state sank into the furthest recesses of the subconscious. The Truth became lost in the myths of Time.

It was this newfound ignorance that gave rise to the first primitive religious rituals: the worship of folk and nature deities. With the awareness of their Celestial origin now enveloped in a miasma of misunderstanding, our ancestors were encouraged by 'Brax to think of themselves as springing exclusively from the planet that nourished them. Eardh-Ain. The Mother of all Life. Which had to be revered, worshipped and placated by gifts and blood sacrifice in order to calm its elemental ferocity and nourish its life-sustaining fertility.

The mysterious forces in nature came to be seen as an intrinsic part of the *physical* world and the rapidly expanding pantheon of folk gods were given animal or human form or a combination of both and endowed with every excess of human and/or bestial behavior. They were stronger, prettier, more energetic, generally larger-than-life and lived forever. They were either here, eternally present in the wind, the sea, the mountains, forests and running water or, when they retired, they were carried across the Western Seas to the sunset islands in the sky where the aphrodisiac wine never stopped flowing, where the men were endowed with monumental virility and the women were young, ever-beautiful and blessed with perpetual nymphomania.

As Man was drawn deeper and deeper into the darkness of physical existence, female sexuality became identified as the active ingredient of the 'Braxian world because, as the bearer of new life, women were the living symbol of the eternally fertile Earth-Mother. The willing collaborators of 'Brax. The coils of the serpent. The vortex sucking the trapped Celestials ever deeper into the World Below. Cutting them off from the Light.

The theme of this eternal conflict has been depicted throughout recorded history in myths and legends based on ancient oral traditions, and in more recent prose, poetry and painting. Much use is made of allegory and symbolism. The Truth is always heavily veiled but there are clues in all kinds of places — as a direct result of The Man's time-travels I am sure. He had mentioned meeting Francis Bacon, who history records as knowing a thing or two, and he may have had a word in the ear of Nicolas Poussin who was suddenly enlightened while in Italy as to the deeper truths guarded by the Knights Templar and the Albigenses, two groups that were branded as heretical by Rome and exterminated with Third Reich thoroughness.

The Albigensian heresy, for which those who clung to it died in droves, centered round the belief that Man was an alien forced to live in an evil world of matter. They also held that Jesus was only a messenger from God, and that it was not *he* who had been crucified at Golgotha but merely the human body which he had inhabited. They were so close, it was clear someone had been talking to somebody.

Poussin concealed an important message relating to this in his painting *The Arcadian Shepherds,* and an earlier artist, Paolo Uccello, portrayed the central elements of the cosmic struggle in his *Saint George and the Dragon.* The superficial graphic image depicts a noble lady chained to a dragon, on the left of the picture, which Saint George, on horseback, attacks with a lance from the right. The pictorial elements represent much more than an incident from the Arthurian legends. The princess symbolizes the female principle; *Binah* in the Kabbalic *Sephiroth,* Understanding. *Binah* was often equated with Sophia — world knowledge — and the diabolist Aleister Crowley identified her as the great Whore of Babylon, the star of Revelations.

Uccello's canvas shows *Binah* chained to the dragon — synonymous with the Biblical serpent, and complete with spiraling tail: the 'Braxian vortex which has sucked spiritual Man down into the physical world, and which also symbolizes the female vagina. And in case you miss that, Uccello has thrown in the dragon's lair — to which the spiraling tail points — a dark, crinkled, semielliptical cavern which does not make undue demands on the imagination.

But don't worry. The good news is on the right. Saint George astride his white horse is the male principle, *Chokmah* — representing Wisdom; usually equated with divine wisdom or illumination, as opposed to the nuts-and-bolts type comprehension possessed by *Binah*. Saint George is armed with a lance, synonymous with the Sword of Truth and the male phallus. The lance that will vanquish the 'Braxian dragon that has made a prisoner of our powers of understanding represents The Power of The Presence — or the power of God, or whatever you wish to call it.

The princess and the knight, *Binah* and *Chokmah*, represent the twin aspects of the Creator. The left and right hand of God. They are linked to each other, and to *Kether* (The Crown, or God-Head) to form the supreme Trinity of the *Sephiroth* which, according to Kabbalic lore, purports to map the twenty-two paths to God, Allah, The Presence, The Ultimate Principle. Once again I have to emphasize that the name doesn't really matter because, when you get there, you won't need to be introduced.

The last key element in the picture can be seen in the sky above the knight: a spiral cloud formation. The second spiral of forces. The one that leads Man upward to the heavens, and to the Empire Beyond.

None of this, I hasten to add, is intended to bring the feminist movement, or things pertaining to their gender, into disrepute. Regardless of our sexual classification, we all contain both male and female elements. In the context of the greater struggle, masculine and feminine are merely generic terms for the complementary aspects of The Power of The Presence. The *Shekinah*. The polarity that underpins the material universe and the language we use to describe it. Good and evil, light and darkness, spirit and matter. The dualism of Zoroaster which was denounced by the nascent Church of Rome as heretical was an essential part of the all-embracing One-ness of The Presence.

But let's go back to when the shaman was getting his act together. We are talking about a time when Zoroastrianism, Gnosticism, and the Christian church that was to crush both lay far in the future. When Uncomprehending Man was busy organizing Dionysiac-type cults where everybody went on seasonal binges to celebrate the agricultural highlights of the year, solar and lunar cycles, and anything else they could think of.

It was at this point that SHEEF — Supreme Headquarters Empire Expeditionary Force — completed their plans for the counterattack, and launched the invasion. And the twelve tribes of Israel woke up one morning to find that they had been selected as the bridgehead. The Jews were the grains of sand on the beaches of a cosmic Normandy. The first piece of Celestial real estate to be liberated.

But, as the French discovered in World War Two, liberation can be an arduous and often painful process. It's not all flags, flowers, kisses and cigarettes. It's also blood, sweat and tears, shells through the roof and tank tracks over the tomatoes. It's great in the end, but if, like the trapped Celestials and their Earth hosts, you can barely remember what it was like to be free, it is only natural to wonder whether it is worth the pain and the inconvenience.

For while the rest of God-forsaken humanity was having a good time, the Israelites got landed with Judaism. Without even being consulted, we were chosen to be the guardians of Man's spiritual heritage and future salvation. The bookkeepers of Man's moral bank account. Moses gets called to Sinai and is told to make sure that we keep taking the tablets. We start living our life by the Book and, before you know it, the Jewish nation has become an island of spiritual and moral rectitude in a sea of heaving buttocks.

With this reawakened awareness of the world of the spirit and the trapped Celestial presence, the world of matter — in the eyes of the Jews, at least — came to be more clearly defined as the prison of the human soul. We might not be able to escape but we could earn remission for good conduct. Two concepts which were echoed in equally ancient theosophies east of the Euphrates.

It was against this background that women came to be seen as the seductive agents of 'Braxian reality. Even though they had a fully integrated role in the daily rituals of Jewish life, any man who succumbed to the lure of female sexuality was thought to be playing Russian roulette with his soul. Carnal knowledge became the forbidden fruit.

From the beginning of Biblical history, women have had to bear the burden of guilt for Eve's quasi-adulterous relationship with the Serpent that put Adam in *shtuk* with God and left them both out on the street with only two fig leaves and a half-eaten apple between them.

The incident resulted in the segregation of men and women in the teaching and practice of Judaism, and other discriminatory acts such as the decree in Leviticus which specified that if a woman gave birth to a female child she was held to be "unclean" for sixty-six days whereas if she gave birth to a son, the ceremony of purification could take place thirty-three days after delivery.

From the very beginning, the rabbinic office and worship in the synagogue was decreed an exclusively male function. It marked the beginning of a kind of spiritual apartheid which was carried over into Christianity. With the notable exception of the Gnostics, who allowed women to preach and maintained the total democracy that had flourished in the post-Pentecostal communes founded by the Apostles, the Church of Rome swiftly debarred women from office; a principle that the papacy has upheld to this day. And likewise, when the revolutionary purity of Islam became corrupted, the Muslims adopted similar discriminatory practices that reduced the social status of women even further.

This religious demarcation dispute can be traced back to Genesis and the Creation legend but it is based on a built-in error. Adam and Eve were *not* the archetypal man and woman. They represent the dual aspects of The Presence. *Chokmah* and *Binah;* Wisdom and Understanding. The Garden of Eden story is an allegory of events that predate the destruction of Atlantis. It goes back to the *First* War of Secession. And it relates to Celestial powers, not protohumans. It is not about the fall from grace of Earth-Man and Woman. It describes the entrapment of our Celestial selves in the universe that 'Brax had helped to create.

The apple — the forbidden fruit from the Tree of Knowledge that 'Brax, the Serpent, persuaded Eve to offer Adam — represented the power given to the Celestials to create and control the physical universe. And Adam's acceptance of it, in defiance of God's injunction, represented the rebellion by 'Brax's blue-collar angels against the authority of God, The Will of The Presence. The Garden of Eden was not an earthly paradise but the Celestial Empire from which the rebellious angels were banished. And their crime was in allowing themselves to be seduced by the wonder of the universe they had helped create into thinking that they were the equal of God.

It was 'Brax, their leader, who was the transgressor. It was *he*, not us, who fell from grace. Adam and Eve represented the twin aspects of his Celestial psyche. It was 'Brax who was driven from the Eden that was the Empire. The cherubim were the Loyalist angels; the flaming sword the First War of Secession. Which caused the Empire to seal itself off behind the Time Gate to protect the Tree of Knowledge, The Power of The Presence from which all things sprang.

It was only later that we poor ham-fisted humans came along and got caught in the cosmic meat-grinder. By which time, 'Brax had done one of his great impersonations and had convinced us that it was all our fault and that God was extremely displeased with Mankind in general. A shrewd move designed to alienate us from The Presence. And to top things off, 'Brax had hung *his* original sin around *our* necks like the Ancient Mariner's albatross.

But here's the good news: it's no crime to be born. Jesus may want you for a sunbeam, but the Empire needs you as people first. The trapped Celestials who got us into this mess need these bodies of ours in order to survive until the Empire regains control of the World Below.

People have had a lot of trouble trying to reconcile the eye-for-an-eye God of Vengeance of the Old Testament with the somewhat more benevolent God of the New. And many have asked themselves why an omnipotent creator should go to all the trouble of creating the world and then proceed to give us such a hard time. But once you know that 'Brax has been impersonating the Old Man, it's possible to work back through the texts and discover the bits where he gave us a bum steer.

One of the recurring themes of the Old Testament is the oft-repeated warning to the Israelites to beware of false gods and false prophets. God, The Presence, or Whoever was *not* omnipotent in the World Below; the claim that He/She was had been disseminated by 'Brax to take the heat off himself. The Second War of Secession has been a constant battle of wits between the Empire and 'Brax; between the Loyalists and Secessionists. One is forced to come back to the analogy of the Allied-backed Resistance movements in Nazi-occupied Europe. The Empire keeps flying in agents to boost the activities of the Loyalist underground with the full knowledge that the network has also been penetrated by V-men (*Vertrauensmänner*) , the double-agents recruited by 'Brax.

The Man had come to boost our awareness of our real selves; our spiritual origin and destiny, and the nature of external reality. But he did not condemn the physical world. He wanted us to see it as it really was, not *"as through a glass, darkly."* He wanted us to understand our part in the great cosmic struggle and how, through The Power of The Presence, we could contribute to the final victory by harmonizing the spiritual and material elements of existence. Restoring the lost equilibrium between *Binah* and *Chokmah* and their link with the God-Head.

'Brax hates equilibrium. As the Lord of Chaos, he specializes in discord. The Man had brought us news of the Celestial Empire; the Judeo-Christian Kingdom of Heaven. And the

Resurrection had demonstrated the supremacy of the spiritual world. 'Brax's response was swift and diabolically clever. Working through well-meaning ascetics, he began to expound the virtues of the spirit and an abhorrence of the flesh and all things pertaining to the world. Which led to the self-mutilation I mentioned earlier, Saint Augustine having to persuade Christians not to throw themselves off cliffs, vows of celibacy by Roman priests, exclusion of women from ecclesiastical office while simultaneously propagating an extreme veneration of the Virgin Mary, and sado-masochistic mortification of the flesh by mad monks and middle-class medieval pietists. Such as the gentleman who had lengths of knotted cord wound tightly around his body so that it cut into his flesh, wore an unwashed hair shirt crawling with lice, and walked around with sharp pebbles in his shoes.

One has to admit it's a hard act to follow.

Any sane person could be forgiven for thinking that a God who made the world, the heavens and all therein and then expected everyone to behave like this was out of his all-embracing mind. No one could reconcile the notion of a benign cosmic intelligence with such aberrant behavior. The licentious celibates, the venality and self-enrichment, the intemperate luxury and abuse of power all helped bring into disrepute the Church that God did not want and The Man had not asked for. He had made it quite clear when he had put down the squabbling disciples: *"The first shall be last, and the last shall be first."* And he had underlined the anti-hierarchical nature of the Empire by washing the feet of his disciples at the Last Supper, a practice that had found few takers among the temporal princes of the Church that professed to follow his teaching. But these same people did not hesitate to use the Bible as a club to beat the middle and lower classes back into line. And when they became strapped for cash, all they did was point the finger at some rich fall-guy and brand him as an heretic, or go out and beat up on a few more Jews.

The willful misinterpretation of The Man's message by the

founding fathers of the Church has robbed the world of The Truth for nearly two thousand years. For centuries, clerics conspired with kings to rule their subjects, teaching their docile congregations that it was God's will that each should have his fixed station and that it was their lot to suffer the misery of poverty, starvation and oppression until Jesus Christ returned to build the new Jerusalem.

Meanwhile, princes and prelates dressed in cloth of gold and lesser men in rags. Man was constantly reminded that he was born in sin and in mortal danger of committing further transgressions. All was not lost, however. The Church had acquired the monopoly on salvation and it was available to all. For a price, of course. The classic squeeze play. And one more example of how The Man's message was perverted.

It was little wonder that people tended to go along with 'Brax. He's brilliant. The charismatic kind of villain we all love to hate — and secretly admire. Let's face it. If you look at things on a short-term basis, he makes a lot of sense. The only problem is that, for most of us, there is a small still voice that occasionally makes itself heard above the din of daily existence and which asks us if there isn't more to life than meets the eye.

It's a tough question; the toughest, in fact, because neither I, nor you who are reading this, will be around at the end of the game to cheer the winner. We'll be there in the spirit, of course, but the earthbound bundle of bones that bears the name of Leo Resnick and you, Dear Corporeal Reader, will be long gone.

That's the hard bit. Because most of us are more concerned with what happens to that hundred and ten pounds (or whatever) of walking pot roast than anything else. That's the thing we're sure of; that we can see in the mirror, squeeze, prod, and feel we understand. Even though, as science probes ever deeper into the molecular mysteries of the body, it gets harder and harder to envisage how anything of such elegant complexity ever got put together.

The answer, of course, lies outside ourselves. Some of us

stumble upon it; for others, it comes at the end of lives which resemble *Pilgrim's Progress*. A favored few are privileged to experience *samadhi;* unification with the Ultimate Principle; the fusing of one's inner being with the transcendent Power of The Presence. But no matter how dull-witted we are, we can all experience the feeling of well-being that springs from an unselfish act of love.

For many of us, that may not be sufficient proof that God, or anything better than this world, exists. That's tough. God, The Presence, or Whoever doesn't have to prove anything. He *is*. You can either go along with that statement and maybe eventually discover the truth of it for yourselves, or you can accept the stainless-steel logic of the philosophers who deny his existence.

Each of us has to find our own way home. For some, it means straying off the path and running the risk of becoming totally lost; for a minority, it is through a life behind high walls, chained to a rosary, chanting *Ave Maria* or *Nunc Dimittis*. Most of us need a push in the right direction, and if anyone finds The Way through reading this then my own journey will not have been wasted.

But let's be certain where we're starting from. The original sin was 'Brax's, not ours, and girls, you're in the clear. God never intended to deny Man the love of a good Woman; and vice versa. That's why he made us that way. Love is a two-way process. A mutual exchange. The fusion of *Chokmah* and *Binah*. It is both giving and receiving. We have to understand what it is, discover it within ourselves and start spreading it around. Love is the great healer; it is the power that can move the mountains of indifference that bar the way to The Truth. And as it shines forth from us, it awakens the dormant power in others and is reflected back. If we could switch the whole world on, we'd have 'Brax hanging on the ropes. The one thing that really creases him is when people start being nice to each other.

Everybody needs to sweat a little, but no one should be condemned from birth to a life of grinding poverty, chronic malnutrition and social deprivation. The Man saw some bad things while he was on the road but it's got a lot worse since. Let's get one thing clear: When The Man urged us to *"take no thought for the morrow,"* he did not mean for us to sit on our collective ass and wring our hands until the Second Coming. The salvation of Mankind is in *our* hands. We have the power. It's inside us and all around us. All we have to do is make the connection.

Some keen students of logic may have noticed that I appear, in the foregoing, to have outlined a situation which implies we have a choice, whereas earlier I reported that, according to The Man, predestination was the order of the day. Bear with me. An answer to the paradox will be forthcoming.

SIXTEEN

THURSDAY the seventh of May. I took a break in the late afternoon and returned to the bookshop where I had purchased the paperback reprint of the *Zohar*. I browsed along the shelves, picked out a book on the Kabbala and several volumes by Rudolph Steiner, then, as I rounded the end of the aisle, I ran slap into Gale McDonald.

"Small world," I said.

"Yes," she replied. "How long have you been interested in this stuff?"

"Ever since someone told me it would give me power over women," I said.

"And has it?"

I shook my head. "Not yet. I'm still trying to find the right book. The guy who told me about it couldn't remember the title."

She followed me to the checkout counter where a young bearded guy whose shoulder-length hair started on the crown of his head manned the cash register. I glanced down at the book she was buying and saw it was an illustrated guide to Tantric Yoga. She stood aside and watched as the bearded guy checked off the prices of my six books and put them into a paper bag.

"They look interesting," she said.

I handed over a fifty-dollar bill and held my hand open for the change. "Yours looks as if it might be more fun."

"Yes, well — I hear it's better than walking the dog," she said. She held the street door open for me. "Listen, I was just on my way over to see you. Can you spare a few minutes?"

"Is this business or pleasure?" I asked.

"Let me buy you a cup of coffee." She steered me across the street and around the corner into a neat little coffee shop with a bronzed glass window.

It was crowded but, as we entered, a couple of guys got up from a table at the window. McD cut in ahead of two purple-rinsed matrons and motioned me to sit opposite her. The waitress cleared the table and took our order. McD lit another of her brown cigarettes.

I gazed idly out of the window and saw the two guys who'd been sitting at the table get into a brown VW delivery truck that was parked right outside. McD lifted her chunky leather bag onto the table, pulled out a tissue, and left the bag lying at our elbows.

I established firm eye-to-eye contact and adopted a matter-of-fact tone. "So . . . how's the miracle market today?"

"Down several points," she said. "The moment I told my editor what I was on to, he told me to forget it. He didn't even bother to look at the stuff I'd typed up. It was quite amazing the way his face changed. It was just like a steel shutter coming down."

"Yeah, well, there you go," I said. "I can understand your disappointment but I think he made the right decision. TV coverage of what happened to Mrs. Perez won't do anything for people who already believe in God and it will only draw howls of derision from those who don't. Metaphysics and the media just do not mix."

She pulled some smoke down into her lungs. "You could be right."

I fished out my pack of dwarf whites and got one going. "So — what else is new?"

She answered me with pursed lips. "Oh, nothing much. I just wanted to dot a few i's. Cross a few t's." She leaned away from the table as the waitress arrived with our coffee. "That was a neat snow job you laid on me the other day."

I frowned. "Let me get this straight — are we talking about Mr. Sheppard?"

She smiled crookedly. "Well — let's say we're talking about the person who occupied Room Three-fifteen at the Mayflower Hotel under that name."

"I see . . ." I blew on my coffee and took a cautious sip. "Does that mean you think there still may be some doubt as to his actual identity?"

She blew smoke at the plate-glass window. "You could say that. Yes."

I did my best to look puzzled. "I don't quite understand. I thought I'd explained what the situation was."

She took off her tinted glass. "Yes, you did. You were very helpful. Which is why I thought you might be able to explain something else."

I noticed that her slate-blue eyes had turned a cold gray. "What's the problem?"

She burned through some more brown paper. "The problem is this, Mr. Resnick. A friend of mine, who works for the NYPD, helped me check out your story. None of the airlines flying the Los Angeles–New York route had a lost-baggage claim for a Mr. Y. Sheppard — or had him listed as a passenger on that particular Monday, or over the previous weekend. The airport police at JFK have no record of finding his wallet, ID papers or passport, and Mr. Y. Sheppard was not listed as a passenger on any of the afternoon or evening flights to Europe and the Middle East on Tuesday — the day you told me he flew out to Israel. Does that surprise you?"

"Not particularly," I said. "You may recall my telling you that was not his real name."

"That's what I'd thought you'd say," she replied. "What name was he traveling under?"

I fanned my cigarette smoke from the air in between us. "I'm afraid I'm not at liberty to tell you that."

"That figures," she said. "Would it come as any surprise to learn that the airport police did not carry out a search of the baggage handler's lockers?"

I spread my palms. "Listen, I can only tell you what he told me. What do you want me to do?"

"Sure . . ." McD dumped the last quarter of her cigarette and pulled out another.

I sat back as she fired a three-inch pencil of flame at the end nearest me. "Do you use that to blowtorch muggers?"

"No. But now that you mention it, I must give it a try." Her grin had a tough edge to it. "This client of yours gets stranger by the minute. Why do you think he made up a story like that?"

"Search me," I said. I glanced out of the window. The brown VW truck hadn't moved from the curb. I checked my watch. "Listen, I don't want to rush you but —"

McD nodded. "I know. This won't take a minute. Jeff Fowler told me about those two meetings he had with you about some, uhh, you know — uhh, blood samples."

"Oh, yeah . . ." I said. Wondering why she had deliberately stumbled over her delivery.

"Yes," she continued. "I just wanted to check over a couple of points because, well, quite frankly — both of us are a little confused."

I considered walking out then and there but decided to sit tight and brazen it out. "What is it you find confusing?"

McD put her glasses back on and gave me the perplexed look of a college student seeking enlightenment from her professor. "Well — when Jeff analyzed the blood taken from the statue, he found that it contained the same striking abnormalities that were present in an earlier sample that came from another client of yours — who apparently died a few weeks ago at his daughter's home in California. A Mr. Abraham . . . Lucksteen?"

"That's correct," I replied.

McD nodded soberly. "Amazing . . . It's almost as big a coincidence as our using the same bookshop."

I swallowed some more coffee. "I'm not quite sure what you're getting at." This time, my puzzlement was genuine.

"Your client, Mr. Abraham Lucksteen," explained McDonald. "He's got the same name as the rabbi who bar-mitzvahed you. You know — the one who lives on Fisk Street, in Brooklyn, and whose daughter lives in California. She was your classmate in junior high and high school, remember?"

My coffee cup almost slipped through my fingers. "You've certainly been busy," I said. The feeling of being suddenly cornered brought a note of aggression into my voice. "Is this what they call investigative reporting? Because from where I'm sitting, publication of any of this would be seen as 'invasion of privacy.' "

Her teeth flashed. Like a shark scenting blood. "Oh, come now, Mr. Resnick. Stop stonewalling. I just want to know what is going on. I made enquiries at your office and was told that Mr. Abraham Lucksteen was not on your list of clients. The rabbi of the same name has assured me that he is alive and well and sends you his regards."

"Well done," I said. Through clenched teeth. "Anything else?"

"Yes," she said. "Something happened at Manhattan General on Easter Saturday. What is it that you and Dr. Maxwell are covering up?"

We sat back as the waitress came to refill our cups. I put my hand over mine. When she'd gone, I slid my elbows back onto the table. "Let me put it this way, McD. If you're off duty, it's none of your business, and if you're wearing your Channel Eight hat, the answer is 'No comment.' "

She added some Sweet 'n Low to her coffee and stirred it in with a patient sigh. "Look — you're a busy man, so I won't waste your time. When Jeff Fowler took a look at the blood samples on those slides that your Dr. Maxwell gave him, he found it was still fresh — and it stayed that way."

I pulled out another cigarette. "He didn't tell me that."

"No," said McD. "But then, you weren't exactly forthcoming with him. The point is, since the samples didn't come deep frozen, they could not have been sent from the Philippines. When you told him that story, he already knew where they'd come from."

"Oh? Where was that?"

McDonald paused for effect then let me have it right between the eyes. "From an unidentified Hispanic male who was tagged DOA when he was delivered to Manhattan General at nine P.M. on Easter Saturday."

All of which, as you can imagine, was familiar stuff. But in the wrong hands, it could be dynamite. I sipped the last of my coffee and feigned a studied disinterest.

McD dragged down more smoke. "Before Jeff came to see you, he went over to the hospital to have a word with Dr. Maxwell. She wasn't there but he ran into an intern named Paul Lazzarotti who was using her office to proposition a nurse. I won't bore you with the details of their conversation but Jeff asked Lazzarotti if — as her assistant — he knew anything about the slides. Lazzarotti mentioned he'd seen Dr. Maxwell with them in her hand on the Saturday when you came up from the morgue. That led to the dead Hispanic, and the discovery that Drawer Eleven was empty, and back to Dr. Maxwell's office, where Jeff — by sheer chance — happened to see a white coat hanging up in a half-open locker. It was one Dr. Maxwell had been wearing which should have gone in the laundry basket but hadn't. And it had bloodstains on it." McDonald shrugged.

"So Jeff took it away for analysis," I concluded.

"Yup," said McDonald. "And there was some fresh blood on it that matched the samples on the slides. So when Dr. Maxwell went along with your story about faith healing in the Philippines, Jeff knew that she was in on the cover-up too."

"I see," I said. It was the best I could manage. Obviously Fowler was much less of an idiot than I thought. As for Mc-

Donald, it was clear she possessed the nose of a bloodhound plus the speed and tenacity of a ferret.

McD paused to drink her coffee. Doubtless to leave me, in the style of John Ehrlichman, dangling slowly in the wind. I knew she was baiting the trap but I could not resist walking into it with my mouth wide open. "Is there any more . . . ?"

"Oh, yes," she replied. "This is where it really gets interesting. Lazzarotti's description of the Hispanic gentleman who went missing from Drawer Eleven is almost identical with Mrs. Perez's description of the man she met in Central Park, and your secretary's description of Mr. Sheppard. When you put all that together with the statue, Fowler's analysis of the blood, and what that implies about Mr. Sheppard's physiology —"

"Oh, yeah, what does it imply?" I said sharply.

She looked about her then lowered her voice. "Listen. We both know that nearly everything you told me about this guy has been either a bare-faced lie or an evasion of the truth. Who is he — and where does he come from? Is he, uhh —" She hesitated. "— part of a *Close Encounter*–type situation?"

I laughed. So near and yet so far. "Fowler's already asked me that. Come on, McD. You know damn well if that was true I'd be beating a path to your door. Jeff Fowler's given you a bum steer. I don't know anything about what happened to the guy who was in Drawer Eleven but I can assure you of one thing — he is not Mr. Sheppard. I'm sorry. I'd like to help you but I have nothing to add to what I've already said."

She formed a loose circle with her mouth and let the smoke drift out slowly, taking it back in through her nose. It had been years since I'd seen anyone do that. "Are the other partners in your law firm involved in this cover-up?"

The smile froze on my face. "You're starting to tread on my toes, McD. Let me give you some sound advice. Stop wasting your time and mine. There is no cover-up. This is not another Watergate. And you are not Carl Bernstein or Bob Woodward. There *is* no story. So just drop it, okay?"

Which has to be the most provocative thing you can say to a pushy reporter. I don't know what got into me.

Her expression didn't change. "Are you sure you don't want to say anything?"

I led with my bottom lip. "Listen. You know as much as I do."

"You mean — like the fact that the amazing Mr. Sheppard is not in Israel but in your apartment on Seventy-fifth Street?" She put the question to me as if she did not quite understand it herself.

I sat there with egg on my face. "You've — spoken to him?"

"No," said McD. "Mr. Sheppard appears unwilling to answer the door buzzer or telephone, but the janitor was very helpful."

You may remember me telling you he was nosy. He would also sell his tenants down the river for five bucks. And what he didn't know he would make up. "Has it occurred to you that he might be mistaken?" I suggested.

She shook her head. "I checked. A lady on the fourth floor of the apartment building opposite was kind enough to let me look out of her window. She even loaned me a pair of binoculars."

"Now that is grotesque," I said.

"Not at all," smiled McD. "It was a touching gesture of solidarity. I told her that I was your estranged wife and wanted to find out if you were cheating on me."

"I think I know the woman you mean," I said.

"Yeah, well, for what it's worth, if you're going to go on inviting girls up, from now on I'd close the blinds."

"Thanks a bunch . . ."

It was her turn to shrug. "My pleasure. Anyway — there in your living room was a bearded man in his thirties who answers the description of Mr. Sheppard. He was lying on the sofa watching television."

"Oh, really," I said. "That's very interesting. Which channel?"

"Couldn't say," she replied. "The back of the set was facing the window."

Which it was. I nodded with grudging admiration. "You're a sharp lady. You should have been a lawyer."

McD shrugged modestly. "Must be in the blood. My father's the local sheriff, my mother's the daughter of a judge, and my favorite uncle is State's Attorney."

I had to laugh. This kid was really rubbing my nose in it.

She smiled along with me. "My brother is with the Justice Department in Washington. I'm the dumb one of the family. That's why I rode horses." She killed her cigarette and her smile at the same time. "What I thought of doing was asking Mrs. Perez along to see if she could positively identify Mr. Sheppard as the man she met in Central Park. How does that grab you?"

"Don't," I said, with a shake of the head. "I've got enough problems." I looked out of the window of the coffee shop and toyed with the idea of telling McD that she'd been spying on Jesus. And it was at that point that I saw what I'd failed to notice before: the video-camera that was aimed at us from the cab of the VW delivery truck.

I turned back to McDonald, pulled her bag toward me, and found the mike that had been taped under the flap.

She tried to play it like Jane Fonda in *The China Syndrome* but underneath she was like a kid who'd been caught with her hand in the cookie jar. "I was, uhh — hoping you'd give me something I could use to beat my editor over the head with."

"Well, you just crapped out, McD," I said, exulting in the fact that it was now her turn on the receiving end. "In the first place, you did not obtain my permission for an on-the-record interview. And in the second place, your friends are photographing my worst side."

The flush in her cheeks started to fade as she bounced back. "What friends?"

I jerked my thumb at the window. "Your friends in the van." As she looked out of the window, I ripped the mike from her bag and said goodbye. "Okay, cut it right there, fellas. It's a wrap —"

The brown VW took off like a Formula One leaving the pit.

"Wait a minute," she said.

I dunked the mike head-first into her coffee and walked out, leaving Channel Eight to pay the bill.

I found a pay phone at the end of the block and called Manhattan General. I hung on for what seemed an age then finally got Miriam on the line. "Our cover's been blown," I said. "I've got Carol's roommate and a camera crew from Channel Eight on my tail. She and Jeff Fowler have been working overtime and both our faithful assistants have been shooting their mouths off."

"Paul?" She sounded surprised. "But I didn't tell him anything."

"You didn't need to. Fowler managed to put it together from the bits Lazzarotti remembered. They don't know it all — like the way he disappeared from the slab, for instance — but they're pretty damn sure where that first blood sample came from, and they know that Drawer Eleven is empty." I told Miriam about Fowler's fact-finding trip and how McD had been checking up on me.

"Oh, God," she sighed. "I wish to hell I'd been there."

"I'm glad you weren't," I said. "You might have spilled the whole story. You're really hopeless when it comes to telling lies."

She greeted this with a brief silence. "So what did you say to this lady?"

"Nothing. I stuck to my original story and didn't admit a thing. But she knows that The Man is in my apartment and she's threatened to send Mrs. Perez around to flush him out unless you and I start talking. Fowler has her partially convinced that they've stumbled across *The Man Who Fell to Earth* —"

"Oh, Jeezuss . . ." groaned Miriam. "This is terrible."

"It's worse than that," I said. "If this goes on the air, we could end up being the first unemployed Jewish doctor and lawyer in the history of New York. Can you imagine anything more ridiculous?"

"Do you think 'Brax is behind this?" she asked.

"Of course he is," I replied. "But not in the way you think. He's not sent someone in disguised as a girl reporter. He's working on all of us. It's the 'Braxian element in McDonald that's driving her on in the hope of uncovering some sensational story that's going to catapult her into the big time, and it's beavering away inside us, sapping our moral courage and reinforcing our instincts for self-preservation."

"So what are you going to do?" said Miriam. "Stand and fight him?"

"You've got to be kidding," I replied. "This is no time to be a hero. I'm taking two weeks off, and you've got your patients to think of."

"True," she said. "Are you going to move The Man up to Sleepy Hollow?"

"I can try," I said. "But that won't necessarily stop him from reappearing in the middle of Manhattan."

"It might — if you stay out of town," she replied.

"Yeah . . ." I mused. Then I remembered something. "Oh, shit!"

"What's wrong?" she asked.

"I left forty dollars' worth of books in the coffee shop when I walked out on McDonald," I groaned. "What a pill . . ."

"Go back and get them," said Miriam.

"I can't," I said. "She and that camera crew may still be hanging around."

"Okay, phone them."

"I can't," I replied. "I don't know the name of the place. Fuck it. Never mind. It'll teach me to avoid dramatic gestures. Are you coming over this evening?"

"You bet," she said.

"Okay, take care — and don't forget to look over your shoulder." I hung up and, as I turned around, I found The

Man standing behind me. I took a split second to recover from the shock then I cased the street in both directions. I couldn't see the brown VW delivery truck, but by now I had begun to develop a healthy paranoia.

"Come on, we've got to get off the street." I grabbed The Man's arm and searched the passing traffic for an empty cab.

"Relax," said The Man. "You're the only one who can see me." He sidestepped to let a young couple go by.

My tongue wrestled limply with the words. "You mean you're — invisible?" A passerby turned and gave me an odd stare.

"No," he said. "You're not hallucinating. I'm really here. All I'm doing is creating a blank spot in the minds of anybody else who looks at me. It's a bit like the electronic countermeasures your Air Force uses to make their planes disappear from enemy radar-screens."

"Neat," I said. Out of the side of my mouth. "You must be able to have some real fun with a stroke like that."

He replied with a shrug. "It comes in handy now and then. Come on — I'll walk you back to the office."

As we threaded our way through the unseeing crowds, I realized that The Man had just solved three of the passages in the Gospels that had been puzzling me. Maybe they caught your notice too because the first of them clearly requires the use of paranormal powers for it to make sense. The incident I'm referring to is in Luke, chapter 4, beginning at verse 16, when Jesus returns to Nazareth, teaches in the synagogue and gets everybody so steamed up that in verse 29 they run him to the edge of town and are about to throw him over a cliff. Then comes verse 30 and the teaser — *"But he passing through the midst of them went his way."* To Capernaum.

I'd been trying to work out how he could have just walked away from a lynch mob that had actually had him by the collor, and now the answer was walking right beside me.

The second passage covers a similar tight corner. This time in the Temple at Jerusalem where The Man had been sounding off and, predictably, had upset a lot of folks. By this time, of course, he was doing his best to make himself unpopular in order to qualify for the ultimate sanction — crucifixion. John, chapter 8, verse 59 is where the magic happens: *"Then they took up stones to cast at him; but Jesus hid himself, and went out of the temple, going through the midst of them, and so passed by."* Note the words. He wasn't stuck out of sight behind a pillar. He was right in among them — but they couldn't *see* him.

The third passage is less explicit but you still get the impression that, once again, he blanked himself out of the landscape. John, chapter 10, verse 39: *"Therefore they sought him again to take him: but he escaped out of their hand."* Three near-fatal encounters from which he escaped by the use of his extraordinary powers — in order to die *on the cross*.

No one could argue that being thrown over a cliff, or being stoned by a mob, is a markedly more attractive alternative. Neither carry a built-in guarantee of instant death. In fact, I would suggest that both could be pretty messy. So it wasn't *just* the suffering on the cross — which Christians have made such a big thing of — that was the reason for the crucifixion. There had to be other factors involved. Things that I did not yet clearly understand. Because although death on the cross might be what the American legal system would call a cruel and unusual punishment, it was not a rare occurrence in first-century Palestine. As Publius Quintilius Varus and his two legions had shown. It could happen to anybody — and frequently did.

I could have asked him outright for the answer but I chose not to. First, because I now knew that he would tell me in his own good time. And second because I wanted to reach out toward the answer intuitively. Put it down to my desire to be a smart ass if you like, but I genuinely believed that if I got to the answer before he gave it to me, I would be on the brink of real understanding.

We reached Forty-ninth Street and paused on the sidewalk across from my office building. "Are you going to come up?" I asked.

He shook his head "You've got work to do."

"Where are you going — back to the apartment?"

"No," he said. "I thought I'd take a ride on a bus — if that's okay with you."

"Whatever you like," I replied. "But I can tell you now, it won't be as much fun as time-traveling."

I walked with him to the bus stop. As he stepped toward the curb, a florid man in an alpaca suit bumped into him. "Hey, watch where you're going —"

"Sorry," said The Man.

I gave him a startled look. "He can see you."

"Don't worry," smiled The Man. "Nobody's following us now."

I looked around for the brown VW truck but it was nowhere in sight. "You should have stayed invisible," I said. "That way you could have saved on the fare."

He patted my shoulder. "I don't want anyone sitting in my lap. Besides, from what I hear, New York needs all the money it can get."

A Greenwich Village bus arrived. The Man waited until the other travelers had climbed aboard.

"Will we see you tonight?" I asked.

"Maybe. I'm not sure. There's a lot happening."

"Okay. Well — you know where to find me." I stepped back and waited as he offered one of my fifty-dollar bills to the driver to pay for the sixty-cent fare.

The driver eyed the bill then The Man. "This is a bus, friend. Not a branch of the Chase Manhattan Bank."

"That's okay," said The Man. "Keep the change."

The driver looked at the note as if it were Monopoly money and brushed it aside. "What are you — a comedian? Gimme the right fare or get off the bus!"

"Here — take this." I passed up a handful of loose change to The Man and addressed the driver. "Go easy — he just stepped off the boat."

The driver rolled his eyes heavenwards — little realizing that a not-inconsiderable chunk of it was making its way to the back of his bus. The doors closed and, as the bus moved off, I saw The Man sitting next to a pretty girl with long black hair. We waved briefly to each other and then he was gone.

And once again, like that time on the porch, I felt this curious sense of loss. I know that doesn't make sense after telling you the increasing anxiety his presence caused, but that's the way it was. Looking back, I'm sure that if any of you had found yourselves in the same situation, you would have experienced the same mental disarray.

Put yourself in my place. One minute you are jogging along, happily minding your own business, and then, suddenly, you run slap into the Risen Christ. Not a brief, starry-eyed vision that took your breath away and made your heart leap but which remained comfortably out of reach. The Man was *real*. A solid, walking, talking being you could reach out and touch. Who could empty a glass of wine without emptying the bottle but who left dents in my sofa and his sandals under my coffee table. Who went in and out of the twentieth century as easily as you or I might walk into or out of the john but who, when he appeared, cast a real shadow. Whose voice was not just inside my head but could be heard on reels of tape. And whose words reduced our private obsessions and public concerns to total insignificance.

Think about it; ask yourself what you would have done and said if you'd found The Man sitting beside you as you rode or drove to work, or sat at home with the kids in front of the TV. Or if you bumped into him at the local supermarket, or if you were cutting your lawn and looked up to find that you were about to run the mower over his toes. Don't laugh. It could happen. The Man doesn't go in for big entrances. The nearest he ever got to the show-biz razzama-tazz of globe-trotting pontiffs with their big set-piece production numbers and white helicopters was a few palm leaves and a ride on the back of a donkey.

When I reached our suite of offices on the twenty-second floor, I found Linda's office empty. She'd left a typewritten note on my desk to say that she'd forgotten to mention the appointment she had made with her dentist. I had a feeling she had heard McDonald's interview had backfired and was avoiding me. Not that I had much of a case against her. McDonald was smart enough to find out that the "dead" Mr. Abraham Lucksteen was not a client of mine without making Linda break the house rules. My suspicion that there had been some collusion hinged on the fact that I had told Linda I was going to the bookshop. One thing I *was* sure of: meeting McDonald there was no coincidence. She had the camera crew holding the table at the window for her. The whole thing was a setup but it must have involved some fast footwork because my decision to go out and buy another armful of enlightenment had been made on the spur of the moment.

I think what annoyed me more than anything was the realization that all my dissembling had been for naught. Both of us now hovered on the brink of exposure by the media; a process that had been hastened by The Man's encounter with Mrs. Perez. As I sat at my desk pondering my next move it seemed to me rather ironic that, after all my lies, the only way I could think of silencing our pursuers was by telling them the truth.

But how? Should Miriam and I confess to them in private? Play back the tapes and show them the Polaroids taken of The Man when he was picked up for dead? Or wait until we could confront them with The Man and just let them discover it all for themselves? Then I thought of the concept of simultaneity and said to myself — *What the hell. God's got it all worked out anyway.* If The Man had not wanted Fowler and McDonald to know, he could have hit them with a mind-block the way he had Lieutenant Russell and Marcello.

I did my best to shove it all to the back of my mind and tried to concentrate my mental energies on my faltering practice of law. At half-past five I got my second surprise of the afternoon. There was a knock on my door and Brad, the young guy who runs our mail room, walked in.

"This package just came for you. Special delivery." He put it on my desk. "Linda had to go to the dentist's."

"Yeah, I know." I hefted the brown paper package. There was only one thing it could contain. Books.

Brad stopped in the doorway. "Do you want a coffee or anything before we all hit the road?"

"No thanks," I said, picking at the tightly knotted string.

"Okay," he said lightly. "Don' work too hard." A real fresh kid. But then, where he came from, it was what separated the winners from the losers.

I gave up on the knot and sliced through the string and the wrapping with the paperknife that Joe's son David had left on his desk when he'd taken off for Israel. Inside I found, as expected, the six books I'd left in the coffee shop. I opened the top book and took out the envelope bearing the Channel Eight logo, and addressed to me. Inside it was a note from McDonald — containing the third surprise of the afternoon.

The note read: *In your haste to leave you forgot these. I do not intend to apologize for doing my job but I think it only fair you should know that the brown VW truck that was being used to videotape our conversation does not belong to Channel Eight or any of its affiliates or subsidiaries and the two gentlemen who gave up their seats to us are completely unknown to me. Fortunately, I took down their license number. I propose to check this out and will let you know if I turn up anything interesting. Meanwhile, if you feel like talking, you know my number. If not, don't worry. I'm still on your case.*

Terrific . . .

SEVENTEEN

I sat back with McDonald's note in my hand, read through it again and again while I smoked a couple of cigarettes, then rang the Channel Eight newsroom on my private line and asked for McDonald.

"You got the books . . ."

"Yeah," I said flatly. "I also got your note."

"I hope you believe me," she said. "I am definitely not trying to put one over on you."

"Just give me the license plate number of the truck," I said. "I've got friends in the police force too."

She gave me the details without demur. The truck had New Jersey plates. "By the way, that wasn't a transmitter mike you dunked in my coffee. It was wired to a deck inside my bag."

"Sure," I said. I hung up on her to let her know how things stood, then called Larry Bekker, my law school buddy who was now Deputy DA. "It's me again," I announced. "Only this time, I'm wearing my Mike Hammer hat. Can you trace a license plate for me?"

"Are you asking me to bend the system?" he said.

"I'll buy you lunch with two of the prettiest faces from *Vogue* magazine," I replied. "All you have to do is name the time and place."

"Give me the number," said Larry.

I passed it over. "Mark it 'Urgent,' Larry. If I'm not here, try my apartment."

I got home about seven and found that The Man had left the TV on. I picked up the remote-control handset from the sofa, hit the Off button, and straightened out the cushions. I checked the hall closet and saw that his brown woolen robe was still hanging there with the sandals placed side by side underneath. I thought of Mrs. Perez, and ran my hand over the coarsely woven cloth then took hold of both sleeves and shut my eyes. Nothing happened. I was not rewarded with a vision of Calvary — or anything else for that matter. I shut the closet door, still persuaded that the robe held some kind of power. If it worked for Mrs. Perez, it could work for me. All I had to do was find the key.

Miriam arrived at half-past seven with a radiant smile which vanished when she found I was the only beneficiary. I explained that, when last seen, The Man had been headed downtown.

She checked her watch. "But that was over three and a half hours ago. Do you think he's gone back to Jerusalem?"

"I doubt it," I replied. "His robe's still in the closet."

Let me just explain what prompted that remark. Despite the fact that my imagination had been honed on treasured copies of *Astounding Science Fiction,* I found it hard to accept that products of external reality such as the clothes we had bought him could exist outside the linear space-time continuum. And if that sounds like psychobabble to some of you let me put it another way. I did not believe it was physically possible for a pair of jogging shoes purchased for eighteen dollars at Macy's on Fifth Avenue in April 1981 to end up, albeit on the feet of the Messiah, in first-century Jerusalem.

Because, if the shoes could make it, then so, by extension, could we. Which opened up the possibility of unlimited two-way traffic, having Tamburlaine for tea, and took us into the realms of total improbability.

I could quite happily accept that The Man could do what the shoes could not. In the same way that his robe, sandals, and other bits and pieces could time-travel because they too were four-dimensional "visualizations" conjured into existence by the incredible power of the Empire. But like The Man, they were not "real" in the way that the clothes Linda had bought him were real. Although he was a miraculous molecule-for-molecule reproduction, he was no longer "of the flesh" in the same way that the wool of his brown robe had not grown on the back of a sheep and his sandals had never been part of a cow's hide.

I made the mistake of sharing these thoughts with Miriam. She listened patiently to my confident hypothesis then demolished it totally. "You've forgotten the bandages I put on his hands and feet before he disappeared from the morgue," she said. "He was wearing them when he turned up at Sleepy Hollow."

"Oh, shit, yes," I said grudgingly. "I'd forgotten about that."

"Never mind," she smiled. "You can't be right about everything."

I let her enjoy that small triumph. Looking back — and I say this with genuine affection — I think she was pretty niggled that The Man had singled me out as the major recipient of The Word. More than niggled, in fact. Insanely jealous. Because although I think she loved me, I'm sure she considered herself the more deserving case. Maybe she was, but in the end, The Man left without giving her the gift of healing she so badly wanted. I never asked him why but my guess is, after what happened to me, he probably decided that her life was screwed up enough already.

I made a cup of coffee while she told me about her day, then I passed her the note McDonald had sent with the books.

She read through it and handed it back with a sniffy laugh. "Do you believe it?"

"I'll tell you when I hear from Larry Bekker," I said. The

phone rang. It was Bekker. Right on cue. "Larry — just talking about you."

"Sorry to be so long," he said. "After you rang a million things happened. Listen — are you sure about the plate number you gave me?"

"Yeah," I said. "What's wrong?"

"The plate's not listed on the New Jersey register," said Larry. "I got them to run the combinations of that serial through the computer. Not one of them is allocated to a brown VW truck."

I eyed Miriam. "So what does that mean?"

"If you've got the right number, it can only mean one thing," he said. "It's a fake — a made-up plate."

"I see . . ." I whispered the news to Miriam. "What conclusion would you draw from that?"

"Huhh," said Larry. "Your guess is as good as mine. In this big bad world there are only two groups of people who use fake plates — professional criminals and employees of certain federal agencies."

"My thoughts exactly," I replied. "Have you passed the details over to Traffic?"

"Yes," he said. "But don't sit by the phone. I don't know what your interest is but if that truck is not part of a common criminal conspiracy then you and I ain't ever gonna hear about it."

"Sure, I understand. Larry, listen — I want you to do me one more favor."

"Those girls had better be more than just pretty," he joshed.

I adopted a tone of mock reproof. "Larry, if I suggested you might get lucky you could haul me in for trying to suborn a city official. On the other hand, what you do on your afternoons off is none of my business. I want you to get me a rundown on two detectives assigned to the Narcotics Division of the Organized Crime Control Bureau, down in the Seventh. They're called Ritger and Donati. Is that going to be a big deal?"

"It'll make me late for dinner," he replied. "But it's only meat loaf, so stick around. I'll call you later."

I rang off and recounted the rest of our conversation to Miriam, including Larry's remark about federal agencies.

She laughed. "Which ones?"

"Well it's not the Department of Agriculture," I said. "It would have to be the FBI, or the CIA."

She shook her head. "You really are getting paranoid."

I shrugged. "Maybe I am. But I haven't forgotten that the ambulance which brought The Man to the hospital was stolen, and that he and I got busted by the wrong section of the NYPD. And now this truck . . ."

"Has it occurred to you that maybe it was Michael and Gabriel that brought The Man to Manhattan General?" she said.

I stared at her. "Why would they do that?"

She threw her hands in the air. "I don't know. To meet you, I suppose. *You're* the one he's spent most time with. As for the arrest, well — you're the expert, but from what I know about the drug scene there's so many narcs posing as pushers and buyers they spend most of their time busting each other."

"It's been known to happen," I conceded. "But I've learned to become wary of facile explanations."

"Yeah, of course, I forgot," she groaned. "You're not happy unless things are complicated. One of these days you're going to end up outsmarting yourself." She pointed to McDonald's note. "She's lying. It's obvious. She got caught out when you spotted her friends in the truck and now she's trying to bamboozle you with a bum license plate."

I met her reasoning with a rolled bottom lip. "It's possible. But don't you think it's curious that, of all the numbers she could have made up, the one she gave me was not on the New Jersey register?"

Miriam gave me a pitying look and got to her feet. "I think I'll make something to eat." She paused in the kitchen doorway and looked back at me. "Only you could think of something like that."

I lay back in my chair and put my feet up. "That's what makes me so smart and so lovable. How about frying up those steaks?"

"You're getting an omelet," she said. "I've seen enough red meat today."

She was still whipping it up when Larry Bekker called me. "I hope you're luckier with model girls," he said.

"How d'you mean?"

He let me have the bad news. "There's nobody by the name of Ritger or Donati working out of the Seventh Precinct."

"Larry," I said, "you've got to be kidding. I was on the street with a client of mine when these two guys busted him. I went down there to get him out."

There was a brief silence. "When was this?"

"Last week. Last Monday. I called you — remember?"

"Ohh, yeah," he said. "I thought you were being a little cagey. Well, listen, we can easily check this out. Their names must be on the arrest report."

"He wasn't arrested," I said. "He was hauled in on suspicion. There is nothing on file. They junked the paperwork when they let him go."

"I see . . ." Larry sounded doubtful. "Did you just deal with these two guys — or was anyone else involved?"

My brain felt as if it was on fire. I must have sounded very confused. "Uhh, yeah, uhh — I've got the names of a couple of other guys, uhh — don't worry, I'll take it from here."

He tried to be helpful. "Maybe if you were to give me the name of your client —"

"No, listen, everything's fine," I said. "Thanks. I owe you an unforgettable lunch. Okay?"

We exchanged bantering goodbyes. When I turned away from the phone, I found Miriam standing tight-lipped at the door to the kitchen. "Did you get all that?"

"It's written all over your face," she said. "No Ritger and no Donati. I was frightened he was going to tell you they'd closed down the Seventh Precinct station house."

"We can soon find out." I picked up the Manhattan directory, found the number, and started dialing.

"Who are you calling?" asked Miriam.

"Lieutenant Russell. He had his name on the door — remember?" I was out of luck. The guy manning the switchboard told me that there was nobody called Lieutenant Russell, or Frank Marcello, with an office on the third or any other floor of the building. "Put me through to the desk sergeant," I said. I covered the phone and looked at Miriam. "It must be me. I must be going crazy."

"Desk sergeant," said a voice.

"Hi," I said, as briskly as I could manage. "Is your name Benny?"

"Nope."

"Oh," I said. "Maybe he's not on this shift. Are any of the other desk sergeants called Benny?"

"Nope."

"I see. Okay, thanks."

"You're welcome." The line went dead.

I put the phone down and slumped against the wall, clutching my head. "They've all gone. They've all disappeared. What the hell is going on?!"

Miriam poured me out a glass of bourbon, stuck it in my lifeless hand, led me firmly away from the phone and eased me into my armchair. "Drink," she said.

I did as I was told and felt somewhat better for it.

Miriam knelt down by the armchair, took hold of my other hand, and addressed me in her best bedside manner. "Has it occurred to you that 'Brax might be behind all this?"

I downed some more bourbon and took my brain off the boil. "I don't understand. You mean Ritger and Donati don't exist? That the arrest never happened? That you and I didn't go downtown and meet Rabbi Whatever-his-name-is?"

"Weinbaum," she said. "No, I'm not saying that. What I'm

suggesting is that they only existed for *us*. If 'Brax is as powerful as he's supposed to be, and he's the master of external reality, then he could have recreated that piece of Forty-second Street where you were arrested, the station house — and all the people in it. They could even look like people in the *real* building." She gripped my hand tightly. "If he wanted to, he could probably re-create the whole city. It would be just as real as the one we're in now."

"Yeah . . ." It was a mind-blowing proposition. I eyed her sulkily. "How come *I* didn't think of that?"

She patted my hand and planted a mocking kiss on my temple. "You're too clever."

"Wait a minute," I said. "Before I buy this great idea of yours — why is he doing it?"

She locked her eyes onto mine. "To make you doubt. To make us *both* doubt the evidence of our own eyes. To so disorient our senses that we would begin to believe that The Man wasn't real — that none of what we had seen and heard had actually taken place." The smile had gone now. I could see she was totally convinced of what she was saying.

"But why *now?*" I insisted. "Why didn't he start working on us from the very beginning?"

Her grip on my hand tightened again. "He *did*. Didn't we doubt what we'd seen? Didn't we try to convince ourselves that it hadn't happened? Didn't we tell each other that it was impossible? Weren't we worried about our jobs? Frightened about what our friends would say? 'Brax was there inside us, exploiting our instincts for self-preservation, bringing out the worst side of our characters. And then when, in spite of yourself, you began to listen to The Man, you were threatened physically —"

"Yes, with the elevator," I said. "But why has he hit us with this trick? Why is he re-creating external reality?"

"Don't you see?" said Miriam. "It's the ultimate weapon. You've forced him to use it because you've started to *believe*. You may not be aware of it but when I sit and listen to you and The Man, I can feel this bond between you —"

"Yeah, well, we get on okay," I said.

"Oh, come on," said Miriam. "You know it's more than that. You're important to him. You must know by now it's no accident he's here. I don't know what's going to happen to any of us, but there has to be a reason why he's been telling you these things. Whatever it is, 'Brax is trying to stop you two from getting together. He's trying to scare you into thinking you're being followed, leading you down a blind alley then making the alley disappear." She paused. "Do you realize that might not have been the real Larry Bekker you were speaking to?"

As you can imagine, that had me reeling. "Oh, come on," I cried. "Where are you getting all this stuff?"

She smiled. "Relax. I'm just trying to demonstrate the power 'Brax has. After all, how can you be sure I'm me?"

I smiled back at her. "The real Miriam Maxwell knows how to make a mean Spanish omelet." I pulled her close and put my mouth on hers. "And she kisses good too."

She eased herself out of my arms and stood up. "Food and sex. I guess that makes you the real Leo Resnick."

I followed her into the kitchen and watched it all happen. "You really amaze me, you know? I've never heard you talk like that before."

She nudged me away from a cupboard door. "I've never had to."

"Yeah, well, you really helped me out," I said.

She started to chop up the green and red peppers. "So why are you frowning?"

"Because we still have a problem," I said. "Let's suppose you're right and that 'Brax has created specific incidents which are indistinguishable from, uhh — what we can call 'ordinary' external reality. Where do we start? What do we use to anchor ourselves if he is able to play around with our perception in the way you suggest?"

She gave me that irritating know-it-all smile again. "It's so simple, Leo. You *believe*. You believe in The Man. *He's* your anchor. If you concentrate all your mental energy on him, 'Brax won't be able to warp your mind. Didn't he say that he represented the ultimate reality and that external reality was the illusion? Forget all this business about conspiracies. Stop looking over your shoulder and concentrate on the road ahead. Because that's where The Man's taking us whether we like it or not."

As I sit here, writing down her words, I ask myself once again — did she know? Had The Man given her the secret knowledge he gave to Mary Magdalene? Was the part she played greater than I knew? Did I ever know who she *really* was? Or even — crazy as it sounds — which side she was on?

When we finished the omelet, I consulted the entertainment section of the *Post* and checked my watch. "Come on," I said. "We've just got time to catch a late movie."

She eyed me cagily. "Of whose choice?"

"Yours," I replied, gallantly offering the paper. It was her turn anyway.

She ran her eye down the movie house listings. "Don't you think this is a little irresponsible? Supposing The Man comes back?"

"It could be embarrassing," I said. "If we don't go to the movies, I plan to strip you naked and make mad passionate love."

She took me to *Cries and Whispers*. Another gloom-laden *smorgasbord* put together by Bergman and distributed by Roger Corman. Presumably by way of penance for making so much money with his own endearingly outrageous brand of cinematic junk food.

You may think it was an odd moment to duck out and take in a movie but the truth was I wanted to give my brain a rest. The Man had come steaming down the centuries like a great ocean liner leaving my life raft rocking in the wake of his presence and in danger of capsizing completely. I desperately needed a moment of calm to get myself back on an even keel. I didn't want to think about cosmic truths, real or unreal cops and nosy girl reporters — or Linda, whom I would have to confront in the morning. I just wanted to empty my mind. The Bergman film was a great help.

When we got back, I checked the hall closet. The robe was still there but the apartment was devoid of his Celestial presence. We went to bed where, despite Miriam's earlier prudish reserve, I got lucky. Better than lucky. Everything clicked so perfectly it almost blew my head off. As we lay locked together with our hearts pounding against each other's ribs, I thought — *What a crazy world.* In which the woman who only hours before had argued so ardently on behalf of The Man could surrender her body with equal passion — notching up several points for 'Brax in the process. But then she was always full of contradictions. That's what made her so interesting.

I reached for the inevitable cigarette. A real cliché gesture. Life's full of them. At least mine is — or rather it used to be. Miriam nestled her head against my shoulder. I circled the small of her back with my fingertips and thought what a pity that the Empire had not seen fit to include this kind of activity in their prospectus. I watched the smoke disperse as it rose out of the glow of the lamp toward the darkened ceiling and wished that all my problems could vanish as easily. Eventually I gave voice to them, and we returned to the menace of Miss McD.

"You should have asked The Man what to do when you saw him today," said Miriam.

"I couldn't," I said. "He was invisible. I'd have been walking down Madison Avenue talking to myself. Which may not seem important to you but there are people around there who know me. I'll ask him what I should do when he comes back."

"It's a pity he wasn't here tonight," she said. "I was looking forward to the next installment."

"Oh, yeah, the 'missing years.'" I crushed my cigarette and blew the last of the smoke from my lungs. "I think he just traveled around. He's already mentioned going to England and Rome."

"You mean he walked?" she said.

"Yes, why not?" I replied. "If you were to do ten miles a day for twelve years that's a —" I figured it out. "— a good forty thousand miles. It would take you around the world and back." A thought struck me. "Hey — I wonder if he came to America?"

"I hope you're not going to tell me he walked across the Atlantic," said Miriam.

"He wouldn't have to," I replied. "He could have made his way across the Kamchatka peninsula and down through Alaska."

"Very clever," she said. "And then what — back the same way?"

I shrugged. "Not necessarily. Thor Heyerdahl is supposed to have proved that the Polynesians reached the Central Pacific from South America. Maybe he worked his passage on one of their reed boats — or hitched a ride in one of the Nazca hot air balloons."

"You're crazy," yawned Miriam.

"No, listen," I said. "Just suppose The Man *did* come to America. It could mean that the Mormons were right after all. The angel Moroni who called on Joseph Smith could have been Michael, or Gabriel — or maybe some other Envoy from the Empire."

"That's true," she agreed. "On the other hand, Joseph Smith and his friends may have made it all up because they liked having women around the house waiting on them hand and foot." She signed off with a kiss under my ear and settled down to sleep.

I switched off the lamp on my side of the bed and lay there in the dark, reviewing various aspects of the mess I'd gotten into. And I wondered whether it was wise to go ahead with my two-week sabbatical. Now that I had McDonald on my back, it made good sense to head for the hills. But what would that solve? There were another four weeks to the Feast of the Pentecost — always assuming that that was when this time-twisting misadventure was due to end.

And that led me once again to consider the idea that The Man might not be time-traveling in the accepted sense. That the theory of simultaneity that Miriam and I had constructed and which he had confirmed might only be a convenient device to bemuse us and, in so doing, enhance the omnipotent image of the Empire and our liege-lords, the Celestials, who had allegedly ordered the history of the universe since the Creation. There was no doubt in my mind about The Man's ability to disappear from twentieth-century Manhattan. But the fact that he did so was not proof that he reappeared in an earlier, still-existent time frame of this planet's history. He might merely have transferred to an extratemporal dimension adjacent to our own. One of the other wavelengths he'd talked about.

So why, you ask, did he turn up on Easter Saturday, broken and bloodied from the Crucifixion? Simple. Without the stigmata how could we unbelievers have recognized him? His appearance, the timing — it all helped us make the right connections. And would lead us to think that he had been catapulted from the rock tomb into the twentieth century. That was his story too. But there was no *proof*. At the beginning, he had said it was an accident. Now it was part of the plan. How many more times were his mission orders going to be revised?

I was not trying, by means of this conjectural maneuver, to deny our peripatetic visitor his place in world history. As far as I was concerned he was still The Man. But these renewed doubts allowed me to regain control of my destiny. For if Time was *not* simultaneous, then we could dump the book analogy overboard. The battle between 'Brax and the Empire was not a foregone conclusion. The issue was still in doubt. God, The Presence, or Whoever did not have my life-plot filed away in some cosmic computer. I was still able, along with the rest of humanity, to choose what I would or would not do. To listen to what The Man had to say, or go to hell in a handcart.

It was a typical 'Braxian thought, but since I had allowed

him to creep back into my loins it was only natural he would try to worm his way into my head and gain control of my mind. And it was so much easier to surrender. Sleep clogged my brain and broke up my train of thoughts. I turned over, tucked the quilt down between our bare backs, and went out like a light.

Somewhere around three o'clock, I surfaced from a dreamless void and my sleep-sodden brain slowly became aware of a bluish light coming from the living room. At first I thought that Miriam had got up and put on the TV then I realized that she lay asleep beside me. I dropped my head back onto the pillow and considered getting up to switch the damn thing off and it occurred to me it could mean that The Man was back.

I rolled out from under the quilt, groped my way into my robe, and padded out of the bedroom, my eyes almost closed in a desperate effort to cling onto sleep. To the point where they didn't even snap open at what they saw in the living room. Was it a dream? I don't know. I'm still not sure. But the light wasn't coming from the TV set. It came from two palely glowing humanoids that stood on either side of The Man. About six foot three inches in height and dressed in a kind of unisex coverall — like racing drivers wear. Only these two weren't covered with advertising. I know they had eyes, a nose and a mouth but beyond that I can't tell you what they looked like. If I had to name a face, I'd have to say John Philip Law, who played the angel in *Barbarella*. But more almond-eyed. More — Pharonic. Not that it really matters because, as The Man said, each of us sees angels the way we imagine them to be. That's why many of the secret gospels that were suppressed by Rome claimed he had the power to change his appearance and emphasized that no two observers saw him in the same way.

The Man's companions had this soft light raying out through their bodies. All the details seemed to be in soft focus. I suppose I should have been shocked, flabbergasted, but — for some reason — I just took it all in my stride. As

I've explained, I had this feeling I was dreaming. I greeted The Man with a wave of the hand and scratched my chest. "Hi . . . can I get you guys anything?"

"No," said The Man. "We're just passing through." He introduced his two companions. "This is Michael — and this is Gabriel. I don't see them as you do. How do they look?"

"Tall, and radioactive," I said. We exchanged nods but I didn't attempt to shake hands. "How are things going?"

"Fine," replied The Man. "We've been attending to a few things in the up-when. I was on my way back to Jerusalem and I thought I'd better stop off to tell you not to worry. Everything's going to turn out just fine."

He said he would never lie to me but I venture to suggest that the truth of that statement depends very much on one's own particular point of view. But once again, that is with the benefit of hindsight. What I said was "I'm glad to hear it. Does that mean you're taking care of McDonald and Jeff Fowler? And how about Linda? Is she going to give me trouble?"

"We're being called down-when," said The Man. He patted my arm just below the shoulder. "Talk to them. But don't wait too long. There's not a lot of time left."

"But how?" I heard myself ask tiredly. "What am I going to say?"

The Man gave me a confident nod. "You'll think of something. I'll try and get up over the weekend." The way he talked, you could almost believe that the Empire had leased the Time Express and was running a shuttle service.

Michael waved his hand. "See you around."

"Yes, sure," I said. Without thinking what that particular exchange might mean — or even noticing whether his lips moved.

Gabriel just nodded.

"One last thing," said The Man. "When you get up, don't miss the news on the radio."

I nodded sleepily. "Okay . . ."

And they were gone.

I stood there for a few minutes while my eyes got used to the dark then shuffled back to bed. The whole encounter had such a strange, offbeat quality I'm almost certain it was a dream and that, in fact, I never got out of bed. But then what are dreams but other dimensions of being? That extend from the plane of temporal existence into the realms of the infinite.

The alarm woke me at a quarter to seven. Miriam stirred briefly then went back to sleep. I forced myself out of bed, hummed away ten minutes of my life under the shower, then padded into the kitchen, put fresh coffee into the percolator, and loaded last night's dishes into the sink so the cleaning lady wouldn't have a fit. I pressed the On button of my Sanyo portable as I went past into the living room in search of a pack of cigarettes and mulled over the strange dream I'd had about meeting Michael and Gabriel. Normally they fade away almost as soon as I wake up but the details of this one stuck in my head.

When I returned to the kitchen, the seven o'clock news had begun. I listened mechanically as the newscaster ran through the morning's headlines. Global news, national news; nothing much had changed since yesterday. Then came the local stuff. It wasn't the first item. These things never are. But during the night, the police and municipal authorities had been bombarded with hundreds of phone calls from people who claimed to have seen a giant UFO hovering above the city. JFK, La Guardia and Newark Air Traffic Control had all reported picking it up on their radar screens but a USAF spokesman at the Pentagon had said that the signal had been caused by freak conditions in the magnetosphere.

Which was just as well, because the estimated size of the spaceship was twice the length of Manhattan Island . . .

I took Miriam in a cup of coffee and described my nocturnal encounter with The Man and his two luminous sidekicks.

"Why didn't you wake me?" she snapped.

"Come on, gimme a break," I said. "I'm not even sure I

was awake myself." I told her about the city-sized UFO that
had been hurriedly explained away by the Air Force.

"Do you think it was real?" she asked.

I shrugged. "After what you said last night, I'm not sure
if I know what that word means."

Dream or no dream, it was clear that The Man knew about
the tug-of-war I was having with 'Brax. Or was it *his* tug-of-
war — and was I just the ribbon around the rope that was
swaying back and forth across the line? Overnight, he had
produced Michael and Gabriel, cast the shadow of one of the
Empire's longships over New York City, and had provided
circumstantial evidence that those feet, in ancient times, had
been fleetingly shod in blue jogging shoes and black 50/50
nylon-and-wool-mix socks.

As I rode downtown in Jake's cab, I remember wishing an
archaeological team could have dug those withered treads
out of the strata containing the rubble of the first-century
city. It would have been indisputable proof of his time-
traveling. The trouble was, no one would have accepted it.
In the same way that scientists could not bring themselves to
accept the evidence of the Turin Shroud.

I met Brad in the lift. He, Joe and I are always the first
three in. Joe and I like to start work early. Brad comes in
because the mail room is a lot nicer than where he lives. An
AM/FM cassette recorder the size of a baby cabin trunk was
perched on his shoulder.

Brad flashed a set of teeth that would cost someone like me
at least two thousand dollars. "Hey," he said. "How about
that flyin' saucer. D'ya hear about that?"

I nodded. "Yes. Did you see it?"

"Nahh," he said. "How come these things always turn up
when 'most ever'body's asleep?"

I grinned at him. "It's to stop guys like you stealing their
hubcaps."

"Yeah . . ." His eyes gleamed. "Twenty-six miles long.
Boy . . . imagine tryin' to park that fuckin' thing."

"Right," I said. I didn't tell him I knew the owner.

Linda made it to the office around a quarter to ten and kept herself busy with the tapes I'd left on her desk. Finally she stuck her head around the door. "Have you got a minute?"

I switched on my Mr. Nice Guy smile. "Sure. Come on in."

She crossed the carpet as if it was a minefield and when she got to my desk she seemed unable to decide what to do with her hands. "Listen," she began. "About what happened yesterday. I didn't know that Gale was going to try to — well, you know —"

"That's okay," I said. "Nobody got hurt. And, in any case, there was nothing I could tell her. She already knew it all." I blunted the barb with an understanding smile but it still cut deep.

"Now wait a minute," she said. "If I'm going to get fired, I don't want it to be for something I didn't do. She called me yesterday saying she needed to get in touch with you urgently. You hadn't said when you might be back so I suggested she try the bookshop. After all, you hadn't told me to keep her off your back. As for that business about Abraham Lucksteen, maybe I did speak out of turn but you should have taken me into your confidence. I've always made a point of knowing who all your clients are and what cases we're dealing with. When I got this call all I did was check the files to see if I could have made a mistake. Since we didn't have any record of the guy I didn't see any harm in saying we didn't represent him. But I did not give out any confidential information."

"I know," I said. "Don't worry about it. Really."

"Well, that's easy to say," she insisted. "But I'm getting very confused. I think I ought to tell you I had a long talk with Gale last night and she told me about these blood samples that have got some guy called Fowler jumping up and down. Why did you tell him the blood came from someone who was supposed to have died when you knew all along that it came from Sheppard? What's wrong with him? Is he carrying some kind of plague or something?"

It was a good question. Because in a way he *was* carrying something that could be regarded by the 'Braxian world as a fatal disease — Truth. But like its companion, Honesty, it could hardly be described as contagious. 'Brax had done his best to make sure that most of us were immune to both.

"If I'm going to go on working for you," continued Linda, "I think I have the right to know exactly what it is that you and Dr. Maxwell are covering up. I'm not asking out of morbid curiosity. I'm concerned. I mean he was such a nice guy. So tell me — is Sheppard in some kind of trouble?"

I shook my head. "No. But I could be."

She frowned. "I don't understand."

How could she? How could anyone guess what Miriam and I had been concealing? A secret that, depending on your point of view, was either truly and utterly amazing or totally absurd. I gazed at her, the words locked in my throat, and thought of what The Man had said to me in his fleeting dreamlike visit. Zacharias and Joseph had both received important messages in dreams. Why not me? Even though Linda had worked with me for two years I did not know whether I could entrust her with the truth about Mr. Sheppard. But I knew I could trust The Man. Or rather, should. I was still a little wary of my newfound belief that The Man would see me through the jam I was in. But he had told me to speak to Linda and now that she had confronted me, I was determined to try.

What could I lose? If she thought I had become unhinged and told Joe, it would only make him more convinced that I needed the holiday I intended to take. If she ratted on me she'd be out of a job, and if she kept it to herself but found it disturbing, she would leave anyway.

I motioned her to pull up a chair. "Linda," I said. "I want you to level with me because what I'm about to tell you could wreck my career. Is McDonald offering you any kind of inducement to pump me on behalf of Channel Eight?"

She shook her head. "No. She figured she could crack the Berlin Wall you'd thrown up around Sheppard all by herself." She waited for my reaction then, when nothing came down the line, she added, "That's the honest-to-God truth, Leo. I know what you're thinking but you're wrong. We've been to a couple of bars but the only thing she's interested in is finding herself a decent apartment. All of which is none of your damn business. I'm just trying to prove I like working here. Okay?"

I accepted this declaration with a nod. "Did she tell you anything about Mrs. Perez?"

She looked puzzled. "Who's she?"

"The lady who followed you from the dry-cleaning store," I said. "Tell me — your parents are Hungarian, right? So what does that make you — a Roman Catholic?"

"Yes, but not a very good one," she replied. "I go to mass at Christmas and Easter. It's kind of a family thing. But I stopped going to confession when I was eighteen."

"But you still believe in God the Father, God the Son, God the Holy Ghost, the Virgin Birth, the Crucifixion, the Resurrection, and all the rest of it . . . ?"

She smiled. "Not fervently but yes, I go along with most of it. But what has this got to do with Sheppard?"

"Good question . . ." I lit a cigarette to steady my nerve. "Do you believe in miracles?"

She looked at me curiously. I could see she was wondering where this was leading. "You mean like in the Bible? I'm not sure. I'm not too happy about the claims made by people who've been to Lourdes but I do believe that there are certain individuals who have the gift of healing — even though I haven't actually met one."

I hesitated then took one step nearer the brink. "Would you believe *me* if I told you that Dr. Maxwell and I had witnessed a miracle?"

"I might," she shrugged. "It depends what kind."

"Okay." I took a deep breath. "Would you believe me if I told you that Sheppard, the man you went shopping with, was lying dead on a slab in a morgue three weeks ago?"

She did a nervous double-take. "Say that again?"

I spelled it out for her. "He was dead when I first saw him."

"Ahh," she said. "I see what you mean. Someone thought he'd died but the doctors revived him. Amazing. I've heard of that happening. Some people have been dead for up to three hours."

I shook my head. "No, you've got it wrong. There was no mistake. He was killed on Easter Friday. Only not this one. He died two thousand years ago. Forget the doctors. He didn't need them." I glanced at my watch then sat back and waited.

Her eyes flickered across my face then onto the objects on my desk, the window and the pictures on the wall behind me. As if she were playing "I Spy."

"It took him three days to get better," I said helpfully.

She eyed me. "I know who died two thousand years ago," she replied. "But it doesn't make sense. Whether he was dead or alive, how is it possible for you to see him here in Manhattan?"

"Exactly," I said. *"That's* the miracle . . ."

She sat there staring at me and let her breath out in a long slow sigh. "You can't be serious."

"On the contrary," I replied. "I've never been more serious in all my life. Now perhaps you can understand why Dr. Maxwell and I felt we had to keep his presence here a secret."

She laughed nervously. "Let me get this straight. Are you trying to tell me that Mr. Sheppard is — the Risen Christ?"

I smiled. "I know how you feel. His disciples had the same problem. Do you see now why I said it could wreck my career?"

She laughed again. As I knew she would. "I can see it could upset things a little."

I leaned forward. "I'm not kidding, Linda. This is no joke, believe me. Do you really think that I'd be sitting here telling you something that, if it got out, would probably get me certified? In the last three weeks I've seen and heard enough things to put me into the nuthouse ten times over. Luckily

Miriam's been there to witness most of it. Do you think Mc-Donald would be following me around if I was making all this up? Ask her to tell you what happened to Mrs. Perez — the lady who followed you, and who dry-cleaned Sheppard's robe — then come back and talk to me."

She stared at me, chewing her lip. Trying to dispel the disquieting feeling that I might be telling the truth. "But Leo," she said. "I talked to him. He told me about his place in California, what he was writing — he even knew people that I knew who worked out at Universal."

"Of course he does." I laughed. "I told him what to say. And he got all that stuff about Universal Pictures out of your own head."

Her cheeks flushed red.

"Don't worry," I said. "He knows everything about me too. When he landed on me, I had to give him some kind of cover story. I mean, come on — what would you have thought if I'd asked you to take Jesus Christ shopping in Macy's?"

She laughed again. "Yes, I see what you mean." She shook her head. "Listen — it's a wonderful idea but I have to be honest with you. I accept that you believe it but — it's not possible."

"Of course it isn't," I said. "That's what I kept telling myself when he arrived here three weeks ago. But what I've seen has convinced me otherwise."

She fixed me with her eyes. "Where is he now?"

I stared straight back at her. "I believe he is in first-century Jerusalem. One of the things he's told us is that Time is simultaneous. The past is still happening, the future already exists. And he has the power to manifest himself in any place and any century he chooses."

Linda closed her eyes and shook her head. "No . . . it's not true. It — it doesn't make sense."

"It doesn't make sense to us," I said. "But it's happening nevertheless. And I may soon have the opportunity to prove it to you."

She looked at me, her eyes besieged with doubt. It sounds

awful but, as with Russell and Marcello, I enjoyed seeing someone else going through the mill. "I don't wish to sound insulting," I said, "but it should be easier for you. After all, you *are* a Christian. There are plenty of Catholic saints who claimed to have a nodding acquaintance with Jesus. Didn't you say yourself that he was a — special kind of person?"

Linda thought it over. "How many other people know about this?"

"Just you, Dr. Maxwell and myself," I said. "He also met Mrs. Perez but I think she has been persuaded that what she actually experienced was an ecstatic vision."

She nodded. "But if this is true, why haven't you told the Vatican?"

I sucked in air through my teeth. "That's one of the problems. From what I've learned so far, they and The Man may not have a lot in common."

She raised an eyebrow. "The Man?"

"It's what we call him," I explained. "You see, he doesn't really fit the image people conjure up when you talk about Jesus Christ."

"Okay," she said. "How about someone in the government?"

I threw up my hands. "Who should I call, Linda? Do you really think the people in the White House would be pleased to hear that Jesus Christ was arriving on the next flight into Dulles?"

"Yes, but, Leo — if this is true — don't you think people have a right to know? Surely — for millions of people all over the world, to know that he was actually here would be the most wonderful thing that could ever happen."

"Linda," I said. "I've been beating my brains out over what to do ever since The Man got here. Believe me, it's not that simple. I don't know what it is he's come to do but if he wanted the whole world to know he could have landed directly on the lawn of the White House." I smiled. "And I think everybody that heard about it would be as skeptical as you are."

"Give me time," she said. "When you hand out something like this, it takes a bit of getting used to."

"Yeah, well, for what it's worth, he told me to share the news with you." I smiled. "That's why you're sitting here instead of clearing out your desk."

She grimaced. "That close, huh? Are you expecting him back?"

"Yes," I said. "Don't worry. You'll be the first to know."

Although the information I'd imparted to Linda was what the Pentagon would label "highly sensitive," I did not attempt to extract an oath of secrecy. I knew what I'd told her was so incredible, she wouldn't breathe a word to anybody for fear of being certified herself. In an odd way I felt better that Miriam and I were no longer bearing the burden alone. Linda had gotten what she'd asked for and, like me, was probably now wishing her curiosity hadn't got the better of her. I had urged her to question Gale McDonald and if, contrary to my opinion, she decided to pass the news on, then that would save me the trouble. McDonald, Fowler, or whoever she chose as the recipient would either find the information riveting or risible. The egg would be on her face, not mine.

You may find this sudden change of heart somewhat surprising after my earlier agonizing, but the fact is something *had* changed inside me. Whether it was what Miriam had said to me, or whether I had been reprogrammed by The Man is hard to say. All I knew was that I had become detached from many of the concerns which cluttered my day-to-day existence. I was beginning to see things more clearly. Narrowing my field of view down to focus on the essentials. Moving toward the stillness at the center.

Toward the end of the afternoon, Joe Gutzman came into my office with his coat on. "I spoke to Friedman. You didn't call him yet."

"Yes, I know," I said. "I've been busy trying to clear my desk. Have you had any more thoughts on the Delaware appeal?"

Joe raised a hand in supplication to the invisible god who

sometimes answers the prayers of Jewish lawyers. "Corinne's going over the transcripts but so far she hasn't found any flaws in your argument. I've said I'll look through it next week. Who knows? Maybe the judge didn't like your after-shave." His eyes told me that my temporary defection had been forgiven. "Are you going down to stay with your folks in Florida?"

It was the last thing in the world I intended to do but I didn't destroy the image he'd built of me. "I'd like to but — they're on a cruise right now." I gestured through the open doorway to where Linda sat busily tapping out the last type-written letters I would ever sign. "Linda here will know where I am — and she'll hold things together while I'm away."

Joe sized Linda up with a nod then drew her attention to me. "Make sure this young man gets a check-up before he leaves town. He's to see Sol Friedman. My secretary will give you his number. Just mention my name when you ring up to make the appointment."

"Joe," I said. "There's nothing wrong with me. It's a waste of his time and the firm's money."

Joe looked beseechingly at Linda then turned to me with his hand on his heart. "Leo . . . first you turn down my daughter, then you turn down my clients. Personal friends. Now it's my doctor who's a nebbish. Is there something you're trying to tell me?"

"Joe, come on," I protested. "You know it's not like that."

"So humor me," he said, giving me his old faithful-blood-hound look.

I patted him on the shoulder. "Okay. I'll call him first thing Monday. I promise."

One more that I didn't keep.

EIGHTEEN

Saturday, the ninth of May. I collected Miriam in the morning and we drove up to Sleepy Hollow. It was another warm spring day and we spent most of it outside gathering wood which I then sawed by hand. It gave me great satisfaction, an aching shoulder and a good excuse for not painting the front porch which, in any case, still needed some work on the railings. The only carpenter I knew was out of town. I can change a fuse but that was about the limit of my handyman skills. It's always been easier to pick up the telephone. It's still difficult to realize that that is something I will never be able to do again.

Miriam raked up the leaves that had been left over from the previous fall and we made a bonfire and pottered around in the fresh air until long after the sun went down. When we got inside, our faces tingled and our hair and sweaters smelled of woodsmoke. Spring and autumn rolled into one. A beginning and an end. Inexorable — and totally unforeseen.

I used some of the branches to build a fire in the living room while Miriam put some supper together. We ate in the glow of the flames then pushed the plates aside, pulled the cushions off the sofa, and lay there propped up against each other, gazing into the fire as the pine wood popped and crackled, sending flurries of sparks up the stone chimney.

"This is the life," I murmured.

Miriam turned her face so that her forehead touched my

cheek. "Well, you don't have to be a big-city lawyer. We could always hang our shingles side by side on a white frame house down a leafy sidestreet in Smalltown, U.S.A."

"Yeah, I know the place you mean," I replied. "Ten miles east of Nowhere. It was great when Spencer Tracy was alive but not since they put the Interstate down Main Street. We'd go crazy inside a week."

She shrugged. "I'll take that risk if you will."

I stroked her hair. "It's a nice idea. But really — can you imagine us fitting in with red-necked ranchers, their D.A.R. wives and the rest of those 'good ole boys'? Besides, they'd never understand my Brooklyn accent."

"True . . . I hadn't thought about that." She snuggled closer. "We could go to Israel."

"Yes," I said. "They'll always have a need for doctors. But what chance would I have among all those Jewish lawyers?"

"You could grow oranges."

I laughed. "I suppose I could at that." It was an idea we had often discussed jokingly before. Like many other young Jewish Americans, Miriam had done a two-year stint on a kibbutz before going to medical school and had gone back there for occasional holidays. Five years earlier, when it had been the turn of my contemporaries, I had stayed at home with my nose stuck in law books. I'd regretted the decision afterward but, by then, it was too late. It would have hurt my career.

Miriam sat up and faced me. "You've got two weeks with nothing to do — why don't you go out there and take a look?"

I reached for the first excuse I could think of. "But what about The Man?"

"Leo," she said firmly, "if it's you he's interested in, he'll be there too. He might even prefer it. He won't have so far to travel."

I eyed her. "I don't really think that's a problem. But I see what you mean." I cast around for another stumbling block.

Miriam clasped her hands together excitedly. "Oh, if only — you'll love it. How soon can you go?"

"Hey, hey, hey — hold on a minute," I said. "That's a big chunk of money you're talking about. Let's think this over."

She took hold of my hand. "Leo, if it feels right, you don't need to think. The moment you do, you can always find a million reasons for not doing anything. It's your birthday on the eighteenth — I'll give you the ticket as a present."

"Are you crazy?" I snorted. "No way. But buy your own and you've got a deal."

She grimaced. It was obviously a big temptation. "I'd love to but — I can't take a break now. But you must go. It's important. Really."

I shook my head. "No, it's a waste of time. Even if I came back starry-eyed and with my pockets full of orange blossom you'll never leave Manhattan General."

She dropped her head on one side and considered me. "I would. It depends on what kind of proposition was put to me."

I gazed back at her. "You really *are* serious about this . . ."

"I'm a very serious girl," she replied. "The only danger is that when you see some of the girls out there, the last thing you'll want to do is marry *me*."

I considered the idea of going. It was mad, but curiously enticing. I tried to fight it off. "Jack Seligmann and his wife hated it."

"Jack is a *shnorrer*," said Miriam. "And what does she know about anything?"

So much for the Seligmanns.

"Listen," I said. "I'll think it over. It certainly would be interesting to see him on his home ground. It's odd that you should mention it now. I've always wanted to go but for some reason I just never got around to it." It does me no credit but I knew exactly what the reason was. I'd always been scared of booking into a holiday hotel and finding myself sharing breakfast with a boatload of Palestinian commandos, or having my West Bank bus ticket clipped by shrapnel from a grenade. It hadn't happened to anyone I knew but the thought had been enough to put me off. Suddenly what might or might not happen to me was not important anymore. It was the quality of my life I was concerned with; not the length of it.

I gave Miriam a pleading look. "It'd really be a lot more fun if you could come with me."

She took hold of my hands. "I will. But it's better for you to see it first through your own eyes. Don't worry, you won't be lonely. I'll give you names and addresses of friends who will be only too pleased to drive you around and show you whatever you want to see. Then, when you come back, we can talk about it and — well, decide what to do."

"Okay, but — I'm not promising anything," I said. Intent on proving I was my own man.

She planted a motherly kiss on my forehead. "I'd rather you didn't. You never keep promises anyway."

"Oh, come on, give me a break," I protested. "I make an innocent remark about how nice it is to be sitting in front of a log fire, and the next minute you're trying to tear my life out by the roots and replant me on some far-flung frontier where they use Syrian artillery fire instead of alarm clocks."

"The break will do you good," said Miriam. "I'll phone Israeli Airlines —"

I held her down. "*I'll* phone them. What's this sudden desire to get rid of me?"

She brushed her fingers across my face. "I don't want to get rid of you, I want to *find* you."

Before I could reply, I caught a glimpse of sudden movement out of the corner of my eye. Miriam and I turned together and saw The Man standing behind the sofa. He was still wearing the clothes Linda had bought him at Macy's.

It was the seventh time he had appeared. I'd tried to remain calm in face of his quite unpredictable comings and goings but they still sent a chill shock up my spine. "We were just talking about you," I said when my jaw muscles had tightened sufficiently. "Come on over by the fire."

Miriam hurriedly gathered up the supper dishes and swept them into the kitchen. I pulled a chair closer to the fire for him to sit in and offered him a glass of wine. When Miriam returned to settle on her now separate heap of cushions I noticed that she'd combed her hair.

"Can I ask you a question?" she said.

He replied with an amused smile: "Sure, go ahead." It was remarkable how patient he was, but I guess that by the time he met us he'd gotten used to people coming to him for answers. Those seeking enlightenment, the incredulous, the ignorant, and the crafty ones — trying to catch him out. And if you bother to count the number of times that I mention it you will also know that he smiled quite a lot. He possessed a wry, good humor and was not above gentle self-mockery but it was my puny, Earth-type dilemmas which appeared to provide his greatest source of amusement. But then, he knew what was in store for me. He had already done his stint and was through to the other side. He knew from experience that, faced with the daily insanities of life in a 'Braxian world, it was better to laugh than cry — and risk drowning in our own tears.

Miriam silenced me with her eyes. "I'm trying to persuade Leo to spend his two-week vacation in Israel. What do you think?"

He glanced at me as he weighed up the question. "How does Leo feel about it?"

"He's tempted. But you know what lawyers are like. He wants to go but on the other hand . . ." She smiled at me. "Leo loves to prolong the agony."

"That's not true," I protested.

She pretended not to hear. "I thought you might make up his mind for him."

The Man looked at us both. "It really has to be Leo's decision but — I think it's a good idea."

My decision . . . *whom was he trying to kid?*

Miriam turned on me triumphantly. "There, you see?" She scrambled to her feet. "I'll go and check the flights."

I grabbed her hand and pulled her back down. "I've already told you *I* will do that." I looked across at The Man. "If I decide to go, is that going to throw your plans out?"

"Not at all," he replied. "I'll show you around."

The idea of touring the Twelve Stations of the Cross in the company of The Man was an offer that was hard to refuse. Miriam could see I was wavering. "So — when can you go?"

"Look," I said. "I don't know yet. Just — get off my back and let me think about it. Okay?"

Her eyes flashed with annoyance. She turned to The Man. "Is there any chance that you might be here tomorrow?"

He nodded. "It's possible."

"Good." Miriam turned back to me with a wintry smile. "You promised to call Linda — or would you like to think about that too?"

It was the kind of smart-aleck remark that often made me feel like punching her right in the mouth. Not that I ever did, of course. I only mention it to show you that, despite my first hesitant steps along The Way, I was not yet overflowing with the milk of human kindness.

I swallowed my venom and told The Man that I'd shared our secret with Linda as he had suggested.

"Do you think she believed you?" he said.

I laughed. "I think she'd like to but she, well — doesn't want to build up her hopes. To be honest, I don't think she's prepared to take my word for it. But at least she didn't suggest I see a doctor." I glanced sideways at Miriam.

"Would you like me to have a word with her?" he said.

I shrugged. "That's up to you. I think it would be fairer to her. It must be terrible to learn that you're here and not know for certain."

"Okay," he said. "Why don't you call her?"

I got to my feet and looked down at Miriam. "I'll see if she can make it tomorrow morning. I'll call Gale McDonald too. And I think you ought to speak to Jeff."

My sudden decision to make it open house took her by surprise. "What shall I say?"

"Simple," I replied, throwing one of her favorite words back at her. "Just ask him if he'd like to meet Mr. Sheppard."

Linda agreed to come without hesitation but her voice was tinged with understandable caution. "What's going to happen?"

"Nothing," I said. "The six of us are just going to sit around and talk. I've told you what the score is. It's up to you to take it from there. But there is something I ought to explain. The Man doesn't stand on ceremony. The way he was when the two of you went shopping is the way he is all the time. So don't embarrass the hell out of everybody by coming dressed as a bride of Christ."

She greeted this with a brief silence then spoke in a small tight voice. "I'll see you around eleven. Do you want me to bring anything?"

"Just an open mind," I said. I had been deliberately provocative to check her Catholic reflexes. They were obviously in good shape despite her professed apostasy and it was clear from the tone of her voice that my gratuitous remarks had gone against the grain. In its fully developed form, it is a mental and bodily affliction known as religious intolerance. Which we Jews know something about.

Let's be fair. We haven't always been on the receiving end. It was we who began the current outbreak by stoning the followers of The Man for uttering blasphemy. What we didn't foresee was that, with a little outside help, the Christians would turn religious intolerance into a fine art. They not only massacred us and the Moors; Catholic and Protestant had burned each other with equal fervor. Heresy and blasphemy brought imprisonment, mutilation and death to those indicted by the Church. And even today, blasphemy could still result in criminal prosecutions by outraged defenders of the faith. A curious fact when one considers the emphasis The Man put on love, forgiveness, and turning the other cheek but perfectly understandable if considered as part of a running campaign by 'Brax to destroy all hope of salvation by turning belief into bigotry. The seed corn of hatred and discord which, if allowed to grow unchecked, would choke the life out of us. The Life Everlasting, that is. Leaving us to feed on our own flesh like a colony of cannibal ants until the sun took matters into its own hands and put an end to us all by engulfing the solar system in its dying embrace, melting the ice on Neptune and bringing Pluto its first and last sunrise.

I phoned McD and made similar arrangements. I didn't get into lengthy explanations. I told her to schedule her arrival for around eleven A.M. but that, like the others, she should call before leaving to check that our houseguest was still there. Miriam gave Fowler the same message. I made it up with her behind the kitchen door but just as I thought I'd gotten around her, she sank her teeth into my bottom lip to teach me that nothing worthwhile is achieved without pain.

I left her to make a fresh pot of coffee and went back into the living room and readied the tape deck so that we could record the postponed session of the missing years.

Some of you will be relieved to learn that I am not going to do a James Fitzpatrick–type travelogue on The Man's journey; others, no doubt, will feel cheated that I chose to waste valuable space telling you about my work, my peccadilloes with people like Fran Nelson, and my relationship with Miriam. Let me just say that The Man told me to tell it my way. That stuff may seem unimportant but they were steps along The Way. Those people and places exist; those incidents took place. Their statements can be checked against this record and the notes and tapes in my safety deposit box to prove that I'm telling the truth. If you want to know what The Man got up to in Rome, all you have to do is listen to Reels 14 and 15. What I've repeated here is the essential core of his story — which is where he disappeared to and why. And who with. For he was not to journey alone.

It was the woman known as Mary Magdalene who traveled with him through the mountainous wildernesses of Asia and over the windswept plains beyond to the myth-laden forests of Central Europe that stretched from the Danube to the Baltic Sea.

Mary of Magdala had first met The Man when she had been eleven years old and he fourteen. Like a lot of young girls of that age, Mary had developed an instant crush on the young Joshua-Ya'el and was devastated when, a year later, he left Nazareth to join his cousin Johanan-Gabriel in the Essene commune at Aenon near Salim. Mary was one of a small group of people outside The Man's immediate family who knew the secret story of his birth; she also possessed the latent gift of clairvoyance. During the years that followed his departure for Aenon, her powers of extrasensory perception came to the fore, making her, in the end, the most gifted of The Man's followers. It was she who perceived his Celestial presence more clearly than anyone else. It was Mary who first saw him in the garden after the Resurrection and it was she who was *"the disciple whom Jesus loved."* Don't be confused by passages in the Gospels where she and this elusive, allegedly male, character are both reported as being present. That is due to emendations of the texts by Pauline scribes who either did not understand, or chose to ignore her key role in the Christ-Mystery.

And so it was that, at the age of nineteen, Mary made her way to Aenon on the bank of the River Jordan to join The Man on the Long March. Their relationship was a sad and curious eternal triangle. Joshua bar Joseph, if he'd been given the choice and the opportunity, would have been more than happy to settle down with a woman like Mary of Magdala. But Mary was in love with Ya'el. The Man behind the man. If Ya'el had not been there, she would not have been drawn to his Ain-folk persona.

Taking their leave of Gabriel, The Man and Mary journeyed northeastward to Harran, the birthplace of the patriarch Abraham, and the city where Gaspar, one of the three magi, was nearing the end of yet another Earth-life. From Harran, they had followed the Euphrates as it flowed southward through the fertile crescent to Babylon, where they were welcomed by Melchior, the second of the magi. Then it was eastward, along the route hewn by Alexander through Susa, Persepolis, past the Straits of Hormuz and the shores of the Arabian Sea to Alexandria Portus on the delta of the Indus, the city that was to become Karachi.

Now far beyond the rule of Rome, The Man and Mary made their way along the banks of the Indus to Kashmir and on into the Himalayas and the depths of Asia where closed communities, similar in spirit to the Essenes, formed islands of awareness in a world that had sunk beneath a sea of superstition and ignorance. An archipelago which, in contrast to Solzhenitsyn's, were outposts of freedom in 'Brax's global gulag.

It was here that The Man and his companion rested, and where he found an awakened Celestial presence which drew its strength from the life-forces within the Earth; the dwindling Power of The Presence which was to come into the world again through The Man. But, as we sat listening to him on that Saturday in Sleepy Hollow, this new transfusion of power that would enable us to grasp Eternity and which, for us, had occurred some two thousand years earlier, had not yet galvanized the world of the Apostles.

Such were the mind-bending rules of the game that the Empire was playing with Time.

The world through which The Man and Mary of Magdala traveled was a far cry from our own, computerized global village but, as the inspired reasoning and dramatic observation of the Greek philosophers and playwrights have shown, there has been very little change in the human condition. During the twelve years he spent on the road, The Man asked himself many of the questions I have reiterated here and found himself worried and depressed by some of the answers. For his journey was not primarily inspired by a spirit of self-sacrifice; it was a quest for knowledge — motivated by the desire to fulfill his mission regardless of the cost and whatever the final outcome.

It was in the hidden power-centers, the mystery schools of

Persia, India and Asia, and along the trail of the Celtic druids through Central Europe to the seeing-stones of Carnac in Gaullish France and the rings of power at Glastonbury in pre-Roman Britain, that The Man was able to fuse his meta-psyche with Eardh-Ain's memory and absorb the history of the planet: the descent of the Ain-folk into Man and their subsequent enslavement by 'Brax.

But while these closed communities had guarded the secret knowledge of Empire for uncounted generations, they could not tell The Man all he needed to know. The mass of humanity was not able to withdraw into a sheltered life of contemplative asceticism; turning one's back on external reality was not a solution that could be universally applied. Man had to live and work in the 'Braxian world but, by liberating the Celestial power within himself through *gnosis* — the acquisition of self-knowledge — he could make it a better place to live in. *"To be in the world but not of it."*

The words came from The Man's mouth but I recognized the phrase as one of the fundamental precepts of the Sufi, the mystical branch of Islam whose members were also known as the Followers of The Way.

It was this sense of purpose that drove him on for those twelve long years in which he and Mary of Magdala traveled thousands of miles on foot, on ox-carts, mules and the decks of boats. He journeyed not as a prince among men, but as a penniless wayfarer; both of them working their way from place to place, seeking shelter wherever it could be found.

It was a tough, bleak and often dangerous road but the harsh conditions were tempered by Mary's loving presence. When one of them stumbled, the other managed to find inner reserves of strength; when one despaired the other gave hope; when one became angry and embittered the other showed compassion and understanding; when they were cold they warmed each other; when they were hungry, they gave each other sustenance. It was not easy for The Man to master the entirely human emotions with which Joshua's Earth-body was endowed and in which his own spirit-being was trapped, but it was only through living as he did that he could fully understand the hold that 'Brax had over the world and discover whether it was still possible to liberate the Ain-folk.

Reaching Britain, The Man led Mary toward Glastonbury where the Celtic druids had harnessed the Earth-forces that flowed through the matrix formed by the Glastonbury Zodiac, the terrestrial mirror-image of the astral configurations that represented the twelve great Celestial Aeons who now inhabited mankind. The Earth-Zodiac was another piece of the esoteric evidence that linked the physical world to that of the Empire and which was alluded to in the cryptic phrase of the medieval alchemists — *"As above, so below."*

The Man's visit to Britain — which included a side-trip to Ireland — set the stage for the subsequent arrival of Joseph of Arimathea at the court of the Welsh king Arviragus with the chalice from the Last Supper. His journey and that of Joseph and his companions provided the cornerstone on which Irish-Celtic Christianity was built — unmarred by the distortions created by the Apostolic Succession. It was also the wellspring from which were drawn the legendary tales of King Arthur and the Knights of the Round Table. The mythical knights and their deeds of derring-do were the human counterparts of the warring Celestials and the quest for the Holy Grail symbolized the inexpressible longing of Man's trapped spirit to be reunited with the transcendent being of God.

From Britain, The Man went back to France, down the Atlantic Coast to the Pyrenees and into Spain. Crossing over to Africa via the Pillars of Hercules, he and Mary made their way eastward to Carthage, in present-day Tunisia, and used his total mastery of language to talk his way onto a Roman freighter heading for Sicily. From here, it was a relatively short hop across the Straits of Messina to the Italian mainland, then north to Naples and Rome. The Eternal City.

No other place on earth ever held so much concentrated wealth and power for so long, and it would be another four hundred years before the empire-building, the throat-cutting wheeling and dealing, the anything-goes villa parties and the bloodstained circuses were closed down by the barbarian invasions.

In all, The Man spent some four months in Italy before crossing the Adriatic to Greece. Athens first, then around the Aegean to Asia Minor, traveling in reverse the route that Paul was to take a few years later: through Thessalonica, Philippi, Pergamum, Sardis, Ephesus, Colossae and Perga.

At Perga, they secured passage on a small Phoenician trading boat which was heading for Paphos in Cyprus. Another Roman ship, which had taken shelter from one of the frequent Mediterranean storms, took them to Alexandria where The Man sought out the aging Balthazzar — the third of the magi who had borne witness to his birth.

It was through Balthazzar that The Man made the final connection with the past history of the Jews. In the desert communities of Egypt and Sinai he met the keepers of the Ancient Wisdom that had been handed down from the Pharonic priests of the Old Kingdom and which had been brought into the world by the Celestial Envoy known as Thoth, and to us as Hermes Trismegistos.

Hermes, the Greek god of messengers with his winged staff; the *cadeuceus* with its interwoven branches — usually depicted as two serpents — coiled around it in opposing spirals. *Binah* and *Chokmah,* the two spirals of force that connected earth with heaven. And the staff itself which, like Saint George's lance, represented the third unifying element, but with wings to show that it came from above — The Power of The Presence. The same power that had armed the rod of Aaron. The apochryphal staff that became a serpent which swallowed up those produced by the lesser magicians of the Egyptian court and which, on another occasion, sprouted branches of flowering almond overnight. Another code message for you to work on.

From the Nile, where Moses had allegedly been found in the bullrushes, The Man and Mary retraced the route taken by Moses in the miraculous Exodus: across the Bitter Lakes, southward into the emptiness of the Sinai peninsula where Moses had his mountaintop appointment with God.

It was about a thousand stony miles to Nazareth via Mount Sinai but I suppose The Man must have thought it worth the detour. Turning for home, they went northward along the Gulf of Aqabah and on through Idumea, the Arab homeland of Herod the Great, to the wells of Beer-Sheba. There was now only a hundred miles to go. They passed through Hebron, paused briefly at Bethlehem, where The Man's astonished relatives told them that Joseph and Eliza, Gabriel's Earth-mother, had both died, then pressed on to Jerusalem. After the silence of the desert crossing, the noise and bustle of the crowded city was almost unbearable.

Although Mary Magdalene had stuck with him every inch of the way and had shared his hardships with amazing fortitude, the journey through Sinai had drained her last reserves of strength. Realizing that she could go no further, The Man sought help from Nicodemus.

Somewhat naturally, Nicodemus didn't recognize the ragged, travel-stained beggar who stood on his doorstep, or the woman at his side, until The Man reminded him of their meeting at the Temple twenty-two years before when, as a child, he had amazed everybody with his interpretation of the Torah. That was something Nicodemus had *not* forgotten. He immediately invited them in, gave them the VIP treatment, and persuaded them to stay for several days. Both got their first hot bath since Rome, all the food their shrunken stomachs could handle, and a change of clothes.

Although he had not fully recovered from the rigors of his journey, The Man decided it was time to seek out Johanan-Gabriel. Reassured by Nicodemus that Mary would be nursed back to health, The Man headed northeast toward Jericho and the green valley of the River Jordan. Then it happened. On the road between Jerusalem and Jericho, he fell among thieves who, as the story goes, *"stripped him of his raiment, and wounded him, and departed, leaving him half dead."* Yes. This was one parable he didn't have to make up.

It was the rich clothes that Nicodemus had pressed upon him that had gotten The Man into trouble; and it was Joseph of Arimathea who was the Good Samaritan.

If the above news leaves some of you a little hazy, let me just explain that Arimathea was a village in Samaria, a province of Palestine sandwiched between Judea in the south, and Galilee. The Samaritans were the descendants of a group of Israelites that missed the boat when the rest of the nation was shipped off to Babylon by the Assyrians. Although their life was based on rigid observance of the Torah, they were regarded by the returning Jews as "unclean." The Samaritans, through choice or circumstance, had diluted their racial purity through mixed marriages, and because their faith had not been tempered by the long years of exile, their brand of Judaism was held to be not strictly kosher. Besides being an object lesson in charity, the parable of the Good Samaritan was a sharp reminder that religious bigotry was alive and well long before Catholic and Protestant, Muslim and Hindu, turned it into a mindless excuse for murder.

This meeting between The Man and Joseph of Arimathea on the Jericho road was the beginning of a clandestine association which finally came out into the open at the Crucifixion when The Man was suddenly short on friends.

So how, you ask, did someone as powerful as The Man let himself be mugged almost within sight of home? The answer is simple. Like Mary, his physical strength had been exhausted, and the inner power of his metapsyche had been drained by the unrelenting struggle with 'Brax. It's important to understand that The Man in the flesh did not have at his disposal the stunning powers of his resurrected form. They were blunted by the Earth-body to which he was bound.

'Brax had made telepathic contact with Johanan-Gabriel impossible but, in fact, The Man had long given up trying to reach him. Indeed, he had given up on just about everything and it was only the mutual support that Mary and he had given each other that had enabled them to keep going until they finally reached home. But he had returned defeated, without any hope of rescue for himself; convinced that the liberation of the trapped Ain-folk was a lost cause. For even if the promised rescue mission arrived, the weight of *karma* he had acquired would make return to the Empire impossible. He was now just another of the Celestial prisoners of the 'Braxian universe.

After The Man had rested up for a few days, Joseph of Arimathea returned from Jerusalem and persuaded him to join his own party which was taking the road north through Samaria to Sebaste, the capital of the region. A mere thirty-five miles from Nazareth. As a result, The Man did not get to call on Johanan-Gabriel. It would have been a wasted journey. The Essenes had moved their base from Aenon near Salim on the Jordan to more secure quarters on the forbidding slopes of the Wadi Qumran on the edge of the Dead Sea. And Johanan-Gabriel was some eighty miles farther north, checking out their abandoned landing module which lay buried under a snow-covered plateau near the summit of Mount Hermon.

Gabriel was responding to a signal he had received from the lead vessel of the rescue fleet, now only twelve months out from Earth. On his arrival at the hidden landing site, he found that the mysterious malfunction that had forced their abandonment of the module had cleared itself, enabling the craft to be recharged by a burst of power transmitted via the chain of longships. For the first time since entering the World Below, Gabriel was in two-way contact with the Empire. To his surprise, the Empire knew of The Man's return to Palestine, and they gave Gabriel precise instructions on what to do when they met.

Joshua-Ya'el, the Jesus-figure who now made his way from Sabaste to Nazareth, bore no resemblance to the gentle, smooth-faced supplicant portrayed in devotional literature. This was a lean, ravaged, fiery-eyed wayfarer, with callused hands and feet, and whipcord muscles like those of a miner from West Virginia under a skin that wind, sand, snow and rain had turned into weathered rawhide.

When he arrived home, Mary, his mother, was overjoyed to see her eldest son alive and well. Despite his strange, other-worldly genesis inside her body — which she had accepted with a kind of childlike wonder without ever fully under-standing — he was still her favorite son. Like the rest of the family she had long given him up for dead and now, here he was. Scarred from his travels, but still with the same intense gaze that, in The Man-child, had filled them with awe and, behind the outward show of diffidence, the same defiant air of authority that had amazed the priests all those years ago in Jerusalem.

The welcome from his brothers and sisters was less than tumultuous. After all, seventeen years is a long time to be away, but they thawed out considerably when they learned that he had no intention of claiming his share of Joseph's estate.

His surrogate-father had died still bewildered by his star-ring role in the Nativity Play. During his lifetime, when the young Joshua-Ya'el had been in his care, Joseph had been constantly troubled by what he took to be signs of madness in his adopted star-child. He did not know, and probably would not have understood, that his son's erratic moods were caused by the conflict between The Man's metapsyche and the Earth-oriented Ain-folk soul-fragment who shared the same body and answered to its given name.

With his mother, sisters Ruth and Sarah, and brother James, The Man went out to the cemetery where Joseph lay buried and said prayers. Afterward, they talked about old times and The Man gave them a brief outline of where he'd been. James accepted it without question but the others tended to take it with a large pinch of salt. Mary, his mother, had been deeply hurt by the fact that he had disappeared without a word to his family but she was, nevertheless, immensely proud of her wayward son. There were not many Jewish boys who had traveled farther than Alexander and had seen more things than a Roman emperor had dreamed of.

The Man asked if they had news of his cousin Johanan. They had indeed. Johanan had become a holy man who, it was said, spoke in the manner of the great prophets. Some even claimed that the spirit of Elijah was upon him. He had become a wild man of the desert, wandering the barren hills of Judea, dressed in rags and with hair like a mangy lion, subsisting on a diet of locusts and wild honey. In the last year, he had acquired a small group of disciples and the title of Johanan the Baptizer. People flocked to hear him speak whenever he appeared on the banks of the Jordan, waiting patiently in line to receive his blessing and undergo, in a simple ceremony, a symbolic rebirth by immersion in the waters of the river. Johanan spoke of the coming deliverance of the people of Israel. The age-old prophecies were to be fulfilled. He was but a messenger, sent to prepare the way for the Messiah who would baptize them not with water but with the transcendent spirit of God.

As they sat around the fire, talking about their remarkable but eccentric cousin, none of Mary's children had the remotest idea that the Savior prophesied by Johanan was sitting among them. But Mary, his mother, knew. She looked into his eyes and remembered the angel who had spoken to her in the dream, the star that had appeared at the time of his birth then had vanished from the sky, and the three wise men who had journeyed so far to kneel before him; and she trembled, her heart full of joy at his return and grief at the knowledge that she was to lose him again — this time forever.

Toward the end of the evening, as we wound up the recording session, The Man dropped another bombshell into the conversation when he made a slighting reference to Paul.

"Wait a minute," I said. "Which Paul are we talking about? Not the Paul who was —"

"Yes," he nodded. "Saul of Tarsus."

I became confused. "But surely — Paul was one of the great founding fathers of the Church. He wrote a big chunk of the New Testament, he was imprisoned —"

The Man shook his head. "One of the best moles 'Brax ever recruited. Believe me." He paused and looked at us both. "I was never on that road to Damascus."

I put a hand to my forehead and stared wide-eyed at Miriam. "I don't believe it. Do you realize what he's saying?"

"Don't argue," said Miriam. "Just listen."

"And another thing," continued The Man. "I never told Peter that he was the rock upon which I would build my church. That was all written in later by Paul and his friends to legitimize their takeover of the movement that the disciples had begun."

"I'm beginning to understand," I said. "Less than a hundred years later, you've got presbyters, deacons and bishops issuing orders and rewriting the rules. The theologians start arguing over the wording of the message and by three hundred and something A.D. when Theodosius gives it his seal of approval, the whole thing goes down the tubes."

The Man smiled. "Not entirely. We managed to keep the message alive through the Sufis."

There'd been the hint of a connection before but this was the first time he had mentioned it directly. But the implications were tremendous. "Do you mean to say that — ?"

"Yes," he said. "The Empire put the fear of God back into the Christians by sending someone to talk to a man called Muhammad. It was the Muslims who kept the flame of awareness alive for the next three hundred years."

I sat there, slack-mouthed.

"What do you think world history is about?" said The Man. "The Second War of Secession didn't end with the destruction of Atlantis. I've already told you this. It's still going on. Through you, around you, over you." He wasn't smiling now. "Man is the prize. *That's* why Earth is so important to us. If we don't win here . . ." He waved the thought away, leaving the sentence uncompleted.

Another of his cliff-hangers.

"The Holocaust, and the new wave of violence against Jews by neo-Nazi groups — even the re-creation of a Jewish homeland in the cauldron of the Middle East, and the fundamentalist intransigence of parties like the *Gush Emunim* — are all part of 'Brax's latest counterattack," explained The Man. "The Promised Land was never part of this earth. It was a symbol of deliverance of the Ain-folk by the Empire. It was the metaphysical acreage of the World Above. But you've allowed yourselves to be drawn into fighting for some rock-laden real estate when the real battle is over the control of your hearts and minds."

"Yes, but come on," I protested. "You know how these people feel about Jerusalem. This is what the Old Testament is all about."

The Man shook his head again. "It's important to remember what I told you about The Word. The Old and the New Testaments were written by men. The Book is not The Truth, but The Truth is in the Book. A subtle, but very important difference."

"You're beginning to sound like Leo," said Miriam.

"True," smiled the Man. "But the point I'm making is absolutely fundamental to your understanding of the statements made by the various authors about what God, I, and other Envoys like Michael and Gabriel are supposed to have done and said."

"It's going to annoy those people who claim every word of the Bible is true," I said, thinking of the Jehovah's Witnesses who kept stuffing their *Watchtower* pamphlets into my mailbox.

The Man smiled and threw up his hands. "I'm always annoying people. A few more won't make any difference. The Book is not something to be learned parrot-fashion. If you read it in the wrong way, you can read it a hundred times and still be none the wiser. Yet if you approach it correctly, The Truth will often leap from the pages at the very first reading. If you would know The Way, you must think of yourself as a traveler lost in a forest that is so dark and impenetrable it blocks out the sun. To free yourself, you must cut a path through the 'Braxian undergrowth toward The Light."

I nodded. "What you're saying, in other words, is that there are a lot of 'Braxian lines that need to be weeded out of the Book."

"Exactly," said The Man. "Take nothing for granted. Not even the things I've been telling you. Just open your minds and let The Word work on your soul. Believe me, it knows more about The Truth, The Presence and the power of God than you ever will."

NINETEEN

SUNDAY, the tenth of May. When I came downstairs, I found
The Man still with us, sitting in his usual cross-legged position in front of the TV set with the sound muted and a glass
of wine within easy reach. To this day, I never found out
where it went. Neither did anyone else for that matter.
Maybe I should have asked him, but somehow we never got
around to it. In the same way that neither Miriam or I
pressed him on the details of his relationship with Mary of
Magdala even though, in the published extracts from the
Gnostic texts found at Nag Hammadi, much has been made
of the claim that "*Jesus kissed her on the mouth.*"

Big deal.

I've mentioned that she was the disciple that The Man
loved. So those of you who've read the Gospels will know that
it was she who had her head on his chest during the Last
Supper. And you may have been struck by the fact that although "*the disciple whom Jesus loved*" knew that Judas was
going to betray The Man, he/she did not tell the others.
Because she was the only other person, apart from Judas, who
knew *why* it had to happen. But we'll get to this later.

Looking back, I realize that there were all kinds of questions I should have asked him but didn't. As to the wine and
the mysteries of his digestive tract, your guess is as good as
mine. I know that poor old Jeff Fowler was left with his

researcher's tongue hanging out and his thirst for knowledge unassuaged. I think it was a deliberate ploy on the part of The Man to teach us that it is our obsession with the nuts-and-bolts questions about the universe that prevents us from getting at the fundamental truths of existence.

There is a reluctance to face up to reality; to the meaningless activity that so many of us are engaged in. To avoid, by constant movement, ever having to think. The plain speaker is anathema. Public debate of fundamental issues is cocooned in cotton-wool syntax that prevents the participants from reaching any meaningful conclusion. Very few have the courage to stand up and tell it like it really is. And those who do usually end up by being gunned down, or crucified by the Establishment, the media, hostile pressure groups. All of us are gagged by a reluctance to offend. For to do so triggers frenzied cries of outrage, hostility, even threats of physical violence. It's like The Man said — " 'Brax will do anything to stop The Truth getting out." He's even prepared to let us blow the world to pieces rather than hand it back to the Empire.

The Man sat with us on the porch while we ate our bacon and fried-potato omelets, followed by coffee and a side order of toasted English muffins and apricot jam. And we listened as he told us some more about his homecoming.

Since leaving Gabriel at Aenon, The Man had not seen the inside of a synagogue and, until he had arrived at Nicodemus's house in Jerusalem, he had not performed any of the prayers and rituals that were part and parcel of orthodox Jewish life. He had returned to Palestine as "unclean" as the Samaritan who had rescued him, the Gentiles of the Roman and Hellenic world, and the barbarians beyond.

The Man was not against the ritual prayers and observances that were the outward demonstration of our faith. He Earth-host. He also understood and sympathized with the aspirations of his nation-race. But he now saw, more clearly than ever, that the whole elaborate panoply of religious rituals had not prevented the Jews from losing sight of The

Truth; indeed, they had helped conceal it. The Jews still held fast to the idea that they were God's chosen people, but their hopes for salvation were now pinned on a secular triumph over their many oppressors. It was the desire for vengeance that lay behind their prayers for deliverance. The New Jerusalem would be built, quite literally, upon the Old. Out of solid stone, and with real bricks and mortar; mixed with the blood of their enemies.

The Man was not against the ritual prayers and observances that were the outward demonstration of our faith. He knew they were the cement that had held our people together whenever the nation had fallen into alien hands, had been enslaved and scattered to the four winds. He was trying to show us that much of it had become a meaningless mumbo-jumbo that was leading us away from enlightenment instead of toward it. We had allowed our spiritual mission to be translated into a temporal quest for political independence and economic prosperity. We had succumbed to the lure of Greek intellectual arrogance and the material wealth of Rome. That was why The Man had those head-on collisions with the Pharisees and the Sadducees. The two things he could not stomach were rampant hypocrisy and the closed minds of those who responded to the notion of God, or The Presence, with the mental agility of blind parrots.

Centuries of oppression had sharpened our sense of survival but had blunted our unique sense of inner awareness. The Celestial presence had become entombed like a Pharonic king deep within his pyramid. It had shriveled into a semi-mummified condition. But it was not totally dead. It was like the parched seed of those desert flowers that lie dormant through long years of drought then blossom, as if by magic, when touched by the rain; filling the arid wastes with color and life.

So although the Book records that The Man broke the rules of the Sabbath, spoke to Samaritans, and mixed with dubious company, it is important to keep his actions and motives in perspective. One has to constantly bear in mind

that the Gentiles, who took over the Judeo-Christian movement, played around with the texts to bring them into line
with their own interpretation of the "truth." With a small
"t." The Canons of the Church; the big guns that were
quickly readied to blow away all opposition to Paul's New
Order.

In the process, we Jews found ourselves stuck with the
charge that we had crucified Jesus Christ. We've lived and
died with that lie for the last two thousand years. Like Herr
Doktor Goebbels said — it's the big one that is the easiest to
sell. I'll come to this in more detail later but let me tell you
this — The Man wanted to die. His orders were to get himself
killed. As he said himself when we first talked up at Sleepy
Hollow — *"That was the way it had to be."* The High Priest
and his allies on the Sanhedrin, the Jews who clamored for
his crucifixion, the Galatians on the execution squad who
pulped his back and broke his ribs with leather flails loaded
with knuckle-bones were just part of a crowd laid on by Central Casting.

And Judas was the willing fall guy.

I was inside looking for a fresh reel of tape when the first
car arrived. Miriam and The Man were on the porch. I went
back out to greet Jeff Fowler and Gale McDonald and saw
that Jeff had also brought along Carol Shiragawa.

Miriam saw my raised eyebrows and smiled sweetly. "Ahh,
there you are. Why don't you make the introductions?"

"What's she doing here?" I hissed.

"I'll go and make the coffee," she replied. She sidestepped
my clenched teeth and went inside, leaving the three of them
facing me and The Man. A really lousy trick.

There was a moment's uneasy silence which I finally man-
aged to break. "Uhh — I'd like you to meet Yale, uhh —
Sheppard." I introduced the others in turn. "Gale McDonald,
from Channel Eight. The girl who's been following up the
Mrs. Perez story. Jeff Fowler, who dragged her into this.
Jeff is a big wheel at the Voss Institute. They spend a lot of

time looking at blood. Which is why he's interested in yours. Carol's the girl to see if you want to fly to Tokyo. She's with Jeff."

Carol gave me a slant-eyed look. "You kept saying you'd bring me up here, so I came along for the ride. Is that okay?"

"*Mia casa es su casa*," I said, showing her a smiling set of teeth that itched to sink into her jugular.

The Man smiled as he shook hands with everybody, and fixed them with his golden eyes. Everybody said "Hello" back.

I turned to Gale. "Did, er — Linda have a word with you?"

"Yes," she said. "I passed the news on to Jeff. The, uhh —" She threw a self-conscious glance at The Man. "— idea takes a bit of getting used to."

"Just give it time," I replied. I didn't plan to give them a hard sell. The Man's presence was enough. I looked at Fowler. "Does Carol know what this is all about?"

Fowler shook his head. "Not yet. I couldn't figure out a way to tell her."

Carol turned back from the view. "Tell me what?"

"I'll go and help Miriam with the coffee," I said. And I left them to it. After all, nobody held my hand. Or Shimon's, brother Andrew's, James's or John's.

By the time I reached the kitchen, the smile on my face had become a petulant snarl. Miriam took one look, then turned her back on me and carried on with what she was doing. I slammed the side of my fist into the door of the refrigerator. "What the fuck does Fowler think he's playing at? Was this your idea?"

"No," said Miriam. "Calm down. Relax."

"The nerve of the guy. Bringing that Japanese meatball . . ."

"Why not?" said Miriam. "*You* were going to."

"Ahh, I see," I replied. "You ran out on me when it got sticky but you stopped to listen from behind the door."

"A woman's privilege," she said. "I was a little shaken

when I saw her get out of the car but now that I've had time to think about it, I'm glad Jeff brought her along. It'll be interesting to see how someone like her reacts to The Man."

I became defensive. "What do you mean — 'someone like her'?"

"I'm sure you don't really need me to explain that," said Miriam with one of those knowing smiles that always irritates the hell out of me.

"Yeah, okay . . ." I replied. "I thought we were through with all that."

Miriam eyed me and went back to spreading chopped liver.

I was reluctant to admit it but what she said made sense. If The Man could sell himself to someone like Carol, then the world was his oyster. It was a big "If." From my brief but intimate acquaintance with the lady I knew it was unlikely that she would rush out and buy a pound of spikenard. And that was why I'd been upset to see her. I didn't want her, or anyone else for that matter, treating The Man like a sideshow at Coney Island. It was a measure of my conceit that I felt, however fleetingly, I should have exclusive control over access to the being who had come to save the world.

I loaded the coffee tray with cups and saucers and carried it out onto the porch. Miriam followed with a trayful of open sandwiches, dips and crisp warm bagels. We found the three of them sitting around The Man in these director's chairs I have. He was sitting in the same spot as on that first Sunday, with his legs crossed and his back against the white clapboards, listening with unfeigned interest as Carol told him, in minute detail, about life in Cedar Falls. Gale and Jeff sat chafing at these apparent inconsequentialities.

I began handing round the coffee as Miriam filled each cup and prayed under my breath that he wouldn't disappear on me until Linda had clapped eyes on him. I didn't mind what happened after that; they would all know I wasn't kidding.

I heard another car scrunch onto the gravel drive below the house. A fire-engine red Dodge Omni had pulled up be-

hind Fowler's Rabbit. "That'll be Linda," I said. "Excuse
me."

I walked down to the Dodge and noticed that it had Virginia plates. Linda was sitting in the passenger seat. "Hi . . .
good to see you." I looked past her at the man who sat with
his hands on the wheel.

"Uhh, this is Peter," said Linda. "My, er — brother."

"Ohh . . . I didn't know you had one," I replied. In an
unwelcoming sort of way. I nodded at brother Peter, who
wore tortoiseshell glasses and a tan leather jacket. A nothing
sort of guy of indeterminate age; late twenties, early thirties
perhaps. He bore no discernible family resemblance to Linda
and, to judge by his expression, carried coffins for a living.

Linda did her lip-gnawing bit. "Pete came into town for
the weekend and, uhh — since he had the car . . ."

"Sure," I said.

"But if you don't want him around, he's quite happy to
come back for me."

I eyed her woodenly. "Does he know what he's getting
into?"

Her mouth wobbled. "Well —"

"That's all I need to know." I opened the car door to
let her out and looked across at her brother. "Join the
party . . ."

We went up onto the porch and waited for a pause in the
conversation. I made the introductions. "Linda and Peter
Kovacs. Linda's my secretary. Peter owns the car."

Everybody shook hands or gave them a friendly wave.

"Hello, Linda," said The Man. He stood up and kissed her
on the cheek.

Linda's cheeks flushed. "Uhh, this is my brother."

"Yes, of course . . ." The Man gripped Kovacs's hand and
gave him a sharp, hawklike stare. "I was wondering when
you'd come."

Kovacs laughed uneasily. "It's not often one gets an invitation like this."

There was something going on but I couldn't work it out. I looked at them both with a frown. "Have you two already met?"

The Man smiled. "In a way." He let go of Kovacs's hand. "I know some of Peter's friends."

Kovacs exchanged a glance with Linda as The Man settled down against the wall.

"Here, take this," said Miriam. She passed the remaining chair over to Linda. "There are plenty more inside."

Kovacs parked his butt on the rail of the porch.

"Uh-uh," I said. "That needs fixing. I'll get you a chair." I turned to Miriam. "Do we have enough coffee?"

"Plenty," she said. "But we'll need a cup for Linda's brother."

Game, set and match.

Kovacs followed me into the house and picked up one of my black bentwood chairs. "One of these?"

"Yes, sure . . ." I went into the kitchen, pulled out a cup and saucer, and opened a bottle of wine for The Man. Kovacs carried the chair to the door of the kitchen and watched as I nearly ruptured myself on the cork. I jerked my head toward the porch. "That was a curious exchange. What do you think he meant?"

Kovacs shrugged. "No idea. But it was kind of creepy, wasn't it?"

"I guess he must have picked up your name and number on one of his trips through Linda's head." I finally got the cork out. "I imagine she must have told you who he is. Do you believe it?"

The question made Kovacs blink. "I'm — prepared to accept the possibility."

I grinned at him. "In that case, you'd better watch your step. From here on in, it's uphill all the way." I picked up a glass and brandished the bottle of red wine. "It's for Yale. He's not into coffee and stuff."

"Why do you call him Yale?" asked Kovacs.

"He told me that was his name. We haven't had much occasion to use it. Miriam and I normally refer to him as The Man. Yale Sheppard was something we came up with so I could book him into a hotel. It's not Yale, it's Ya'el — pronounced Yah-*ell*. If you use that name, or think of him as The Man, it stops you getting hung up on the conventional image that springs to mind when anyone starts talking about Jesus. Though if we were being pedantic, it could be argued that Jesus of Nazareth was the Spirit of God in the flesh. That body out there on the porch originally belonged to a Galilean called Joshua bar Joseph. The Man may look like one of us, but he isn't. Believe me."

Kovacs pursed his lips. "Ya'el . . . mmmm, interesting. I wonder . . . ?"

I put the things I was carrying on the kitchen counter. "Wonder what?"

"If it's an abbreviation of Yahoel . . ." Kovacs put the chair on the floor and leaned on it.

"Who's that?" I said, lighting a cigarette.

"Yahoel is the first of the seventy-two names of Metatron," said Kovacs. "The king of angels, prince of the divine face, or presence."

It gave me a very curious feeling to hear those words coming out of someone else's mouth. The Man had admitted to being a Prince of the Ninth and of The Presence but I'd always considered it to be our secret. Once again I was being overly possessive, but at the time I felt a flash of resentment. Almost as if I'd discovered that Kovacs had been eavesdropping on my conversations with The Man.

"Metatron," continued Kovacs, "is the Celestial power that links the human and the divine. Assuming, of course, that you believe in angels in the first place. He even holds sway over Michael and Gabriel — two of the great angelic princes. Yahoel, or Metatron, is believed to be the angel who was the spiritual guide of Abraham, and the guardian of the Israelites during the Exodus from Egypt and their journey through the wilderness. He's also been identified, by some authorities, as the power that occupies the throne on the right hand of God — and also as the Messiah of Christian theology."

Four weeks ago, all this would have sounded like gobbledy-gook, but not anymore. I helped myself to some of the wine and offered the bottle to Kovacs along with my cigarettes. Kovacs, it turned out, didn't drink or smoke. "That's quite a mouthful," I said. "Do you keep tabs on angels for a living?"

He smiled and took a more comfortable grip on the back of the bentwood chair. "No, it just happens to be a hobby of mine. It started when I picked up a secondhand copy of a marvelous book called *A Dictionary of Angels* at Leakey's —"

"You mean the shop on Second Avenue at Seventy-ninth Street?" I interjected.

"Yes," he said.

"Amazing," I replied. "I've been getting books from there. I can't understand how I missed that one."

"It's out of print," said Kovacs. "I got my copy a good ten years ago. And I've been hunting down copies of the books mentioned in the bibliography ever since."

"It sounds fascinating," I said. "And it all fits with what our friend out on the porch has told me. Could you send me a Xerox copy of anything you have on Yahoel?"

"My pleasure." Kovacs adjusted his glasses. "I hope this doesn't sound impertinent but — what was it that convinced you that he was the, uhh — you know . . . ?"

"The Risen Christ?" I smiled. "You don't have to feel embarrassed. I know how tough it is to discuss something like this without generating waves of laughter or cries of outrage. All I can say in answer to your question is something inside me responded to his presence. He has never told us, in so many words, who he is but he has never denied it. We were just fortunate enough to recognize him — and we've also seen him do some pretty incredible things. But that was later. The knowledge of who he was came first. If you're lucky, it may come to you and Linda. But it won't be through my telling you. It comes from within."

Kovacs gave a deprecating smile. "Doesn't sound too difficult. I'll give it a try." He picked up the chair. "As you've
probably gathered from Linda, we Catholics tend to be easily
impressed."

"You're also easily upset," I replied. "I'd better warn you,
it's not all good news. Rome comes in for a lot of stick."

Kovacs laughed. "Can you think of a time when it didn't?"

I flagged him down as he turned away. "Hold on a minute
— does the name 'Brax ring a bell?"

Kovacs's eyes fluttered as his brain made the right connections. "That's an interesting one. The only name I can think
of that fits is 'Abraxas.' The Gnostics regarded him as the
Supreme Unknown. He's usually classified as a demon but his
name is also connected with the cycles of Creation. He was
believed by some authorities to be the ruler of three hundred
and sixty-five heavens and by others as the mediator between
living creatures and the God-Head. There is also a story
about an Aeon — which again, by tradition, is usually identified as Abraxas — who mirrored himself on chaos and became
Lord of the World."

As you can see, this guy Kovacs was a walking encyclopedia.
His mention of the word "Aeon" brought to mind what The
Man had said about the origin of the Ain-folk. "And an Aeon
is what?" I asked.

"The highest order of Celestial power," replied Kovacs.
"It's a term used to describe the first created beings. Spiritual
entities formed from the divine Presence. God's own being.
Abraxas was their leader. The word 'Aeon' is also synonymous with the *sefira* — the divine emanations through which
God manifested his existence in the creation of the Universe."

More pieces of the jigsaw puzzle. And they seemed to fit
into the picture I'd begun to build of 'Brax. "I must get a
copy of this book," I said.

"The best thing is to let Leakey's know you're after one,"
suggested Kovacs. "And try the other secondhand bookshops.
It was published in nineteen sixty-seven by The Free Press,

New York. The author's name was Gustav Davidson. Price was fifteen dollars. At least, it was then. Could be twice that now."

I waited in case he was going to quote me the Library of Congress catalog number but he didn't. I handed him his cup and saucer, took out a new glass for The Man, and picked up the bottle of wine. "What do you do for a living, Pete?"

Kovacs moved aside to let me pass. "I'm an analyst."

"Investment, political, food, systems, or psycho-?" I asked.

"Agricultural," he replied. "I'm mainly involved with studies of Eastern Europe, Russia and Asia. Keeping tabs on changes in crop mixes, ground utilization and farming technology. Producing forecasts of grain and root crop yields. Mostly from journals, official reports and statistics published by the countries concerned — plus whatever information comes to hand."

It sounded like the kind of job where you could die of boredom before picking up your first paycheck. "Fascinating," I said.

Kovacs shrugged as we walked through to the front of the house. "It pays the rent. It also helps us fix the right price for our grain shipments if we know how desperate they are. All part of the international poker game."

I nodded agreement. "I see from the car that you live in Virginia. Do you work for the Department of Agriculture in Washington?"

"Well, sort of," he replied, with an interesting lack of precision. "I'm on a kind of retainer. But I guess that still makes me a faceless federal bureaucrat."

"Don't knock it," I said. "Kissinger started on a part-time basis too."

Kovacs caught The Man's eye as we joined the others on the porch. "Are you sure you wouldn't prefer a chair?"

The Man shook his head. "No thanks."

I poured out some wine and got Linda to pass it to him. Miriam filled Kovacs's cup with coffee and handed me the pot. "Leo, be a sweetie — go and make some more, will you?"

Leo, be a sweetie . . .

Gale McDonald found me watching the percolator doing its stuff while I nursed my paranoia.

"What do you think?" I said. "Was it worth the trip?"

"He's certainly a pretty remarkable guy," she admitted. "And he's been coming out with some amazing stuff but —" She pressed her lips together and raised her eyebrows clear of blue shades. "— what proof have we got that it's true?"

"How about your editor? Do you think he'd buy it?" I asked.

McDonald shook her head. "I doubt it. I have a feeling that if I wheeled Yale into the office and got him to repeat what he's just been telling us, we'd both get thrown out on our ears." She sighed frustratedly. "If only we could come up with some tangible evidence. Maybe some kind of medical report from Jeff Fowler about his blood. A complete rundown on his physiology or whatever. Something that would really prove that Yale was not just an ordinary guy who was making all this stuff up."

"Yes, I see what you mean," I said. "And a few miracles would come in handy too."

"Don't be such a pisser, Resnick," she sniffed. "I came up here to help."

"Has it occurred to you that he might not want your help — or even mine?" I said. "That it might be the other way around and that you and I needed his?"

She reseated her glasses on the bridge of her nose. "Don't you want to see him on TV?"

"No," I replied.

She looked baffled. "Why not? If you handle this the right way you could reach a global audience of four, five, six hundred million people. You could get the whole world to switch on."

I shook my head. "Gale, come on. You know in your heart of hearts it would never work. It would be cheap, trivial and totally superficial. Besides which, I can't bear the idea of him being interviewed by David Frost. Can you imagine it? It would be absolutely horrific."

"Now who's being trivial?" said McD. "Look, let's be serious for a minute. If we could sell this to my editor, he could probably persuade Channel Eight to get a team of Biblical scholars together in a lodge up in the Adirondacks, or Lake Placid, and pay their expenses while they check out his story."

"Gale," I sighed, "I don't think you understand. If you put The Man together with the top five or the top fifty theologians, what would it prove? Every scrap of knowledge they possess comes from the study and reinterpretation of the surviving written evidence. Which has already been messed around through oral transmission before being selectively edited and amended by the first writers to put pen to papyrus and then getting its tenses twisted by translators. Not to mention the chunks missed out by copyists or burned underneath Arab cooking pots. When you come right down to it, there is very little hard, incontrovertible evidence —"

"But what about his healing of Mrs. Perez's hands — and the statue that she and her husband and Father Rosado saw bleeding. And Jeff's medical evidence. That's proof too."

I brushed her words aside. "That could be explained away. And in any case, it's not directly attributable. Supposing he refuses to give the panel a sign — the way he turned down that request from the Pharisees? Can't you see what would happen? You'd get into a ludicrous situation where the experts insisted that the texts were authentic and that The Man was an impostor."

"Sure, I can see that," replied McD. "But there's an equal chance that it could be the other way around. After all, there's no reason why they shouldn't react the way you have. Obviously we'd put people with open minds on the panel. Maybe a humanist, some agnostics, atheists or whatever. You know — so that we get a broad spectrum of belief."

I threw up my hands. "Gale, it's pointless. It's a self-defeat-ing exercise. If you're trying to get The Man the Good Housekeeping Seal of Approval, your experts also have to be acceptable to the churches whose viewpoints they represent. Which means that your panel will be packed with hard-liners and would never reach a consensus."

She frowned. "Why?" It was obvious that learning to ride a bucking bronco had not left her a great deal of time to absorb the ups and downs of the ecumenical movement.

"Because," I began patiently, "the differences that separate right-wing and Marxist-type Christians are almost as great as the differences between Christian and Jew. And between Jew and Moslem, and Moslem and Hindu. It may not be exactly headline news, but the Vatican has been cracking down on its maverick theologians over the past few years. How are they going to take the news that the power that launched Christianity was the same power that inspired Muhammad and set Islam on the road to Morocco? And which in turn, through its incursions into Spain and southern France, carried enlightenment back to Christendom. Fueling the Renaissance, the Reformation and — through the teaching of the Sufis — a new search for The Truth?"

McD's eyes narrowed in an effort to bring this giant canvas into fine focus. Bright though she was, I had a feeling that her knowledge of European history stopped at the North Dakota line. "Did he tell you that?"

"That, and much much more," I said. "The big headline to come out of all this is that you Christians don't have a monopoly on the truth about God. You've been running with the ball but in the wrong direction. The Man staked a claim to the whole world but the one you've created is not quite what he had in mind."

"Don't look at me," she said.

"Or me either," I replied. "Apart from my sister's wedding, it's nearly twenty years since I saw the inside of a synagogue. But what The Man is selling is light-years away from the present setup. It means a radical rethink of God, heaven, earth and the whole salvation package. We have to go back to the beginning and revise our views on everything from Arianism to Zen. The Man is part of an ongoing Universalist movement. The elements are here, right under our noses. We just have to work out how to put them back together again."

"So tell me about it," said McD.

I pointed past her at the kitchen door. "Go out there and talk to The Man. If he runs out of time and you have a spare week, you can come up here and listen to the tapes we've made. If there's anything you don't understand, I'll try and explain it. But let me make one thing clear right now: If you really want to know what this is all about, *you* are the one who is going to have to come up with the answers."

"Okay," she said. "But meanwhile, what are we going to do about him?"

I took a deep breath. "Gale — I'm not going to do anything. This visit of his is strictly off the record. Whatever you decide to do is your business. But I can tell you right now that even if you manage to sell this to your editor, his appearances are too erratic to even contemplate setting up a panel of experts. I've been wrestling with this problem for weeks — trying to decide whether I should keep it to myself or attempt to share the news with other people. In the end, he solved the dilemma for me. He wanted you, Jeff and Linda to know."

"Did he tell you why?" asked McD.

"No," I replied. "But if I were you, I'd think twice before asking. Nothing that has happened is an accident. Carol and Peter Kovacs are here for a reason too. Whatever it is, it's now their problem, not mine."

"So what you're saying is — 'do nothing.' " It was clearly a solution she disliked.

"No. What I'm saying is that you should give up any idea that your meeting with The Man is going to bring you fame and fortune. Each of us has to draw what we can from this encounter. Which may be nothing, something that is of passing interest — or an experience that will affect the rest of our lives."

McD accepted the point with a sober nod. "Okay . . . you've convinced me. So I'm not going to be the next Barbara Walters."

"You'll survive," I said. "You may even live to thank me."

Jeff Fowler appeared at the door to the kitchen. "Uhh — Miriam sent me to check on how the coffee's doing."

I showed him the fresh-perked pot. "It's right here."

Fowler eyed the pair of us. "You both look very glum for such an auspicious occasion."

"Gale wants to have The Man certified," I said.

The news raised Jeff's eyebrows.

"As Jesus," explained McD. "Not as a lunatic."

"I can see the problem." Fowler nodded. "Still — it might be possible to prove medically that he is — how shall I put it — not one of us?"

"I already suggested that," said McD.

"And?" inquired Fowler.

"It doesn't solve Gale's problem," I replied. "All it's going to do is make him the Man from Mars."

"We've got to start somewhere." Fowler shrugged.

"I agree. But not on The Man," I said. "We have to start on ourselves."

"I need a cigarette," said McD wearily.

"There's a pack of Marlboros right by your elbow," I said.

"Thanks, but mine are out on the porch." McD held out her hand. "Give me the coffee."

I poured myself a cup first. "Jeff?"

"No, thanks. I've had plenty."

I passed the coffee and the jug of milk to McD. "Stick around. Jeff and I don't have any secrets."

She eyed me. "I think I may learn more outside."

I gulped down some coffee and cranked up some more of the Resnick charm to lay on Fowler. "Uhh, Jeff — I know I should have leveled with you when we first got into this but —"

"That's okay," said Fowler. "In the circumstances I'd have probably done the same thing."

I treated him to an affable smile that came straight off the shelf. "So, tell me — what was so special about that blood sample?"

Fowler licked his lips. "I know you played dumb when we first met, but how much do you actually know about the subject?"

"Jeff," I said. "I know it's red, that we've got about nine pints of the stuff, and that, if you're lucky, it clots when you cut yourself — or if you're not, you bleed to death. And that's it. *Finito. Terminada.* If you want to know the truth, the reason I know so little about it is because, when I was small, I used to faint at the sight of it. I was eighteen before I saw my first Dracula movie and discovered that girls liked being bitten on the neck."

"Mmm, interesting . . ." Fowler lit a cheroot and began lecturing me. "The three main constituents of blood are the red and white cells and the plasma — the liquid carrier medium. The red cells enable the blood to carry oxygen around the circulatory system and the primary function of the white cells is immunological. They fight off infection. The red cell contains no nucleus when it enters the blood stream. The white cell does, and is independently motile. It can wander in and out of the circulatory system at will — concentrating in vast numbers in infected areas of the body."

"So far so good," I said. "When do we get to the exciting bit?"

"Any minute now," replied Fowler. "If I don't give you the basic setup, you won't be able to understand the importance of what I discovered. After all, you're the man who didn't even know the going price for a pint of blood."

"I was just kidding, Jeff. Go ahead," I said. "I'm all ears."

Fowler resumed his dissertation. "Okay. The red cell has a finite life of around one hundred and ten days. During that period it ages and is finally removed from the system by the action of the spleen. Now it is possible — by careful analysis — to establish the percentage of new blood cells in any given sample. These are called reticulocytes. And the percentage in

any normal red cell count is usually around thirty percent."
He paused before delivering the punch line. "In the sample
Miriam gave me that was supposed to have come from the
unlucky Mr. Lucksteen, the proportion of reticulocytes was
zero percent. They were all mature red cells. And they were
all identical."

I could see from his face that this was meant to be startling
news but its full impact was lost on me. "So — is that what
you meant when you talked about an abnormality that could
arrest the aging process?"

"Absolutely," replied Fowler, his eyes gleaming. "That's
what made me suspect the pair of you. I could understand
your not wanting to get technical, but when Miriam didn't
press me for any details, well . . ." He puffed a cloud of
smoke at the ceiling. "Can you imagine it? No *new* blood?
Naturally, I wanted to know more, but the sample wasn't big
enough for the full range of tests to be applied. But I managed to establish that the blood contained no nutrients.
Things like glucose, calcium and iron that are produced by
the digestive tract then passed out into the bloodstream and
carried to where they are needed in the body."

"That figures," I said. "He hasn't eaten anything since he's
been here. But he's downed several bottles of wine." I
frowned. "Something's wrong somewhere. Isn't there calcium,
iron and glucose in that?"

Fowler brushed my question aside. "And then, the miracle
happens. Father Rosado drops out of the blue with the phial
of blood from the statue — and there was more where that
came from. I was able to establish that it was identical with
the sample Miriam had given me. Again, a one hundred percent mature red cell count. No nutrients and — most important of all — no DNA in the lymphocytes. They're a special
type of white blood cell, the little bastards that gang up to
reject heart transplants." He paused. "I take it you know
what DNA is — deoxyribonucleic acid?"

"Yes," I said. "It's the chemical that carries encoded genetic
data."

Fowler nodded approvingly. "It's a constituent of the chromosome which is present in the nucleus of the cell. The chromosome is the hereditary blueprint. Without it, the cell can't reproduce itself. And if none of the other cells in the body contained DNA —"

I completed the sentence for him. "The organism would have to be an original. A one-of-a-kind."

"One-of-a-kind, yes," said Fowler. "But not an original. An almost perfect reproduction of a real human being — with closed-circuit body chemistry."

I shook my head. "A *more*-than-perfect reproduction, Jeff. One that will never grow old, fat, or senile. Or be fed to the flames, or left to the worms." I understood what Fowler had been saying. The Man's physical entity was eternally present. It was a stunning demonstration of the Empire's powers over the life and death cycle of the 'Braxian universe.

Carol Shiragawa wandered into the kitchen, snaked an arm around Fowler's neck, and slid a hand behind his belt buckle. "What gives? Is this where the action is?"

"No," I said. "It's all out front."

Carol rolled her eyes. "You mean we're just going to sit around and listen to that kook with the beard?"

"Well," said Fowler, "that was the general idea."

"Jeezuss," groaned Carol. She turned to me. "Who is this guy? Is he some kind of religious pothead from California?"

I exchanged a glance with Fowler. "Why do you say that?"

"Aww, come on." She smiled. "Gale just told me he thinks he's Jesus Christ."

"Yes, that's right," I said. "He is."

Carol turned to Fowler. "What is this — some kind of put-on?"

"How do you mean?" I replied.

She laughed. "Leo, I know I'm supposed to be dumb, but don't try and tell me you really believe that."

I squared up to her. "Yes, I really think I do. And I say that with the greatest possible reluctance."

Carol eyed me skeptically then looked at Fowler. "How about you?"

Fowler shrugged noncommittally.

"You're both as nutty as he is." She shook her head in disbelief and stopped her stealthy assault on Fowler's body. "Do you have a bike here?"

I nodded.

"Great." She planted a kiss on Fowler's cheek.

"Where are you going?" he said.

"For a ride. What do you think?"

Fowler looked confused. "But — don't you want to stay here with us?"

Carol patted his face. "Honey, if I'd wanted to hear people talk about God, I'd have gone to church."

"You'll find the bike in the garage," I said. "If you want a track suit, mine's behind the door of the upstairs bathroom."

"Thanks." Carol gave Fowler a quick feel on account and left.

He turned back to me, pink with embarrassment. "Sorry about that."

I spread my hands. "You can't win 'em all . . ."

TWENTY ═══════════

IN a way, Carol's reaction was perfectly understandable. Neither she nor the others had seen what we had seen — his scourged and crucified body on the slab in the morgue; its inexplicable disappearance; his return a week later, miraculously whole; the stigmata he had produced at will and which had made my stomach turn; his tricks with the bottle of wine, and with the books; his manipulation of my mind — enabling me to speak Hebrew with the fluency of a first-century rabbi. Linda had already met The Man. God knows what the others came expecting to see. But all they found was an olive-skinned, thirty-four-year-old black-bearded Semite who needed a haircut, wearing the plaid shirt, green cords and blue jogging shoes he'd picked up when Linda had taken him shopping. He was not flanked by angels, no saintly halo hovered above his head, his eyes were not turned meekly heavenward, no doves descended; his voice was not underscored by a swelling Celestial soundtrack.

It was little wonder that Kovacs, Gale McDonald and Fowler each sought me out in the kitchen instead of remaining glued to their seats, spellbound by The Man's words. One would have thought that Kovacs couldn't wait to speak to him, and that McD and Fowler would not have wanted to miss a thing. Carol? Yes, okay — maybe she was dumber than the rest of us, and easily bored. But the others, in their own oblique way, had come to be reassured. They knew who I was. Whereas the claim I'd made on behalf of The Man was too hard to take. What they wanted from me was some rational explanation. Something that would convince them that I was telling the truth when The Truth itself was sitting outside on the porch. Fowler's scientific mind had been engaged by the mystery he'd found under his electron microscope; McDonald the newshound had gotten the whiff of a good story and had dragged Linda into it. All three had come beating at my door for an answer and I'd let them have it right between the eyes.

The trouble was it wasn't the answer they wanted. McD and Fowler could have handled the Man from Mars. The media input over the last thirty years beginning with visionaries like Asimov and Hugo Gernsback and culminating with the philosophical pyrotechnics of Spielberg had made a close encounter of the third kind not only plausible but positively welcome. Indeed, it was viewed by some as the only thing that might divert the world from what they saw as a headlong plunge into the abyss of nuclear war. But to find your curiosity has led you to confront an individual who might be the Risen Christ was something else entirely. Especially when that individual's appearance was something less than divine, and when his message seemed calculated to reduce the whole elaborate edifice of organized religion to a heap of rubble.

There was nothing I could do that would make them see what their hearts and minds had, so far, failed to recognize. To accept that Ya'el was The Man meant more than just revising their belief systems and accepting a tolerant attitude toward the possible existence of God; it required a quantum leap of the imagination, an act of faith that, for the moment at least, none of them seemed able to produce.

It was fascinating to watch. They all listened as he told them many of the things he had told me, and did their best to stifle their incredulity, but the magic, the sheer wonder of the moment slipped through their fingers. Gale McDonald and Jeff Fowler, who had come hoping to gain some professional advantage, were clearly frustrated. Peter Kovacs became worried over the theological implications of The Man's dismissal of the Trinity; Linda, bless her, was obviously hoping for a miracle.

It would have made things so easy. And I said as much to Miriam when the two of us chanced to meet over the dishes in the kitchen. "It's crazy," I muttered. "All he has to do is make those wounds appear on his wrists."

Miriam shook her head. "People believe what they want to believe. They could say they were hypnotized — like people claim after they've seen the Indian Rope Trick."

"But he showed us," I protested. "I've seen all kinds of things."

"Maybe he feels you're a lot more important than they are," said Miriam.

Which, in hindsight, was another cryptic remark.

"I don't see why I should be," I replied. "But even if I am, it's no answer. The reason Gale, Jeff and Linda are here is because he told me to tell them."

"I thought you had dreamed that," she said.

"Don't split hairs," I snapped. "What's good enough for Joseph is good enough for me. They're going to go away thinking we're a couple of lunatics."

"I doubt it," said Miriam. "Give them time. Even after what we saw at the hospital it took us a week to come to terms with it."

"Yes, I guess you're right," I mused. "I'll have to curb my missionary fervor — otherwise I may end up making house calls."

Carol Shiragawa, who disappeared for several hours, returned, having pushed the bike for the last five miles with a flat front tire. By this time, the conversation had moved into the living room and around the log fire. Carol showered and changed back into her clothes then joined us with the obvious intention of giving us a yard-by-yard account of her cycling saga which — apart from a few expressions of sympathy — found no takers.

Let's face it, if you're given a choice between hearing about a front-tire blowout or the birth of the Son of Man, it's a no-contest. Carol stuck it gamely for a good thirty minutes then went into a huddle with Miriam and disappeared into the kitchen. A move which more than made up for her total disinterest in the proceedings because the result was a truly inspirational sukiyaki.

During supper, I announced that I was thinking of spending my two-week vacation in Israel. The news caused some surprise among my guests but I did not enlarge upon my reasons for going. Somehow it didn't seem the right moment to tell them I was thinking of growing oranges. The Man sat at the head of the table with Miriam on his right and Linda on his left. Jeff sat next to her, facing Kovacs, leaving me flanked by Carol and Gale McD. Since one came from Iowa and the other Montana, I engaged them in a bantering conversation about the manners and morals of the Midwest which Carol interrupted from time to time to blow kisses across the table to Fowler while rubbing her shin against my left calf, seemingly unaware that Gale McDonald was applying the same inviting pressure to the right. Unfortunately, I was too far down the road to be able to respond to the joint invitation but I mention the incident for its anecdotal interest. It may not say much about religion but it says a great deal about human nature. Or maybe we had an uninvited guest and this was his way of letting me know he was there.

It was the first time that I actually saw The Man eat something and, like the smart cookie he was, he complimented Carol at length in what I assume was faultless Japanese then chatted to her again afterward while the rest of us did the dishes. I never got the chance to question her properly about what he said but I had the feeling he gave her something to think about.

Jeff followed me outside when I went to get another basket of logs. "I thought you said he didn't eat."

"Not when he's been with us," I replied. "But so what? The Book says he ate some fish and honey in Bethany and broke bread with a couple of guys at Emmaus."

Fowler looked over his shoulder then lowered his voice. "Don't laugh, this is important. Has he been to the john?"

I bit back a smile. "Funny you should ask. I've been curious about that too. The answer is — not to my knowledge. Maybe he does all that back in first-century Jerusalem. Or waits till he's outside what we laughingly refer to as the space-time continuum. Or maybe he doesn't go at all."

Fowler sighed patiently. "Leo — I'm not going to get into whether this guy is Jesus Christ or not. That's your problem. But he sure as hell is something special. What concerns me is that he has a body which some absolutely unique blood has come out of, and which food and drink has gone into. Don't try and tell me it doesn't go anywhere."

I humped the basket back in through the kitchen door. "I'm not trying to tell you anything, Jeff. If it really worries you why don't you ask him?"

"Are you kidding?" said Fowler.

I built up the fire, Miriam fixed everybody up with a drink, and we rounded things off with a warm, cracker-barrel kind of an evening. The Man had a genius for blending in, but underneath the relaxed manner there remained that central core of gentle incorruptibility. Some people only smile with the teeth, leaving their eyes on ice. The Man smiled with both, but his gaze always had the same alarming directness. It seemed to reach right into you, giving you no place to hide and leaving you with the feeling that he could spot a phony at a thousand yards.

Just after eleven, I noticed his attention wander. He seemed to be listening to an inner voice, the way animals react to sounds that we cannot hear. He uncrossed his legs and got up from the sofa. "I have to leave, but please — don't let me break up the party."

We got to our feet. He said goodbye to us all in turn, leaving me till last.

"Can I give you a lift somewhere?" asked Kovacs.

The Man smiled. "It's good of you to ask, but — I've got my own transportation." He brought Miriam's hands together and gave them a fatherly kiss. *"Shalom . . ."*

Finally, it was my turn to grasp his hand. "I'll probably fly out to Israel on Tuesday or Wednesday."

He patted my shoulder. "Okay, I'll meet you there."

"Don't forget we still have a date at the hospital," said Miriam.

"Don't worry," he said. "I haven't forgotten." He stepped away from us and raised his hands in a gesture that was both a blessing and a goodbye wave rolled into one. "Love one another."

And suddenly he was gone. Miriam and I were merely startled, but his disappearance left the others gasping.

"Now that," said Fowler, recovering his voice, "is absolutely fucking fantastic."

What you might call an overvigorous understatement.

"I don't believe it," said McDonald.

"It's impossible," said Kovacs.

"Oh, my God," said Linda, her eyes filling with tears. "It really was him. It really was."

Carol stared at the empty space The Man had occupied and blinked hard several times to clear what she must have thought was a vision defect. She turned to me with a puzzled frown. "Give it to me straight, Leo — did that guy just vanish, or did you put some shit in the chocolate cake?"

I smiled at her. "It would make it a lot easier all around if I'd laced the cake, Carol, but you're not hallucinating. I'm afraid you're going to have to face up to the fact that he really did vanish."

"But," she insisted, "people can't do that."

I spread my hands. "He's not people, Carol. He's The Man."

Fowler looked at McD, Kovacs and Linda and slumped

down into an armchair, shaking his head. "Miriam, come on — say something. You're a doctor. You know this can't happen."

"A few weeks ago I would have agreed with you," said Miriam. "But what I've seen since Easter Saturday has forced me to suspend both belief and disbelief. I can't give you any rational explanation — and don't try and look for one, you'll drive yourself crazy."

"But it doesn't make *sense!*" protested Fowler.

I let out a long-suffering sigh. "Of course it doesn't. Do you think we don't know that? This whole event defies all logic and all reason. But it's happened all the same. You saw The Man. You spoke to him, touched him, ate with him. I've got his voice on tape." I pointed at Kovacs. "Peter here even took pictures of us with him on the porch."

"I hope to God they come out," said Kovacs.

"The Polaroids the police took were okay," I said.

Gale McDonald jerked back into life. "Are you telling me that the NYPD have got pictures of him on file?"

"They had," I replied. "They're now in my possession."

"Do you have them here?" she asked.

"No," I said.

"Why did the police take pictures of him?" said Kovacs.

So many questions. And so few answers. I clutched my forehead. "Ohh, yeah, you don't know about that . . ."

"Why don't you begin at the beginning?" suggested Miriam. "That way you can fill in the bits that Gale and the others don't know about."

"Good idea." I served up another round of drinks, Miriam made some strong black coffee, then we sat down with the five of them around the fire and told them everything that had happened to us from the moment the two mysterious ambulance men wheeled the crucified body of The Man into Manhattan General.

They listened gamely, and were prepared to accept most of it, but the whole business of the simultaneity of time threw up too many stumbling blocks. And although nobody went so far as to say I was talking through the top of my head, it was clear that there were very few takers for the idea that he was commuting back and forth between 1981 and first-century Jerusalem.

Which is a pity, because within some forty-eight hours, he provided me with conclusive proof that he was.

We must have talked solidly for about two hours then wrapped it up with an agreement to meet again on my return from Israel. This time for a whole weekend — that we were to spend listening to the tapes I made of The Man.

"What do you think, Peter?" I said as people got up and stretched, fumbled for car keys, and rushed to the john.

He raised his eyebrows. "It's an amazing story. So much so that it's hard to imagine anyone making it up."

I nodded. "I know what you mean. Listen, it's up to you. You can either believe that you spent today in the company of The Man or you can take the way out suggested by Carol and decide that all this was some elaborate hoax. If it is, someone's been feeding me dope-filled cake for the last three weeks."

Kovacs smiled. "I did consider that but, unfortunately, it's not a viable solution to the dilemma you've presented us with." He put his hand on my shoulder. "Would you have any objection to me talking with Father Rosado and Mrs. Perez?"

"None whatsoever," I replied. "Just keep my name out of it until I get back. Is that a deal?"

"Yes." He shook my hand. "Thank you for letting me share in this experience."

"It's not over yet," I said. I caught up with Gale McDonald as she and Carol went through the front door. "Well, you wanted a story. Is this one big enough for you?"

She gave me a loaded look. "You realize, of course, that no one's going to believe a word of this. Let alone print it."

I ruffled the hair on the top of her head. "That's one of the joys of being a reporter."

She ducked out from under my hand and shook her hair

back into place with a mischievous, narrowed-eyed smile. "Do you think he'll be back?"

"I don't see why not," I replied. "I'm only going to be away for ten to twelve days."

"Good," said McD. "Keep in touch."

I switched on the outside lights as she stepped off the porch and turned my attention to Carol. "Hey, come on, you're supposed to look happy."

She shook her head as we walked down to where the cars were parked. "This is all too much for me. I'm just plain folks from Cedar Falls, Iowa. All that stuff about alternative realities, and 'Brax — Jeezuss, who needs any of that?"

"That's exactly how I felt," I said. "But, strange as it may seem, it really does help you get things sorted out."

"Terrific," she said. Using a word she'd picked off my pillow. "Let's make a deal. You leave me out of this — and I'll forget I came. Okay?"

"Okay." We reached Fowler's VW Rabbit. A rather apt choice of car. "Does that mean you don't want to come up with the others when I get back?"

"That's right, honey." She gave me a pouting kiss that reminded my lips of better days. "Spending my weekends with a bunch of Jesus freaks is not my idea of a good time."

As she and Gale got in, I saw Fowler looking at me over the roof of the car. "I've got to talk to you," he said.

"Call me," I replied. "I'll be at home most of the day."

Miriam walked past with Linda and Peter Kovacs. Linda was still dazed by The Man's disappearance. "It was really *him*," she said.

I opened the car door for Kovacs. "I have a feeling that I've just lost a secretary and the Church has gained a daughter. When you get her home, tell her I said to take Monday off."

"I think I may take Monday off myself," replied Kovacs. He put the key in the ignition. "I don't know how the two of you can take it so casually."

I shrugged. "Peter — when you've seen one miracle, you've seen 'em all." It was his turn to worry now.

We waved them away into the darkness and watched until the red taillights disappeared around the bend in the road, then went back up into the house with our arms around each other's waist. "So — what do you think, Doctor Maxwell? Are we going to pull through?"

"Only if you follow the recommended treatment," she replied.

"I'm going," I said. "I'm going."

She washed up the cups and glasses while I collected the tapes and straightened the living room. Then we packed our bags, turned everything off, and locked up the house, leaving the fire on its last legs in the grate.

"Why are you laughing?" said Miriam, as we stowed our weekend bags in the back of the Porsche.

"I was just thinking of Jeff and Gale and the others." I settled into my seat. "Right now they must be wishing they hadn't come. Still — that's what comes of asking questions."

Miriam looked across at me. "Are you sorry you did?"

I responded with a quick laugh. "If we're to believe The Man, I was born to ask questions, and he was born to answer." I turned the car around in front of the garage and headed down the lane. "I'll tell you when I get back from Israel."

"Yes . . ." She turned her head away and stared out of the side window.

"Don't let Jeff and the others give you a hard time."

"I won't," she said.

I glanced at her as she was lit briefly by the headlights of a passing car. Her cheek was streaked with tears.

"You're crying," I said.

"Yes, I'm allowed to," she sniffed. "I'm off duty."

'Do you want to tell me why?"

"Not particularly," she said. "It will only make you more conceited than you are already." She pulled out a couple of tissues and honked into them like a bereaved baby elephant.

We cruised sedately back into town along the Saw Mill River Parkway then down the West Side. It was a desperate waste of all that horsepower packed behind me, but I think subconsciously I was trying to make the weekend last forever.

We reached Riverside Drive. "Your place or mine?" I asked.

Miriam took her head off my shoulder. "Yours. You don't have to get up this morning."

I turned off at the Marina and coasted home.

Before Miriam left for the hospital, she called Israeli Airlines and inquired about flights to Tel Aviv. I lay in bed with a cup of coffee on my chest and let her organize me.

Miriam handed me the phone. "There's a seven forty-seven daily via Paris. It's a ten-hour trip. You leave JFK at four-thirty and arrive at nine A.M. their time, the day after. There are seats available on tomorrow's plane."

"Anyone would think you wanted to get rid of me." I eased myself up on one elbow and spoke with the reservation clerk, who took my name and number and confirmed that the computer had alloted Resnick, L.N., a tourist-class aisle seat on the starboard side of the rear smoking section. I hung up and reached for a cigarette. "I'm still not sure why I'm doing this."

"Maybe you'll discover why when you get there," said Miriam. Yet another of her sphinxlike remarks.

I pulled on a robe and saw her out of the front door then fished out the reel of tape we had recorded on the Saturday, threaded it onto the deck, switched the sound through to the bedroom, and crawled back under the covers.

Before we go any further, let me do something we lawyers are fond of — and that is to define our terms of reference. If we straighten things out now, it will avoid confusion later on.

Up to this point in the story, I've used the term "The Man" to describe the spiritual entity Ya'el who appeared to us in an externally perfect replica of the body of his pre-Crucifixion host. The Man then, is synonymous with the Risen Christ — in contrast to the historical personality known elsewhere as Jesus of Nazareth and who consisted of a perishable human host occupied by Ya'el's metapsyche and his companion, the normal Ain-folk fragment identified by the given name of the host body — Joshua.

Thus we have the Joshua-Ya'el combination which, for the sake of simplicity, we can continue to refer to as "The Man"; and, similarly, Johanan-Gabriel. The double-barreled combination is used whenever necessary to signify that Ya'el and Gabriel are "on board."

As I mentioned earlier, both Ya'el and Gabriel could and did detach their spirit entities from their host bodies from time to time. When they were absent, the host continued to function under the control of the Ain-folk element — becoming fully Joshua, or Johanan, neither of whom had any paranormal gifts. They were just ordinary people like you or me. Actually, that's not quite true. The presence of such powerful spiritual beings in their host bodies had stunted the development of their Ain-folk companions to the point where Joshua, left to his own devices, gave the impression of being incoherently subnormal. What the French term *aliéné*.

Because of their power and completeness, Ya'el and Gabriel were able to fuse their metapsyches with those of Joshua and Johanan, absorbing through them the bodily sensations of their human hosts and their experience of the external world. When they spoke, it was with the voice of Joshua or Johanan but, on those occasions, it was the personality and force of character of Ya'el and Gabriel that impressed itself upon the listener. It was at these moments that people said *"the spirit was upon them."*

In the same way, Ya'el and Gabriel could break contact with Joshua and Johanan while remaining within the host body. This withdrawal usually took place when they felt the need to shut themselves off from the influences of the external world: the inputs from the bodily senses. It was a defensive move designed to avoid unnecessary contamination of their metapsyches. When this withdrawal took place, Joshua and Johanan took over control as they did when Ya'el and Gabriel detached themselves completely.

One last point, which concerns Ya'el in particular. I have

already mentioned The Man's striking gaze. It appears that the disciples and others who were close to The Man could tell when Ya'el was absent by the way that Joshua's eyes dimmed. Almost as if somebody had switched a light off inside his head.

Within a week of arriving home, The Man announced that he was leaving to seek out his cousin Johanan. Mary, his mother, did not let go of his sleeve until she had elicited a firm promise that he would return in time to go with the rest of the family to the wedding in Cana. In fact, she wanted to send his brother James along to make sure that The Man came back on time, but James managed to persuade her to let him go alone.

As the second child, James was more aware of the disturbing "otherness" that had periodically descended on his brother during their childhood years together. Like his mother, James knew that Joshua was able to generate, now and then, an inexplicable power to make things happen. He remembered seeing The Man-child twirling himself around to raise a howling dust storm that blinded his tormentors; how he made stones fly like a flock of birds and sent them buzzing around the heads of boys from a neighboring Gentile village, who were chasing them both with sticks; and the whispered, worried conversations of Mary and Joseph in the middle of the night when they voiced their fears that, in his childish anger, their strange star-child might turn his powers against them and their other children.

They need not have worried. Although the struggle with 'Brax and the internal conflict between Ya'el and Joshua had often made the growing Man-child moody and recalcitrant, he never forgot the trauma of his physical birth that he had shared with his teenage mother, and the love with which she had nursed him while he had lain totally helpless in her arms.

From Nazareth, The Man headed southeast across the Plain of Esdraelon toward the River Jordan. As he met people on the road, he inquired if they knew where he could find the holy man Johanan the Baptizer. No one was quite sure.

Some thought that he might still be around Aenon; others said they had heard that Johanan had moved north toward Galilee. But that had been a month ago — when Gabriel had been summoned to Mount Hermon.

At Aenon, The Man discovered that the Essene community had moved south to the Dead Sea, and the villagers confirmed that Johanan had last been seen moving north. The Man turned around and followed the river until he came to the road across the Jordan that led to the eastern shore of the Sea of Galilee. As he drew level with the township of Agrippina perched on the hillside west of the river, he saw a crowd down on the bank and a line of people crossing the road ahead of him. He questioned a woman at the tail-end of the group. She told him they had come down from Gadara to be blessed by the holy man.

Following her down to the river, The Man saw Johanan-Gabriel standing hip-deep in the Jordan, flanked by two of his disciples. Four more were busy trying to bring some semblance of order to the line of people waiting to be baptized. The years of arduous physical and mental discipline, first with the Essenes and then in the solitude of the barren hills of Judea, had burned every gram of fat from Johanan's body, enabling him to survive in conditions that would have broken ten ordinary men.

Although he had never disclosed the fact to Ya'el, Gabriel had always known the ultimate purpose of the mission. Ya'el was the instrument through which The Word was to be brought back into the world; he was to provide the initial impetus that would lead to the eventual liberation of the Ain-folk. During the last two years, Gabriel had been the herald, announcing through Johanan that good news was on the way.

And so it was that Joshua-Ya'el came to the Jordan below Gadara and stood in line with the rest of the poor sons of Canaan: the shepherds, goatherds, the quarrymen who hammered loose the great blocks of stone for the younger Herod's grandiose building projects, the tanners and dyers, those who took the place of oxen at the plow, and those with green, nimble fingers who tended the vines; the women who worked the fields, wove the cloth, pounded the corn, and baked the unleavened bread.

The Man didn't say anything when the two of them came face to face and, as he told it, Johanan-Gabriel was halfway through the simple ceremony of bestowing God's blessing before he realized who it was he was laying hands on.

It's hard for us to appreciate the hierarchical intricacies of the Celestial Empire, where the differences in nature, rank and function are not quantifiable in terms we can fully understand, but, as the Book records, Johanan-Gabriel was reluctant to go through with it. The Man insisted, saying, *"Suffer it to be so now: for thus it becometh us to fulfil all righteousness."* Which is a mite impenetrable but, when translated into the modern idiom, comes out as "Don't wait for me to start walking on the water. Just throw me a goddamn life jacket."

When The Man submitted to baptism at the hands of Johanan-Gabriel, it was an act of utter humility, an admission of his failure to keep faith with the Empire. It symbolized the rescue of Ya'el's metapsyche from the dark spiral vortex of the 'Braxian world. Ya'el was like a drowning man reaching up a hand; pleading to be saved. But aside from its cosmic significance, it was an emotional reunion too as Joshua and Johanan clasped each other like two long-lost brothers, half laughing, half crying, and drenched to the skin.

Leaving Andreas, an ex-fisherman, in charge of the other disciples, Johanan-Gabriel led The Man around the western side of the Sea of Galilee, to Bethsaida and Caesarea Philippi; the capital of the province ruled by the third surviving son of Herod the Great — Herod Philip.

When Joshua and Johanan had found lodgings and were safely asleep, Ya'el and Gabriel transferred their metapsyches to the land module buried near the summit of Mount Hermon.

Once again let me stress, as The Man did constantly, the

need to reach beyond the *Star Trek* connotations of the words we're obliged to use. The landing module was not a mechanical contrivance filled with instruments. Like Ya'el and Gabriel, it was brought into being by the Empire. It was a metaphysical construct, part of the Celestial packaging designed to protect their temporal aspects during penetration of the space-time dimension; powered by the Will of The Presence.

As you can see, "landing module" is less of a mouthful.

Using the newly transmitted energy, Ya'el contacted the Empire via the approaching starfleet. He learned what Gabriel already knew — which was that the breakdown in the landing module had been prearranged to force Ya'el's integration with a human host. Michael had been left in the dark in order to create a genuine feeling of crisis, the double objective of which was to mislead 'Brax, tempting him into a mood of overconfidence, and to trick Ya'el into thinking that he and Gabriel might be permanently marooned. This deception had been necessary in order to ensure that Ya'el totally identified himself with the plight of the trapped Ain-folk.

His twelve long years on the road had been a vital part of his mission. For it was only through living as a man that he could fully understand the human condition. Because of who he was, he had suffered more at the hands of 'Brax than any of the other Celestial Envoys to Earth. He had returned to Palestine weakened, demoralized and almost without hope, but the Empire regarded his journey as a triumph. It did not matter that he had been beaten to his knees. The fact that he had sought out Johanan-Gabriel to seek God's blessing, humbly taking his turn among the *'amme ha'aretz* — the people of the land — meant he had kept faith. He had taken everything that 'Brax could throw at him and he had come through.

But at what cost. The Empire might regard the mission as a triumph, but Ya'el knew that, with the crippling degree of *karma* he had acquired, he could never return to the Ninth

Universe. Worse still, he could not pass through the Time Gate. He had become trapped in the endless cycle of reincarnation; one more Celestial prisoner of the World Below.

It was at this point, when he had reached the depths of despair, that the miracle happened. In an extraordinary act of faith that put the Empire at risk, The Presence moved to free Ya'el from 'Brax's temporal dominion. Once again, we're stuck with our own words but bear with me. This is pretty mystical stuff but I've reduced it to the simplest possible terms and thrown Teilhard de Chardin out the window.

Imagine a laserlike beam of cosmic power, triggered by the Will of The Presence, blasting out through the Time Gate and across the yawning vastnesses of physical space. This is the real thing. One hundred percent pure God. The stuff that angels' dreams are made of. Follow it now, as it punches a hole right through the bad static 'Brax has spread around the Universe, is relayed along the line of rescue craft, and is deflected by the lead ship into the buried module on Mount Hermon. And now, think of it raying through Ya'el's metapsyche, wiping out his earthly *karma;* cleansing him of both past *and future* actions; restoring his spiritual perfection and replenishing his powers.

This was the moment when Joshua-Ya'el was transmuted by The Power of The Presence into the figure described in the opening chapter of John's Gospel. The Logos. The Word made flesh. Full of Grace and Truth. The Son of Man; what we were all, in the fullness of time, to become. And it is depicted in symbolic form in the paintings of the Baptism of Christ in which The Man stands haloed in the Jordan, with a dove descending from God's hand.

Some of you may ask — did the painters know the secret? The answer is: not necessarily. As The Man said, The Word has the power of God, or The Presence, behind it. That's why Truth is often linked symbolically with a sword. It keeps breaking through the barriers set up by 'Brax and working on us in all kinds of ways. Sometimes subconsciously. No matter how much he tries to twist the message, he can't destroy it. The Word lives.

It was now that Ya'el learned that he had twelve months — and not the three years some authorities have claimed — to set up the nucleus of a liberation movement that was to be fueled by a massive power input from the Empire. The transmission would take place when the rescue fleet was in position with the longship at the head of the chain in solar orbit but a pre-requisite step was the liberation of Ya'el's meta-psyche through the physical death of his Earth-host — by crucifixion.

After all the good news, the manner in which he was required to die came as a profound shock and, as some of you know from the Book, the decision did not go unquestioned. Both Ya'el and his companion psyche Joshua were still haunted by the shared childhood memory of the two thousand Jews crucified by Varus outside the walls of Jerusalem.

Gabriel drew an easier death sentence. In order to assist in the planned resurrection of The Man, he was instructed to arrange for his Earth-host to die within the next three months. The death of his Earth-host before that of The Man was also intended to check that their spirit-beings could escape unhindered from the chains that bound them to the world of 'Brax. Remaining true to the character he had created through Johanan, Gabriel proposed to provoke his arrest by Herod Antipas by publicly denouncing his dissolute relationship with his wife and niece Herodias, and her daughter Salome who, by all accounts, was an X-rated version of Shirley Temple. His plan met with the Empire's approval.

Breaking contact, the two Celestials slipped back into their unconscious hosts at Caesarea Philippi and, the next day, prompted Joshua and Johanan into making the return trip. As they passed through Capernaum, they crossed the path of Shimon-Petrus, who stopped folding his nets and stared back curiously at the golden-eyed stranger as he walked by. Like me, Shimon had no inkling of what lay ahead. Or that, in fact, the bearded stranger was a second cousin long given up for dead.

When they rejoined Johanan-Gabriel's small band of disciples at Salim, Andreas, who was also gifted with a high degree of ESP, was quick to discern the aura of Celestial power that now radiated from Joshua-Ya'el. Johanan-Gabriel introduced The Man to his disciples and explained that they were now to follow him. He, Johanan, would soon be arrested and put to death by Herod Antipas. The six young men were shocked and bewildered by this unexpected news. Johanan-Gabriel reassured them: this was not the end but the beginning; The Man was the Messiah whose arrival he had predicted — *he* was the Master they must now follow. But in the meantime, they were to go home and wait there till summoned by The Man. Later, when they had gone, Gabriel told Ya'el that he would send along someone else who might prove useful. A man who had joined the Essene commune after Ya'el had left, and whose given name was Judas.

Once more Ya'el and Gabriel were at a parting of the ways. It was the last time they saw each other alive; the last physical embrace. Joshua-Ya'el made his way into the Judean hills; Johanan-Gabriel set off to tour the towns of Galilee. The Man told us how he had stopped and looked back as Johanan's ragged, wild-haired figure strode resolutely away down the road, never once looking over his shoulder. Doubtless rehearsing the fire-and-brimstone speech that was to put Herod the Fox on the spot, Herodias into a towering rage, and his own head on a plate.

Alone in the high places, The Man meditated upon his mission and eventual death and how best to accomplish both. He now had the most extraordinary power ever given to a Celestial this side of the Time Gate. For not only had his past *karma* been removed, he had gained eternal freedom from the hitherto immutable law that governed existence in the temporal Universe. Nothing he did now, or in the future, could dilute the purity of his spiritual essence.

It was to these hills, as the Book says, that 'Brax sent emissaries to parley with Ya'el. Eight Black Princes formed from his all-embracing cosmic presence. Up to that moment, 'Brax had been convinced that he had the upper hand. Ya'el had been tied to a human host and buried alive under a crushing burden of *karma*. 'Brax's master plan had been to offer Ya'el a truce, in the hope of recruiting him to the Secessionist cause. For, reasoned 'Brax, until his *karma* had been purged in the World Below, where else could Ya'el go?

'Brax had persuaded himself that, with Ya'el on his side, there was a real possibility of rallying the remaining pockets of Loyalist resistance to his dark banner. Starting with the twelve great Aeons of Eardh-Ain. The Ain-folk trapped within Man. But now, all his scheming had come to naught; his plans were in tatters. The second-greatest power in the Empire had been his prisoner. For one heady moment, victory had been within his grasp and had been snatched away in a manner that 'Brax could not have possibly anticipated. For in removing Ya'el's *karma* at a single stroke, The Presence had changed the rules of the game.

This was why 'Brax now came, in the guise of his fawning minions, cap in hand and honey-tongued. The defeated Ya'el would have been a great acquisition, but a Ya'el freed from the law of *karma* and armed with the transcendent power of The Presence held the key to the Time Gate and the ultimate 'Braxian vision: conquest of the Empire and subjugation of The Presence.

Now you know where we get our rebellious arrogance from.

The Man never revealed what went on in his mind during this crucial encounter but, as we all know, he turned down the offer. Which I can now reveal was a two-way split of the World Below with Ya'el holding fifty-one percent of the stock and 'Brax as his trusty lieutenant. Some deal. There was as much chance of Ya'el saying "Yes" to that as there was of my mother doing the Viennese waltz with Adolph Eichmann.

What The Man knew, and what he was trying to tell us via this episode, was that God, The Presence, or Whoever represented, and was the source of, the essential eternal values that lay at the very foundation of existence. And that the 'Braxian universe and the Netherworld beyond were no more than a cosmic house of cards that was already programmed to self-destruct.

In essence, the Empire gave life, 'Brax represented death, decay and corruption. This was not important in the physical sense. The cycle of birth, death and rebirth of all life on this planet mirrored the larger life and death cycle of the Universe. And in any case, it was only our host bodies that died. The real "us" — the trapped Ain-folk fragments, the intangible essence that was regarded as the soul of Man — lived on. We had not lost our legendary immortality. We had merely mislaid the key. We simply no longer understood its nature. We had become fixated with our physicality; an obsessive desire to prolong, at whatever cost, our earthly existence.

Mankind's attempt to cheat Time mirrored 'Brax's fight against the inexorable Law of Simultaneity under which all events were preordained by The Presence. All 'Brax's efforts were, in the end, directed toward trying to transform the multidimensional nature of Time, to wrest control of the future from The Presence. It brought us back to the book analogy again. Only in this version, the characters were trying to take control of the Author in a desperate attempt to stop the story from ending.

It seems irrational, but down here on the ground we were trying to do the same kind of thing. Groups with more money than sense had been sold on the idea that cryogenics was a substitute for salvation. (It isn't. And if you don't need the money, give it away to the poor. Your soul is not going to hang around until some kindly serviceman in the far future switches your central heating back on.) But the lunacy doesn't end there. The medical profession and its richer patrons are so besotted with the manipulation of life that they have not faced up to the Frankensteinian future of transplant technology. In fifty to a hundred years from now, medical science may discover how to keep you alive for, say, two or three centuries. Can you imagine it? Two double-centenarians humping? Each of them a sutured collage of silicone plumbing and pieces from other people's auto accidents? Terminal men and women living in fear of a power outage?

Even if science achieved the ultimate 'Braxian miracle — control of the genetic matrix, giving us test-tube replicas of Arnold Schwarzenegger and Bo Derek, or John Wayne and Jane Russell — all the wit and ingenuity of cloned, transplanted Man in the ages to come will not enable us to survive the death of the sun or the collapse of the Universe.

How much better to come around again as a fresh, new-born human being with all your options open. To be able to see, once again, the world through the unveiled eyes of a child. With the possibility that, this time, you may get it right.

Innocence and idealism tend to be derided as impossible and impractical states that have no place in the "real world." Yet these abstract notions are not products of our brain's biochemistry. The moral dilemma, the concept of perfectibility could not exist unless it had been put into our minds by some external agency. Man would not strive toward these goals, would not seek the perfect love, the perfect friendship, unless he was driven by some inner force. This desire for the seemingly unattainable is the outward expression of our soul's longing to be reunited with God. The yearning of the Ainfolk to be freed from their prison cells.

The Man came down from the hills with a clear idea of what he had to do. His first priority was the recruitment of twelve disciples. As I've mentioned elsewhere, they were a symbolic representation of the twelve Aeons he had come to liberate. They also had a more practical purpose. The Man intended to use them as test vehicles to evaluate the effects of an input of Celestial power, and they were to serve as his bodyguard. The Man had not forgotten his near-fatal mugging on the road to Jericho. Even though he now had the ability to blank himself out of the landscape, his Earth-host was not totally invulnerable. As long as he remained bonded to his physical body, his power was finite and could be drained away in the same manner that electrical current flows down an energy gradient. From a source of high potential to one of low. As in the incident when the woman crawled through the ring of disciples and touched the hem of his robe. Remember how he felt the power drain from him? If you don't, it's recorded in Mark, chapter 5, verse 30. That was why he kept pulling out when the crowds became unmanageable.

Despite what the Book says at this point about his movements after the forty days and nights in the wilderness, he did not go to Capernaum, but to Jerusalem. To seek out Mary of Magdala, whom he had left in the care of Nicodemus. He found her rested and ready to travel. It was with Mary by his side that he journeyed northward to Galilee to summon Shimon-Petrus and his brother Andreas from their nets to be fishers of men.

Andreas, you may remember, had been instructed to await The Man's arrival. Shimon, who is enshrined in Christian theology as Saint Peter, was not the first to be recruited, nor was he called "The Rock." That is a mistranslation for "The Truth" — something that he, along with the eleven other disciples, was to be the foundation for. Peter's preeminence in the New Testament Canon is due to the creative editing of the Pauline organization men; the essential underpinning that provided the foundations for the Apostolic Succession.

From the very beginning, The Man's teaching was anti-hierarchical. Time and time again he stressed that the first would be last and the last first. Don't be misled by indications in this account of a pyramidal command structure inside the Empire. There are no class divisions, only degrees of essence. In the way that a cloud and a wave have their beginning in the same ocean.

I don't want to use up valuable space arguing over the Aramaic texts, but the Apostles were not given the task of building a church and all that that implies. The original message has been distorted. The Man's ultimate aim in spreading The Word was to build an army (*kahal*) of assembled organic unities (*edhah*) or, as a chronicler of the Empire might say, to reunite the fragmented Ain-folk.

Over the next few weeks, with Mary of Magdala's help, The Man gathered together the disparate group of twelve who were to follow him doggedly until that panic-filled night in the Garden of Gethsemane. And during the next few months, he also gathered other adherents who were to form the nucleus of the group known as the Followers of The Way. Mary of Magdala was given the task of selecting and organizing this group and, as she had direct access to The Man, interceding on their behalf whenever necessary.

The character and eventual fate of the twelve disciples has been chewed over by Biblical scholars and endlessly romanticized by a succession of novelists. In historical terms, their personalities, like mine, are irrelevant. Their importance lay in the part that each played in enabling The Man to carry out his mission; the fact that they were twelve in number and because, as a group, they represented a varied cross-section of society. They were not all dirt-poor sod-busters, or fundamentalist fishermen. Matthew-Levi was a tax collector, Philip a Greek-speaking student of law, Shimon the Zealot was a political activist, and Judas was a member of the Sicarii — a first-century version of the Stern Gang, specializing in covert assassination of Roman soldiers and civil servants. Andreas, Philip, Nathan barTolomai, Jacob of Alphaeus, Timmaeus and Thaddeus were the disciples The Man inherited from Johanan-Gabriel. Jacob and Johan bar-Zebedee came, as did Shimon-Petrus, from the fishing community based around Capernaum.

It was Judas, arriving from Jerusalem, who brought the news that Johanan the Baptizer had been arrested for his vituperative assault on Herodias and her preteen strumpet daughter, and was now languishing in the slammer at Machereus, Herod's forbidding fortress-palace on the eastern slopes of the Dead Sea. The curtain was going up on the third and final act. It was time for The Man to assume the role of an itinerant preacher whose wandering route through the Galilean and Judean countryside was to end on Calvary. But first, there was that marriage to attend in Cana.

On the way there, he made that ill-fated attempt to preach in the synagogue at Nazareth which ended, as I've already mentioned, with him being run out of town. Cana was the last time he was to meet his mother face to face until he looked down at her through pain-wracked eyes from the cross. It was also the occasion of his first recorded miracle when, under protest, he turned six stone flagons of water into wine. It was a somewhat frivolous use of his powers but, as those of you who've got one will know, Jewish mothers are not easily denied.

TWENTY-ONE

THE phone rang, cutting across The Man's recorded voice. I got up and switched off the tape deck and took the call in the living room. It was Jeff Fowler.

"About yesterday," he began, not wasting time on any preliminaries. "When you get back from Israel do you think you could persuade your friend to come down to the institute for a complete examination?"

"What do you hope to prove, Jeff?" I asked.

"I'm not sure we can 'prove' anything," replied Fowler. "But that food and wine he swallowed last night has to go somewhere. If his internal organs are as perfect as his external appearance and motor functions imply, then he must have gastric juices in his digestive tract. In which case, what are his kidneys doing? And what's happening to the excess oxygen that's floating around his system?"

"What makes you think there is any?" I replied.

"Leo," said Fowler, "his blood contains nothing but mature red blood cells. That means he's already carrying more oxygen than normal. But if his blood and tissue cells aren't aging, then the energy that would normally be used up in the building of new cells, muscle fiber, bone and tissue will just accumulate. How does he store it? The guy must be like a superball!"

"Maybe he has a totally different type of metabolism," I

suggested. Airing some of the knowledge I'd picked up from watching *Doctor Kildare*.

"Maybe he has," said Fowler. "In which case I'd like to find out how it works. Let me give you another 'for instance.' If he has no DNA in his white cells, what happens when he cuts himself? How can the cells reproduce to cope with the infection? It's driving me bananas."

"Jeff," I said, "I think you are going to have to accept that The Man is outside the rules. You're looking at him in the wrong way."

"I don't accept that," said Fowler. "Okay, I know he disappeared. I admit I have no answer for that as yet, but the rest leaves us with two options. He is either real — in which case his physiology has to make some kind of medical sense. Which is why it's important to be able to examine him. Or we are singly and jointly the victims of an incredible illusion."

"You're right," I said. "We've allowed ourselves to be totally deluded by external reality. *That's* the illusion. Don't you see that's what The Man is trying to tell us? We have to look at everything with a fresh eye."

Fowler greeted this with a short silence. "Leo, let's be practical about this. Real is real. That's the only way we can operate. If we don't hold to that then we might as well book ourselves into the funny farm."

"Jeff," I replied, "this is it. We were all booked in at birth."

"Yes, well — I suppose that's one way of looking at it," said Fowler. "I'll talk to you when you get back. Have a good trip."

I put the phone down. Poor Jeff. I knew how he felt. I had often experienced the same uncomfortable wave of embarrassment when I had encountered some banner-waving nut in the street hawking ten-cent pamphlets proclaiming the Good News. Salvation for the righteous and eternal damnation for the wicked. Who needed to hear all that? I had been face to face with The Man himself and even I had proved a reluctant customer. While much of what he had said was totally new, some of it reinforced certain ideas that had already occurred to me. But as Miriam had said, I had tried to keep my involvement at arm's length. My intellectual curiosity had been engaged but I had done my level best to avoid any real commitment.

I think the reason that I was able to keep my distance for so long was because, while The Man's presence may have contributed to my courtroom defeat, it had not affected the practice of law. Whereas it threatened to turn Jeff Fowler's world upside down. Miriam's too. Their professional lives were based on their sure and certain knowledge of human physiology and the physical sciences. They could perform their healing function, arrive at a diagnosis because, although much still remained to be discovered, the practice of medicine was founded on the logical analysis of biochemical processes. The observation of cause and effect. Action and reaction. There was always a reason why — even if it could not immediately be found. It was little wonder that Fowler was now clinging, like a shipwrecked sailor, to the notion that The Man's share of Carol's sukiyaki must, inevitably, work its way through his digestive tract.

It didn't, Jeff. But don't worry about it. Like I said, it's not important.

I don't intend to go over everything The Man said and did during his last twelve months in Palestine. The core of it is in the Book. His words have been messed around with but the message is there if you dig for it. Now that I've given you an idea of the real setup, you will know what to look for. The events in the Book are not all in the right order but if you approach the New Testament narratives as if you were a detective sifting through statements in a murder investigation, you will be surprised at what you'll find.

I've already touched upon the feeding of the five thousand. The healing is not in dispute. The state of some of the people he came across was heartrending. He had to do something about the lepers, the crippled, the deaf, dumb and blind, but on each occasion he asked the beneficiary not to attribute the cure to him. The reason was twofold. Healing took the power out of him. Wherever he went, people clustered round him. Trying to reach through the protective ring of disciples. Over and over again he found himself surrounded by a waving forest of hands and arms stretching out desperately to touch him. After days like that, he needed time to recharge.

The other factor was his growing notoriety. Obviously, when you restore the ravaged flesh of lepers, make the blind see, send beggars dancing down the street on their once-crippled limbs, give voice to the dumb so that they can praise God; when you heal the minds of raving lunatics, turning a herd of pigs into Spam in the process, perform remote-control cures of a young girl in a coma and a Centurion's servant, people are bound to sit up and take notice. And the moment you ask them to keep the news to themselves you can guarantee that it's going to spread like wildfire.

The Man knew that certain Pharisees — the influential sect that were the self-appointed guardians of Jewish orthodoxy — had been meeting with members of Herod's court to discuss the problems caused by The Man's abrasive comments on the current state of Judaism and the increasing number of people who appeared to be taking them seriously.

The establishment was also disturbed by the loose talk that he might even be the promised Messiah. Palestine was a powderkeg. An explosive mixture of subversive religious and political factions seething under the Roman yoke. The Man — who was reportedly mixed up with political activists — could be the spark that might blow the country apart.

Nicodemus, through his seat on the Sanhedrin, was well placed to garner the substance of these backstairs discussions, and Joseph of Arimathea, who himself was a wealthy merchant, was able to monitor the growing unease of the business community. Both kept The Man advised of the plots being hatched against him. It enabled The Man to keep one step ahead of his adversaries and make the most effective use of his public appearances. He needed to get his message across to as many people as possible but he also knew that over-exposure could precipitate his arrest. He had to stay out of trouble until the right moment, when all the elements would fall into place.

Johanan-Gabriel was already in prison and would soon force Herod to kill him. The Man knew that if Herod was seen to be able to kill someone like Johanan the Baptizer with impunity, his opponents would be quick to conclude that Joshua of Nazareth could be dealt with in the same way. The establishment's view, as reported by Nicodemus, was coldly realistic. Good news about God was one thing, but if this so-called Messiah was going to create a situation where the Romans would feel obliged to send in another hard-line general like P. Q. Varus to reimpose order, then salvation could go to the bottom of the list.

While we're on the subject of The Man and his progress through Galilee there's a point that needs to be made concerning his promise to make the disciples, fishers of men. Some of you may remember the story of the miraculous draught of fishes in the last chapter of John and my fantasy about The Man having sonar built into his ankles. It didn't happen.

It is an allegorical statement about the Ain-folk. Another clue to the real story. The early Christians who were driven underground, first by Paul's campaign of repression and then by Rome, used a symbolic fish as their call sign; the first example of religious graffiti. This has been explained by scholars as being a kind of visual mnemonic; the five letters of the Greek word for "fish" formed the initial letters of the key phrase — "Jesus Christ, God's Son, Savior." However, like so many of the passages in the Book, there was more to it than that. The fish symbolized both the single Ain-folk element and the shoal. You must have all seen, in the TV documentaries of Jacques Cousteau, pictures of a shimmering mass of quicksilver, sometimes made up of thousands of fishes. All moving as one. Turning in graceful coordinated movements — as if guided by an overmind. It was this symbol that was the link with our distant past when the twelve ancient races of Man had each been the home of one of the great Aeons. Their guiding spirit.

The story of the miraculous draught of fishes landed by the disciples was an allegory for his mission and the part they were to play in it. The gathering together of all the fragments by the Twelve. Each fish part of the shoal. Each individual Ain-folk element part of the greater whole.

In the fortress-palace of Machereus, overlooking the Dead Sea, Johanan-Gabriel now only had a few weeks to live. Despite the fact that Johanan had heaped scorn, ridicule and the wrath of God upon Herodias and her daughter Salome, Herod Antipas had no personal animosity toward him. In fact, up to the time of his sudden execution, Herod proved a remarkably benign jailer. Herodias was the daughter of one of Herod's half brothers by one of his old man's five Number One wives — Mariamne I. Which made Herodias The Fox's half niece. But before marrying Herod, she'd been wedded and bedded by another half brother — Herod Philip — making her, officially, Herod's sister-in-law. All of which was not exactly incestuous but it was regarded by the Galilean Bible Belt as being too close for comfort. Especially when Salome had a habit of creeping into their bed to keep warm.

While Johanan-Gabriel's moral strictures had not been exactly music to Herod's ears, the Baptizer's honesty made a refreshing contrast to the toadying courtiers that clustered around him, vying for favor. Not that he was overly concerned with truth, honesty or clean living. Like Herod the Great's other sons, Herod had been educated in Rome where he had picked up a taste for the good life. Along with a passion for building, he had inherited his father's sharp sense of survival. Palestine, then as now, was a region in constant ferment, and Herod Antipas liked to keep his ear close to the ground.

Herod was particularly interested in the rumors that linked Johanan-Gabriel to the alleged birth of two beings from beyond the stars, whose arrival in Bethlehem had been celebrated by the secret visit of three magi in the last years of his father's reign. At that moment in history, an august body known as the College of Haruspices was still employed by the Roman state to prognosticate upon the future by reading the entrails of slaughtered animals. Naturally, no Roman with a whiff of sophistication took such things seriously. They were superstitious, yes. They still looked for lightning in the right part of the sky. But they were no more irrational than we are about black cats, spilled salt, and walking under ladders. With his Roman background, Herod Antipas took a similar view. His Pharisaic advisers and functionaries might believe in angels and demonic spirits like the Persian and Babylonians before them, but Herod took a more cynical view of what made the world tick. Rulers then, as now, assured their futures by trade-offs, payoffs, and making people offers they couldn't refuse.

And yet, and yet . . . there was a strange other-worldliness about Johanan that intrigued Herod. His insistence that there was a spirit-being inside the human body. The constant repetition of the claim that salvation was at hand. Johanan had denied being the Messiah but admitted to having been born in Bethlehem. And Herod knew from his informants that the Baptizer was related to this new prophet that people had begun to talk about. Joshua of Nazareth. From what Joshua was reported to have said, one could almost believe that he and Johanan were one and the same person. With one important exception. This new prophet, it was alleged, could heal people at a touch. Herod was prepared to accept that it might be true. He was aware that the ignorant and uneducated were inclined to marvel at anything they did not understand and that the devout Jew was habitually inclined toward religious hyperbole, but — anything was possible.

Herod had sent men out to bring this Nazarene before him so that he could see some of these miracles for himself but, so far, Joshua had proved remarkably elusive. Herod was not too worried. Sooner or later they would come face to face.

That would be the moment to judge whether there was any substance to the extravagant claims now being made on his behalf. Meanwhile, Herod decided that it would be better to tread cautiously. For if there *was* an empire greater than Rome beyond the stars, it would be unwise to harm its emissaries.

What Herod Antipas didn't know was that, in-between his occasional chats with Johanan-Gabriel, Herodias had been making a few prison visits of her own. Her intention had been to convince the Baptizer, with the aid of some heavily perfumed charm, that a public withdrawal of his condemnation of her would be in everybody's best interests. Johanan-Gabriel's response was both predictable and unprintable and led directly to the fateful evening when, in front of the chariot-set that had been invited to supper, Salome tricked Herod into ordering Johanan's execution.

With the demise of their host body, Johanan — the Ain-folk fragment that had been Gabriel's companion — slipped into the shadow-world that Theosophists know as Devachan to await its next reincarnation. He had lost his Earth-life but in a good cause. The blows that had severed their host's head had also cut the bonds that tied Gabriel's temporal aspect to the living body. As he broke free, Gabriel felt the same exultant surge of relief that a pilot does when he manages to eject from a stricken jet fighter and feels that chute pop open safely above his head.

The first thing that Gabriel did after breaking his Earth-bonds was to contact Ya'el and give him the good news. With the death of his host body he, too, would be a free spirit once again.

In his postbaptismal dialogue with the Empire, Ya'el had been told that his mission was to culminate with the transmission of the Power of The Presence from the Empire to Earth — for which he was to be the ground station. A kind of cosmic lightning conductor. In preparation for this event, Ya'el had been instructed to test the effect of a limited input of Celestial power on the twelve disciples and the sev-

enty-two Followers of The Way who were to be the spear-
head of the post-Resurrection phase of the mission. For in
order to spread The Word they needed to be armed with the
power to open men's minds, heal the sick, and drive out "evil
spirits" — the elemental 'Braxian forces that were constantly
trying to infiltrate the human body.

That may make you smile, and scientists and sociologists
will say that mass murderers, sadists and child rapists are the
product of society; the victims of deprivation. That's true,
but it is the lack of love, of justice and compassion, that cor-
rodes an individual's humanity and creates a kind of darkness of the soul. And when that happens, the elementals, the
'Braxian creatures from The Pit, move in and take control.

Once again, let me stress that we are not talking about
the joke demons conjured up by popular fiction, the naked
fang-toothed ladies with snakes in their hair, or the red-eyed
goat-headed ringmaster conjured into cinematic life by such
masters of the macabre as Roman Polanski. These forces
exist. They are around us all the time just as The Power of
The Presence is.

And they are a very real danger. For it is the elemental
within us that makes us cruel, vicious, violent and destruc-
tive. The twin subjects of possession and exorcism have been
richly exploited by novelists and film-makers. In the hands
of the *Shlockmeisters* they have been stripped of their true
meaning, becoming bastardized rituals like the U.S. Cavalry
charge and the slaughter of Hollywood Indians. Yet both are
rooted in the actions of The Man as he moved through Galilee. For it is only The Power of The Presence that can drive
'Brax out once he has a grip on us. And I say "us" advisedly.
It is not only the sadistic killers behind prison bars, or those
lurking down dark alleys or behind the curtains of suburban
bedrooms, that are in trouble.

Since fang-toothed ladies, exorcism and Hollywood all
feature in the previous paragraphs, let me persuade you to
make a brief mental leap from Palestine to Transylvania, the
mist-shrouded legends of vampires, and virgins who never

keep their windows locked. You may have wondered why such stories exercise such timeless fascination. The answer is not hard to find. It is yet another allegory. Count Dracula is no more than a symbolic front man for 'Brax. It is not the warm red stuff that runs through our jugular veins that Count 'Brax is after, but the lifeblood of our humanity. He wants to sink his teeth into our soul. To drain the power of the Ain-folk spirit from us and, with it, our immortality. He wants to turn us into zombies; part of the legion of the living dead.

It is Count 'Brax who is condemned to live forever in the darkness of the world. The rays of the rising sun that send him scurrying back to his cobwebbed coffin is the Light of The Word; the cross from which he recoils, the shining Power of The Presence. That is the core of truth that lies under all that Transylvanian embroidery. But please — don't let it stop you enjoying the movies.

It was Gabriel's spirit-being that Ya'el used to power an experimental healing mission by the Twelve and the Followers of The Way. Matthew, chapter 10, relates how the disciples received the gift of the spirit and were sent on their way; Luke, chapter 9, echoes this account, and Luke, chapter 10, described how the seventy (-two) initiates were given almost identical mission orders. Through a mix-up in the oral transmission of this material, the writer of Luke has split into two what was, in effect, one operation.

Once again, numerologists may already have spotted the significance of the number combinations, but for those of you who are not familiar with the workings of this arcane science let me explain: Gabriel's spiritual power was divided among both the disciples and the Followers: $12 + 72 = 84$ which, by Fadic reduction $(8 + 4)$ equals 12. Once again, The Man's message is repeated. The many gathered together to make those who will be saved. The elect. The Ain-folk. The twelve great Aeons of Eardh-Ain who themselves were part of The Presence. For 12 $(1 + 2)$ equals 3. The Trinity. Not the misleading Christian version, but the True

Trinity. The Creator, the Creative Force, and the Created. United and Indivisible.

Gabriel's presence within his followers told Ya'el what he wanted to know. Men could be switched back on. The sleeping Ain-folk driver could be jolted awake by a heavy input of Celestial power. And the disciples had been able to use it to heal the sick and drive out "demons." But Ya'el noted that when Gabriel's spirit withdrew, the resident Ain-folk element rapidly sank back into a state of torpor not all that far removed from its previous semimummified condition. The Ain-folk element inside the disciples was like a dead battery. Gabriel's brief presence had given them a boost but they couldn't hold the charge. Only the massive transfusion of power from the Empire that was due to take place after the Resurrection could provide the long-term input to raise their awareness to its original level. And The Man knew that 'Brax would do everything he could to prevent that happening.

After withdrawing from the disciples, Gabriel's spirit-being transferred to the module near the summit of Mount Hermon to await the arrival of the first of the longships. The Man followed with the Twelve. He stopped briefly at Caesarea Philippi where he left nine of the disciples to await his return then pressed on with Andreas, Jacob and Johan bar-Zebedee. Next to Mary, it was these three who possessed the highest degree of ESP. In the Book, Shimon-Petrus replaces his brother but that is due to the creative editing I've mentioned.

As the longship at the head of the chain of rescue vessels moved into solar orbit between Earth and the planet Venus, it made contact with Gabriel. And while The Man was making his way toward the snow-capped summit of the mountain with his three closest disciples, Michael was beamed down into the module.

Ya'el, who had been in constant touch with Gabriel during his journey northward, could hardly contain himself but, by a supreme effort of will, he forced himself to stay with Joshua and the others until they reached the high plateau.

It was the reunion of Ya'el with the two Celestial Envoys that was the mystical event recorded in the Book as the Transfiguration. Andreas, Jacob and Johan had not been given any prior warning or explanation. Consequently, they were somewhat startled when two luminous humanoids suddenly materialized on either side of The Man. Beings from beyond the world of men that the awed trio were later to describe as "fiery angels."

As Michael and Gabriel embraced their commander, Ya'el's great spirit-being disengaged from its host body, presenting the now terrified disciples with an even more incredible sight. For — as Ya'el detached his metapsyche — Joshua's body was pierced by shafts of dazzling white light which seemed to come from a central point within, raying outward through his clothes and his bare limbs. There was a bright aura around his head and, as the three disciples watched through half-closed eyes, his face began to shine like the sun.

The shafts of light that pierced The Man became more and more brilliant, then coalesced, blotting out Joshua's body completely and making the incandescent forms of the two "angels" look pale by comparison. Finally, the light was so blinding that Andreas, Jacob and Johan were forced to shield their faces. But the light pierced their hands. They felt it burn into their brains and, in a sudden flash of awareness, they recognized Michael and Gabriel as the Celestial powers who had been present in the physical bodies of Abraham and Moses, Aaron and Elijah, the leaders and guardians of the twelve tribes of Israel. And they understood that, over the tens of thousands of years since the Atlantean catastrophe, Michael and Gabriel had guided the destiny of the chosen people: keeping alive the vital spark of inner consciousness that 'Brax had constantly threatened to extinguish; nurturing the seed-grain of memory that held the secret of our origin and destiny until the moment when the power and spirit of Ya'el was to come into the world again.

Hard on the heels of that revelation came an even greater

one. Andreas, Jacob and Johan "saw" Ya'el and realized who he was. Convulsed by a kind of clairvoyant ecstasy, the three disciples were each hit by a massive brain seizure and passed out. As they fell to the ground, the Ain-folk spirit element within them mushroomed out through their skulls like an atomic fireball. A rapturous fission-fusion process in which their inner being merged with that of the cosmos.

Samadhi. Union with the Ultimate Principle.

Each of them saw himself as an infinitesimal speck of space-dust floating in the star-filled vastness. A gossamerlike mote of awareness that knew itself to be part of the infinite cloud of cosmic consciousness that filled every dimension of space and all eternity. The Power, the Wisdom and the Being of The Presence; the God of Israel and the Savior of the Christians, Allah, Brahmah. The *Nirvana* to which Buddhists aspire.

"The dewdrop in the shining sea."

It was a timeless moment of inexpressible joy. Inexpressible because although it is possible to experience the presence of God and be granted a glimpse of his ultimate purpose it is not possible even to begin to describe either by the written word.

Language is a product of the 'Braxian world in which our spirit is held prisoner. It is one of the bars of our cage. This is something we tend to ignore — or even deride — but deep down, we know it to be true.

There are moments in our lives when we experience feelings of great joy, happiness, love. Moments of exaltation. States of being when a veil seems to lift from our eyes, revealing a new dimension of existence. They are moments we would like to share with the people close to us but are unable to — because we cannot find the words. Not because our vocabulary is limited through a lack of education, but because there *are* no words to describe what we feel.

There is a saying that friendship, like love, "is better felt than e'er expressed." And we know this to be true. Because if we try to put into words what, or how, we felt during one of those unforgettable moments we begin to realize that in attempting to describe it we are debasing the experience.

But it is the very fact that we *can* experience the inexpressible that proves our "otherness," and the existence of some kind of divine presence. And it exposes the hollowness of the materialist philosophy which holds that Man can hope for nothing more than a brief, accidental moment of biochemical consciousness in a universe devoid of purpose whose beginning and end are as irrelevant as his own.

When the three disciples regained consciousness, they found The Man standing over them. He was quite alone; his appearance perfectly normal. The landing module, of whose existence they were unaware, had taken off in a blaze of ethereal light, carrying Michael and Gabriel to a rendezvous with the longship that, in another time frame, had obligingly appeared for my benefit in the night sky over Manhattan.

What Andreas, Jacob and Johan had experienced now seemed like a dream, but they knew it was something more than that. They were convinced that they had witnessed a quite extraordinary event, the details of which now hovered tantalizingly just beyond the horizon of memory. And they were left with the impression that, at one point, they had understood everything.

The Man ordered them to keep silent about what they had seen, then led them back to Caesarea Philippi. When they had rejoined the others, The Man announced his intention to go to Jerusalem where he would be arrested and crucified. He had already warned Mary of Magdala of his eventual fate when he had sought her out after his baptism in the Jordan. The news left the disciples astounded and dismayed. They could not understand how someone who had escaped as if by magic from hostile mobs, who could be in two places at once, who had the power to perform miracles of healing could be put to death. Who, on Earth, could have power over him? Crucifixion was a Roman method of execution. How could the Romans hold him where others had failed?

The Man answered their questions. He explained that although his death would take place at the hands of the oppressors of Israel, the decision to die was an essential part of his mission. But it was not the end. He would be restored to life on the third day and his resurrection would be the beginning of even greater things to come — in which each of them would play an important part.

It was now about the middle of January. The Man had another eight weeks to prepare himself for death. His last journey took him south from Caesarea Philippi, through the Greek-speaking area to the east of the Sea of Galilee, down the river Jordan to Jericho and on to Jerusalem. During his meeting with Michael and Gabriel on Mount Hermon, the timing of his arrest and execution had been coordinated with the crew of the longship — which was now heading around toward the far side of the sun. With his entry into Jerusalem it would swing back toward Earth and three days after his death would be in the correct orbital segment ready to send Michael and Gabriel down to ensure the smooth transfer of his metapsyche and the body of his Earth-host to the longship.

On this last trip down the road, things were different. The Man no longer fled the crowds. In each village, or wherever people gathered about him, he preached The Word in the form of parables. He reached out to touch as many people as possible. He healed all those who were brought to him. He let people sing his praises. He let people believe whatever they wanted to believe: that he was the Messiah, the Son of God, the new King of Israel; the prophet of the new order that would throw out the Pharisees and Sadducees and give power to the people; the leader that would weld the multifarious underground groups into a single revolutionary army and drive the Romans into the sea. He even let people think that he intended to make good his prophecy that the Temple in Jerusalem would be utterly destroyed — even though the actual event was not due to take place for another forty years.

More and more people flocked to join the exuberant crowd that now surrounded him, first lining the route and then tagging on to the procession as it wound its way toward Jerusalem. A city already crowded with pilgrims, and with more arriving daily from every part of Palestine for the coming Passover celebrations. A city that was playing host to Herod Antipas, who had taken up residence at the family palace in the Upper City and was lavishly entertaining the City Fathers, and Pontius Pilate, the Roman procurator of the province, who was lodged at the Fortress Antonia over in the Second City next to the Temple, with several cohorts of hard-nosed Galatians. Nobody with anything to lose wanted trouble while those two were in town.

Jerusalem was the bastion of the establishment. New York and Washington rolled into one. And as the reports came in of The Man's triumphal progress toward the city, the fat cats who ran the country from within its walls became increasingly nervous.

The situation was very like that in many states of South America today. The country was controlled by the Sadducees — a tightly knit group of wealthy families. They, or their appointees, held all the key posts in the Temple hierarchy and the Sanhedrin — the council that governed the interwoven secular and religious affairs of the Jews. It was a neat, watertight setup. The Sadducees controlled the priesthood; the priesthood controlled the Temple; and the Temple was the richest organization and the largest single industry in Palestine. The High Priest held a unique position. His office combined the authority of Ayatollah Khomieni, the infallibility of the Pope, and the financial clout of King Khalid of Saudi Arabia.

The High Priest was not just there to light incense and intone the Torah in the Holy of Holies. There were investments to protect. Tax revenues from every Jew over twenty years of age, who was obliged to contribute half a shekel annually; a percentage on the yearly turnover from the sale of birds and animals sold to pilgrims for use as burnt offerings; commission from the moneychangers in the courtyard who lived off the tourists. It all added up. And now, here was some lunatic preaching what amounted to anarchy. An antimaterialist philosophy which exhorted rich men to give away all their possessions and urged the poor to give no thought for the morrow.

Dangerous notions.

But it wasn't just what The Man was saying that posed a threat to the fortunes of the Sadducean junta. It was what he was doing. For it now appeared that he actually *did* possess some kind of extraordinary power. The Man had cured literally hundreds of people. It was little wonder that the ignorant, impoverished people that now surrounded him had been impressed. In his message of salvation and of the kingdom that was to come, they saw the promise of freedom from the burden of their daily lives, the often back-breaking toil in conditions of semislavery to which their humble birth and the system had condemned them. The Man's presence and his words were an affront to the authority of the High Priest and an assault on the sovereignty of the State and those charged with the direction of its affairs. Caiaphas, the then holder of that prestigious post, was in no doubt as to what had to be done. The Man would have to go.

The decision was simple but its implementation was beset with problems. The Jewish state, despite its sectarian class structure which concentrated the power and wealth in the hands of a privileged minority, was, for its time, relatively humane. In Judea, the only capital crimes were blasphemy and adultery, for both of which the sentence was death by stoning. For all other offenses, the most severe punishment was flogging. Usually thirteen strokes; with an absolute maximum of thirty-nine. Convicting The Man on a charge of adultery was, by all accounts, out of the question. There were a number of Pharisaic experts who thought that they could make a charge of blasphemy stand but — as always — it was a question of interpretation. The Man had already outwitted the rabbinic undercover men who had been sent out to ask him trick questions. Unless his conviction could be guaranteed it was a dangerous course to follow. If the confrontation with The Man was allowed to develop into a public debate, it might end by diminishing the authority of the High Priest and making the Sanhedrin look ridiculous.

It was Annas, the High Priest's father-in-law, and ex-holder of the same office, who came up with the idea of maneuvering The Man into the hands of the Romans. They had the power to execute criminals and did so by hanging, beheading and crucifixion. If Joshua the Nazarene could be arrested and found guilty of a crime against Roman law, then the problem was solved.

There was one small snag. Roman law usually ensured a fair trial. But the plan had three weighty points in its favor. First, Pontius Pilate, the man charged with governing the province, owed the Sanhedrin. Caiaphas proposed to call in his marker. Second, Roman justice was highly efficient. Once a man had been found guilty and sentenced, punishment was swift and inevitable. And third — if the Nazarene was tried and executed by the Romans his death would be *their* responsibility. And it meant that if, by some inconceivable trick of fate, Joshua actually was the Messiah, God's retribution would fall on the backs of the Romans and not the Jews.

One of the great miscalculations of all time. But Caiaphas could not help but reason thus. He was just playing out the part that had been programmed for him. Like the rest of us, he was a puppet on a cosmic string.

TWENTY-TWO ═══════════════

THE Man entered Jerusalem on the back of a donkey, flanked by Mary of Magdala and his disciples and hailed as a conquering hero by his followers who lined the route into the city, waving palm leaves and throwing their coats on the ground for him to pass over. Reaching the temple courtyard, The Man overturned the tables of the moneychangers and the piled-up cages of the merchants selling sacrificial pigeons and goats, then preached to an ecstatic crowd.

Outraged by this frontal assault on their authority, the High Priest and the Elders of Jerusalem wanted to send in the Temple Guard to arrest The Man. Annas counseled caution. The Nazarene was surrounded by an unwashed out-of-town mob. If the arresting officers were obliged to use force to take him into custody, it might spark off an uncontrollable riot. They must, said Annas, wait for a more opportune moment.

At sunset, The Man left the city with his disciples and spent the night in a house in the nearby village of Bethany. The next day, he returned to the Temple where a crowd quickly gathered around him in Solomon's Porch. Hearing of his return to the city, Caiaphas sent a group of priests — all experts in the Mosaic law — to challenge The Man in front of the crowd, in the hope of luring him into making a statement that they could publicly condemn as blasphemous.

The Man's replies confounded them but, under the pretense of seeking enlightenment, the experts kept trying to trap him with apparently innocent questions.

Once again The Man predicted the destruction of the Temple. A prophecy that, somewhat naturally, enraged the High Priest and his acolytes, the Sanhedrin, the Elders of Jerusalem and everyone else who had a finger in the pie. For besides the money and power that flowed from it, the Temple was the shrine for the soul of the Jewish nation. The reconstruction work, started under Herod the Great, had been going on for nearly fifty years and was still far from completion. To talk of its destruction was the equivalent of proposing the demolition of the Ka'bah in Mecca to a group of Muslim fundamentalists. It is not hard to imagine how the pillars of the Jewish establishment reacted. The Man's threat — for it was translated as such — caused them to experience every shade of outraged emotion from incredulous anger to purple-faced apoplexy. But, by sunset on the second day, The Man had still not been arrested.

Bitterly disappointed, he returned to Bethany to spend the night with his disciples. While the others slept, The Man woke Judas and Mary of Magdala and led them silently out of the house and back toward Jerusalem. The gates of the city were closed but Judas took The Man and Mary through a secret entrance used by the Sicarii — the underground resistance group to which he had belonged. Their destination was the house of Nicodemus; The Man's secret ally on the Sanhedrin.

The reason for this midnight call was to discover why the Sanhedrin had not yet arrested him. Nicodemus gave them an account of the latest twist in the labyrinthine plot to eliminate The Man. Since opting for Annas's devious solution, Caiaphas and his supporters had finally discovered that The Man had not been born in Nazareth, Galilee, but in Bethlehem, Judea, and, what is more, might conceivably be a descendant of King David. In addition, they had learned, through their own informants at Herod's court, of the mystery surrounding his birth and his relationship with Johanan the Baptizer. Political expediency was one thing, but prophecy was the bedrock of Jewish history.

Annas and Caiaphas were now faced with the possibility that the Nazarene might not be an impudent imposter. Worse, Gamaliel, acknowledged to be the unchallenged authority in the interpretation of the Torah, had even gone so far as to suggest that, on the available evidence, The Man might even *be* the promised Messiah.

Gamaliel's reading of the runes had caused Caiaphas and his father-in-law to buttonhole the revered sage and take him off into a quiet corner to seek further clarification. Was he serious? Was it possible? To which Gamaliel's considered reply had been "Yes, but —" as President Nixon was wont to say, "— don't bet the ranch on it."

In face of the evidence of The Man's remarkable powers and presence, some of you may find this mixture of cautious reserve, doubt and outright disbelief hard to understand. But as the Book showed, Israel had not been short of charismatic prophets. As any contemporary Jew could have told you, Jehovah had been making promises for centuries. A land of milk and honey they could call their own, salvation, vengeance via his divine hand upon their enemies. All of which he had so far failed to deliver.

There was also another reason for caution. Caiaphas and his supporters had begun to be seriously worried by the testimony of those who claimed to have been healed, or to have witnessed miraculous acts by The Man. If the stories were true, they could only be explained by the presence, within the Nazarene, of one of the legendary Persian angels — or demons. Who could tell? Whichever it was, Caiaphas was reluctant to inspire its wrath by a rash move against its earthly agent.

The Man now knew what had to be done. And Judas was tailor-made for the job. As a one-time member of the Essene community in which Gabriel and The Man had resided, Judas understood the situation in a way that the other disciples — as yet — did not. There was no need for lengthy explanations. The Essenes were soldiers in the army of the Prince of Light. The kamikaze of the Celestial Empire. All The Man had to do was to tell Judas that he needed his help.

Judas was instructed to go to Caiaphas and to offer to betray The Man. He was to demand payment so that his motive would not be suspect. He was to say that he could tell when Joshua's "spirit" had left his body and that, without it, Joshua had no power to harm them. He was to explain that the "spirit" could not bear pain. If they seized Joshua and beat him, the "spirit" would not dare reenter his body and if they killed him, the "spirit" would be forced to return to the place from which it had come.

The Man explained that in order for his deception to work, his other disciples and followers must not know of this arrangement. For the High Priest's spies were everywhere. Judas had to be seen as the betrayer — and risk the inevitable consequences of his action. And so, in one of the most celebratedly notorious acts in history, Judas went to the house of the High Priest and offered to betray Joshua of Nazareth in return for thirty pieces of silver.

At what has come to be known as the Last Supper, The Man warned the Twelve that in a few short hours he would be arrested and, within a few days, he would be dead. Coming after The Man's triumphal entry into Jerusalem and the last two days when, faced with the best brains the Temple could muster, he had seemed invincible, the news was not only profoundly shocking; it was utterly unbelievable. And Shimon-Petrus was even more upset when, after swearing that he would go to his death alongside The Man, he was told that he would deny Joshua three times.

Shimon did not realize that The Man was not accusing him of faithlessness but inserting a delayed-action command into his subconscious. It was a move designed to protect Shimon from his own foolhardiness. Ya'el wanted his disciples alive, not dead. That was why they were all programmed to run out on him when he was arrested. The guilt-laden supporters of a suffering Christ — what Colin Wilson has termed "Crosstianity" — have made much of the fact that everyone abandoned The Man when the chips were down but they are wrong. It was part of the plan.

The other point that needs to be clarified concerns the consumption of the bread and wine that The Man passed to those around the table. Two items which were used to symbolize his flesh and blood and which were to become the basis of the Eucharist — the central rite of Christian worship and, incidentally, a bone of contention within the early Church. Many of The Man's followers in the immediate post-Resurrection period could not accept the Pauline interpretation of the Last Supper and found the ceremony offensive. Well — the news is that The Man never intended it to become one.

The writers of Mark and Luke got it nearly right. The Man made no mention of any remission of sins. That was overlaid later. But it was certainly true that his death was on behalf of all of us. Only we don't have to feel guilty about it. Once we understand why, we should all be dancing in the streets. His death on the cross brought the release his spirit-being longed for. So let's set the record straight. Although the celebration of the Last Supper rapidly acquired a unique significance within the Christian church-state, this kind of sacramental rite was by no means exclusive to them. Variations of the same ceremony can be found in other belief systems and all have their roots in religious practices that reach back to Methuselah and beyond.

If you want to know more about this, look up any references you can find to the sacred yellow plant *haoma*.

The Last Supper was another occult metaphor that linked Ya'el with the earlier Celestial missions to Earth. Which the Roman Church ignored as it proceeded to distort The Man's message. The deliberations of Ignatius, Clement, Irenaeus, Hippolytus *et al.* which, through the adoption of the Nicene creed, gave a monolithic character to Christianity which was to last till the Great Schism in 1054, were based on two fundamental errors. The first being their implacable opposition to what was called "syncretism" — the attempt to reconcile the diverse threads of philosophic and religious thought and practices. Everything that had happened prior to The Man's birth was either ignored or branded as heretical when, in fact, The Truth was there all the time, staring them in the face. The reason is not hard to find: 'Brax had already got to work on those who saw the Apostolic Succession as a vehicle they could use to propel themselves into positions of power.

If you believe nothing else in this account, you must believe that The Truth has been around from the beginning. It has lain buried in the heart and mind of Man in every age and has been expressed, often obscurely and incompletely, in every faith from stiff-necked Episcopalianism to the wacky spontaneity of Zen.

The second error which, like the first, was the result of some cold-eyed pragmatism concerns the Eucharist. As I've said, The Man never intended his last meal on Earth to become institutionalized. It was the Pauline organization men who saw in its symbolic representation of the timeless mystery the magic ingredient which, served up with some liturgical salad dressing, was to be the cornerstone of the power-structure they were building.

What they proceeded to do with The Man's message — with a little help from 'Brax — can be explained in the terms of a modern marketing operation. Celebration of the Eucharist allowed the organization men to get the corner on salvation. That was the product for which the bishops held the exclusive franchise. The churches were the retail outlets. And the people putting this deal together claimed to have been granted the license to do so by Peter — whom Paul had built up into The Man's sole legal representative. The only one to whom the secret formula had been confided.

Over the next three centuries, when theology became the new growth industry, the careerists maneuvered themselves into the commanding positions. They became the medium for the message. They could not stop the individual search for God, but the Word According To Rome was loud and clear. If you did not come to church to celebrate mass, your soul would be eternally damned. And, of course, only officially approved priests could celebrate mass and give absolution. Once you had committed yourself to buy the basic package, you were on the hook for life.

The piece of bread and the cup of wine that The Man shared with his disciples was built up into the greatest protection racket of all time. And if you find that hard to accept, just think of all the money and power that has passed through the hands of Rome & Co., and the violence it has unleashed on those who chose to dissent from its teaching. There is no doubt about it. 'Brax may have failed to recruit The Man, but he did a great job on the people who were left minding the store.

By arrangement with The Man, Judas stayed behind in Jerusalem to await the return of the owner of the house — whom he had to reimburse for the wine and food they had consumed. The rest of the party left the city before the gates closed for the night. Instead of returning to the village of Bethany, The Man led the way to the Garden of Gethsemane on the Mount of Olives. When they reached the garden, The Man left nine of the disciples by the gate then went deep into the olive grove with Andreas barJonah, Jacob and Johan barZebedee — the three who had witnessed the Transfiguration. As on Mount Hermon, Shimon-Petrus took his brother's place in the rewrite.

A hundred yards or so from the gate, The Man left the three to keep watch, and went off on his own. This, as the Book says, was the crucial point in the mission. When The Man questioned the necessity for the Crucifixion, and his ability to go through with it. It was his last contact with the Empire before his death, and they were so concerned that they ordered Gabriel down from the orbiting longship to strengthen his resolve.

The three disciples did not really fall asleep as Matthew,

Mark and Luke state. It was a coded way of saying that their minds were unaware of The Man's mental agony, and Gabriel's brief, reassuring visit.

As The Man rejoined the three disciples, he heard a confused babble of voices and saw the light of torches on the slope below the garden. Shimon-Petrus, one of the nine left by the gate, ran up to warn The Man that a mob led by men from the Temple Guard and armed with swords and staves were looking for him. Andreas urged The Man to run, but it was too late. They were already surrounded by some thirty to forty men, two of whom had Judas pinned by the arms. The mob advanced cautiously to within ten or twelve paces of The Man then pushed Judas forward to check that the "spirit" had left the Nazarene.

Judas had arranged with the captain of the Temple Guard, who was there to make the arrest legal, that he would embrace The Man if it was safe to seize him. But as he closed in, Judas found himself looking into the fiery eyes of the complete man — Joshua-Ya'el. With a cry of surprise, Judas fell on his knees and grabbed hold of The Man's hands. *"Rabbuni!"* — "Master!" The Man hauled him to his feet and whispered urgently: *"Do what you have to do —"* Trembling with shock, Judas embraced him, planting the kiss that was to earn him a place in history. For all the wrong reasons.

Although orthodox Christianity ignored the central role played by Mary of Magdala, and branded Judas as the archetypal traitor, it's interesting to note that Islam, which was to bring the power of The Word back into the world, regarded Judas as a somewhat more heroic figure who played an essential part in The Man's mission.

The mob surged forward to seize The Man and a struggle developed as Shimon, Andreas, Jacob and Johan tried to protect him. Just as the violence began to escalate, The Man created a diversion. Ya'el separated out from Joshua as a pale apparition in a flowing robe and sowed a few vital seconds of panic which is recorded in Mark chapter 14, verses 51-52. Verse 50 is out of sequence and should follow it. *"And there*

*followed him a certain young man, having a linen cloth cast
about his naked body; and the young men laid hold on him:
And he left the linen cloth, and fled from them naked."* To
which is added verse 50 — *"and they [the disciples] all forsook
him, and fled."*

And Judas managed to escape too.

That was why Ya'el had not withdrawn his spirit-being
before Judas arrived. In the confusion that followed the appearance of "the young man in white" and the frantic attempts of the mob to lay hands on him, the disciples broke
free and, with The Man's voice in their ears urging them on,
disappeared into the darkness.

After tying The Man's arms, the mob dragged him back
to the sleeping city at the end of a rope and took him to the
house of Annas — Caiaphas's father-in-law. As High Priest,
Caiaphas was reluctant to get involved officially at this stage.
He had too much at stake if things were to go seriously
wrong. It was much better for the arrest to be seen as the
spontaneous action of a group of decent, honest, God-fearing
individuals.

Nicodemus was one of the ten members of the Sanhedrin
summoned to witness The Man's preliminary investigation
conducted by Annas. At first, Nicodemus was unaware that
Caiaphas was also present, watching discreetly from behind a
pierced wooden screen. And, as all students of the New
Testament know, Shimon-Petrus had insinuated himself
into the small crowd that had gathered outside in the courtyard and was warming his hands over a fire.

The other ten disciples had made their way back by various routes to the house in Bethany where they sat shivering
with fear and panting like a pack of hunted dogs that had
gained a temporary respite. They stared into each other's
glazed, tear-streaked faces, hating themselves for their cowardice. Not knowing that, in responding like well-drilled
robots, they had done exactly what The Man had intended
them to do.

Mary of Magdala and several other women from The Man's

entourage were on hand to provide some friendly warmth and moral comfort but it did little to reduce the mental anguish of the ten escapees. Slowly, as the night gave way to a gunmetal dawn, their utter amazement that Judas — of all people — had turned traitor gave way to a cold unreasoning anger and vows of vengeance.

Caiaphas had come braced for some verbal fireworks but there were no sparks flying from the Nazarene as Annas accused him of blasphemy, preaching subversion and of possessing demonic powers. Joshua denied the charges. Not forcefully, but in an evasive manner, turning each question around to form its own answer. Caiaphas had the distinct impression that the Nazarene had no idea what they were talking about. Annas, too, was unsettled by the interrogation. The Nazarene was only a pale shadow of the fiery-eyed troublemaker that had led an unruly mob through the Temple courtyards, overturning stalls and disrupting business.

Annas retired behind the screen and went into a huddle with Caiaphas, the captain of the Guard, Nicodemus and the other representatives from the Sanhedrin. Had they been tricked by Judas into arresting the wrong man? The captain and Nicodemus reassured Caiaphas. The man who stood bound and guarded in the other room was definitely Joshua of Nazareth. Annas, who had listened to The Man preaching in the Temple, was forced to agree that he and their prisoner were one and the same. Only Nicodemus knew that what stood before them was only the host body of Joshua. The spirit of Ya'el was absent.

After a lifetime of hardship and frustration, this was to be Joshua's finest hour. Ya'el had told him that they were both near the end of the road and explained what was to happen. Joshua now understood that he, too, had a vital part to play in Ya'el's mission. As with Judas's Ain-folk psyche, there were to be no medals, no special return-ticket to the Empire, but his contribution to the war effort would not be forgotten in the final accounting.

Resuming the interrogation, Annas asked Joshua if he was

The Messiah. The answer, in modern English, was — "You said it, not me." That was enough for Caiaphas. Joshua's reply was tantamount to saying that he *was* The Messiah. The ultimate blasphemy. And, if that wasn't enough, his refusal to answer questions properly showed the Nazarene to be both insolent and unrepentant. Caiaphas ordered the captain of the Temple Guard to administer a salutary but not too savage beating. They needed Joshua on his feet for his trial before the full Council of the Sanhedrin that coming morning.

As Nicodemus left Annas's house, he saw Shimon-Petrus standing in the shadows outside the gate to the courtyard and gave him the news. The Man had condemned himself. It was all over. There must, urged Nicodemus, be no attempt to rescue him. Shimon-Petrus left to spread the word.

The impact of The Man's arrest on the Followers and the huge crowd that had flocked with him into Jerusalem was absolutely shattering. They had come to town with such high hopes, burning with a newfound belief that deliverance was at hand; braced and ready for the dramatic overthrow of the ruling Jewish families and the defeat of the Romans by miraculous acts of power. And what had happened? His closest disciples had fled and were now in hiding. The Man had been arrested without a fight, had submitted passively to interrogation and had allowed himself to be beaten by common servants and ignorant soldiers.

While this bewildering news spread through the narrow, crowded streets, Joshua was brought before the Council of the Sanhedrin, his hands still bound, at seven A.M. None of the hastily assembled members had ever attended a meeting this early but Annas and Caiaphas were anxious to get Joshua into the hands of the Romans before his supporters had time to work out a coherent response.

The arraignment did not go as smoothly as they had hoped. A series of all-too-eager witnesses presented a mass of conflicting evidence. Joshua remained silent, refusing to answer any of the allegations. Aware that the case against the

Nazarene was on the verge of collapsing, Caiaphas played his last card. Summoning up the full authority of his high office, he sonorously intoned the $64,000 question — *"By the living God I charge you to tell us: Are you The Messiah, The Son of God?"*

To which Joshua answered — *"It is you who say that I am."*

"Blasphemy!" cried Caiaphas, simultaneously tearing his robes with carefully controlled hysteria. It was a symbolic, ceremonial act which impressed the waverers on the back benches. Annas took up the cry and called for a show of hands. The verdict was unanimous. Guilty on two counts. Blasphemy and treason against Rome.

Pontius Pilate had barely finished breakfast when Joshua was delivered at the door to the Fortress Antonia, courtesy of the Sanhedrin, charged with claiming to be King of the Jews and urging people not to pay taxes to Caesar. His accusers, who were backed up by a noisy crowd suffering from a sudden rash of loyalty to the emperor, demanded that, as putative leader of the dissident minorities, Joshua should be put to death before the situation got out of hand.

As governor of the province, Pilate was duty bound to investigate the charges but, after questioning Joshua, he was distinctly unimpressed. The Nazarene's answers were incoherent and he certainly did not appear to be brimming over with revolutionary fervor. In fact, to put it bluntly, he did not appear to be all there. Who, asked Pilate of his lieutenants, would follow a man like this? On the available evidence, the case against Joshua under Roman law was thin and contrived: what we, since the thirties, have called a frame-up. That, in itself, did not disturb Pilate. All kinds of people, from the humblest Jew to the noblest Roman senator, were railroaded every day of the week. But Joshua had already been found guilty of blasphemy, a crime for which, under Jewish law, he could be stoned to death. If the Sanhedrin wanted him killed why hadn't they done it themselves?

Pilate made some discreet inquiries of his own. What he

learned was hard to believe, but if it was true, then the Nazarene was far more than a dull-witted one-time carpenter. His reported powers of healing could only be described as supernatural. It was even claimed that he had caused storms to abate, and had saved some men in a boat by walking across the wave-tops of the Sea of Galilee. Could this, wondered Pilate, be the reason why the Sanhedrin had delivered Joshua up to the Romans? But, if these stories *were* true, why had the Nazarene submitted to a beating? If he could heal the sick with a touch of his hand, why had he not mended the broken skin on his own bruised and bloodied face? There had to be a catch somewhere. Too many things did not add up.

Despite his cynicism, Pilate, born in 9 B.C., was a man of his age. Like Herod Antipas, he had been educated in Rome, acquiring the same veneer of sophistication and the same careless disregard for religion. The Roman pantheon of gods did not make heavy intellectual demands on a man; worship was a mere formality; religious festivals little more than an excuse for getting riotously drunk.

As a professional administrator and one of the ruling elite, Pilate knew that power came out of the short swords of a well-drilled legion. Even so, one has to remember that, despite the intellectual brilliance displayed by the Greeks in their inquiries into the nature of matter and the structure and origin of the universe, the accepted cosmological theory still put planet Earth at the center of seven concentric spheres. And Zeus-Jupiter was believed to be alive and well and living on Mount Olympus.

Second sight, or clairvoyance, was not only more readily accepted then, it was much more widespread than it is today. The predictions of the Jewish prophets were a matter of historical record and, compared to other races, the Jews were believed to possess a greater degree of paranormal skills. Pilate did not really buy the idea that Joshua was possessed by a spirit-being from beyond the stars but he was relieved when a member of his staff pointed out that, legally, this potentially troublesome prisoner did not come under his jurisdiction. Herod Antipas was Tetrarch of Galilee. As a Nazarene, Joshua was his problem.

Chained hand and foot, Joshua was delivered to Herod at the Western Palace in the Upper City. Herod Antipas was pleasantly surprised to see the man whose career he had followed with interest but who, up to that moment, had eluded him. What Herod wanted to see more than anything else was one of the Nazarene's miracles.

Herod and his circle of courtiers were to be disappointed. Joshua, by nature or design, proved to be depressingly inarticulate. How, wondered Herod, could anyone think that this man could walk on water? He didn't have the wit to step over a puddle. Why did the Sanhedrin want him killed?

Whatever the answer, it was not Herod's problem. For Joshua had been born in Bethlehem. Which made him a Judean and, since the exile of Archelaus, Judea was directly under the rule of Pontius Pilate. Herod ordered Joshua to receive twenty strokes of the whip for wasting his time then sent him back to the Fortress Antonia dressed in a purple robe. It was, after all, only fitting, joked Herod to his courtiers. If Joshua was supposed to be King of the Jews, then he should be dressed like one.

And so Joshua was returned to Pontius Pilate, standing on the back of an ox cart, surrounded by an escort of Syrian mercenaries from Herod's palace guard. Glad of a little excitement, the soldiers hammed it up, shouting at the people in the streets to make way. Some of the disciples were in the crowd that gathered as Joshua went by. They could hardly bear to watch as the soldiers urged the crowd to salute their "king" and demonstrated how it should be done by spitting on him and beating him about the head and body with their fists. Forcing their way to the front of the crowd, the disciples tried to catch Joshua's attention but, although he looked right at them, he gave no sign of recognition.

Pilate was not overly pleased to find Joshua back on his doorstep. Stripped of his "royal" robes, he was dragged before Pilate for a second, and final, interrogation. Did he realize the gravity of the charges against him? No reply. Did he have anything to say in answer to the evidence of his accusers? No reply. Did he claim to be King of the Jews? Answer: *Thou sayest it.*

Pilate had passed sentence on a large number of people since he had been appointed procurator but never, in his whole life, had he seen an accused man under threat of crucifixion act like this. Joshua did not have the gallows-defiance of a rebel who knew he had no hope of acquittal. He was just allowing himself to be led like a lamb to the slaughter.

So be it.

Like the news about Paul, this next section may leave some of you gasping but this is where we have to part company with the Book, which now proceeds to cast Pilate as the noblest and most reluctant Roman of them all. All that business with Barabbas and the crowd is pure moonshine. It didn't happen. The agonizing by Pilate, his wife's warning dream, the orchestrated howls of the mob in front of the Fortress Antonia, Pilate washing his hands of the whole affair — all this was the work of later writers whose job it was to whitewash the Romans and, by extension, the rest of the Gentile world, neatly shifting the blame for The Man's death unfairly but squarely onto the backs of the Jews and playing right into 'Brax's hands in the process.

It is important to realize that Paul was a Roman citizen as his father had been. The Jew from Tarsus, who had studied under the great Gamaliel in Jerusalem and had been regarded by the sage as one of his most promising pupils. Intelligent, quick-witted, endowed with enormous energy and vision and, above all, a burning ambition to succeed. He also had one other, important advantage. You don't grow up as a Roman citizen without realizing that the secret of Rome's success lay in efficient, disciplined organization. Paul was not only a great letter writer; he was also a great organizer.

It is no secret that he willingly accepted the task of crushing the rapidly expanding number of Judeo-Christian communes that the Apostles and Followers were setting up everywhere. Paul knew that if he succeeded, he would not only earn the Sanhedrin's grateful thanks, it could mean rapid promotion to a position of power within the Temple hierarchy. But there remained one insurmountable stumbling block. No matter how well Paul did in his given assignment, even with Gamaliel's backing, he could never make it all the way to the top. His Roman citizenship, plus the fact that he was not a Sadducee, meant that he could never be High Priest.

But, on the other hand, as Paul was quick to see, the belief system of the Judeo-Christians he had been detailed to beat sense into had great possibilities. And the more Paul considered them in detail, the greater those possibilities became. Judaism, as they say, was a living, but the market for it beyond the borders of Palestine was nonexistent. The Man's message, however, with its built-in element of universality, was something that *would* sell. The text just needed a little adjusting. The essential thing, apart from widening the franchise, was to make Joshua of Nazareth as important as Jehovah. To say that he *was* God, and not just God's messenger. With that one shrewd move, Paul put Christianity on a par with Judaism. Let's face it, if you're planning to sell stock in Western Union, it makes more sense to have the Company Report signed by the Chairman of the Board instead of by one of the telegraph boys.

The light that hit Paul on the road to Damascus was a blinding flash of inspiration. A billion-watt bulb that lit up with the word "IDEA!" printed on it in Latin. When Paul and his newfound friends took the big step and started recruiting uncircumcised Gentiles into the Judeo-Christian movement it marked the break with Judaism. From that point on, the Jews were to be the enemy. And to make sure nobody forgot that fact, the Pauline scribes sharpened their quills and applied themselves diligently to the task of setting the record straight. Eliminating much of The Truth in the process.

Pilate did not agonize over Joshua's fate. He knew that the Jewish establishment had a powerful lobby in Rome. If the Senate heard he had been less than zealous in maintaining the emperor's authority it could damage his career prospects. When it came down to it, keeping Caiaphas happy was more important than dispensing justice to a tongue-tied carpenter.

Anxious to rid himself of Joshua's unsettling presence, Pilate quickly sentenced him to death by crucifixion and handed him over to the duty officer of the garrison. As it happened, an execution squad had already been formed to deal with two thieves who had been sentenced by Pilate some days before. Their scourging — a grimly painful softening-up process — had started when Joshua was committed to the squad's care with the request for special treatment in deference to his rank. It was not every day that a Roman soldier got a chance to lay hands on royalty.

The squad members were all tough ex-campaigners from the province of Galatia — now part of modern Turkey. They were no strangers to pain, or the methods of inflicting it. But the same kind of thing is still going on in the basements of political prisons all over the world today.

Basically, a prisoner up for crucifixion was beaten with alternate strokes from the *flagellum* — a whip made up of several thin strands of square-section leather that sliced straight through the skin — and the *flagrum* — which consisted of three lengths of heavy cord onto which human knuckle bones were knotted some three to four inches apart. A real rib-breaker. On top of which, they rammed a crown of thorns around his skull. If you've ever pricked yourself pruning roses, just think about what that means.

Throughout Joshua's scourging, Ya'el remained in the Garden of Gethsemane; his metapsyche drifting invisibly among the trees. A formless cloud of superconsciousness that took upon itself the full force of Joshua's agony.

What Joshua felt as he hung chained in the cellars beneath the paved courtyard of the Fortress Antonia was the physical impact of the blows that drove the breath out of his body. The resulting pain was dulled in the way it is when your dentist administers a local anesthetic. You feel the pressure and vibration of the drill but the pain is mostly imaginary.

For Ya'el, each blow was like the shrieking jolt you feel when a raw nerve is jabbed. But because of the nature of his spirit-being, the pain you or I might have felt was magnified within him a million times over. That was why he had been so reluctant to face this ordeal. It was this, and not the earlier moment of distress, that was the Agony in the Garden. The moment when, as the writer of Luke noted in a passage that should not be taken literally — *"his sweat was as it were great drops of blood falling down to the ground."*

The Man's account of this moment had left me puzzled but before I could seek clarification, I had been distracted by the arrival of our visitors. But as I listened again to his voice on the tape I asked myself the same question: If God, The Presence, or Whoever could change the rules of the game and wipe out Ya'el's *karma* at a stroke, why couldn't he have arranged his escape without killing Joshua? Why was it necessary for them to suffer, each in his own way, the agony of the Crucifixion?

I had to wait until I reached Jerusalem before I was given the answer to that one.

TWENTY-THREE ═══════════

On what turned out to be my last Monday evening in Manhattan, Miriam hung up her white coat an hour before her day officially ended, went home, and cocooned herself in the bath and bedroom; emerging, when I called at eight, as an impeccably groomed social butterfly. I knew that it was meant to be a special going-away present and I complimented her accordingly while secretly wishing she would stop cutting her wonderfully thick, dark hair.

I am conscious of the fact that Miriam's coiffure is of relatively minor importance in the overall scheme of things but I mention it to illustrate how life is made up of both the mundane and the metaphysical. One should remember that even while such notables as Augustine and Jerome were bucking for sainthood and speculating on the nature of God, their minds were also dwelling on the unholier attractions of good food, drink, the racier Greek classics and strong-limbed, eager women.

As my special treat, I'd made a reservation at The Leopard. We had a superb meal, after which Miriam allowed me to take her to see my hero in *Escape from Alcatraz*. On the way there in the cab we passed the hospital. To my surprise, it was still standing. After the movie we stopped off at the bar where we'd first met when the group of people she was with had come in out of the rain to phone for a cab. Her escort was a guy I'd known in high school. Which was good luck for me and bad luck for him. Her hair had been long then. Glistening with drops of rain. But that's another story.

We had a couple of drinks and looked at each other a lot and then it was back to my place, where we lay in bed, happy to be together.

In the morning, we were awakened by the phone. It was the hospital for Miriam. One of the team had come down with a viral infection. Could she cover? She swore quietly under her breath and grimaced at me. "Is it okay if I don't see you off?"

"Sure." I smiled. "I hate goodbyes." You know how it is. You either get there too early and run out of things to say, or you're all tensed up trying to make it through the traffic to the terminal before they close the boarding gate.

Miriam got dressed. I pottered around in my robe and made some coffee. We had a toast and orange juice breakfast together during which she checked my wallet to make sure I had the list of names and addresses of her friends in Israel, some of whom she had already telephoned from the hospital to tell them I was coming. No wonder the goddamn city was going broke. I called her a cab and, minutes later, the janitor buzzed through to say that it had arrived. I took her in my arms and kissed her gently. On her lips, her forehead and each side of her nose.

"Take care," I said.

"You too," she replied.

"Listen," I began. "If anything —"

She kissed me to stop the dread words coming out.

"I love you," I said. And saw the tears spring from her eyes. "Hey, hey, hey, come on. I've told you that often enough."

"I know." She flicked the tears away with her fingers. "It's just that this time I get the feeling that you mean it."

"Perhaps that's because I've finally understood," I said.

"Me too . . ." She blinked her eyes dry.

"Good." I smiled. "Maybe there's hope for us yet."

"Yes," she said. "Maybe there is."

"See you, red-eyes." I gave her a quick shoulder-hug then closed the hall door and went over to the window, waiting for her to appear in the street. She looked up as she crossed the sidewalk, blew me a kiss, then got into the cab and was carried away down the street.

When I was all packed, I sealed the tapes of The Man's conversations in several large buff envelopes along with the NYPD Polaroids and the color film I had shot of him at Sleepy Hollow, arm in arm with Linda, Gale McDonald and the others, and that I'd put in for processing the day before. And I wondered how Kovacs's film had turned out.

Just after midday, the phone rang. It was Gale McDonald. "Hi," I said. "Had any more thoughts about the weekend?"

"Several," she replied. "Tell me — how well do you know your secretary?"

The question caught me by surprise. "Linda? Uhh — pretty well, I guess. She's worked with me for a couple of years now. Why do you ask?"

"Because I've been digging around since that brown VW truck with the bum license plate eavesdropped on our conversation in the coffee shop," said McD.

"And?"

"Did you know that she was never employed as a secretary by Universal Pictures?"

"Yes, I knew that," I said, with a dry laugh. "If you dig far enough, you'll probably find she tried to break into movies and ended up as a party girl. Not exactly the best reference for getting a job with a straitlaced New York law firm."

"Is that what you think she was doing out there?" asked McD.

"I really don't care," I replied. "All I know is that she can type, spell and is willing to work late."

"Did you know that she and Peter Kovacs are not brother and sister, but husband and wife?" said McD.

The news sent an inexplicable chill up my spine. "No, I didn't. How d'you find that out?"

"I can't tell you over the phone," said McD. "But there's

plenty more where that came from. What are you doing right now?"

I collected my thoughts. "Uhh — I was just about to take a cab into midtown Manhattan. I have some stuff I want to leave at my bank. Then I was going to grab a quick lunch and go on out to the airport. My plane leaves at four-thirty."

She sounded surprised. "What — today?"

"Yes. I have to check in an hour before takeoff. When you fly to Israel, they search the bristles on your toothbrush."

"Okay, listen," she said. "You know Costello's — ?"

The line went dead.

I put the phone down and waited for her to call back. Ten minutes later I picked it up to call her at Channel Eight and found myself without a dial tone. I stopped by the janitor's office on the way out and used his phone to get through to the operator. She told me that there was a fault on my line and that she would report it. There was no reply from the apartment McD shared with Carol, and when I called the Channel Eight newsdesk, they told me she was out working on a story.

When I'd been to the bank and stowed the tapes and papers away in my safety deposit box, I dropped my luggage off at the reception desk in the foyer of our office building and took the lift to the twenty-second floor. Joe, fortunately, was out to lunch. The cover was still on Linda's typewriter. I remembered I'd told Peter Kovacs she should take Monday off, but today was Tuesday. I used the phone on her desk to call her apartment but it didn't answer. I toyed with the idea of asking the telephone company to come up with a number for Peter Kovacs then decided not to bother. I said goodbye to Nancy, our switchboard girl, on the way out and promised to send her a postcard from Bethlehem.

At Costello's, I had a word with the three bartenders. None of them had served any single ladies in the past hour and could not recall seeing anyone answering McDonald's description using the pay phone. I checked the lunch tables at the rear, then nursed a large bourbon at the bar for a good forty minutes, getting a crick in the neck through watching the door to the street. At two-thirty I decided that whatever it was she had to tell me would have to wait.

As I walked back to Third Avenue to get a cab, I saw a brown VW truck parked across the street. I stopped to let a car go past then crossed over to take a look at it. There was a young German shepherd dog sitting in the cab. The side cargo door was open and the back was filled with office stationery that two guys were off-loading into a nearby building. I watched them for a couple of minutes but they didn't give me a second glance.

As I reached Third, a cab was just depositing a fare. I rode over to Madison to pick up my luggage then went straight out to Kennedy.

At Paris, there was a thirty-five-minute stopover to let people on and off and give the Israeli Airline ground staff time to count the wheels. It gave me a chance to stretch my legs in the circular, space-age Charles de Gaulle terminal and appreciate just how goddamn expensive France had become since my last visit. I was tempted to buy Miriam a pint of duty-free Chanel No. 5 then realized it would be safer to pick it up on the return trip.

When the time came to go back on board, I noticed several new faces in the seats around me. The Franco-American from the Pyrenees with a laundry business in San Francisco had vacated the middle seat, and a lady in her late fifties and a flowered dress, who looked like Golda Meir's sister, was sitting by the window. The sharp-eyed stocky guy with hairy wrists was still in his seat across the aisle. I gave him a nod as I strapped myself in then sat back with my eyes closed until we had thundered along the runway and angled safely up into the air. Ever since that DC-10 barrel-rolled into the ground at Chicago, I hold my breath until they tuck the flaps in.

The thunder from the engines eased to a soothing rumble as the guys up front throttled back for the slow climb to altitude. Over the Alps into Northern Italy, down the Adriatic to Greece then across the Mediterranean. In four hours we would land at Tel Aviv. I checked to see that I didn't have someone like Sophie Tucker sitting behind me, then let the seat back as far as it would go and crashed out.

I remember a confused dream. The kind that makes sense at the time but which is impossible to describe. And in it was the sound of someone screaming. I woke up to find that it was real. As I sat up, a distraught woman with a young child in her arms rushed down the aisle toward the rear of the plane. I put my hands on the seat in front and began to straighten my legs.

The stocky guy across the aisle snapped at me. "Sit down!" Which I did.

As the woman with the child passed me, I peeked around the side of the seat and saw three people — two young men and a woman — standing by the entrance to the First Class section. There was a lot of shouting going on and they were waving their arms around. The cabin staff had disappeared. Then the two young men moved down the port and starboard aisle and I saw they were holding automatic pistols and brandishing canvas satchels in their other hands. We'd been hijacked.

Ohh, Jeezuss, I thought. *That's all I need . . .*

As the guy moving down our aisle came nearer, I got a better look at him. He had dark hair, hollow cheeks, swarthy complexion and the beginnings of a beard. He looked like a protesting Iranian student but he could have come from anywhere around the southern Mediterranean; Libya, Syria, a PLO training camp — who knows? Maybe you do. I didn't get a chance to find out.

"Nobody move — hijack — *ne bougez pas,*" he kept repeating, aiming his pistol along each row of seats and holding up his satchel of grenades, or whatever.

"*Oh, merde,*" growled the woman by the window in a throaty male voice. "*Encore ces cons d'Arabes . . .*" And in the next five seconds she told me she'd been at Entebbe.

I didn't have time to sympathize. As the hijacker passed me, I saw he was trembling. And you can imagine how that made me feel. His companion in the other aisle had paused to shout in Arabic at a protesting passenger. I lay back, clasped my hands together and took a deep, calming breath. *"Please God,"* I said to myself, *"get me out of this in one piece."*

As I opened my eyes, the stocky guy across the aisle came out of his seat with the speed of a striking cobra, pulling a short-barreled .38 out of the folded magazine that had been on his lap. Before I had time to react, he shot the guy in the port aisle through the head then whirled around and dropped the hijacker who'd gone past us.

More shouts. A woman somewhere behind me went hysterical. And, as the two hijackers went down, someone up near the front fired several times at the girl. The shots slammed her four different ways against the bulkhead. As she slid to the floor, there was utter confusion as the people near her struggled to get out of their seats, falling over each other in the aisle.

The stocky Israeli security guard ran toward them. "Keep down, keep down! Stay in your seats! Everything's under —"

The rest of his words were lost as he and the people in the front section were engulfed in an orange cloud of fire. There was a thunderous, deafening roar of sound. The shriek of rending metal mixed with the screams of the people in front of me. My brain froze in horror as the orange fireball billowed out toward me, filling the interior of the plane. I turned away from the aisle, throwing myself into the empty middle seat in a vain effort to escape the searing heat — and fell into the arms of The Man.

And then, although I couldn't feel his arms around me, I knew we were together. Falling, falling, falling. Then, that first moment of paralyzing terror faded away and with it, the sensation of falling. I could no longer feel my body and for an indeterminate moment of time I seemed to float in a formless void. Unsure whether I was still myself, or part of this — eventless eternity. *Is this death?* I wondered. *The shadowy spirit-world of Devachan?*

Light pierced the gray fathomless fog that surrounded me.

Light, streaming in through my eyes. A fiery pink and orange, streaked with gold. I recoiled and covered my face, thinking, for a brief instant, that I was still trapped in the explosion aboard the plane. Then, as my eyes snapped into focus, I realized that I was looking up at a dawn sky.

I lifted my head up and saw that I was lying on a hillside dotted with olive trees. The Man stood by my feet, gazing down at me with a strange enigmatic expression. I had the feeling he was trying not to smile. He was dressed in the pale brown robe he'd worn on his first visit to Sleepy Hollow. A dark-haired woman knelt by my side. He didn't need to tell me who she was. I could tell from her clothes that it was Mary of Magdala.

Behind her, night slipped away over the western horizon, leaving layers of wind-smoothed iron-gray cloud piled up like folded prison blankets. I looked the other way and shaded my eyes as the sun came up over the horizon and threw a pattern of light and shade over the roofs and towers of the walled city that straddled the top of the hill on the other side of the valley. Already, smoke had begun to rise from a thousand cooking fires, and from somewhere higher up the slope behind me I could hear the timeless tinkling of goat bells.

I gazed for a moment at the city then looked up at The Man. "Is that — ?"

"Yes . . ." He leaned forward and offered me his hand. "Welcome to Jerusalem."

I got to my feet and slapped the dust of the Mount of Olives from the seat of my pants. "This is not quite what I had in mind."

Don't ask me how it was done. Just take my word for it. What you are reading is all the proof you need. These people can move themselves — and us — through time. But don't get too excited. A war-games buff will never be able to go back and help Napoleon win the Battle of Waterloo. It doesn't work like that. You can't change history when the future is already a part of it. All you can do is play it as written.

"How do you feel?" asked The Man.

"Me? Fine. Tremendous," I replied. I didn't of course, but what else *could* I say? I had to look cool — if only for the sake of the twentieth century.

"Glad to hear it," said The Man. "For a moment there, I thought I'd lost you."

A jumble of thoughts raced through my head, making my brain buzz as I tried to adjust to this unexpected twist in my traveling arrangements. "This may sound a stupid question but — am I dead? Did I die in that hijack — and am I imagining all this?"

The Man shook his head and smiled. "No. We brought you here just before death overtook you. You're alive, Leo. The rest of your time-line has been transferred to the first century."

"Oh, God," I sighed heavily. "Did you know this was going to happen?" He didn't reply. "You did, didn't you? You knew from the very beginning."

"Not from the very beginning," he said. "The knowledge was not mine to share but, had you known, it would have changed nothing."

"But — I could have made arrangements," I bleated. "A will. Jeezuss, I've left an eighteen-thousand-dollar car parked in the garage, there's my apartment, the house at Sleepy Hollow —"

The Man waved aside my protests. "Someone will take care of all that. Don't worry about it. You've got more important things to do."

I closed my eyes, breathed hard and prayed for strength. Then I turned to his companion. "Excuse me. You must think me very rude." I stretched out my hand. "Hello. My name is Leo Resnick — but then I guess you already know that."

Mary looked at me with brown darting eyes, then turned to The Man, hiding her laughter behind her hand.

I threw up my hands. "She doesn't understand a word I'm saying."

"Try it again in Hebrew," he said.

"Oh, yeah — I forgot." I ran it through in translation.

Mary clasped her hands around mine. She was obviously unused to twentieth-century-style handshakes. "Welcome to our world, Leo. The Master tells me you come from another time. There will be many things you do not understand but have no fear. I shall be your guide and companion for as long as you have need of me."

"Thanks," I replied. In my second native tongue. I looked down at myself and saw that I was still wearing the shirt and trousers I had boarded the plane with. I'd left my jacket in the overhead luggage locker and my shoes, which I'd kicked off, under the seat in front.

Mary unwrapped a bundle and pulled out a black and brown striped ankle-length *djellaba*. The Man handed it to me. "Here — put this on. We can't take you into Jerusalem dressed like that."

I pulled the roughly woven robe over my head and wrinkled my nose at the musky animal odor. Mary offered me a pair of crude leather sandals. I stripped off my socks and put them on. "How do I look?"

The Man eyed me critically. "Like an Egyptian camel driver."

I guess I deserved that.

"Keep still . . ." He placed his hands on either side of my head and fixed me with that golden gaze of his. A swarm of tiny ice-needles zigzagged back and forth through my brain. It lasted for ten, maybe fifteen seconds. At the end of which I discovered that, in addition to Hebrew, I knew how to speak, read and write fluent Aramaic, Latin, Greek, Persian, Coptic, you name it.

Pure magic.

The three of us walked down toward the stream that ran through the Kidron Valley. Even at this distance, I could hear the sounds of the waking city. I turned to The Man. "Can I ask you something?"

"Ask me anything you want, Leo," he said.

"There must have been over two hundred people on board that plane. Are they all dead?"

"Yes," he replied. "But don't worry. They'll be back."

"Maybe," I said. "But was it necessary to kill two hundred men, women and children just to get me here?"

"Of course not," he said. "That wasn't my doing. Boats sink, cars crash, trains collide, planes fall out of the sky, cities are leveled by earthquakes every day of the week. I don't make that happen and I can't stop it. When your time comes, that's it. Your name was already on that passenger list from the moment you were born. If more people realized that, it might make them love those nearest to them while they are alive instead of weeping over their coffins, crippled by remorse."

"Does Miriam know I'm here?" I asked.

He shook his head. "No. She thinks you died when the plane blew up."

"But that's going to make her feel terrible," I said. "She is going to blame herself for the rest of her life."

He smiled. "I hope not. Otherwise it means I've been wasting my time. Don't worry. She's a very strong lady."

I imagine he thought that would make me feel better but let's face it — everybody likes to be missed. It was only fair that Miriam should miss me. Desperately. Later on, of course, I mellowed. But at that moment, I could only cling onto the past — which had yet to happen — and think of what had been taken away from me. Instead of what I had been given.

My flight had taken off on the twelfth of May, 1981. Somewhere along the line I appeared to have lost two weeks of my life because I eventually found that I had landed — if one can use that phrase — on a Wednesday sometime in early June. Preparations were already underway for *Shavout* — the Feast of the Pentecost — which meant that his disciples had not yet been given the mind-blowing injection of power that, in the following weeks, was to amaze and alarm the inhabitants of Jerusalem and provide an unknown student from Tarsus with the opportunity to make a lasting name for himself.

Why had he brought me here? The answer was simple. I, too, had a mission. To tell his story in the words and images of my generation. I was to be the voice of the future, reaching out from the past. Proof of the Empire's mastery over Time and Space. To transmit, through my feeble glimmer of awareness, the Light of The Word.

And now I can give you the final chapter in the story of The Man's crucifixion. But first, a small technical point that filmmakers keep overlooking. The Man did not drag his whole cross through the city. He and the two thieves had their outstretched arms bound under and over the transverse beam placed across their shoulders.

When Joshua started his journey from the Fortress Antonia to Golgotha, Ya'el came back to him. They were together every step of the way as their host body stumbled along the route through the Second Quarter to the Joppa Gate. Joshua-Ya'el fell several times and finally, the execution squad pulled a man out of the crowd to carry the beam for him. Not as an act of mercy, but to keep themselves out of trouble. When the governor sentenced a man to be crucified he was expected to die on the cross, not in the street. Joshua was doused with water, hauled upright, and frog-marched the rest of the way.

The streets along the route were lined with silent ranks of spectators, many of whom had been part of the joyous procession that Joshua had led into the city six short days ago. Regardless of the disappointment and the temporary hatred they might have felt for The Man for what they saw as a betrayal of their hopes, the sight of any Jew struggling under a Roman cross was no cause for celebration. It was a cruel reminder that they were an occupied nation. What was happening to Joshua and the two luckless thieves could just as easily happen to other Jews tomorrow.

It is not hard to imagine that to hang by the arms for any length of time soon causes excruciating muscular pains. To which are added the circulatory cramps caused by the ropes bound round the upper arms and chest and — in the case of

The Man — the nails driven through the wrists and feet. But that was not all. An additional layer of suffering came from the flies swarming over the open wounds caused by the scourging.

If you were strong, it could take two, three, even four days to die, especially if you managed to take the weight off your arms by getting a temporary purchase on the upright beam with the soles of your feet. To stop you from doing this, in the case of judicial as opposed to punitive crucifixions, the execution squad usually broke your legs sometime during the first day.

In spite of the screaming pain that came from having your shinbones shattered with a heavy cudgel, the *crucifragum* was regarded by the Romans as an act of mercy. And, since the soldiers had to guard the victims until they died to prevent any rescue attempt, it also cut down the time they had to spend on the job.

The Man's death on the cross served a threefold purpose. First, the crucifixion meant sure and certain, officially certified death before dozens, if not hundreds, of witnesses. In rising again, three days later, The Man demonstrated to the world the absolute power of The Presence over life and death. Second, he was sentenced and executed by Romans under Roman law with the full might of the Roman state behind it. His resurrection proved that even the mightiest empire on earth, the greatest power which — up to that time — the world had ever known, was helpless against the power of the Celestial Empire.

And third, through his suffering on the cross, Ya'el reaffirmed the bond between God, or The Presence, and Man. For the magnified pain that pierced his spirit-being was not his alone. Every Celestial spirit had been created from and was part of the Infinite Being of The Presence. The *corpus dei*. And because of this, they possessed a unique, interlocking sensory system. As Ya'el took Joshua's pain upon himself, it was transmitted through him from the World Below to the World Above.

Imagine, if you can, the pain radiating out from Joshua's crucified body in the form of a spherical shock wave — like you've seen in the film footage of nuclear bomb tests. Except that this shock wave doesn't lose momentum. It builds up as it goes on traveling. Spreading outward in every direction, engulfing Michael and Gabriel in the orbiting longship, and going on out of the solar system, through and beyond the galaxy to fill the whole universe. Bursting through the Time Gate like a great tidal wave; flooding the Celestial Empire; reaching the heart of The Presence; filling it with limitless, soul-searing pain that only ceased when Joshua and Ya'el were freed by the death of their host body.

It was not the sins of the world but the pain of existence that God, or The Presence, took upon him/her/itself through The Man. In sharing our suffering, The Presence showed that he had not abandoned us. Our true selves. The trapped Ainfolk. The spirit within us that was the spark of our humanity. That was the reason The Man died on the cross and not on a bed of roses. The darkness that the writers of Mark and Luke mention, and which hung over the earth from the sixth to the ninth hour, was the poisonous 'Braxian darkness that The Presence drew out of the soul of the world and into itself through the crucified body of Joshua-Ya'el.

For the next few days, I stayed at the house of Nicodemus while I adjusted to the cultural jet-lag that came from being catapulted backward through two millennia. I didn't see much of The Man, but I spoke often with Mary of Magdala. And you'll find this hard to believe but do you know who she reminded me of? Joe Gutzman's daughter Joanna — whom I'd successfully kept at arm's length. There was another lesson there too, for as I got to know her better, I realized that she was beautiful in a totally different way. And in the end, it's the only way that counts.

It was Mary who explained to me the concept of "raying back" The Power of The Presence. It's something I feel you should think about so let me run it by you — as the saying is some two thousand years from now. According to Mary, the power of God shines forth like the rays of, let's say, the sun. The reservoir is, in theory, inexhaustible but, in order to keep everything on an even keel, the power, the force, the love of God has to be recycled. It needs to be rayed back, reflected by the mirror of the soul. But, as must be obvious, nothing can shine forth if, to put it bluntly, your head is full of shit. The only way to put a shine on your soul is through the power of The Word. In plain language that means opening your heart and mind to God's love.

Yes. I know that's the kind of phrase that makes people cringe. *"Oh, Jeezuss,"* they think. *"How embarrassing."* And if anyone had said something like that to me before I got into this, I'd have felt like throwing up. It's little wonder that the word "Love" sticks in people's throats. 'Brax not only hogtied us with language; he has made us frightened to use it as well. It has become sectioned off, with separate vocabularies for separate occasions. Like baby language, we have a language that politicians use, and another fingertips-together language for talking about God and tut-tutting about the decline in moral standards. I've never understood why the good guys are constrained to use only the politer half of the dictionary. The good time that 'Brax is offering you doesn't come for free. He's out to fuck your mind, folks. So for God's sake, don't just lie there and let him do it to you. Stand up and fight for what's right.

Don't let yourself get sidetracked by the semantics. Whomever, or Whatever, this power comes from — God, The Presence, Allah, You-Name-It — by the time it reaches us, it's called Love. And it's the only thing that can revive our real self, which is suffocating inside us. If everybody lets it flood in, and starts beaming it back out, the world would come alive again.

Being me, I naturally asked what might happen if we all turned our backs and just didn't bother. As you can see, despite my sudden transfer to the first century I was stubbornly ignoring the facts of predestination that were staring me in the face.

Mary's answer was this: By raying back The Power of The Presence we were helping to restore the vital equilibrium of the World Above and the World Below; holding the line between the Empire and 'Brax. It we didn't ray it back, more and more of the good stuff would be trapped in the fabric of the physical universe which, as it got increasingly out of balance, would gradually get sucked in through the Black Holes into the Netherworld. Only none of us — sentient life — would survive the trip.

Those students of logic I addressed earlier will be quick to realize that this opens up yet another new ball game. The Man left me guessing on this one, so I hereby bequeath you the problem.

Mary also told me about Judas's death. For reasons best known to himself, Judas hung around Jerusalem after The Man's arrest and was spotted by Shimon and several other disciples on the terraced roof of a merchant's house. It appears that the merchant in question was not at home but as he owned several cargo boats Mary was convinced that Judas must have been trying to arrange his passage out of the country. According to a stall owner who'd been opposite the house, Judas appeared on the terrace and walked to and fro, constantly returning to the parapet — giving the stall owner the impression he might be preparing to leap over it. Suddenly, without any warning, he threw several handfuls of silver coins into the street. Where, somewhat naturally, it was regarded as manna from heaven.

By sheer chance, Shimon, Johan, Matthew, Nathan and Thaddeus were only a couple of streets away. Attracted by the noise, they hurried to see what was happening. Shimon hauled the stall owner out of the frenzied heap of treasure-seekers and learned that a crazy man had thrown money from a roof. They looked up and there was Judas. Bursting into the house, Shimon and the other four disciples pushed aside the startled servants and found their way onto the roof where they discovered that Judas had fled into a two-story tower that rose from one corner of the terrace. As they battered down the door, he leaped out of an upper window, arms out-stretched, falling head-first onto the flagstones of the court-yard below. Judas died instantly, and the impact ruptured his intestines. He didn't, as reported in Acts, chapter 1, verse 18, have time to buy a farm, but the author got the rest of it right when he spoke of Judas *"falling headlong"* and *"burst asunder."* Matthew, chapter 28, begins with Judas's attempt to give back the money, after which he hanged himself. It could be argued that by accepting the assignment, Judas sentenced himself to death and that by remaining in Jeru-salem he hung himself. So in a sense, both versions of his death are true.

Either way it was a sad loss because, from what Mary told me, he sounded like a good man to have around. But then, as I myself had come to learn, the Empire moves in mysterious ways.

On the day before the Feast of the Pentecost, The Man came to say goodbye. I had been moved to a house a few miles from Jerusalem, owned by Joseph of Arimathea. The Good Samaritan. It seemed ironic that apart from The Man, and possibly Mary, I was the only one who knew what was going to happen the next day and for some time after that. I would have swapped the knowledge gladly for news of my own future but it was not to be. By this time, Mary had intro-duced me to all the disciples, including Matthias, the new twelfth man, and I was feeling a little left out.

"Is everything set?" I said, as we walked out into the garden.

The Man nodded. "Yes. We're going to make the power transfer tomorrow. The Empire is setting up a big move to decoy 'Brax out of the relevant time frames."

I shook my head. "I don't think I'm ever going to under-stand how all of this really works."

"You will one day," he replied.

"The Twelve are due to find out tomorrow," I said. "Don't you think I deserve to be included?"

He treated me to his last smile but one. "I like you just

the way you are, Leo. When you start putting this down I don't want you getting lyrical over me."

"It's a waste of time," I said. "Nobody's going to believe it. Okay, so I'm a lawyer. But what does that mean? Nothing."

He eyed me soberly. "Shimon-Petrus is a fisherman who can't even write his name. None of the people who are due to write all this down are Doctors of Divinity. The first theological college has yet to be founded. Forget about the people who will claim to know better because they've read what I'm supposed to have said in the original Greek. Just tell it in your own words, Leo."

I accepted this instruction with a glum nod. "So . . ." As I told you, I hate goodbyes.

"Mary will help you get started," he said. "She'll see you've got everything you need. Within reason, of course."

"Don't worry," I replied. "I haven't forgotten where I am." A feeling of desperation came over me. I could not believe that this was the last time I would see him. "Do you really have to go?"

"Yes," he said. Then he smiled. "But you can always get in touch if you need me."

I grabbed hold of his arm. "Listen — there's something I'm not quite clear about. This 'raying back' business. From what Mary's told me, things may not be so cut and dried as you've made out. Come on — level with me. Do the good guys win, or don't they?"

He took my hand from his arm and held it tightly. "Of course they do. It's just going to take time, that's all. Maybe a little longer that we first expected. Don't worry, the Empire knows what it's doing but —" He beckoned me closer. "— just to be on the safe side, be sure to tell everybody to keep trying."

The Man put his hands upon my shoulders and fixed me with his golden eyes. As he did so, I heard this voice inside my head. I closed my eyes in order to concentrate and I experienced a timeless, out-of-body moment while The Man, or whoever it was, spoke to me, saying —

Look upon my world through the window of your soul. A world hung with drifting clouds of shimmering gold, pierced by the burnished rays of a thousand suns, yet filled with a light as soft as the face of a sleeping child.

A world without weight. Where the horizons are rimmed with an endless sunrise, and where you float upon the clouds of a sunset so beautiful it can only be seen through tears of joy.

A glorious world of infinite, harmonious hue. Where form is perceived as feeling. Where feeling is expressed as color. Where color is heard as a vibrant sound. Where the sound is music, and the music is filled with the scent of wild flowers.

A world that is within your world and yet encloses it. That is all around you yet which you cannot touch. Which enters you with each breath and which all may enter. Which awaits your coming and to which I long to return.

I am the hand of The One who has no eyes yet sees into your hearts, who has no ears yet answers your cry, who has no tongue yet whose Word is Love, who has no legs yet stands astride the Universe, who has no arms yet embraces all Eternity.

Your tongue has made a prisoner of your mind and has robbed you of the power to understand how and why our world came to be but there will come a day when you will look upon The Face of The Presence and All Things will be made known to you. At that moment Time, as you know it, will end. For Us now, Time Is.

I became conscious of my body again. Of my feet pressing against the ground. I opened my eyes as The Man let go of my shoulders and took a step backward.

"Goodbye, Leo . . ."

"Wait a minute," I said. "Just answer me one question — the police, Lieutenant Russell —"

"What about them?"

"Were they real people? I mean, like me — or were they three-dimensional phantoms created by 'Brax?"

"No," he said. "They were part of the external reality to which you belonged."

"Then who were the other people in Russell's office when he questioned you? The ones that left as I arrived."

"Frightened men," he said — and was gone.

Leaving so much unanswered.

For a moment, I thought I would die. It was as if someone had torn my heart out. I stood there for what seemed like a long time. Thinking about The Man, my life, and Miriam — and how ridiculous it was for someone like me to be crying.

I've been with the people at Qumran for over a year now, working as a scribe, using my newfound linguistic skills in translating documents and making copies of whatever is needed. My previously acquired legal expertise has also made it possible for us to screw the Romans at every turn.

I suppose I should have written more but getting hold of enough papyrus and sticking the goddamn sheets together has been a real problem. As you may remember, I was never very good with my hands but I'm learning, I'm learning. I just hope this stuff lasts. I probably should have waited until I was more experienced but I was anxious to get all this down before anything bad happened to me. Like an accident, or something. This place is a long way from Manhattan General. Thank God I had my appendix taken out when I was sixteen.

The Essenes run their life pretty much by the Book but they make a few allowances for me. It's a bit like Marine boot camp — only the people are a lot smarter. The air here is much better than in the city but I'm not too crazy about the food. Wild honey may be sweet to the tongue but locusts are definitely an acquired taste.

You may find this hard to believe but I think what I miss most is the traffic.

Love and Peace.

Leo

TWENTY-FOUR ═══════
Preface

— The "Resnick" Scroll. Catalog No. Q-11-7 QUMRAN, 7th Tishri, 340th year of Minyan Shetiroth

To Doctor Miriam Maxwell, Apt #411, 57th St. & 1st Ave., New York, NY; to my parents, Philip and Pearl Resnick, of 946 Riverland Road, Fort Lauderdale, Florida, and to my sister Bella Cohen, of 293 Winthrop Shore Drive, Boston, Massachusetts, U.S.A.

I write to you across the years not knowing when this message will be found. Perhaps you have yet to be born, or are already long dead. I can only pray that, by God's good fortune, you are alive when this scroll is found and that the finder will send you news of my fate. I was chosen to bear witness to The Word and to The Man. It is for this reason that I believe my testimony is destined to survive although I am sure the experts will do their best to refute it. If just one person believes, my journey will not have been wasted.

Do not weep for me. I am among friends and, at last, my life has meaning.

I send you my love and His.

LEO

Appendices

(Publisher's note: What follows is only a partial record of the correspondence relating to the foregoing manuscript. It is our belief that many key documents have either been destroyed or removed from the relevant files. We would like to make it clear that official spokesmen for the federal government have declined to comment on what would appear to be high-level interagency communications, facsimiles of which are reproduced here. It is for the reader to judge the authenticity of these documents and draw the appropriate conclusions.)

AMERICAN SCHOOL OF ORIENTAL STUDIES
JERUSALEM — ISRAEL

To: Professor Moritz Kaufmann
    Curator — Dead Sea Scrolls
    HEBREW UNIVERSITY, JERUSALEM

From: Dr. Arthur Lovell   9 August 1958
CONFIDENTIAL
The Resnick Scroll/Catalog No.Q—11—7

Dear Moritz,
    I have to tell you that Frank Walker and I
are in a terrible quandary over what to do with
this document. In fact, we both heartily wish
that Dr. Sterckx's team had not opened Cave
Eleven at all. At least we would be able to
sleep nights!
    Clearly, a Dead Sea scroll written in
American English — a language which was not in
existence at the date inscribed on the
document (30 A.D.) is a logical absurdity.
    Despite the fact that the syntax and idiom
employed by the writer includes certain phrases
that are quite unfamiliar to us (e.g.: "Let
me run it by you") the internal stylistic
evidence points to a supremely impudent hoax
by someone with, at the very least, a college
education and who is also a religious
iconoclast.
    Frank is of the opinion that the culprit is
probably a contemporary American writer of
science-fiction but I was struck by the
reference to the Gnostic texts from Nag
Hammadi. As you know, the contents of these
have been kept secret since their discovery
and they are currently under lock and key in
the Coptic Museum in Cairo. Neither Frank nor I
have yet seen them and there cannot be more
than a dozen or so international scholars who

know of their existence. So the joker may be nearer home. However, that is the least of our problems!

The fact is, we are totally floored by the results of the laboratory tests we have carried out. All the results serve to confirm the scroll's total authenticity and date it as coming from the same period as the other documents found in Q.11. I have enumerated our findings as follows:

1 — The Papyrus is, without doubt, early first century. Frank is inclined to think it is pre-50 A.D. The weave and multiple sheet composition are identical to the other papyri we have recovered from this period from Qumran and elsewhere.

2 — Condition of the Scroll: Of all the papyri found to date, Q—11—7 is by far the best preserved. The only surface flaking that has occurred is around the edges. The text has been preserved in its entirety (including the four-letter words). It is this remarkable state of preservation that gives rise to our suspicion that Q—11—7 is an imposter but —

3 — Analysis of Ink Samples: These were taken from the preface to the scroll and at intervals throughout the text. The standard tests were applied and produced a perfect match to the composition profile we have constructed of inks used on fully authenticated documents.

4 — Carbon Dating: Analysis of both papyrus and ink confirm the comparative evidence for the age of the scroll.

5 — Pottery Storage Jar: This is identical to several others we have found and, by our present criteria, totally authentic. The potter's mark matches that on other storage jars found in Q—11, Q—1 and Q—4.

6 — Provenance of Scroll: There is absolutely no doubt that the scroll was inside the jar which

was opened, like the others from Q—11, under controlled conditions and under the personal supervision of Dr. André Sterckx. (Who, I might add, is just as upset as we are.)

7 — Jar Plug and Sealant: The standard ceramic plug and pitch sealant was used. Both gave positive results when tested.

8 — Location of Scroll Jar: This, I am afraid, is the one that puts us right behind the eight ball. Q—11—7 was found buried under a 12-inch layer of dust and other debris along with six other jars containing papyri scrolls with Aramaic texts. There was no sign of any disturbance of the covering layer. As you can imagine, this is a real headache. For we are obliged to ask the following question: If the scroll is a forgery (as we firmly believe it to be) how did it get in the cave alongside five indisputably authentic documents? References in the text to World War Two indicates that it is of recent origin. General Eisenhower is mentioned as having been president. It therefore seems unlikely that the text was composed prior to his term of office. But to avoid any detectable signs of soil disturbance, the jar would have had to be inserted at least twenty to thirty years ago. Which makes the forging of the scroll even more difficult. The writer would not only have to be an archaeological expert, he would also have to be something of a seer!

9 — Handwriting Analysis: I do not accept this idea but Annette Schuman claims that there is graphological evidence to support the notion that the writer of Q—11—7 could be the scribe/copyist of at least three other Hebrew documents from Q—4 that are currently under analysis. Annette's expertise in this field is not in question but the idea is quite preposterous. Frank and I both feel that further comparative

analysis along these lines would be a fruitless exercise.

CONCLUSION: We are faced with an apparently insoluble paradox. Clearly, the scroll is a forgery. However engaging the story might be it is both improbable, impractical and — more to the point — scientifically impossible. Indeed, it raises more problems than it purports to solve. But how do we reconcile this conclusion with the results of the scientific tests? If we reject the Resnick Scroll then, by the same criteria, we must reject all the other scrolls that we have already accepted as genuine.

We are therefore left with the following options:

(a) Destruction of the scroll: A move which, despite the scroll's counterfeit nature, we would be most reluctant to make. Frank and I both believe that it should be preserved, if only for its curiosity value.

(b) Remove all reference to Q—11—7 from the manuscript catalog and put it into cold storage. There are many years of work ahead for the restoration and translation teams. I think this one can be safely put at the bottom of the pile.

I therefore return it to your safekeeping.

Cordially yours,

Arthur

State University of New York
Downstate Medical Center/Brooklyn/NY

To: Dr. Arthur Lovell
American School of Oriental Research
Jerusalem, Israel

Ref: Document Q-11-7

Dear Arthur,   15 Sept 1958
Thank you for your letter and enclosures of the
15th August. I have read the typed transcript carefully and examined the photostat showing a section
of the scroll. It's an interesting problem. The
scroll is obviously a very clever fake but I am unable to supply a plausible explanation for the apparently unshakable scientific evidence which
points to its utter authenticity. However, since
your letter shows you to be keenly aware of this I
shall not labor the point, apart from saying that
you have my sympathies.

It has taken me a little time to trace the people
on the list you enclosed. Hence the delay in replying. So far, I have discovered the following —
(a) A Mr. and Mrs. Philip Resnick live at 112 Pol-
hemus Place, Brooklyn, N.Y. They have a daughter, Bella, aged 18, and a son, Leonard Nathan
Resnick, aged 13. He is currently attending
Friends School in Brooklyn Heights.
(b) Rabbi Abraham Lucksteen lives at 206 Fisk St.,
Brooklyn, N.Y. This is just around the corner
from the Resnicks. He and his wife have a
daughter Abbey, aged 13. I called the secretary
of Resnick's school and she confirmed that he
and Miss Lucksteen were classmates. I also
called the rabbi and he was kind enough to confirm that he had conducted Leonard Resnick's
bar-mitzvah.
(c) No joy on Dr. Miriam Maxwell. From the approxi-
mation of her age given in the transcript she
would now be 10-11 years old. Her father may

be a doctor. I propose to check the AMA listings for the State of New York and will let you know what I turn up. The address given in the scroll preface for her apartment is presently a construction site.

(d) Nothing so far on Linda or Peter Kovacs. The indications are that these people may be refugees from the Hungarian uprising. I will check with Immigration.

(e) There is a D. E. Russell currently undergoing recruit training with the NYPD but there is insufficient evidence to positively identify this individual.

(f) Nothing available on Lazzarotti, McDonald, Fowler or Shiragawa. So I cannot confirm that these are real people either.

(g) Perez: I checked 49th St. between 5th and 3rd Avenues. There are no dry cleaners or laundry shops operating under or owned by anybody with this name.

Just out of interest I include the following —

(h) Dr. Henry Kissinger is a lecturer at Harvard and a part-time national security consultant to the Eisenhower Administration.

(i) Richard Nixon, as you know, is currently Vice-President under Ike. He is undoubtedly an adroit politician but, unlike the writer of the scroll, my Republican friends do not view him as Presidential timber in his own right.

(j) Clint Eastwood: I understand from my youngest daughter that he is an up-coming TV actor currently playing a character called "Rowdy Yates" (!) in a new series titled <u>Rawhide.</u>

(k) David Frost: The writer implies that he is some kind of celebrity/interviewer similar to Walter Cronkite or Arthur Godfrey. Nobody here has heard of him.

Incidentally, I must say that I took exception to the scurrilous remarks about Ike. He's a good man and far above that kind of thing.

Even though this document is pure fiction I feel bound to remark that it portrays a chilling, and somewhat depressing, view of life twenty years from now. The use of explicit language between men and women and the free-for-all sexual license I find rather upsetting. And I simply cannot believe that a stag film of the kind described in the text and titled <u>Deep Throat</u> could ever be allowed to be shown publicly. I can only say "God help us" if it is.

Similarly, as I will be eighty in twenty years time, I find the idea of 12-year-old muggers absolutely horrifying. As much as I admire the aggressiveness with which the writer expresses some of his ideas, his description of life in this future New York reveals a morbid preoccupation with sex and violence.

Let me know if I can be of any further assistance.

My best wishes to Sheila, and Frank Walker.

Your friend,

<u>Jake</u>

Professor S. J. Wassmeyer
Department of Psychology

AMERICAN SCHOOL OF ORIENTAL STUDIES
JERUSALEM — ISRAEL

To: Professor Moritz Kaufmann
    Curator — Dead Sea Scrolls
    HEBREW UNIVERSITY, JERUSALEM

From: Dr. Arthur Lovell   25 September 1958

CONFIDENTIAL
Ref: Q–11–7

Dear Moritz,

I enclose a copy of a letter from Jake Wassmeyer. His comments, I am sure, will be of interest. I must say Frank and I are more than a little disturbed to discover that some of the characters in Q–11–7 appear to be derived from real people. What is more, at the time the related events are supposed to occur — twenty-three years from now — the real Leonard Nathan Resnick will be the same age as the purported narrator of the scroll. I hardly need to point out that the implications of this development are quite frightening.

I am glad your committee agrees that we should all do our utmost to conceal the existence of this document while stopping short of its destruction. Frankly, it raises too many disturbing questions for which there are no reasonable answers.

With your permission, I propose to put a transcript of the text and photostats of the scroll together with copies of this correspondence into a safety deposit box at my bank in Boston on my next visit home. If, by the Grace of God and John Foster Dulles, the world is still in one piece twenty years from now, I will make arrangements for this extraordinary document to be brought to the notice of the appropriate authorities.

Cordially yours,

Arthur

CENTRAL INTELLIGENCE AGENCY — LANGLEY — VIRGINIA

INTERNAL MEMORANDUM   COPIES: Original
                                                        One copy to FC File

MOST SECRET/YOUR EYES ONLY

To: Internal Operations Director
From: Field Coordinator "Gordon"
Date: Monday 13 April 1981

SUBJECT: OPERATION EASTER BUNNY

Sir,

The following first-response surveillance measures have now been successfully deployed and

are at go-status. Daily field reports will be submitted if and when target arrival is confirmed.

1 — Agent "Sugar-George," who was recruited into
the Field Services Department of the Agency
in October '77 has now been working as Resnick's
personal secretary for the past two years.

2 — The janitor of Resnick's apartment building
was replaced by Agent "Hotel-Queen" at the
beginning of this year.

3 — Agent "Victor-Bravo," a fully qualified doctor from our Medical Intelligence Unit, has
been assigned as an internee on Dr. Miriam
Maxwell's team at the Manhattan General.

4 — Communications intercepts have been installed
on the appropriate private and business lines
of all individuals on Target List Q-11-7.

5 — By arrangement with the NY Police Commis-
sioner, Agents "Orange-Dog" and "Able-
Zebra" have been assigned to the Narcotics
Division of the Organized Crime Control
Bureau based in the Seventh Precinct. These
two agents are the nucleus of the proposed
external surveillance team. Lt. Dan Russell
from the NYPD Internal Services Department
has been appointed as Police Liaison Officer.

6 — The cooperation of civilians on Target List
Q-11-7 will be solicited and/or additional
Agency personnel will be inserted into the sur-
veillance net as required.

7 — Arrangements have been made to secure the contents of Resnick's safety deposit box at the
midtown branch of the Chase Manhattan Bank
should the tapes and allied documentation
listed in the Target File materialize as physical evidence.

MEMORANDUM ENDS

OFFICE OF THE DIRECTOR OF INTERNAL OPERATIONS
CIA/LANGLEY/VA

To: Blue One/Washington Date: 18 April 81/1800 HRS
Copies: None/Read and Destroy

FOR YOUR EYES ONLY
OPERATION EASTER BUNNY

Sir,

There are now increasing indications that the
Q—11—7 event may be about to occur on a sequential
real-time basis. If so, we will need a decision on
the next seven days on the containment strategy to
be adopted in respect of the individuals concerned.

The graduated options open to us are as listed in
Memorandum 12.

We also need to decide, within the same time
frame, whether or not we should inform Israeli Airlines of the possible danger to their Flight 072
on the 12th May.

CENTRAL INTELLIGENCE AGENCY/TELEX TRANSCRIPT
INT-OP FILE

ORIGINAL TRANSMISSION TIMED AT 1700 HRS 18 APRIL 81

TO: INT-OP ONE
ORIGIN: FIELD-CO GORDON
SUBJECT: OPERATION EASTER BUNNY

MESSAGE BEGINS
AGENT VICTOR-BRAVO CONFIRMS RESNICK DUE TO MEET
MAXWELL 2130 HRS TONIGHT MANHATTAN GENERAL HOSPITAL
STOP
AGENTS ORANGE-DOG AND ABLE-ZEBRA WILL MAINTAIN
SURVEILLANCE OF TARGET ARRIVAL POINT EAST SIDE
MANHATTAN STOP
LATEST WEATHER REPORT FOR NY FORECASTS HEAVY RAIN
STOP
MESSAGE ENDS